The Heart of the Sands

Book 3 of *The Gods Within*

Only when the steel no longer rules can the shadows within be mastered.

by

J. L. Doty

TELEMACHUS PRESS

This book or eBook is a work of fiction. Names, characters, places and incidents are either the product of the author's imagination or are used fictitiously. Any resemblance to actual persons, living or dead, or to actual events or locales is entirely coincidental.

The Heart of the Sands, Book 3 of *The Gods Within*

The publisher does not have any control over and does not assume any responsibility for author or third-party websites or their content.

Cover designed by Telemachus Press, LLC

Cover art:
Copyright © ThinkstockPhoto/106546676/iStockPhoto
Copyright © ThinkstockPhoto/101495952/Hemera
Copyright © ThinkstockPhoto/137088827/iStockPhoto
Copyright © ThinkstockPhoto/89908712/iStockPhoto
Copyright © ThinkstockPhoto/96635409/iStockPhoto
Copyright © iStockPhoto/2172405/Mlenny
Copyright © iStockPhoto/15208251/hadynyah
Copyright © iStockPhoto/16101435/PatrickPoendl
Copyright © iStockPhoto/22438702/1001nights
Copyright © iStockPhoto/22492620/Ugurham

Published by Telemachus Press, LLC
http://www.telemachuspress.com

Visit the author's website:
http://www.jldoty.com

ISBN: 978–1–939927–51–4 (eBook)
ISBN: 978–1–953757–03–6 (paperback)
ISBN: 978–1–953757–11–1 (hardcover)

Version 2023.11.23

KEpuz!po!EFTLUPQ.6CV292J:
Formatted using eTools for Writers 3.8.8, Nov 22 2023, 15:40:12
Copyright © 2013–2016 by J. L. Doty

Printed in the United States of America

10 9 8 7 6 5 4 3 2 1

The Heart of the Sands

Book 3 of *The Gods Within*

Prologue:
To Know the Steel

Command not the steel, for the steel always commands. Listen well, for only then can the Master know the steel.

The Master must know the heart of the steel, the soul of the steel, and the child of the steel. For should his knowledge falter, the steel will rule his heart, and he will know only the pain of the steel.

1

An Oven of Sand

MORGIN FORCED HIMSELF to walk, to drag one foot forward through the sand and put it in front of the other, to shift his weight onto it and then repeat the process just one more time. Each step required an effort of will, for he sank to his ankles in the sand, and it sucked at his boots as if reluctant to release its hold. The heat was unbearable, and sand had worked its way into every fold of his clothing. It stuck to his sweat-soaked skin, and abraded the most sensitive parts of his body. His lips had swollen and cracked, his eyes encrusted with dried tears and sand, and he knew he wouldn't last much longer. But he also knew that all he had to do was keep heading northwest and he'd eventually run into the Ulbb, so he kept the afternoon sun in front of him and to his left. He'd walked out this far to escape the jaws of the skree; he could walk back.

Then it struck him and he stopped dead in his tracks. He thought for a moment, and he couldn't be certain if he walked beneath the morning sun rising toward noon, or the afternoon sun falling toward dusk. If the latter, then his path led him northwest toward water. If the former, then his path carried him deeper into the Munjarro: more sand, more sun, more heat.

The heat was so intense merely breathing proved difficult, and his tongue had begun to swell and block his throat. He had no choice but to stagger on, and so he walked, and tried not to think of anything but the next step . . . and the next . . . and the next . . . and the next . . .

••••

Valso's Kullish guards opened the door to his private sitting room and admitted the pretty, young Vodah girl. She crossed the room hurriedly and dropped into a curtsy, lowering her eyes appropriately, exposing her cleavage and allowing him a good look at it.

"You summoned me, Your Majesty," she said breathlessly.

Chrisainne et Vodah, now esk et Penda; he'd searched carefully to find someone who fit his requirements perfectly. She was tall, lithe, beautiful, traits easily found. But in addition to her physical charms, she was ambitious, though her father had managed the family's finances rather poorly and could provide her with only a meager dowry at best. Had Valso not intervened, she would have had little chance of marrying anyone better than some backwoods nobleman.

"Rise," he said.

She rose slowly, keeping her eyes downcast and making sure he had plenty of time to examine the rather generous swell of her breasts so carefully exposed by the dress. Good! She'd dressed with an eye toward impressing her king, perhaps even seducing him. That was the other trait he needed in her: ruthlessness.

He said, "Raise your eyes, child. Let me look at you."

She did so. He ignored the shamelessly blatant look of invitation she gave him and said, "You are newly wed, just last month, eh?"

"Yes, Your Majesty."

Not only had Valso enriched her dowry enough so she could marry reasonably well, but he'd pointed her father at just the right Penda nobleman, and made sure the wedding vows were taken here in Durin.

"And you leave on the morrow for your husband's estates in Penda?"

"Yes, Your Majesty."

Valso frowned. "Is that all you can say, just 'Yes, Your Majesty'?"

She blushed, which made her even more attractive. "I would add that I am most grateful to Your Majesty for improving my station so I could marry well."

Valso turned away from her and dismissed her comment with a casual wave of his hand. "Yes. Your father has expressed his gratitude repeatedly, though I'm not sure how much his gratitude is worth."

"But I meant that I am personally most grateful to you, Your Majesty."

And she was smart. Good! He turned back to her. "Personally?"

She blushed again, and he began to think she might actually control that. "Yes," she said breathlessly, sensually. "I would do anything to make it up to you."

She thought she'd make it up to him by bedding him. He just needed to broaden her horizons a bit, show her how she could advance much farther by bedding someone else. He retrieved a very special coin from his desk. "I have need of a set of eyes and ears in Penda court. Can you be discreet?"

He saw in her eyes the way she quickly shifted her thinking, catching the meaning of his words without missing a heartbeat. "Yes, my king, I can."

"I need someone close to BlakeDown himself. Very close."

He saw her finish the transformation in her thinking, saw her make the leap in that instant. She said, "My husband occasionally attends BlakeDown's court. And I think I could ensure that BlakeDown desires our presence much more frequently."

He extended his hand and held the coin out to her. "Then do so," he said as she took it, a questioning look in her eyes. "Kiss that coin when you want to speak to me, and I'll know, and I'll come into your thoughts when I am available."

He waved a hand impatiently and said, "Now leave me. I have other business awaiting my attention."

She curtsied quickly and hurried toward the door, but he stopped her by calling out, "Lady Chrisainne."

She halted and spun to face him. "If you get close enough to BlakeDown, and you serve me well, your rewards will be far more than some paltry dowry."

She smiled, and he was happy to see the avarice in the look she gave him. Then she bobbed a quick curtsy and left.

••••

He must be dreaming, for he rested comfortably on a blanket on the sand. The heat had dwindled to something bearable, and when he opened his eyes he lay in a cool and comfortable shadow cast by the folds of a small cloth lean-to. Almost within arm's reach the shadow ended in a thin, sharp line, and beyond that the oven of yellow sand extended forever. Out there nothing moved but transparent waves of heat that danced about slowly on a still, windless calm.

A man sat just within the edge of the shadow with his legs crossed, his back to the sand and the heat. Behind him the sun beat down with such blinding intensity his features were lost in the blackness of a dark silhouette. He leaned forward slowly, held something out toward Morgin's face, and a trickle of water passed between his lips to wet his tongue. Morgin swallowed and gulped at it greedily, and as the water washed down his throat the man sat back, rested his hands on his knees and returned to his still, silent vigil.

In the distance behind him Morgin's eye caught a flicker of movement out on the sands. Something out there approached the lean-to, an animal of some kind that flowed with the grace and fluidity of a shadow. But it was yellow like the sands, not black and dark, and when it remained still it blended into the glare of the Waste so completely it might as well have been invisible. It moved like a predatory animal stalking prey, holding as still as the heat for a few heartbeats and blending into the ripples on the edge of a dune. Then it would cautiously move forward, cross to another dune and stop, blending once again into the stillness of the Munjarro.

Whatever it might be, Morgin realized it stalked him and the man in the small lean-to, something big and sleek. Its muscles rippled like the heat waves that danced across the dunes, and he was too weak to move, too weak to speak, too weak to give warning of any kind. The man sat with his back to the sands waiting for something, and as the monster behind him approached, Morgin struggled to cry out, but a nameless weight upon his soul paralyzed him. So he lay there watching the beast approach, and as it came closer he saw that it was a giant cat with sand-yellow fur and blood-red eyes. Two giant, saber-like teeth protruded from its upper jaw, it ran on large paws that kept it from sinking into the sand, and in it Morgin sensed a deadly malice toward all things mortal. But when it reached the lean-to, instead of pouncing upon them as

Morgin expected, it settled down on its haunches just beyond the edge of the shadow, as if it preferred the hellish fire of the sand rather than the cool shade of their shelter. It just sat there, watching him with those blood-red eyes, until finally it lifted one forepaw, and with the faintest flick of its wrist, it extended its claws, five of which were razor sharp and the length of a man's fingers. But the sixth claw was tiny, no more than the size of a small thorn, and as Morgin looked at it a minute drop of venom dripped from its tip, and he understood that the smallest claw was the most deadly of all.

The beast smiled at him, and he knew her name to be Shebasha. He knew it was all just a dream, or a hallucination, and that in reality he was probably lying face down in the sand somewhere with the sun baking his brains.

••••

Standing before a large hearth and warming his hands, Valso fully expected to hear the door behind him slam loudly, fully expected to hear DaNoel demand, "He is dead, is he not?"

He turned to face the young Elhiyne lord who stood just within the threshold of his suites. Clearly, he'd begun to have doubts about betraying the whoreson, as well as doubts about conspiring with a Decouix. Valso said, "If not now, then soon."

"What do you mean by that? What about those little dogs of yours, the skree?"

The fire warmed Valso's backside, and he thought that, when he ruled all seven tribes, he might spend winters in Elhiyne. Here in Durin, in the far north, the chill of winter often lingered even into late spring. By now those Elhiynes were probably enjoying warm spring days, and Valso envied them that.

Valso gave DaNoel an indifferent shrug. "The skree devoured something. We found a large, bloody smear in a field on your brother's trail—"

"He's not my brother."

Valso ignored the interruption. "But it wasn't him. I would know that."

DaNoel crossed the room angrily. "Then who, what?"

Valso smiled merely to irritate DaNoel further. "Upon returning to Durin, I learned his wife took a horse from the stables while we were organizing the skree. Apparently, she rode out after her husband with some foolishly romantic idea of aiding him. A horse is fast until it tires, but the skree are relentless. It's likely the skree devoured his wife and her horse in that field."

DaNoel had grown so agitated that as he spoke, little drops of spittle flicked out between his lips. "I care nothing for Rhianne one way or the other. It's the whoreson I want to know about."

Valso feigned indifference. "We chased him out onto the sands of the Munjarro."

"Then he's still alive?"

"I doubt it. With no supplies, he won't last two days in that oven of sand. He's probably already chased a mirage or two, and by now the Waste has consumed him."

DaNoel's eyes grew dark, fearful and haunted. Valso suspected DaNoel's fear stemmed from the fact that he now understood he'd ensnared himself in a trap of his own devising. They both knew he'd have to continue to cooperate with Valso, or Valso would expose him to his family, and that old witch Olivia would eat the fool alive.

"That's not good enough," DaNoel said. He spun on his heels and marched across the room, pulled the door open, but hesitated before leaving. He turned back to Valso. "You promised."

Valso turned his back on DaNoel, and rubbed his hands together in front of the warm fire. "I will ensure that he does not return from the dead, and in the meantime I don't want rumors of his possible survival floating about. Remember this, Elhiyne: as far as everyone else is concerned, your brother and his wife both died in the jaws of the skree."

"You fear him, don't you?"

Valso laughed. "No, it's you who fear him."

DaNoel hesitated for a moment, then stepped through the door and slammed it angrily.

When he was gone, Valso glanced to one side at a set of drapes that hid a balcony. He said, "You heard, Lord Carsaris?"

One of Valso's most powerful sorcerers stepped out from behind the drapes. Carsaris stood taller than most on a skeletal frame of long limbs. His thin nose and sunken cheeks only added to his spectral appearance. "We'll have to watch him closely, Your Majesty. He clearly regrets having cooperated with you."

"Yes," Valso said. "But his hatred for his brother blinds him to how truly, deeply he is ensnared."

"Then, Your Majesty, it might be wise to enlighten him. If he knows he cannot go back, he will be less likely to betray us."

"As always, Lord Carsaris, your counsel is invaluable."

Valso stepped away from the fire to face Carsaris squarely. "How goes our little project?"

"Progress is slow, Your Majesty. The swordsman, he is stronger than anticipated, though that isn't a bad thing. The stronger the swordsman proves to be now, the stronger Salula will prove to be later."

••••

Morgin drifted in and out of his dreams of Shebasha for some unknown time. Sometimes she sat just outside the shade of the lean-to, and sometimes not. The man remained unchanged; always sitting just within the shadow, though Morgin wondered if he truly was a man, for a dark silhouette always hid his features. He also dreamt of the skeleton king sitting upon his throne in the tomb in Attunhigh: vivid images that seemed very real, as if the sands wanted him to remember the crypt with clarity far greater than that of a dream. He had seen the skeleton king's crypt for the first time when he lay dying in the enchanted alcove in Castle Elhiyne. But now something in the image had changed. He couldn't say what, and that bothered him.

Then the sense of a dream ended and he came fully awake. The large cat was nowhere to be seen and he realized she was just a figment of his delirium. The small lean-to was real, though the shade it cast was far from cool, yet certainly far cooler than the oven out on the open sands. The man no longer sat in the shade with Morgin, but Morgin spotted him out on the sands in the distance.

Morgin first noticed the shape of his head; it was enormous and triangular, though that hadn't been the case when the fellow sat in the shadows within the lean-to. He wore sand-yellow breeches tucked into calf length boots, an odd, knee-length robe collected at the waist by a black belt, with a hood thrown up over his strangely shaped head. He bent down over something in the sand with his back to Morgin, and when he stood erect he lifted a small creature in his hand that struggled to escape. He gave its neck a sharp twist and it went limp, then he turned back toward the lean-to. It was then that Morgin understood what made his head appear to be so oddly shaped. He wore some sort of broad, stiff-brimmed hat, over which the hood of his robe had been thrown. The brim of the hat had the effect of making a large tent of the hood, which, in the bright sun, hid the man's face in a deep and mysterious shadow.

As the man approached the lean-to Morgin sat up, found that he was still dressed in the torn and battered clothing he'd worn during his escape from the Decouix dungeon. Around his neck, someone—he assumed it had been the man—had added a thick ring of intricately braided leather. It was too small to slip over his head, and it had no clasp so he surmised it had been braided in place while he lay unconscious.

"You'll grow used to the debt-ring," a voice said.

Morgin looked up and found the man standing over the entrance to the lean-to. The timbre of his voice told Morgin he was still a young man, probably in his mid-twenties like Morgin. "Debt-ring?" Morgin asked.

"Yes," the young man said. "I saved you from the sands. I gave you water"—he held up the small, reptilian beast in his hand—"and now I'm about to feed you. You owe me a great debt, and it's not honorable to be indebted so."

Morgin wondered if this made him some sort of slave, and for a moment he considered resisting the young man. But as the fellow threw back the hood and pulled off his hat, Morgin saw the bone-white color of his skin for the first time. With his memories of haunting the soul of the ancient Benesh'ere warrior Morddon still fresh in his mind, he knew this man would be a fearsome warrior. Though, even if he were able to defeat him, they were somewhere out in the middle of the Great Munjarro Waste, and Morgin was wholly dependent upon him for survival.

The young man stabbed a finger into his own chest. "I am Harriok, your new master. You will address me as Lord Harriok."

Morgin decided to play along, then escape at the first opportunity. "Yes, Lord Harriok."

"Very good."

Harriok bent down, crawled into the lean-to, sat down with his legs crossed opposite Morgin, drew a knife and began gutting the small creature he'd captured. Morgin had been right about his age, a young Benesh'ere warrior with the characteristic bone white skin, and coal-black hair tied into a braid that hung down his back just past his shoulders.

Morgin cleared his throat. "May I ask a question, Lord Harriok?"

Harriok nodded. "Go ahead."

"How long ago did you find me?"

"Late yesterday."

Morgin ran his fingers through his hair. "I feel much better than I think I should."

Harriok held up the creature he'd cleaned. "A few more hours and this cratl and his fellows would have started picking at your flesh. But you weren't bad off. A little too much heat, not enough water, both easily remedied."

Harriok finished gutting the cratl. "Speaking of water," Harriok said. "You've put me a day behind schedule, and you've used water I hadn't counted on. As soon as the sun sets we'll pack up and leave."

"Where are we going?"

"To join the tribe. I was scouting our northern flank when I came across you lying in the sand. But now that I've wasted a day here they're probably well ahead of us. It won't be easy catching up. In fact we may not be able to join them until Aelldie."

"What's Aelldie?" Morgin asked.

"It's the largest oasis in the Munjarro, and the last oasis before we leave the sands for the summer."

"You're leaving the sands?"

"Of course we're leaving the sands. We always leave the sands in summer. It gets too hot to survive so we go to the Lake of Sorrows. And you're asking too many questions."

Morgin nodded meekly and said, "Yes, Lord Harriok." He smiled inwardly, for though Harriok complained, he clearly enjoyed having someone to talk to.

Harriok cut the cratl meat into strips and gave half of them to Morgin with a small ration of water. "Raw cratl meat," Harriok said, holding up a strip. "A good source of water."

They dined on raw cratl and hard brown journeycake. Near dusk the temperature dropped and he took Morgin out onto the sand. It was then that Morgin first saw the other, larger lean-to in which Harriok's horse rested quietly on its haunches in the shade.

Morgin helped him clear several traps that had snagged other reptilian creatures like the cratl and a few small rodents. Harriok snapped each creature's neck then tossed it in a sack.

"Aren't we going to clean them?" Morgin asked.

Harriok shook his head. "Not now." He looked up at the darkening sky. "Now we travel. We'll stop when the sand starts to heat up at sunrise. There'll be plenty of time for that then."

Both lean-tos folded up into an impressively compact bundle. Harriok gave Morgin a knee length hooded robe like his own, adding, "I have to take care of my property," and they were on their way.

2

Walking the Sand

HARRIOK RODE WHILE Morgin walked close behind him, and by the stars he could tell they headed due west. A three-quarter moon lit the yellow dunes beautifully, though there was really nothing to see but an endless ocean of sand. It was not easy walking on the sand. It shifted and slid beneath his feet, and it often required two steps just to travel one. Harriok rode a special breed of horse Morgin had heard of but never seen. It had large, broad hooves that didn't sink far into the sand, with a lean, compact body that didn't require excessive water or feed. Mounted, Harriok could have pushed Morgin to travel much faster, but instead set a reasonable pace that Morgin maintained without difficulty.

He trudged along in silence for a good while, concentrating on keeping his footing in the loose sand, when Harriok surprised him. "What's your name?"

"Morgin," he answered, then realized he should have lied. A wanted man shouldn't use a name others might recognize.

"What were you doing out on the sands?"

Morgin knew the Benesh'ere hated the Decouixs, so he decided a common enemy might put him in a better light with this young warrior. "I ran afoul of some Decouixs, and it was either the sands, or get my throat cut."

"Are you a clansman?"

"No. Just a wandering swordsman."

"Well, you can't have wandered all your life. You must have come from somewhere."

It would be wise to stay as close to the truth as possible, so Morgin made up a life for himself not unlike that of some of his childhood companions. "I'm the son of an Elhiyne freeman. My father was a soldier and my mother a kitchen maid. I was raised at Elhiyne itself, and taught some soldiering skills."

Harriok turned about in the saddle and looked down at Morgin, his voice filled with curiosity. "You grew up in the castle?"

"Aye," Morgin said.

"What was it like? Was it big? It must be strange to live surrounded by stone like that."

Morgin told Harriok about Elhiyne. He described every detail of the place, and the people who lived there, which fascinated the young Benesh'ere warrior. But for himself, he became sadly homesick.

"You miss them," Harriok said. "I can tell."

For all his bluster, Harriok treated Morgin almost as an equal. To maintain a good pace they took turns riding the horse, though Harriok tied one end of a good length of rope to Morgin's debt-ring, and the other to his wrist. If Morgin tried to spur the horse into a run and escape, the young Benesh'ere could easily yank him from the saddle. And only occasionally did Harriok remember that Morgin was in his debt and demand that he call him "Lord." They stopped near midnight to eat, then traveled on. They continued at a steady pace until well past dawn since the air remained cool during the first few hours of morning. As the sands warmed Harriok called a halt. He taught Morgin how to pitch the lean-tos, then how to set traps in the sand. By that time the air had grown thick and hot, so they retired to the shade of the lean-to.

Morgin wanted to drop instantly into sleep, but first they cleaned their catch from the previous day, cut the meat into strips, ate some of it raw and lay the rest out in the sun to dry. After they lay down in the lean-to, and before sleep took them, Morgin asked, "Do you own me? Am I a slave, or something?"

"Of course not. You owe me a debt of honor, and until it's repaid you are mine to do with as I please."

The next night went much as the first. They kept up a steady pace while Harriok quizzed Morgin incessantly about life among the clans. Near dawn, just as the sky began to lighten, Harriok stopped abruptly, stood up in his stirrups and sniffed the air.

"Water," Harriok said excitedly. Then he climbed down out of the saddle, and with some urgency untied his pack.

"Help me," he said.

Morgin could only provide minimal help since he had no idea what Harriok was trying to do. "What are we doing?" he asked.

Harriok grinned. "A mist still, for water. Just wait and see."

They quickly assembled what appeared to be a strangely shaped and oddly inverted tent. It was a contraption made of wooden stakes and a circular piece of oiled cloth about as wide as the spread of a man's arms. The stakes supported the outer edges of the cloth about knee high off the sand, while in the middle Harriok placed a small stone that weighted the center of the cloth downward. With that done, they then went about the business of making camp, though it was much earlier than the previous morning.

As they worked, Morgin noticed a light mist forming just off the surface of the sand. But by the time camp was fully set it was knee deep and as thick as a heavy fog, and Morgin had difficulty seeing through it to set the last trap. Then the sun rose, and the mist dissipated.

"Quickly now," Harriok said, and taking up a nearly empty water skin, he stood over his strange contraption. "Come here and help me."

As Morgin approached he looked down into the bowl of the little inverted tent, and in it he saw the small rock Harriok had placed there to weight down the center. It now lay beneath the surface of a good-sized puddle of water.

Harriok pulled the stopper on the water skin, handed it to Morgin, bent down and took hold of one edge of the oiled cloth to support it as he pulled one of the stakes. Morgin didn't need to be told what to do. He carefully held the water skin in place while Harriok lowered that edge and let the water drain into the skin. With that done, they quickly disassembled the mist still, repacked it, and retired to the lean-to. Again, Morgin dreamt of Shebasha and Aethon's tomb.

That night, as they traveled under the star-lit sky, Morgin felt the tug of something arcane, a pull that started out as a faint sensation, but grew stronger with each step. By the time they began erecting the two lean-tos in the morning, he knew they were in the vicinity of something unusual. When the tents were ready and he could take a free moment, Morgin climbed to the top of a nearby dune to scan their surroundings. To the south he caught a glint of something shiny on the horizon, though that didn't seem to coincide with the direction of the pull he felt. When he shaded his eyes with his hand and squinted, he could just make out a jagged silhouette, like that of a city with tall, glassy spires.

"Ah," Harriok said as he joined Morgin at the top of the dune. "The ruins of Kathbeyanne, the phantom city. We call it the city of glass."

The words *city of glass* triggered an old memory. After Csairne Glen, when the archangel Metadan had fought Ellowyn in his dreams and knocked her unconscious, he'd given Morgin a message, something about the Unnamed King and his consort the god-queen Erithnae, and seeking the god-sword, and failing, and asking three questions in the *city of glass*. Morgin struggled to recall the message in its entirety, but the memory eluded him.

"Have you gone there?" Morgin asked.

Harriok shook his head. "That's a fool's errand. It's enchanted. If you walk toward it, it will always remain on the horizon and you'll never get there. Eventually, you'll find that you've walked in a vast circle. It's a dangerous trap for the unwary."

Facing the city squarely, Morgin closed his eyes and concentrated on that arcane pull that had drawn his attention. With Morddon's memories he recognized the scent of the fabled city, recalled looking through the ancient warrior's eyes at the grand palace of the Shahotma for the first time, the spires that reached toward the heavens, balconies and balustrades that soared high above the city, with level upon level of parapets and battlements. In front of it had been a massive parade ground, with the barracks of the Benesh'ere and the twelve legions of angels to one side. It was there, haunting Morddon's soul, that he'd first met TarnThane, the griffin lord, AnneRhianne, the Benesh'ere princess, and Gilguard, warmaster of the Benesh'ere, all ancient and long since gone.

Standing atop a dune in the middle of the Munjarro with his eyes closed, he would have sworn the city lay to his left, not straight in front of him. He opened his eyes, and the vision of Kathbeyanne lay on the horizon directly before him. If the gods had left an enchantment on the city so it appeared to be where it was not, one would certainly walk in circles trying to get there. On the other hand, if he ignored the mirage and walked toward the pull of the arcane, might he actually reach the fabled city? Morgin decided to say nothing of this to Harriok. Maybe someday he'd come back and seek out Kathbeyanne, the *city of glass*, and ask Metadan's three questions. Though first he'd have to find Metadan and ask him to repeat that message.

Morgin had drifted off into a light doze in the middle of the heat of the day, when Harriok sat up suddenly and startled him fully awake. The young whiteface cocked his head to one side and appeared to be listening for something, and the look on his face frightened Morgin. "What is it?" he asked.

"Silence," Harriok hissed.

Morgin obeyed without question while Harriok listened further. After several heartbeats of silence, the young Benesh'ere reached for his hooded robe and snapped out, "There's a storm coming, and we don't have much time."

In the stifling heat of the midday sun, they broke down their small lean-to. Harriok pulled his horse out into the sun to get it out of the way, then led them down into a deep valley between two dunes. They scooped out a depression in the sand and combined the two lean-tos to make a fully enclosed tent. Harriok pressed the already short tent poles deeper into the sand, giving the tent a flat, low profile. "Start tossing sand on top of the tent," he ordered. "We need at least a full hand's depth."

Harriok climbed into the tent itself, began scooping out more sand. Morgin could now hear a faint roar in the distance, and a dark cloud appeared on the horizon. He frantically tossed handfuls of sand on the cloth of the tent, glancing over his shoulder at the dark shadow that grew higher and closer with each heartbeat. Then it hit them with a fury that threatened to sweep them off their feet. But by that time he and Harriok and the horse were safely sealed within the tent in relative comfort. The storm raged above them, howling out its hatred as if it were a living thing. And though the midday sun burned in the sky above them, in the tent beneath the sand they waited in complete darkness.

"The Munjarro is angry this day," Harriok said. "Let us hope it is not angry at us, eh?"

They carefully arranged their provisions, then settled down to an uneasy sleep.

••••

Rhianne came to the Lake of Sorrows near dusk of a calm, clear day. The trail she followed opened out into a small village on the eastern side of the lake, but as she nudged her horse forward she realized the huts had been abandoned long ago. The glassy and smooth surface of the lake glistened in the fading light, and a seemingly enchanted stillness hung over all. The huts were in poor condition, there was no wood for a fire, and it had been quite some time since she'd eaten anything more than the few nuts and berries she'd gathered.

The sword hovered in the back of her thoughts, always there, never forgotten. It hungered for death and destruction, a thing of pure chaos, hatred and malevolence. It called to her like a newborn child, obstinately demanding her attention, begging her to take it up and wield it so it could sate its bloodlust on the innocent. No wonder it had nearly driven Morgin to madness, and she understood now what strength he must have possessed to resist its relentless demands.

Wearily, she sat down on a flat rock near the edge of the water and watched the sun set over the Worshipers, and as the chill of night settled upon her she wondered what she would do for food and shelter, wondered if she could find the strength to resist the sword as Morgin had. She buried her face in her hands and shed the tears she had held back for so long.

When she ran out of tears she sat up straight and opened her eyes. It was then that she saw the lights on the north end of the lake, and the regularity of their spacing told her there must be an active village there, not just a few campfires. She had heard that some sort of town existed near the lake, so she took her horse's reins, pulled her cloak tightly about her and began searching her way through the forest toward the lights. A good-sized moon gave her plenty of light, but cautiously she led her horse rather than riding it, and after some time she discovered a trail that hugged the lakeshore. It still took her several hours to reach the village, and by that time the chill of night had cut to the bone, and she hovered on the edge of collapse.

She searched out what must be the village inn, the only two-story structure in the place, with a healthy cloud of smoke billowing from its chimney. The door was barred, so she rapped on it with the heel of her hand, and after a pause it opened a crack and a grimy face stared out at her.

Close to tears, she asked, "Is this an inn?"

"Aye," a gruff male voice answered her. "And who's askin'?"

"A traveler," she said, "seeking shelter from the cold."

"Where's yer man?"

A woman never traveled alone; it was much too dangerous. Rhianne tried to think of a good lie, but realized they'd learn the truth soon enough. "I'm traveling alone."

The innkeeper looked her over silently for an interminable moment, then grumbled his disapproval and opened the door. Inside, blessed warmth washed over her and she paused just within the door for a moment to let her shivers die. Across the room a healthy fire crackled in a large hearth, and without hesitation she approached it. She stood in front of it until she could no longer stand the heat, then she backed away, turned around, and took stock of her surroundings.

There were a number of patrons seated on crude benches in the inn's common room, all of them male, all of them staring at her with undisguised distrust. The ceiling was low, the air sooty and stale, and the floor simple packed earth. The fat innkeeper had retreated behind a bar at the far end of the room, and like his patrons, he stared at her suspiciously while he used a dirty rag to polish a tin cup. She crossed the room toward him, stepped up to the bar and smiled politely. "I'm very hungry. I haven't had a full meal in days."

"Sure," the innkeeper grumbled, thick folds of skin at his neck wobbling as he spoke. "We got food to sell."

Money! Rhianne had never thought to carry money. A woman didn't carry money, unless she was the kitchen maid going to market for her master, or some servant on an errand. "I have no money," she whispered.

The innkeeper shook his head. "I don't give food away free."

A man stepped up to the bar next to her, standing over her uncomfortably close. "So yer hungry?" the man said. "And penniless, eh?" He grabbed her by the arm, spun her to face him, leaned up close to her and grinned a gap-toothed grin. His breath smelled of onions and beer and it turned her stomach. "But yer a pretty one, me girl, and I know how you can earn a few coins."

"Jokath," someone shouted, "going to keep her all for yourself?"

"Please," Rhianne pleaded. "Let go of me."

"Ah, you just don't know what you want, little girl."

"Let her go, Jokath," the innkeeper said.

The bully glanced his way. "I'll let her go when I'm done with her."

He grabbed both her shoulders with his hands, pulled her face toward his, and as rising panic took her she instinctively reached for the only weapon at her commend, and she surprised herself at how easily her magic answered her call.

Sparks crackled at her shoulders where his hands touched her, and while her power protected her, the bully screamed out, jerked and twitched, then fell away from her and landed on his back on the floor. He groaned and clutched his smoking hands to his chest. At that moment, every man in the inn decided he had other business to worry about and looked away. Rhianne's blood was up: Morgin's death, days without food and rest, hungry, tired, and dirty. She stood over the bully and he cringed beneath her as she pointed a finger at him. "Lay a hand on me again, bully, and I'll turn you into a toad and feed you to the innkeeper's cat—if he has one. If not, I'll eat you myself. Now be gone with you."

The bully whimpered, got up onto his hands and knees and crawled to the door. Rhianne wondered how he'd feel if he knew she didn't know how to turn him into a toad. She turned back to the innkeeper. Clearly as frightened as the bully, he remained behind the bar as if it would protect him from the witch who'd come in the night. "I'll work for a meal and a roof over my head," she said.

The innkeeper's fear dissipated, turned into curiosity as he considered her proposal for a moment. Then he came to a decision. "Can you heal?" he asked. He leaned across the bar toward her, cocked his head to one side and pulled the collar of his tunic down to expose the side of his neck and a large, ugly, swollen boil. "Can you heal this?"

She looked it over for a moment. It was obviously painful. "You're asking for magic. And magic is difficult and dangerous. Dangerous for me, not you. So healing that will cost you far more than a single meal and a single night's sleep." She tried to judge the degree of suffering the boil had caused. "Three days and nights room and board, and stabling and feed for my horse."

He lifted his collar, straightened up and looked at her narrowly. They argued further, settled on a day and a half. He finished with, "Ok, what's yer name? Gotta have a name to seal a bargain."

Rhianne hesitated, knew she shouldn't give her real name, hadn't thought far enough in advance to come up with one. She blurted out the first thing that came to mind, "Syllith."

The innkeeper noticed her hesitation, but didn't say anything. "And I'm John, but everyone calls me Fat John."

He lifted his hand, spit into his palm and extended it toward her, saying, "Done, Mistress Syllith."

Not sure what she was supposed to do, she spit into her own palm and shook his hand, then wiped her hand on her dress. "I'll begin in the morning. For now have someone show me to my room. And that's where I'll eat, so have them bring my dinner as soon as possible."

The innkeeper nodded to a young boy seated near the end of the bar. "Take her to the room in the northeast corner."

Rhianne's magic flooded her soul, and she sensed some deceit in the innkeeper's words. She looked at him angrily. "I won't demand the best room in the inn. But if there's anything wrong with the room you give me, I'll give you another boil to match that one . . ." She glanced down at his crotch, ". . . but in a far more painful place."

The innkeeper looked at her for an instant, then shivered and grumbled at the boy, "On second thought, take her to the southeast room."

3

The Spirit of the Sands

NICKOLOT SAT IN her room, trembling as she listened to Rhianne's screams. When the Kulls were done with Rhianne, she knew in her soul that Valso would give her to them next . . .

The Tulalane tried to paw her, slapped her and hurt her . . .

NickoLot awoke from her nightmares trembling. She sat up in bed, re-called that night so long ago, and yet it seemed only last night that she'd had to sit in her room, listening to the Kulls raping Rhianne in the room next to her. Rhianne's screams had eventually died down to whimpers, barely heard through the thick wall between them, then nothing. And yet, Nicki had still sat there imagining what they would do to her when her turn came.

She climbed out of bed, went to her closet to select a gown for the day. After Csairne Glen there'd been a great deal of mourning to do, and Olivia had arranged for all of them to be properly attired. Nicki found black a comfortably unflattering color, and she now preferred it, wore it exclusively. She liked the high necklines that hid her small breasts, with a black veil to hide her face.

It suddenly struck her that the black dresses and veils were her equiv-alent of Morgin's shadows, a comfortable place to hide.

••••

Morgin awoke to the blackness of the tent, vivid dreams of Shebasha and Aethon's tomb fluttering through his memory. Outside, he still heard the storm blowing out its fury, while inside he sensed a tension in the air that could only be coming from his companion. "What's wrong?" he whispered into the darkness.

Harriok shifted his position. "Night is approaching, and there's no sign the storm is letting up."

"So?" Morgin asked. "We seem to be safe."

"So we'll miss travel time, and we're short enough on water as it is."

Morgin could almost see Harriok through the darkness, and he wondered if some small part of his lost sense of shadow might have returned. But more than seeing him he heard the tension in his voice. "There's something else, isn't there?"

Harriok nodded. "The big cats. They hunt at night, though they're loners, so ordinarily they'll stay away from men, especially if there's more than one of us. But they become quite bold during a storm like this because we're so helpless."

"Aren't they helpless too?"

"No. Where the blowing sand would cut the flesh from our bones their thick fur protects them; and where the grit and the dust blind us, they have a transparent membrane that protects their eyes. But we should be safe. We're dug in nicely, so it's not likely one will find us."

Remembering his dream Morgin asked, "Do they kill with their venom?"

To be the target of the lightning speed of a Benesh'ere warrior was a frightening experience. Almost before he'd finished speaking, Harriok pressed the cold steel of a knife to his throat. "What did you mean by that? The cats have no venom."

Morgin glanced down at the blade. "I dreamt of a big cat with one venomous claw."

Harriok released him, shook his head and muttered, "We're doomed."

"What do you mean we're doomed? I'm not giving up that easily."

"It doesn't matter," Harriok groaned. "If you dreamt of the demon-cat then she is coming for us."

"And why is this cat so special?"

Harriok curled up in a corner of the tent. "Her soul is haunted by the spirit of a demon, and her venom is the darkest magic of death. Once it has touched you, your soul is hers until she dies."

Morgin argued, "Then we'll have to kill her."

Harriok shook his head. "How can you kill something that is already dead? The storm itself is probably her doing."

As the hours passed the fury of the storm abated somewhat, though not enough, Harriok assured him, for them to travel. The howling of the wind outside often sounded like the cry of a large animal, and with increasing frequency Morgin found it difficult to convince himself it was only his imagination. Eventually he drifted off into a fitful sleep where he dreamt of the storm and the sand and Harriok . . . and the cat.

She was a hot spark of life in the blackness of the wind and the sand in the night, a soul filled with hatred, desire and madness. In his soul he watched her stalking them, darting from one dune to the next, undeterred by the fury of the storm. *Just a dream,* he tried to tell himself, but he found little comfort in that, for long ago he'd learned how dangerous his dreams could be.

Another spark of life appeared in his dream, a hint of netherlife with a strange familiarity to it, a netherbeing whom Morgin could never fail to recognize: Rat. Shebasha changed course, intent upon intercepting Rat. But he darted from one dune to the next, popping in and out of reality as if reality and dream were stepping stones across a path of fear.

Rat crossed the terrain of Morgin's dream and slipped into the tent. He crouched within a shadow in the confined space and his scent reminded Morgin of the sewers of Anistigh. He wore a jumble of filthy rags, his eyes hot sparks in the blackness of the tent. "You forgot this," he growled. He dragged forth Morgin's sword and dropped it in the sand before him.

Morgin awoke to the howl of the wind, his fingers wrapped about the hilt of his sword, memories of Rat haunting his dreams. Shebasha's scream rose above the cry of the wind, an anguished shriek Morgin knew must come from the demon haunting her soul. No longer dreaming, he sensed her stalking them, preparing to attack.

Morgin shouted above the howl of the wind, "The cat's near. She's going to attack."

In the altered tent they couldn't get higher than their hands and knees. Harriok tensed and shouted, "Stay low."

Harriok tried to burrow into the sand, and Morgin followed his example. They heard the cat shriek above the howling wind. She leapt, and her claws ripped through the cloth of the tent, opening it up to admit the night, the fury of the storm, and the hatred that haunted the great cat's soul.

The sand cut painfully at Morgin's cheeks so he folded the hood of his robe across his face to protect it. Harriok rose beside him, sword in hand, probably unaware Morgin now had a sword of his own. Harriok gripped Morgin's tunic, pulled him close and screamed in his ear above the howl of the wind, "Stay low, or the blowing sand will shred your skin."

Shebasha ran a zigzag charge through the sand toward them. Then she made her final charge, and as she leapt, Morgin wrapped his arms about Harriok, let his knees fold and they landed in the sand. Arcing over them, she missed them and plowed into the horse. The horse screamed, went down with the cat on top of it, and Morgin caught a momentary glimpse of a massive, clawed paw tearing out its throat. As the horse kicked out its last moments of life, the cat clamped its jaws about its throat and dragged it off into the storm.

Morgin screamed into Harriok's ear, "Get up. We have to fight." But the young Benesh'ere remained unmoving and lifeless. Morgin held on to his sword with one hand and with the other gathered the tattered remnants of the tent about them, tried to wrap them both within its folds to protect them from the storm. He sensed Shebasha just on the other side of the dune next to them, and tangled in the cloth and sand he feared there was little he could do to defend them.

He concentrated on his only chance: the sword. He sought out its magic, searched for it, opened his soul to it. Shebasha, possibly born of the same netherlife as the sword, must have sensed his tactic. She climbed to the top of the dune and leapt just as the metallic scent of magic touched his nose. The sword came to life, literally lifted him off the sand, and stood him straight up in the heart of the storm directly in the cat's path. He struck out as she hit him, but the force of the impact sent him and the great cat tumbling down the side of a dune. At the bottom she landed on top of him and consciousness left him.

••••

JohnEngine cringed as Olivia said, "This has been a disaster." Even in his mid-twenties, JohnEngine reacted like a trained dog taught to fear the voice of its master.

"Yes it has, mother," AnnaRail said, Roland standing beside her. "But you must calm yourself."

JohnEngine glanced around the room as the two tried to calm the agitated old woman. Even here in Durin, Olivia had managed to recreate her sitting room in the suite she'd been given. The furniture was clearly not the same as that in her room in Elhiyne, the colors and materials different. But she'd moved various pieces, and they were no longer positioned as JohnEngine had first seen them almost twelve days ago. The old woman had shifted them here and there until the atmosphere of her sitting room had been recreated, an atmosphere in which all present felt as if Olivia sat on a throne above them, passing judgment at every turn.

"How can I remain calm with Morgin and Rhianne both dead?"

At the mention of their deaths, JohnEngine saw the hint of a tear in AnnaRail's eyes, and suppressed a tear of his own. DaNoel's stoic attitude disturbed him. His brother showed even less feeling than the old woman, and JohnEngine found that curious. Certainly, he and Morgin had never gotten along, but it appeared odd that he showed absolutely no sorrow whatsoever at the death of his adopted brother.

Olivia continued her rant. "The Decouix turned the tables on us. BlakeDown will surely use this to his advantage."

Yes, Valso had turned their victory at Csairne Glen into a horrible loss of face. They'd come to Durin in triumph. Then the Kulls had dragged Morgin into the throne room and dumped him onto the floor, a bloody, beaten mess.

"We leave this city on the morrow," Olivia said. "Instruct our servants and retainers to be ready for travel."

JohnEngine bowed and said, "As you wish."

DaNoel did the same, and they both turned and left the room while AnnaRail and Roland remained.

Out in the hallway JohnEngine turned to DaNoel and said, "You feel nothing for Morgin?"

JohnEngine expected to see defiance, but thought he saw something akin to guilt flash in DaNoel's eyes.

"I mourn him," DaNoel said. "Perhaps not as deeply as you, but I do."

DaNoel's words just didn't ring true. As DaNoel turned away and strode down the hall, JohnEngine wondered why he felt the need to lie; and from where did such guilt stem? JohnEngine pondered that as he followed in DaNoel's footsteps.

••••

Morgin awoke to the vast silence of the morning dunes. The storm had blown itself out, the sun had risen, the morning still and calm with the temperature just beginning to rise. He lay on his face at the bottom of a dune, twisted up in the tangled remains of the tent. He hadn't dreamt of Shebasha, but had dreamt of Aethon's tomb.

He looked around; there was no sign of the big cat, so he rolled over onto his back, discovered painfully that she'd clawed him across the back of his left shoulder. Probing with his right hand, he found five straight, deep furrows in the skin there, each throbbing painfully and caked with dried blood and sand. He thought he felt a small sixth furrow next to them, perhaps the length of his thumb. To his surprise it didn't throb with pain, but was numb to the touch. He tried to recall what Harriok had said about Shebasha's venom, and he wondered if he would now die some horrible death as her venom consumed his soul.

His left arm was of limited use and it took him some moments to pull free of the tent, then he climbed slowly to the top of the dune to survey his surroundings. On the other side of the dune the remnants of their camp were spread across the sands, though he saw no sign of his sword and assumed he'd lost it in the sand somewhere. Harriok's horse lay nearby, its throat ripped out, long since dead. Sand had completely filled the depression Harriok had created for their tent.

Morgin dug frantically and quickly found Harriok wrapped in a good-sized piece of the tent. He was still alive, though unconscious. He'd been clawed across the chest, and he bore the marks of all six claws. Morgin examined the mark of the sixth claw carefully; it was shallower than the rest, and while the others had closed and the blood about them had dried, the small, sixth mark continued to ooze a thick, yellowish fluid.

Morgin laid Harriok to one side and dug further. He uncovered one of the water skins, torn and empty with no hint it had ever contained moisture. Digging further he found Harriok's saddle, and along with it the rest of their provisions, including one, half-full water skin.

He pieced together as much of the tent as possible, managed to reassemble a small lean-to to protect him and Harriok from the sun, spent the day going through Harriok's provisions, discarding anything not absolutely necessary and tying the rest into a small pack. As night approached and the temperature dropped, he converted the lean-to into a litter, tied Harriok securely within its folds, attached a piece of rope to it and tied the other end about his waist.

His only chance was to make for the oasis at Aelldie. He looked up at the emerging stars. Harriok had taken them due west, so he guessed the oasis must be somewhere in that direction.

••••

Tulellcoe stared silently out the window of the inn at the rippling waters of the lake. He heard Cort approach him from behind, felt her wrap her arms around his waist. She rested her chin on his shoulder and said, "It is a sad day."

They'd taken a room in an inn at Lake Savin, about half a day's ride northeast of SavinCourt. With almost an entire season of rest, and under Cort's care, his wounds had healed nicely. It could have been a pleasant time, had it not been for the steady stream of unpleasant news: Morgin captured and a prisoner of the Decouix in Durin. Then, just the previous day, they'd heard that Morgin and Rhianne had both died in the jaws of the skree.

"Yes," he said. "Those two young people deserved better than that. I should have done something to help them."

Cort sighed patiently. "And how would you have done that, my love, with a hole in your side from a Kull saber?"

He could not dispute that. Nevertheless, he felt responsible, as irrational as that might be. "You're right," he said. "But I think I might have to avenge Morgin . . . and Rhianne. I think I want to avenge them."

She removed her hands from around his waist, gripped his shoulders and turned him to face her. "Now you listen to me. You're not going to go riding off on some ill-conceived quest for vengeance." She put her arms around his waist and pressed her body against him, reminding him of the pleasures they shared. "I'll not let you deprive me of you that way."

He couldn't help but smile. He kissed her on the forehead and grinned. "I'm not foolish enough to ride off in haste. I'll bide my time, and some day an opportunity will arise, especially if I help it come to pass."

She kissed him on the cheek, just lightly brushing her lips along his skin. "You're frightening when you get that look in your eyes. At times, Morgin had a similar look, and he was tall and lanky, like you. Are you sure he doesn't have some of your blood in his veins? Perhaps you spent a little too much time with the wenches."

Tulellcoe shook his head. "It wouldn't have been me. I never whored around, ever. But the gods know there were enough Elhiyne clansmen who did, men who were related to me. It's quite possible there was some Elhiyne blood in his veins."

He wrapped his arms around her. She smiled and said, "Well, you're whoring around now."

He shook his head. "Oh no, my lady. I'm taking great joy in the pleasures of a beautiful woman. A woman whom I hope will share my days to come."

4

Rescue

CARSARIS WATCHED FOUR Kulls carry the plain wooden chair with the unconscious swordsman strapped into it. Standing beside him, Valso was preoccupied with the little, demon flying snake perched on his shoulder. The combination of Valso and the snake always unnerved Carsaris. Valso had occasionally used the snake to execute someone who displeased him. The snake's venom produced a long, slow and horrid death.

The Kulls put the chair down in the middle of the dungeon's main chamber, a large room filled with various tools for extracting information from enemies of the crown, or for merely punishing those who had displeased the Decouix king. The swordsman's head hung down, his chin almost touching his chest, his greasy and unwashed long, blond hair hanging limply, covering his face.

Standing beside Carsaris, Valso said to the little snake, "Shall we see how much progress Lord Carsaris has made?"

"Yesss, Massster," the snake hissed.

Fearful of one of Valso's whims, Carsaris said, "I hope you'll not be displeased, Your Majesty. It is a . . . difficult task."

"Fear not, Carsaris," Valso said magnanimously. "It is a near impossible task. But the *near* impossible merely takes more time. And you are one of my best, so I have every confidence that you will prevail."

Carsaris knew better than to trust Valso's mood. He'd seen the king shift in a heartbeat from happy and forgiving to venomous anger. Someone usually died when that happened.

Valso waved a hand at one of the Kulls. "Wake him."

The Kull lifted a wooden bucket and tossed its contents into the swordsman's face. When the stream of filthy water hit him, the swordsman didn't react at all. He didn't splutter or cough or choke, but with his head still bowed he remained still and motionless for several heartbeats, the water dripping from his hair. Then he merely took a deep breath, his chest rising slowly. He released the breath, then just as slowly, he lifted his head, and the eyes that looked upon them bore no semblance of humanity.

The swordsman smiled and spoke in a voice no longer that of the swordsman. It was almost a deep, grumbling growl. "Your Majesty, I see that you are now king. My compliments to you. It will be a joy to serve you again."

Valso stepped forward, though he remained well out of reach of the monster in the chair. The snake took to the air and hovered above the swordsman nervously. "My dear Salula, it is so good to see you again, though I do apologize we must treat you so." Valso waved a hand, casually indicating the chair into which they'd tied the monster.

The monster shrugged. "He is a strong one, this swordsman, this France fellow. I wonder at times if he is perhaps more than he appears. He is—"

The monster stopped speaking, closed his eyes and trembled. Then his eyes snapped open, his teeth clenched so tightly Carsaris saw the muscles of his jaw bunched and straining. He grimaced and shook his head violently, then he threw his head back and screamed, a cry of anger, fear and hatred.

Valso stepped back, and the snake retreated with him as the thing strapped into the chair struggled against his bonds. But his hands, feet, arms and legs had been tied with thick lengths of knotted rope, reinforced with powerful spells. It took him the space of many heartbeats to realize the futility of his struggles. Only then did he cease his efforts, and an odd calm settled over him. The eyes that looked upon them were now quite human, and it was the swordsman, not the monster, who said, "I'll fight you to the death."

Valso shook his head patiently, as one might when instructing a child.

"No, my friend, not to your death; at least not as you mean it. To the death of your spirit, yes. But my dear friend Salula has need of your soul and your body. So I'll not allow them to escape so easily."

Valso turned to Carsaris. "You have done well. I know it seems that little progress has been made, but patience is required in this matter."

He looked at the swordsman. "And when Salula owns you, body and soul, we'll let you go get that sword from the Elhiyne. That blade is the only thing that prevents my master from properly manifesting on the Mortal Plane. And after that, you can kill this ShadowLord."

Valso laughed. "That's funny, don't you think. You'll get to kill the man who killed you."

••••

Morgin allowed himself one tiny sip from the water skin, just enough to wet his throat and relieve the burning. The sun had reached midday, and out on the sand waves of heat danced a silent homage to whatever gods they worshiped. Inside the remnants of the patched-together lean-to it seemed the temperature was no better. He was burning up with fever, and in no condition to pass judgment on the heat. The venom of the sixth claw had finally taken its toll.

He trickled a few drops of water across Harriok's lips, but the young Benesh'ere made no effort to swallow, and he lay so silently that once again Morgin tested the pulse at his throat. He put the stopper into the water skin, then shook it carefully, listening to the water gurgle within. Perhaps only two or three mouthfuls remained.

The hottest part of the day was approaching, and out on the sand he spotted the same flicker of movement he'd seen every day now. Shebasha was on the prowl, darting across the dunes like a ghost in a children's tale.

Every night and every day had been the same. Morgin pulled Harriok across the dunes through the night, pitched camp as the sun rose, though he hadn't the energy to set traps. He would sleep for a while, dream of Aethon's tomb then awake near midday to watch the great cat circle the lean-to carefully. Each night he broke camp and continued on.

"How many days?" he asked aloud, but there was no one there to answer him. *Two*, he thought, *maybe three*. The days were all the same, and the only thing that changed was the diminishing weight of the water skin, and his ever weakening strength.

Shebasha sat down on her haunches just outside the shadow of the lean-to and preened herself. "Good day, mortal," she said.

"Good day," Morgin answered. They had the same conversation every day. But again he wondered how many days.

"Do the days matter, mortal?"

Morgin shrugged. "I don't know what matters. I suppose water matters."

"All that matters is what matters to you. So what matters to you, mortal?"

"Getting out of this alive," Morgin said. "Getting Harriok out of this alive. Will you kill me, and eat me?"

"Now why would I do that," she asked, "when you've done so much to help me?"

"What did I do to help you?"

"Why, you killed me, and for that I am grateful."

She stood then, and he saw the wound in her chest where he'd struck blindly with his sword when she'd leapt upon him in the midst of the storm. After that glimpse she drifted away like another wave of heat, and he slid deeper into his dreams.

He awoke shivering. The sun had set long ago and the night had come upon him.

That was different. In days just past he'd managed to awake shortly before sunset, in time to break camp and be on his way by nightfall. He tried to lift himself to his feet, barely managed to get up on one elbow, realized then he was hopelessly weak, that even if he got to his feet he wouldn't have the strength to do more than just stand there.

He lay back down, hoping a little more rest might give him the strength to go on.

••••

Rhianne looked at the old woman kneeling before her, realized she was not that old, just poor, filthy, and underfed. And her husband was in no better shape. "Will you help us, Yer Ladyship?"

Rhianne sat in a chair in her room in the inn, while the two peasants knelt before her. "I'll help if I can," Rhianne told the woman. "But I can't be sure until I examine the cow myself."

The woman's husband spoke up. "Our farm's about two leagues north of here."

Rhianne nodded. "Very well. Tell Fat John to have my horse saddled. I'll join you shortly and you can lead me there."

For the last few days she'd lived a precarious sort of existence. It had taken her two days to heal the innkeeper's boil, and by that time she wondered where she would find shelter when that was done. She had considered trading her horse for more time, but beyond the clothes on her back, the animal was her only possession. Then, on the day she finished with Fat John's boil, the town's smith brought his son to her with a broken arm. The man was quite fearful his son's arm would heal improperly, and he would not be able to take up his father's profession. So Rhianne set the bone, bound it carefully with a splint, gave the smith instructions on how to care for it, and told him to bring the boy back at six-day intervals while it healed. The smith had given her a chicken as payment for her services, and she'd given that to the innkeeper for another day's room and board.

The word spread quickly that a witch-healer had taken up residence in the inn, and after her success at healing Fat John's boil, and the smith's son's arm, every man and woman in the district with any kind of ailment had come to see her, and she now did a rather steady business. They paid her mostly with food, dead animals, goods, barter, and occasionally a few coins. Only the day before, she'd acquired a coarse shirt and a set of men's breeches, along with a pair of small riding boots. None of it fit well, but there was a woman in the village with some skill as a seamstress. All of these poor people needed healing of one kind or another, so she bartered that for some alterations to her newly acquired peasant garb. It would have to do. She was about to change into the breeches when instinct told her these country folk might not understand the sight of a woman in men's pants, so she decided to continue wearing her only dress over the breeches. The boots would come in handy for slogging through the mud and dung of a farm, and her skirt would keep them well hidden.

As she left the inn, the innkeeper showed considerable concern, and looking at the patrons of the common room, she realized she attracted a fair amount of business for him. It occurred to her then that she should negotiate some sort of contract with the man, perhaps a reduced rate on her room and board as long as she stayed in the inn.

The peasant couple walked and Rhianne rode her horse, its saddlebags filled to bursting with herbs and prepared potions. It was the first time Rhianne had ridden west from the lake toward the mountains, and the terrain grew steeper as they traveled. Just short of the couple's hut, the road opened out into a large area cleared of all trees, with three, enormous open pits of blackened earth.

Rhianne had heard of the coalmines, knew that they and the iron mines drove the local economy. But she'd expected to see dark, forbidding tunnel mouths in the side of the mountain, not open pits with seams of black coal running through them. To one side the miners' camp consisted of a large cluster of huts and tents, and she saw more than a hundred men scattered throughout the pits, swinging picks and bending their backs to shovels.

Rhianne stopped and commented to the peasant couple. "Quite an enterprise!"

"Aye," the man said. "The iron mine is farther up the mountain. The coal feeds the smelters and the cokers, and together they trade coke and soft iron and pig iron to the clans."

Rhianne learned that the couple grew vegetables on their small farm, and traded with the miners for other goods.

The peasant couple lived in a mud and wattle hut with one cow, several chickens, two pigs, and their two children: a boy and a girl. The boy looked to be about sixteen, the girl about fourteen, and while none of the family were well fed, it was obvious the girl got only what was left after feeding the couple, their son, and their animals. Daughters were evidently of little value to a peasant family, though it occurred to Rhianne that even among the clans, daughters were only considered of value if they could be married off to a rich or powerful family.

The cow was quite ill, running some sort of fever. Rhianne had never been taught about the healing of animals, so she must depend almost wholly upon her magic in this. But she didn't want word to spread that a powerful witch had taken up residence in the small village, so she played down the magical aspects of her efforts.

She turned to the peasant woman. "Your cow is quite ill. Clear the hut so I can work alone with the animal without interruption. It would be best if you and your animals took shelter elsewhere."

"Yes, milady," the woman said obediently.

"Wait," her husband said. "First, what's yer price? If it's too high I'd do just as well to butcher the animal."

Rhianne shook her head. They really couldn't pay the price of magic, but she had to charge them something. She had to survive, and she couldn't afford the reputation of not demanding fair payment. "Oh," she said. "I'll take a couple of chickens."

It was an extremely fair price, considering the value of the cow, but the man's eyes narrowed in a calculating way. "I'll give you one chicken and me daughter."

The daughter gasped, and her mother pleaded, "No!"

That the man would consider his daughter of less worth than a chicken stunned Rhianne. And if she took the girl on, she'd have two mouths to feed. The girl started crying. "Shut up," her father said, and he raised a hand to cuff her into silence.

"Hold," Rhianne shouted, and the man halted with his hand in the air. "She belongs to me now, so you'll not strike her without my permission."

"Then we've a deal?" the man asked.

Damn! Rhianne swore inwardly. But she nodded and said, "We have a deal. Now clear out, all of you."

The young girl's name was Braunye, a stick-thin waif of a child. Late that day Rhianne led her back to Norlakton. The deal she struck with Fat John was that Braunye's room and board would not cost Rhianne extra, and Braunye would sleep on a mat at the foot of her bed.

The poor girl was terrified of Rhianne, and seemed unable to adopt any expression but eyes wide and mouth open with fear. She jumped at every word Rhianne spoke, and constantly trembled like a frightened rabbit.

Rhianne retrieved the shirt and breeches she'd acquired, took the girl to a stream near town where Rhianne herself bathed frequently, made the girl strip, and instructed her to bathe herself. It was then that Rhianne discovered the girl didn't know how to bathe, so Rhianne joined her in the icy water and showed her. Then she told her to wash her clothing, which was little better than rags, and made her put on the shirt and breeches. Only then did they return to the inn where they hung her clothes to dry.

Rhianne had a hot dinner brought up to her room, though it took some coaxing to get Braunye to eat. But once begun, she gobbled the food down with blinding speed and no regard for the quantity she ate and the size of her shrunken stomach. Rhianne stopped her before she made herself sick all over the room.

Later, while Rhianne lay in bed waiting for sleep, with Braunye curled up in her blanket on the floor, Rhianne heard the young girl sobbing quietly. "What's wrong, Braunye?" Rhianne asked.

The girl jumped at the sound of her voice, but she didn't answer.

"Come now, Braunye. Answer me. Why are you crying?"

The girl spluttered and sobbed, then in a tearful voice said, "Please don't eat me. I'm not more than skin and bones anyway. Please."

"Oh dear!" Rhianne sighed. "Very well, Braunye. I won't eat you. You can be my servant instead. How does that sound?"

"Oh thank you, milady. Thank you."

The room grew quiet with the end of Braunye's tears, and Rhianne hungered for a dreamless sleep. Her dreams were normal, and like most dreams, strange and inexplicable, but the sword hovered ever in the background. It wanted something from her, wanted it desperately, and like an infant it constantly cried and begged for her to satisfy it. But like that same infant, it didn't know how to tell her what it wanted. After such a night she would climb out of bed exhausted, and struggle through the day yawning and nodding off here and there.

••••

Morgin dreamed of water touching his lips, washing away the thirst and the heat. And he dreamed of the Benesh'ere giants, lifting him, carrying him away to a place of tree-lined groves and large, pavilion-like tents. He dreamed that someone forced him to eat foul tasting herbs, to drink warm, meaty broth, and water with the chill of winter to it. And then he snapped awake and realized it wasn't a dream, that Harriok's people must have found them.

The sun had just risen, and when he sat up he found that the leather debt-ring around his neck had been tied to a stake in the ground by a length of rope. In every direction, for as far as the eye could see, small Benesh'ere tents dotted the dunes, with the occasional large pavilion nestled among them.

He stood with great care, testing each muscle before putting it to use, though he discovered the rope was much too short to stand fully erect. He felt reasonably good, a little wobbly in the knees, but otherwise in relatively good shape. Twice now, that oven of sand had tried to take his life.

A bandage covered the claw marks on the back of his shoulder. He sat down in the shade of the lean-to and tried to peel back an edge to get a look at the wound, but it was too far back to see anything clearly.

"Now leave that alone," a young girl snapped at him. He looked up, found her standing over him holding a tray, noticed that, like him, she wore a leather debt-ring braided around her neck. Her skin was the white of the Benesh'ere and she wore one of those broad-brimmed straw hats with the hood thrown back. She couldn't be more than sixteen, though if he'd been standing she'd stand as tall as him.

"Feels nearly healed to me," he said.

She answered him with a sneer, put the tray down on the sand nearby, lifted a knife off the tray, stood behind him and began cutting away the bandage. Her hands were not gentle.

"Who are you?" he asked.

"My name is Yim," she said, "And yes, it is nearly healed. I think you can do without a bandage now."

Morgin looked over his shoulder at her face. "How is Harriok?" he asked.

Her eyes darkened. "Lord Harriok," she corrected him, "is very ill. You were lucky. You were not touched by the sixth claw." She frowned for a moment and looked at the wound on the back of his shoulder carefully. "There is a sixth mark here." She probed at it, but it was numb to her touch. "But it's long since healed, an old scar. No, you were not touched by that claw."

He was almost certain he had been touched by the sixth claw. The sixth wound had been open and fresh the morning after Shebasha's attack. But all he said now was, "Will he live?"

She shook her head. "We don't know. He should be dead by now."

She lifted a cup of steaming liquid off the tray and handed it to him. "Drink this, and you look strong enough for food. Let me see what I can find." She picked up her tray. "And Lord Harriok's father, Jerst, will want to question you." The girl turned and walked away before Morgin could protest.

Jerst! Morgin struggled to remember where he'd heard that name before. How many times had he seen Benesh'ere in this life? His memories were all confused with those of Morddon in the far past. But then he had it: Jerst was warmaster of the Benesh'ere, and Morgin had insulted him and his hot-blooded daughter Blesset shortly before the battle at Csairne Glen, and Jerst had sworn that when next they met, he'd kill Morgin.

Morgin began fumbling at the knot connecting the rope to the debt-ring about his neck, but as he did so a shadow blocked the ever-bright sunlight. Blesset stood over him with her hands on her hips. "Go ahead," she said calmly. "Untie the knot. Free yourself. And you'll also free me to kill you here and now."

Morgin knew he could not match the fighting prowess of a Benesh'ere warrior, male or female. And for some reason the debt-ring stopped her from killing him, so he carefully lowered his hands from the knot.

"At least you're not stupid," she said. "It is fortuitous the sands have chosen to put you in our hands. My only sorrow is that you owe my brother a debt, so I cannot kill you until it's repaid. But that time will come, Elhiyne. Either he'll heal, and grant me permission to kill you, or he'll die, and his wife will inherit your debt and she'll gladly allow it. Yes, that time will come."

5

The Jest of a Name

THE OASIS WAS a large strip of fertile land somewhere near the western edge of the Munjarro. Sand still covered almost everything, but the oasis contained a large lagoon with open water, and a great many shrubs and trees with broad-bladed leaves that cast shadows everywhere. Hundreds of the white-faced giants moved about, with quite a number of tents both large and small pitched among the trees.

Harriok had told Morgin that out on the sands the tribe broke up into smaller clans and family units. But each year, with the coming of spring, they all converged on Aelldie and waited there until the last had arrived.

Word had spread that Morgin was to be mistreated by everyone. Whitefaces passing by spat on him, or kicked sand at him. As the morning progressed the mistreatment ratcheted up a notch; they not only spat on him, but occasionally gave him a healthy kick, though the punishment never grew to the point of serious harm. By nightfall his body felt as if it had become one giant bruise.

As the sun set the camp filled with the smells of cooking, and while the Benesh'ere ate, Morgin sat alone and the torment abated. Then, for a while, many of them congregated around several of the fires where they talked in low tones, until one by one they retreated to their tents and the camp grew quiet. Yim brought him a bowl of table scraps and a blanket. "Thank you," he said gratefully.

"Don't thank me," she snapped. "If it were up to me I'd cut your throat myself. But Lord Jerst wants you healthy so he can kill you himself."

"Why doesn't he just kill me now? I'm here for the killing."

She frowned at him as if she thought him an idiot. "Why, that would dishonor him. You have to repay the debt first." She turned her back on him and walked away.

Morgin sat on the ground and wrapped the blanket tightly around his shoulders. He gnawed on the table scraps and tried to clean every last bit of meat from the bones. He could easily untie his leash, but where would he go? Aelldie lay too deep in the Munjarro, and without the Benesh'ere to help him he would quickly die.

As the last of the whitefaces disappeared into their tents, the camp and the night grew quiet and still. Morgin sat on the ground and watched the glowing embers of the many cooking fires slowly die, and he tried to understand how he'd come to this. It seemed ironic to have gone from guttersnipe, to prince, to outlaw, to debtor, and now a man under sentence of death.

The night was warm, the air still and the camp silent. In the distance Morgin noticed three men walking his way, weaving their way among the tents. He could tell by their relative heights that one was not Benesh'ere. Only when they were within a short stone's throw did Morgin realize the shorter man was Val accompanied by two Benesh'ere warriors. "Val!" he called. He jumped to his feet, was jerked painfully to a halt by his leash and forced to remain in a crouch.

The two warriors walked on either side of Val, watching him closely as if guarding him. Val approached warily, stopped about five paces away and said, "I dare not come closer. Jerst is allowing me to speak to you only because I told him I have very bad news for you. Rhianne is dead."

It took Morgin a moment to hear Val's words, to let them punch a hole in his heart.

"No," he pleaded. "It can't be."

Val continued. "She rode out of Durin following you. She went after you in some misguided hope of helping you, or saving you, or something. She rode out ahead of the skree, and they caught up with her before they got to you. They left nothing for us to bury."

Morgin's heart lurched, and as his eyes welled with tears he closed them and sat down in the sand. He pictured once again what the skree had left of the old mare, just a smear of blood on the grass of a field. They would have left nothing more of his beautiful Rhianne, just another smear of blood on the grass of another field. He recalled again the night she'd kissed him in the stables what seemed an eternity ago, and the way that untamed lock of hair always escaped the tangle of tresses atop her head. That kiss, the only truly passionate moment they'd ever shared, that kiss had held such a promise of happiness for them, a promise that now would never be fulfilled.

With tears streaming down his cheeks, he opened his eyes and said, "I'm going to kill Valso. I'm going to kill him with my bare hands."

Val said, "I would enjoy helping you."

Morgin didn't want to think of Rhianne, not with Val and two Benesh'ere looking on to watch him cry. He asked, "What are you doing here?"

"Once all of Decouix had your scent they left the rest of us alone. We took Tulellcoe south to Yestmark where Cort has some friends. When he was doing better she and he decided to take up residence near a pretty lake, and since I was close to the Munjarro I thought I'd come and see some old whiteface friends."

Val held up his hands, and Morgin finally saw that his wrists were tied together by a length of rope. "Apparently, anyone who was with you the night you insulted Jerst is guilty by association."

"Enough," one of the Benesh'ere guards growled. "Jerst said you could give him the bad news about his wife. You've done so. Now end it."

Still holding his tied wrists out, Val said, "I do hope you can mend the situation with Jerst."

Morgin watched the two warriors lead Val off toward the center of camp. Rhianne had died because of him, and it appeared that Val would soon die because of him as well.

Morgin lay down on the sand and pulled his blanket tightly about his shoulders. He'd learned that nights on the desert took on a decided chill, though this night it was the chill in his heart that kept him awake.

••••

Brandon stood on the parapets of Elhiyne and watched Olivia and her retinue approach the castle. Morgin dead! Rhianne dead! Olivia had sent riders ahead with the news, which by now had spread throughout the valley.

Standing beside him, NickoLot said, "I don't believe he's dead. He can't be dead."

Brandon turned and looked at her carefully. In her late teens, of marriageable age, she was still a tiny thing, stood barely chest high to Brandon; and rail thin, she was light as a feather. But she'd gone weird in the head after Valso and his Kulls had occupied Elhiyne and the Tulalane had tried to rape her. She'd taken to wearing only black, and always obscured the features of her face in the shadows of a dark veil. It was a lovely face, almost childish—until one looked deeply into her eyes, and there, one might glimpse the power within her soul, a frightening thing at best. In the last two years she had grown from a middling witch, to one of the most powerful in the clan, rivaling even AnnaRail and Olivia in that respect.

Brandon asked. "What about Rhianne?"

She didn't move; just stood there staring out at the train of horses and carts and carriages. "No, nor her. They can't be dead."

"But grandmother wrote that, even with AnnaRail's help, she can find no trace of their souls in mortal life."

She didn't answer him, but stood there silently staring out over the distant fields.

"Nicki, answer me, please."

She turned to look at him, and beneath the veil he caught a glimpse of her eyes and had to look away. "I don't care what grandmother thinks. I don't believe they're dead." She turned away from him and began walking.

"Nicki, wait. Please."

She stopped and turned to face him.

As much as Morgin and Rhianne's deaths hurt them all, he feared Nicki would harm herself further by living in denial. "I'm sorry, but they are dead. You have to accept it."

She stared at him for the longest moment, didn't acknowledge his words in any way. Then she turned and walked away.

••••

Morgin opened his eyes slowly, sensed something arcane had awakened him and was careful not to move. The sun had yet to rise, but a hint of light in the sky told him dawn waited just over the horizon. He sensed netherlife hovering close at hand. He closed his eyes again, listened to the stillness about him, heard the sound of someone shifting his weight nearby.

Morgin rolled over quickly, fearing one of the whitefaces had decided to give him a kick. He rose into a crouch, ready to defend himself, found one of them sitting with his legs crossed a few paces away, staring silently at him.

Like most Benesh'ere men and women, the fellow wore loose-fitting, sand-colored breeches made of a coarse cloth and tucked into knee-high or calf-length boots. He also wore a knee-length robe made of the same material, gathered at the waist with a belt of intricately woven cord and strips of leather, a hood thrown over his head, formed into that triangular tent-like affair by the broad brimmed hat made of woven straw.

The fellow threw the hood back, then removed the hat and laid it to one side in the sand; now Morgin could see that he was quite old. His hair had long since turned a white to match that of his skin, and while the top of his head was bald and shiny, a thick mane of hair still grew out of the sides and back of his head to cascade down over his shoulders. His face remained expressionless, his eyes boring silently into Morgin's soul.

Morgin took a seat facing him, waiting for him to speak, but the old man seemed content to just sit and stare. Finally, Morgin's impatience got the better of him. "What do you want?"

Slowly, a smile formed on the old man's lips, but still he did not speak.

Morgin looked straight into his eyes, refused to be intimidated by his damn stare. "What do you want, old man?"

The old man nodded, as if he'd seen something, or come to some decision. He spoke slowly. "My name is not *old man*; it is Toke, and I've come to see if you can see."

Morgin shrugged, couldn't put the feeling aside there was something magical here. "Well I'm not blind, if that's what you mean."

The old man's smile broadened. "We're all blind in one way or another, boy. I find you interesting because you see all, and yet you see nothing."

Morgin had once threatened to kill Tulellcoe if his uncle again called him "boy." But to this old man everyone was probably a child.

"I brought a friend," Toke said. "It's curious about you." He looked to one side as if someone sat next to him. "Aren't you, old friend?"

Morgin saw nothing there, but his instincts told him to look closely, and for just an instant he caught the telltale shimmer of a netherdemon holding contact with this world, and he understood then why his sense of magic had been aroused. "You're a sorcerer then?" Morgin asked.

Toke frowned. "Ah, what I would give to taste true power. But alas! No, in that *I* am blind."

The demon hovering near Toke's shoulder gave off a familiar nether scent. "But you've summoned life from the netherworld."

Toke shook his head. "No. The *namegiver* is an old friend of mine, and often seeks me out."

"The *namegiver*?" Morgin asked. "You mean ElkenSkul?"

Toke turned to the demon. "He remembers you, friend." He cocked his head slightly as if listening to something, then nodded. "Yes," he said to the demon. "He is, but he'll learn."

Again, Toke appeared to listen to something. He laughed softly for a moment and asked, "Really?" Then he reached down, and with the palm of his hand he smoothed over a small area of sand. A moment later the demon scratched something in the sand. Morgin craned his neck and tried to see what the demon wrote, but his leash wouldn't allow that, and dawn was still too far off, and the light too dim for him to see the marks clearly.

When the demon finished Toke looked carefully at what it had written, then threw back his head and cried out with laughter. "Oh that is good, *namegiver*. That is a wonderful joke. Truly wonderful!"

Sitting on the sand, Morgin couldn't see the *namegiver's* scratchings. He climbed to his feet, leaned out to the maximum extent his leash would allow, peered down at the small area of sand where the demon had written its message. As the sun broke over the flat horizon of the desert he saw that the demon had scratched the symbol of the sunset king with the two crossed lines beneath it. It had added the two extra lines that made it appear to be Aethon's name with crossed swords beneath it, the extra lines no one but Morgin had seen.

As a young boy he'd put those extra lines out of his thoughts, put them away and forgotten them, thought of them rarely, if at all. How would he have explained to Olivia what he'd seen and she hadn't? Attempting to do so would only have focused her attention on him even more. Perhaps this old man could tell him what those extra lines meant, tell him his real name.

Morgin sat down at the limit of his leash. "Why do you find my name so funny?"

"I don't find it funny."

"But the demon wrote it in the sand, and you just laughed at it."

"But I wasn't laughing at your name."

"Then what were you laughing at?"

Toke smiled mischievously. "It likes to play jokes, especially on demanding old women who summon it with so much arrogance."

Morgin recognized the reference to Olivia. "What kind of jokes?"

Toke's smile broadened until it split his face, and his eyes glinted with mischief. "It likes to mislead."

Morgin shook his head angrily. "It tells lies then? But I thought it couldn't lie about a name."

Toke nodded his agreement and turned to the demon. "Did you hear that, friend? He thinks the only way to deceive is to lie outright." Toke listened for a moment, as if the demon spoke to him, then he threw his head back and laughed uproariously. "Yes. But we're all stupid that way."

Toke stood up abruptly and looked down at Morgin. "The *namegiver* finds it easier to just let fools lie to themselves. Look at your name, boy. Look at your name." Then he turned, and continuing his one-sided conversation with the demon, he walked away.

Morgin jumped to his feet and shouted, "But wait. What does it mean? Tell me my true name."

Toke ignored him and continued walking. Standing there, Morgin watched him leave and cursed the old fellow. He again leaned out to the limit of his leash to look at the symbol the demon had scratched. "Ae-thonLaw," he whispered softly to no one.

Why wouldn't the old man help him understand his true name?

Morgin couldn't reach the spot with his hands, but laying down and extending his legs, he obliterated the demon's scratchings with his feet.

6

Brothers of the Sands

"YEE SEEMS OLDER than I was first a-thinking," Braunye said as Rhianne ground the dried ginberry leaves in the mortar and pestle.

Rhianne looked up from her work. Braunye's cheeks had filled out a little. While neither of them ate any grand fare, Rhianne had been able to provide them with a steady, if monotonous, diet. Rhianne had also quickly realized that if she allowed the villagers to gain even an inkling of her true power, word would spread quickly and someone would come to investigate. So she needed to appear to be no more than a witch of moderate power and middle age. Out in the open countryside among small villages, such hedge witches were not uncommon and of considerable value as simple healers.

Appearing to be of moderate power was not difficult. The incident in which she'd defended herself against the bully in the tavern that first night had been almost completely forgotten, and even a hedge witch could come up with something under such circumstances. But since then she'd been careful to avoid putting on any kind of show. She used Olivia as her example of what not to do: no flamboyant gestures, no shimmers of power, no speeches or grand discourses. If she needed to cast a spell she would have the room cleared, give credit to herbal remedies and such, and claim only a limited capability with magic, even when she did call upon her not inconsiderable powers for healing.

Appearing older, but most importantly different, proved more difficult. She began right away by always wearing a hooded cloak and keeping her face well hidden. And little-by-little she'd concocted a careful spell-casting, a glamour to give her the appearance of added years. She knew she was considered pretty, so the glamour also dulled her features enough that she appeared simple and plain, neither ugly nor pretty. She now wore plain homespun clothing, with a coarse and almost abrasive weave. But most important of all, the glamour hid the bright-green of her eyes, an unusual trait that might have easily given her away. What Braunye saw was a simple, middle-aged hedge witch with plain brown eyes. And any-one who recalled her youthful appearance that first night; well, the common room had been dark and smoky, and many of the patrons had been drunk like the bully.

To answer Braunye's question, Rhianne said, "Perhaps you're just looking more closely, now that you know I'm not going to eat you."

Braunye giggled at that.

They'd moved out of the inn and into an abandoned three-room hut at the edge of town. It needed a bit of repair, so to keep the healer happy and willing to stay, the innkeeper and several men had spent a day fixing the front door and sealing up the walls to keep the weather out. Rhianne now had a certain amount of autonomy she'd never be-fore experienced. If only the sword would leave her alone, she might be content. If only Morgin were still alive, she might have found happi-ness.

If only this. If only that. She couldn't feed her and Braunye with *ifs*. She missed the luxury of not having to worry about the next meal. She missed putting on a beautiful gown, tying up her hair in something elabo-rate, putting on makeup and looking pretty. She thought of that night in the stables before the sword had gone berserk. Morgin had been hand-some and she'd been pretty, and she'd kissed him brazenly. She'd thought to excite him, and while she certainly had succeeded, the kiss had sent an electric thrill through her body. Her thoughts had turned most unladylike at that moment, and she regretted now that she hadn't acted upon that impulse back then. She would never again know the taste of his lips; at that thought her heart swelled and tears moistened her eyes.

She put thoughts of Morgin away, for that was the past, and this was her present, and she didn't yet want to think about the future. Heal someone today to put tomorrow's meal on the table. That's what her life had become.

••••

As the camp came to life that morning, Morgin sat quietly and wondered about Toke and the *namegiver* and their little joke. The Benesh'ere rekindled the cooking fires. Morgin heard pots clanging together, an argument somewhere, then the air filled with smells that made his stomach growl.

Shortly after dawn Yim brought him a bowl of boiled wheat. It was bland and tasteless, but hot enough to take away the chill of the night so he ate with fervor. When finished he wiped his mouth with a grimy piece of his sleeve, then sat in the sand savoring a full belly, letting the sun's rays warm him further.

Near one of the few large tents at the center of the camp Morgin noticed a lot of whitefaces coming and going; apparently some sort of gathering taking place. Then a small group of people broke away and walked purposefully his way. He sat up straight and tried to be ready for anything.

A young Benesh'ere woman led the group. She wore an ankle length, hooded robe, not the sand colored breeches and knee-high boots most common among the whitefaces. Yim and two warriors followed her, so Morgin thought it best to stand respectfully as they approached, though his leash forced him to remain in a rather undignified crouch.

The young woman and Yim stopped well out of his reach while the two warriors flanked her protectively. She looked Morgin up and down curiously, without the scorn and hatred he detected in the others, just interest. He bowed carefully. "My lady, how may I serve you?"

Her eyes narrowed as she studied him. She was neither pretty nor ugly, but she carried herself with an air of rank and authority, and in her own way she was attractive. But stress showed in the creases about her eyes. "Bring him," she said, and then, as an afterthought, she added, "Don't bind him. And treat him well."

She spun about, and with Yim scurrying behind her, marched back to the tent. The two warriors untied Morgin's leash, and he could finally stand erect. But the warriors each gripped him by an elbow and wrist, and hustled him along at a quick pace; and while he wasn't bound, their grips hovered on the edge of pain as a constant reminder he was not free to go his own way.

They led him to a long and wide tent, one of the largest within the tribe. They hustled him inside, and there Morgin found the young woman facing Blesset; the anger radiating from them both chilled the atmosphere of the room.

"You cannot do this," Blesset said, though the steel in her eyes belied the calmness of her voice. "I won't allow it."

"This is not your household," the young woman replied coldly. "And since my husband has asked for him, it is not up to you to allow or disallow anything here."

Blesset leaned close to the young woman. "My father—his father— will have something to say about this."

The young woman stood her ground. "Nor is it up to Jerst."

Blesset turned her back on the young woman scornfully and walked out of the tent. The young woman took a deep breath and let it out with a long sigh, then she turned to the two guards holding Morgin and snapped, "The two of you: out. Leave him and get out." To Yim she said, "And you too."

Yim jumped like a startled rabbit and shot out through the tent flap. The two guards released Morgin and exited hastily behind her.

The young woman waited until she and Morgin were alone, then demanded in a soft whisper, "Did you give my husband Harriok water?"

Morgin shrugged. "He was dying. I had to."

She closed her eyes, as if his answer saddened her. "My husband is conscious now, and he recalls the cat's attack, and the location, and we found you several leagues from there. And he was in no shape to walk. Did you carry him?"

Morgin shrugged. "I dragged him." He explained how he'd constructed a litter from the remains of their tent and dragged the unconscious Harriok behind him.

She opened her eyes. "My name is Branaugh," she said, then she stepped aside, pulled back a curtain and indicated that Morgin should step through. "My husband has asked for you."

Morgin stepped carefully into the next room and the smell of sickness immediately assaulted his nose. Harriok lay on the floor in a pile of pillows, wrapped tightly in blankets. Morgin crossed the room and sat down beside him, noticed his skin had the sheen of a man deathly ill. For the moment his eyes were closed, his breathing ragged and unsteady.

Branaugh sat down opposite Morgin. "He's not sleeping, not at this moment."

She reached out, touched his cheek tenderly. "The Elhiyne is here, as you requested."

Harriok swallowed with considerable effort, then opened his eyes and looked at Morgin. He smiled, though his eyes were distant. He tried to lift his hand, managed to raise it only the span of a finger above his chest. Morgin reached out and took it while Harriok struggled to speak. "I dreamt about you. I wanted water so badly, and you gave it to me."

Morgin smiled. "But you gave me water too."

Harriok smiled, tried to laugh, managed only to cough. "Yes . . . I did. That makes us brothers of the sand." He coughed again, then shivered. "I'm so cold," he said, and his body shook with spasms.

Branaugh eased herself into the bed beside him and wrapped her arms around him to lend him heat. On impulse, Morgin climbed into the bed on the other side of Harriok, and wrapped his arms about them both. Quietly, Branaugh mouthed the words, *Thank you.*

It was some time before Harriok's spasms ended, and by then he'd drifted off into a restless sleep. Morgin pulled himself out of the blankets, then helped Branaugh do likewise. "Thank you," she said.

She was about to say more when they heard a man call out, "Branaugh, we beg entrance to your tent."

Morgin followed her as she stepped into the outer chamber of the pavilion. "You are welcome, Jerst."

Jerst stepped through the tent flap, followed by Blesset, Yim and the two warriors. Blesset pointed at Morgin and said, "Seize him."

Morgin didn't resist as the two warriors crossed the room with the lightning speed of the Benesh'ere, and once again locked his arms painfully behind his back. Yim gave him a smug, scornful smile.

Jerst looked at Morgin, and Morgin was surprised that he didn't see the undisguised hate he saw in Blesset's eyes, though there remained plenty of anger to make up for it.

Branaugh kept her voice calm. "This is my household, and you'll not give me orders here."

Jerst said, "I would never attempt to."

Blesset tried to step around him, but he gripped her arm tightly and forced her to remain behind him.

Branaugh said. "This debtor is my responsibility, and you'll not touch him without my permission, or that of my husband."

Jerst looked at Blesset pointedly, angrily, then released his grip on her arm; she didn't move. He turned to Branaugh and said, "He insulted us. All of us."

Branaugh nodded. "Aye, and out on the sand he gave my husband water."

With those words an odd thing happened: a subtle change fell over the entire room. The two warriors spontaneously relaxed their grips, though they didn't let go completely, but any hint of pain disappeared. The scorn disappeared from Yim's face.

Jerst didn't react at all, while Blesset frowned and seemed a little less certain of herself. She said to Branaugh, "This is not yet finished, woman." And with that she turned and calmly walked out of the tent.

Morgin thought it interesting that Branaugh hadn't told them how he'd dragged Harriok through the sand for some unknown number of days. He decided to follow her lead and keep that to himself.

Jerst watched Blesset leave, stood there staring at the tent flap as it flopped back into place, then turned slowly to the two warriors holding Morgin. "Bring him," he snapped, then spun about and followed Blesset out of the tent.

Apparently, not even Branaugh would attempt to countermand the warmaster. Morgin knew it would be futile to resist as the two warriors locked his arms painfully behind his back. Clearly, with Jerst snapping orders at them, neither of them cared that Morgin had given Harriok water as they hustled him out of the tent and into the light of day. His feet barely touched the sand as they propelled him in Jerst's wake, his shoulders protesting the harsh treatment.

Jerst led them to a pavilion even larger than Harriok's, halted in front of it and called out, "It's me, Jerst, and I bring the Elhiyne."

The voice that answered him crackled with age, "Come in, old friend."

Jerst lifted the tent flap and held it for the two warriors. They threw Morgin through the opening and he landed on his face on a thick carpet. He heard Jerst order the two warriors to, "Wait out here." Moments later the interior of the tent darkened as the flap blocked the morning light.

The crackly old voice said, "He doesn't look like much."

Morgin moved slowly and got to his hands and knees, not sure how much abuse he'd have to take.

"No," Jerst said, "but we both learned long ago not to judge a man by his skin. And maybe some fools shouldn't be judged by their hot-tempered words."

Morgin looked up at the possessor of the crackly old voice, an ancient Benesh'ere seated on a heavy, wooden chair, smaller than a throne, yet still very throne-like. His hair had gone completely white, framing a face almost as wrinkled as Olivia's. An older woman stood on his right, hovering over him protectively. Beside him lay a crutch and a long walking stick. And Toke stood in the shadows far to one side, as if in hiding, though certainly no one could miss him.

The ancient, old man said, "A valuable lesson that. I wonder if it's one he's yet learned."

Still on his hands and knees, Morgin desperately tried to recall everything he'd learned about the Benesh'ere. Their leader, Angerah, ruler of the Black Council, was reputed to be quite aged, and to have been partially crippled by a Kull saber-thrust to his back years ago. His wife, named Merella, was a little younger. For once, Morgin was thankful for the lessons Olivia had drummed into him.

Morgin rose slowly to his feet and spoke softly, "There are many lessons I have yet to learn."

The old man smiled, though not a pleasant smile. "Somewhere along the line he's learned humility."

Jerst stepped around to stand beside the old man. "Yah. It's a shame he didn't learn it long before this."

The old man stared at Morgin for several heartbeats, then said, "I can override Harriok, remove the debt collar. The council will back me on that."

The woman frowned, clearly not liking that idea.

Jerst considered that for a moment, then he shook his head and said, "No, Blesset would just kill him." He sounded disappointed.

The old man said, "You're still going to have to kill him."

Jerst sighed tiredly and said, "I know, no way around it." Again, that disappointment!

He looked at Morgin and said, "You can go."

Morgin started to turn, but Merella said, "Wait. I'm not done with him yet."

"Fine," Jerst said, walking past Morgin to the pavilion's entrance. "We're only hours from marching out onto the sands, and I have too much to do. Send him back to Branaugh when you're done with him."

Morgin kept his eyes on the old man and woman in front of him, didn't turn to follow Jerst as he left the tent. The tent brightened again as Jerst threw back the tent flap, then darkened as he dropped it.

The woman said, "Come closer."

The room was about four paces wide, so Morgin took two steps and stopped in the center. He glanced at Toke briefly, and Merella's eyes narrowed, as if looking the old man's way had been oddly significant.

Morgin bowed, as he'd been taught to do so before any clan leader, though he did so without any flourish. He had the feeling such embellishments were not the Benesh'ere way.

"I am Merella, and this is Angerah" the woman said, confirming Morgin's deductions.

Morgin said, "I know who you are, if only by reputation."

Toke said, "I told you he's not stupid. Foolish, yes, stupid, no."

Morgin glanced Toke's way, and followed the old man with his eyes as he crossed the room to stand next to Angerah.

Merella turned to Toke, though oddly she didn't look directly at him. "I see that you were right," she said to the old fellow.

Toke laughed and said, "And yet he still sees nothing."

Merella nodded and considered Toke's words carefully for several heartbeats. Then she looked at Morgin, clearly appraising him. "But he must pass the final test."

Morgin's curiosity would not allow him to be silent. "What test is that?"

Toke grinned. "The test that is Jerst."

Merella said, "You may go. Report back to Branaugh."

Morgin stepped out of Angerah's tent, wondering what that had been about. If nothing more, that little encounter told him he would never understand these strange whitefaces.

••••

You shouldn't avoid me, you know.

DaNoel grimaced at the sound of Valso's voice in his head. To enter another's mind from such a distance required unprecedented power, and it frightened DaNoel that Valso did so with such casual indifference, though he would not let the Decouix see his fear. Luckily, he was alone in his room in the southwest tower, or someone might have seen him flinch. He put down the boot he'd been about to pull on, leaned back in his chair and closed his eyes to concentrate on the Decouix. *I'm not ignoring you,* he thought. *Our business is done. We have no further need of each other.*

We don't? And here I thought we had become such good friends.

Friends—never. We share a mutual dislike of the whoreson, nothing more.

But we also share a mutual desire to see him ruined in the most devastating manner.

He is ruined, disgraced, dead.

Really?

You told me he baked his brains out in that oven of sand. Everyone knows he's dead, along with that slut wife of his.

In his mind's eye DaNoel pictured Valso considering his words carefully. *All I told you was that it is likely he died out on the Munjarro. Don't you find it interesting that no one actually witnessed his demise or saw his body? He merely disappeared. Convenient, is it not? And just when everyone thinks him long dead and gone, he has the most amazing ability to prove them wrong. He's done it time and again. Might he do so once more?*

What are you saying, that he's alive?

Valso laughed. How he managed to do so in his thoughts, DaNoel could not fathom. *You do fear your brother, don't you?*

He's not my brother. He's the son of some whore. And it seems to me you fear him more than I.

Valso's anger flared so strongly it seemed to burn a hole in DaNoel's soul. DaNoel cried out as every muscle in his body spasmed, and he understood then that the Decouix could feed him limitless torment through their connection. Valso held him like that for an eternity of a heartbeat, then released him. DaNoel whimpered with relief, tasted blood on his tongue and sat in his chair gasping for air as the pain receded.

Elhiyne, you should exercise more caution in your insults.

With that, the Decouix disappeared from his thoughts, leaving him alone with the knowledge that Valso owned a piece of him. He sat there for a moment, his eyes still closed, breathing heavily, wondering how he might escape this trap. Only when the pain was truly gone did he open his eyes.

NickoLot stood over him; her fists on her hips, her elbows flared out, staring at him angrily, knowingly. She demanded, "What is it you've allowed into our home?"

Even in the full blossom of womanhood, she was a tiny thing. And he thought then that he could crush her, that he could strike her down and be rid of her and her accusations. With that thought he stood, raised his hand to do so, and in response, she merely drew power. But it was not the amateurish summons of some child; she called forth far more power than DaNoel thought possible, power on a level with that of Olivia or AnnaRail, far more power than DaNoel might call upon. He stayed his hand, knowing that any blow he attempted would fail, that she could harm him far more than he could harm her, and he'd better not give her an excuse to do so.

"Brother," she said, her eyes pinched and narrow. "What have you done? There is a corruption about you, but I don't know what it is."

He leaned forward, careful to make it clear he was not attempting to strike her, and he spit the words in her face. "Exactly! You know nothing, your suspicions are unfounded, and you have no proof. You're just a little girl playing at being a woman. And if you're going to make accusations, make sure you can prove them."

He pointed to the door. "Now get out. This is my room and you have no right to trespass on my privacy."

7

An Old Friend

BRANAUGH GAVE YIM orders to put Morgin to work. She turned him over to an old woman named Satcha, the cook for Jerst's extended household, and she in turn led him to a great pile of cooking pots, and set him about cleaning them. It was hard work in the hot sun, but far better than being staked to the ground at the end of a leash, and they gave him one of those straw hats that protected him from the sun. And while most of the whitefaces treated him with indifference—some with thinly veiled scorn—at least they no longer abused him, though that was strictly due to Branaugh's favor. Furthermore, he had the feeling that if Harriok died, she might find it difficult to continue to protect him.

Morgin busied himself sharpening some of Satcha's knives. He saw Yim returning from the lagoon with several girls her age. Some wore the debt-ring about their necks, though most did not. They'd bathed in the lagoon, and their hair was wet and black and glistening in the sun. As they walked and talked and laughed like young girls do, they worked at drying their hair. It occurred to Morgin that he hadn't washed since Valso had thrown him in the dungeons in Decouix. He called after her, "Yim."

The group of girls paused and silently stared at him. Yim looked his way coldly. "Yes?"

"Will I be allowed to bathe?" he asked.

She shrugged. "Of course." Then, to the laughter of her friends, she added, "In fact, we would all appreciate it if you did. But don't wait until late in the day. You'd be well advised to be dry before the chill of night sets in."

Morgin looked at Satcha and shrugged the same question at her.

She cocked her head toward the lagoon. "Finish that last knife. Then go."

Morgin did so, then wandered down to the lagoon.

He guessed there must be some sort of underground source to feed the lagoon. It wasn't large enough to be called a lake, but it was certainly no pond. There were a number of Benesh'ere scattered about its shore, most concerned with some business other than bathing. But there were a few in the water, some standing on the shore drying themselves, and while there were a number of trees and bushes lining the shore, the whitefaces paid little heed to hiding their bodies from one another.

It appeared to be common practice to first douse oneself with a bucket of water before entering the lagoon. Morgin grabbed one of the leather buckets, found a short stretch of beach where he could bathe without company, then stripped off his clothes. He poured a bucket of water over his head, and rubbed his skin down with sand until he'd washed away the grime and dirt. He filled the bucket again and dumped his clothing into it, and the water in the bucket immediately turned a dirty brown. He refilled the bucket three times before the water in it didn't cloud up with dirt. Then he spread his clothing out to dry, and walked into the water.

It was quite warm near the surface, but the bank sloped away quickly, and deeper down the water had a decided chill. He sucked in a chest full of air, pulled his head beneath the surface, then shoved off the bottom toward the center of the lagoon, held his breath as long as he could before arcing upward and breaking the surface.

Treading water, he turned slowly full circle. He'd only made it about halfway toward the center of the lagoon, and was thinking about crossing it completely, when he noticed all activity along the shore had come to a stop. The whitefaces had paused at whatever they'd been doing to look at him, and each stood frozen like a statue as if time had come to an abrupt halt. Then the moment ended, and slowly they turned away from him to return to whatever they'd been doing.

He swam back to the shore, stood self-consciously in the shallows and again rubbed himself down with sand.

"How did you do that?" a young voice called out.

Morgin looked up, saw a young boy standing on the shore holding some sort of bundle in his arms. The boy couldn't have been more than eight or nine years old. "Do what?" Morgin asked.

"Walk out to the middle of the lagoon," the boy said. "I thought the water was too deep to walk out that far."

"It is too deep to walk," Morgin said. "I swam."

The boy frowned. "What's swam?"

"I used my hands and feet to keep my head above water."

The boy's eyes widened. "I did that once, but only for a few heartbeats."

It was quite possible that none of the whitefaces knew how to swim. They spent the majority of their lives out on the sands, and probably never considered the possibility.

"One question at a time," Morgin said. "Who are you?"

The boy grinned openly, and other than Branaugh it was the first kind look Morgin had seen on a Benesh'ere face. "I'm LillianToc," he said. "Jerst's youngest son. Yim sent me with some clothes for you. She said you should wash those rags you're wearing, then get back to help with dinner. What's swam?"

Morgin climbed out of the water. "Well it's kind of difficult to explain," he said as LillianToc handed him a towel. While he rubbed his skin briskly with the towel he tried to describe the technique of moving through water, but the young boy didn't understand.

The clothing LillianToc had brought was the standard sand colored breeches and knee-length robe worn by most Benesh'ere. Morgin tucked the breeches into his boots, thought he might look the part of a small Benesh'ere if he'd had one of the intricately braided belts they wore. Instead he cinched the robe around his waist with his own belt. The pants felt a little big in the hips.

"Yim gave you some of her own clothes," LillianToc told him, "since none of the men's would fit you."

Morgin gathered up his old clothing. The knee-length robe Harriok had given him out on the sands was a total loss after being shredded by the cat's claws, then cut away to get at the wound. The breeches, though, with a needle and a bit of thread, were at least salvageable. He decided to give them one more wash, and while he did so LillianToc quizzed him incessantly about the clans. He answered the boy's questions to the best of his knowledge, though, while doing so, he noticed out of the corner of his eye three teenage boys walking their way along the shore. They approached with a swagger that spelled trouble.

"Hello, LillianToc," their apparent leader said as they stopped nearby. "I take it this is the Elhiyne."

"Hello Tallik," LillianToc said.

Morgin stood, wringing water out of his breeches.

"When I speak to you, Elhiyne," Tallik said, "Look at me."

Morgin turned toward him, watched Tallik's eyes sizing him up. Tallik was taller than Morgin, though he still had some growing to do so the difference in size was not as great as it might have been, and Morgin's shoulders were broader.

Morgin kept his voice calm, tried to swallow his pride and avoid a fight. "I'm sorry. I didn't know you were speaking to me."

"I've heard about your insults, Elhiyne," Tallik said, and he stepped in close to emphasize the difference in their heights.

"Tallik!" LillianToc pleaded. "You're supposed to leave him alone."

"I'll leave him alone when he's learned some manners," Tallik said as he gave Morgin a shove.

The shove pushed Morgin back a step, and he realized then that Tallik would have his fight regardless of what he did. He tried to relax, to be aware of every movement the larger boy made, to be ready for any shift in his weight no matter how subtle.

While Tallik had the advantage of size, he appeared to be about sixteen and had probably never needed to actually fight for his life, so his reflexes were the kind developed in practice, not combat. Morgin had quite a few years on the boy, many of them spent fighting for his life, and a certain ruthlessness that came with the territory. For him there was no pulling a punch, no bravado, no need for saber rattling before battle. In fact, he fed Tallik's overconfidence by trying to appear a bit helpless at that moment. He lowered his eyes and appeared afraid, while inside he tensed for action. But Tallik needed to impress his friends, so he broadcast the first punch a little, confident his size and Benesh'ere reflexes would protect him, and wanting the onlookers to have every opportunity to observe the blow properly.

Morgin side-stepped the punch slightly, deflected it only a touch with his right hand, let it brush past his cheek as he spun and fired a kick into Tallik's solar plexus. It connected solidly, even more so than Morgin had intended, and Tallik fell back, crumbled to the ground with a loud grunt and a great outlet of breath.

The contest was over. Tallik lay curled up on the sand, clutching at his stomach and gasping for air, his friends standing over him with no inclination to take up the fight. Morgin didn't feel any great triumph at winning this match, nor did he feel any guilt at his own ruthlessness. Tallik would walk away from this with nothing more than a few bruises and a bit of hurt pride. Hopefully he'd learn a lesson about playing the bully, though, if he focused too much on the damage to his pride, he might learn the wrong lesson, and that would be a shame.

Morgin gathered up his belongings and, with LillianToc following closely, headed back to Harriok's tent.

"What's swam?" LillianToc asked as they walked.

"I don't think I can explain it," Morgin said. "Maybe someday I'll just teach you how."

••••

"You're restless," Cort said.

Tulellcoe stood at the window of their room, staring out at the lake silently. He didn't turn as he answered, "Aye."

"It's Morgin and Rhianne, isn't it?"

"Aye."

She put her hands on her hips. "I've had enough."

He finally turned to face her, and she continued. "Ever since you heard about them you've done nothing but stare out that window and grunt one-word sentences at me. It's time we did something about it."

"Like what?"

"Pack up our stuff and go to Durin ourselves. See what we can find out."

Tulellcoe stood silently considering her words, staring into some far distance. At such moments he turned eerily lifeless, as if he'd turned into stone and no longer needed to breathe. Then his eyes focused on her and he said, "Ok. But first I need to prepare a charm—two charms actually. One each for Morgin and Rhianne, keyed to our memories of them, something that will help me understand if I cross their path."

Cort said, "I can help with that."

They spent the rest of the day preparing the two charms, and Tulellcoe tied them to a leather thong that he placed about his neck. The next morning they headed for Durin.

They spent three days in the city, carefully and discreetly dredging up whatever rumors they could. It hadn't been long since Morgin's escape, so they heard quite a few, many of them contradictory. But one thing remained clear: Morgin must have had help to escape the castle, and then the city. And, the rumors were consistent in that he'd headed south, confirmed by the fact that Valso had led his skree in that direction. So Cort and Tulellcoe decided to check out the countryside between Durin and The Munjarro.

In the forest south of Durin, Cort became a bit separated from Tulellcoe, but they were in no hurry, so she let her horse continue at an easy walk. In any case, the forest had thinned considerably throughout the morning. She occasionally caught a glimpse of him up ahead, and they were following a well-defined game trail, so Tulellcoe wouldn't veer off it or change directions without waiting for her to catch up.

The forest didn't end abruptly, but over a distance of several hundred paces it thinned even further, and she found Tulellcoe seated on his horse waiting for her at the edge of cleared farm land. As she approached him, Tulellcoe said, "I don't think he came this way."

"Well let's check the farms hereabouts," she said. "Perhaps we'll unearth some bit of information. After all, it's been less than a moon since he was killed."

The first farm they checked turned up nothing so they continued south. At the next they found a rather talkative farmer. Tulellcoe nudged the fellow's memory, carefully counting the days back to the evening Morgin had escaped. The fellow finally said, "No, don't recall anything myself. But ya know, old Tobin lost a mare to thieves about then."

"Old Tobin?" Tulellcoe asked.

"Yah, next farm over. Due south. You can't miss it."

Late that afternoon they walked their horses down a long cart path, at the end of which they found two dilapidated structures constructed of mud and wattle walls with thatched roofs. It wasn't clear which was the barn, and which the house. An older man with a bald head and round belly stood in the path, watching them approach, a pitchfork held tightly across his chest as if he meant to defend himself with it. "What you want here?" he demanded in a surly tone.

Tulellcoe dismounted to face the man squarely, though Cort noticed he kept his distance well out of reach of the pitch fork. "We just want a little information," he said.

Tobin had lost a mare, stolen in the night. He hadn't seen or heard the thief or thieves, so he couldn't say if it had been just one, lone man, or two, or more.

The next day they found another farm where the thieves had struck. Again, the farmer couldn't say if it had been just one man or a group. Someone had stolen a tattered piece of canvas and picked through a bin of cattle feed, exactly what a lone, desperate fugitive might do.

••••

Satcha put Morgin to work preparing the cooking fires and carrying water up from the lagoon. He found such menial labor increasingly frustrating. Something more demanding might at least prevent him from obsessing on his name. How did those two extra marks change it? He had to find an answer to that, but to do so he'd first have to escape from the Benesh'ere. Then it occurred to him that if he did escape, he had no idea where to go to find the answers.

Yim showed him how to collect horse and cattle dung for the fires. She gave him a large canvas sack, instructed him to separate those leavings fully dried from those still fresh, showed him where to pile the dry dung, and where to spread out the fresh stuff to dry further in the sun. It wasn't pleasant work, but it gave him a chance to explore the entire camp and get a feel for the place.

If he could escape, could he go to Olivia with the question about his name? She certainly knew more about names than anyone else he could think of. But then, she'd find some way to use him, so he couldn't go to her. AnnaRail! Or Roland! Perhaps if he went to them in secret.

Moving about the camp collecting dung, he discovered the corral on the far side of the camp. It was enclosed by a permanent, stone wall that must have taken generations to build. It included a grove of trees where horses, cattle and other livestock grazed in the shadows. Morgin took a break from gathering dung, stopped to look over the Benesh'ere herds, and while he stood there a strange, though not unfamiliar, feeling came over him, as if he were being watched, but not by anything mortal. Then a tall, black mare stepped out of the herd and trotted his way. It reminded him of the almost identical scene in his dreams when Mortiss had found Morddon in Kathbeyanne.

She stopped in front of him just on the other side of the stone wall, snorted at him scornfully as if to say, *Of course I'm here, you fool.*

He reached out and scratched her behind the ear, and she let him do so almost impatiently. He tried to recall when he'd last seen her: at the river, shortly before France had drowned, and Tarkiss and his Kulls had captured Morgin and taken him to Durin.

Mortiss spluttered her frustration at him. *No, it was at Aethon's tomb when you laid him to rest.*

Morgin found it oddly comforting to once again suffer Mortiss's derision. "But that wasn't me," he said. "That was Morddon."

She neighed angrily, *How can you be so ignorant?*

Most often, he thought of her merely as Mortiss, but he recalled now that her full name was Mortiss, the DeathWalker. When he'd first met her he'd had no idea what that meant, but now the meaning seemed quite clear: death followed her everywhere.

He shrugged and said, "I guess if you're here, the sword can't be far away."

Off to Morgin's left one of the Benesh'ere tending the herds took no-tice; he put down whatever he'd been doing and walked Morgin's way. There was something familiar about the man, and as he approached, Morgin thought they might have met before, and he struggled with his memory to recall the meeting. The name Jack the Lesser came to mind, and Morgin remembered the tall bowman who had accompanied Jerst and Blesset when they'd first met before Csairne Glen. But while this man looked in every way to be Jack, there was something about him that put a lie to such a thought, an air of anger, bitterness and disappointment.

The Benesh'ere stopped a few paces away—a good safe distance—looked Morgin over carefully, then looked at Mortiss. "She lets no one touch her that way; won't let anyone saddle her. One of these days I'll just butcher her for her meat."

Morgin suspected that if the fellow ever decided to follow through on such a threat, Mortiss would simply be absent. Or more likely, when not in her immediate presence, the fellow would probably completely forget her existence. But he said nothing of his suspicions and merely shrugged. "She's always had a mind of her own."

It was unsettling to recognize this man so readily, and yet to know with absolute certainty he was not the man Morgin had met. "Do I know you?" Morgin asked.

The Benesh'ere's eye's narrowed. "You think you've seen me before, eh?"

Morgin shook his head carefully. "No. I've met someone who looks like you, but not you."

The fellow frowned, then he smiled. It was the second kind look Morgin had seen on a Benesh'ere face. The man shook his head slowly with a certain wonder in his eyes. "You're the only man I've ever met who hasn't made that mistake, at least on first meeting. How did you know I'm not my brother?"

Twin brothers! Morgin merely said, "I don't know. You're just differ-ent. And I have a certain instinct about names, and your name is not Jack the Lesser."

"No," the man said. His face again hardened and a deep bitterness entered his voice. "I am Jack the Greater."

Morgin failed to hide a frown. "How did the two of you come by such names?"

Jack smiled bitterly. "The same way you came by your name, Lord AethonLaw."

Morgin stepped back, felt as if he'd been struck. "The demon?"

"Aye. The demon." He looked at Morgin carefully, waiting for some sort of reaction, then he added, "Beware of that great name of yours, Lord AethonLaw. And don't waste your time trying to live up to it."

Jack waited for another moment, perhaps to see if Morgin had some comment to add. But then, in silence, he turned away and walked back to his work.

8

Close to the Steel

WHEN MORGIN RETURNED to Harriok's tent a crowd of whitefaces had gathered waiting near its entrance, all seated quietly in the sand like statues. As he approached he noticed the bully Tallik sat among them and a knot formed in his stomach. Morgin guessed he'd now pay for humiliating the bully, and he wondered if he might get by with a simple apology.

Waiting with Tallik were LillianToc, Yim, the two boys who'd accompanied Tallik that morning, and an older Benesh'ere man who stood as Morgin approached. The rest stood with him, but the man stood above them all, tall and angry and impatient. The man's eyes narrowed, and looking at Morgin he grew even angrier. "You're the Elhiyne?" he demanded.

Morgin stopped out of reach of any impulsive attack. "Yes," he said tentatively. "About this morning. I—"

"Silence!" the man shouted, and Morgin obeyed.

The man turned to Tallik. "This is the man struck you down?"

Tallik averted his gaze respectfully. "Yes, father."

The man nodded and looked from Tallik to Morgin. Then to Tallik he said, "And he bested you rather nicely, I hear."

Tallik lowered his eyes. "Yes, father."

The man walked over to Tallik carrying a long, thin strap of brown leather Morgin hadn't noticed before. He stood behind the boy, and wrapped a length of leather around his throat, then began weaving it with intricate knots. When he finished Tallik now wore a debt collar not unlike Morgin's.

Tallik's father stood and looked down on his son angrily. "You'll take his duties now, and he yours. And you'll do so until I'm satisfied you've learned to be a man, and not a bully."

Morgin suddenly realized he was looking at these whitefaces through Morddon's heart. Back in Kathbeyanne all those centuries ago, he'd rather liked the whitefaces with whom he'd ridden and fought. And while Morddon had been an angry grouch, he'd actually loved his Benesh'ere brethren. Looking at Tallik through Morddon's heart, Morgin felt oddly sorry for the boy, especially since it appeared his father would take pains to be sure he learned the right lesson from the fight. The kid would probably grow up to be a nice fellow, though Morgin still wasn't sure if Tallik's punishment was for picking the fight, or for losing it.

••••

Tallik's father tasked Yim with leading Morgin to his new duties. She led him through the tents of the main camp, and as they approached its edge he picked up the faint ring of hammers pounding on steel, a sound that grew louder with each step. She led him to a cluster of tents separate from the main camp, tents different from a typical Benesh'ere tent. The tents were complete in and of themselves, but each had a large flap that extended out from the tent proper, with two corners supported by long poles. It created a shaded workspace next to the tent, with a table and a rack of tools, and, most obvious of all, a smith's anvil. There were about a half-dozen tents in all, with about half of the shaded workspaces occupied with smiths working metal.

Yim stopped outside one of the tents and spoke loudly, "Master Chagarin, I have the Elhiyne."

She turned to Morgin and whispered quickly, "Be respectful, for he is very close to the steel."

Close to the steel! Morgin had heard that phrase before. He knew he didn't fully understand what it meant, and hopefully he'd now have a chance to learn.

Chagarin threw the tent flap aside and stepped out into the sun. He was short for a Benesh'ere, which meant he stood only a few finger-widths taller than Morgin, who was taller than most clansmen. Like any smith, Chagarin was broad-chested, with thick ropey muscles rippling over his entire upper body.

He looked Morgin up and down and demanded, "And where's Tallik?"

Yim lowered her eyes. "His father feels he should wear a debt collar for a time."

Chagarin threw his head back and laughed. "Picked another fight, did he? Who did he pick on this time?" He looked at Morgin and his eyes narrowed. "Not the Elhiyne, here? Don't seem too hurt to me."

Yim described the fight of that morning and Chagarin laughed even louder. Then to Morgin he said, "Was it luck, or do you know how to fight?"

Morgin shrugged. "I've had to fight a time or two in my life."

Again, Chagarin looked him up and down carefully. "*Had* to fight, you said. Didn't choose to fight."

"I choose to fight only when I must."

Chagarin eyed Morgin, clearly evaluating him. "That's the kind of at-titude comes from an experienced fighter. Bet you've had to fight for your life a time or two, huh?"

Again, Morgin shrugged. "I suspect that gave me a little advantage over Tallik."

Chagarin turned to Yim. "He'll do. Now be gone with you, girl."

Then to Morgin, "Come with me."

Chagarin led him into the shaded workspace, indicated a table on which tools were strewn haphazardly, with the anvil mounted at one end near a firebox and bellows. "Know anything about steel?" he asked.

Morgin flashed back to Morddon and his memories of centuries spent at the forges—or were they Morgin's memories? Of that, he couldn't be certain, and that frightened him. "A little," he said, not will-ing to visit that place in his memories. "I helped our smith now and then, but not as an apprentice, just a simple helper."

They'd attracted a small crowd. The other smiths had put down their work and gathered around Chagarin and Morgin to look over *the Elhiyne.*

Morgin would love to learn why Benesh'ere steel was considered so superior to any other. He asked, "Are you making blades?"

Chagarin shook his head. "Not out here on the sands. Working the good steel requires a lot of fuel for a hot, controlled flame, and for that, we need good coke, and lots of it. Out here we just fix things, buckles and harness and horseshoes and such. No, the coke and the raw steel await us at the Lake of Sorrows."

The implications of that statement were clear enough. He now understood that Tallik's punishment was a harsh one, to go from working the steel to collecting dung for the fires. "Is Tallik your apprentice?"

Some of the other smiths chuckled at that question, but Chagarin merely looked thoughtful and shook his head. "No. He hopes to be, but I don't think he's close enough to the steel. In any case, the steel will decide that."

Morgin wondered if he had finally met a true SteelMaster. "Yim called you Master Chagarin. Are you a SteelMaster?"

Everyone got a good laugh at that. "No, young man, there are no SteelMasters. The last died centuries ago. I'm just the Master Smith. But that's master enough, and questions enough, too."

He clapped Morgin on the back of the shoulders, the first comradely gesture any Benesh'ere had ever made toward him. "Let's get you to work, man. We're leaving for the Lake of Sorrows tonight and we've got to clean this mess up."

••••

The smiths put Morgin to work helping them pack up their equipment: tongs, peen hammers, flat hammers, farrier's hoof nippers and end nippers. Morgin was surprised he knew the names of all the tools so clearly. He even knew their proper use, had quite a string of old and long-forgotten memories of using similar tools at one time or another. That was odd, because, as he recalled, when he and JohnEngine had spent several days helping the Elhiyne smith, the fellow had taught them next to nothing of the smith's crafts. To the smith they'd been no more than a pair of strong backs, and the smith guarded the secrets of his craft quite carefully. No, this knowledge came from the memories he shared with Morddon.

Late in the afternoon, the smiths took up swords and began practicing in pairs. With seven smiths that left one of them, a fellow named Baldrak, without a partner. He told Morgin, "Swinging a hammer all day might make you strong, but if that's all we do we lose our sword skills."

The other smiths were sparring, practicing, no animosity in the various contests. And Baldrak looked like he'd dearly love to join them. But he had no partner, so Morgin said, "I wouldn't mind a bit of practice."

Baldrak frowned and considered Morgin for a moment. "Why not? You won't be much of a match for me, but I'll take it easy on you. Come with me."

He turned and led Morgin to his tent, retrieved three long, thin bundles wrapped in oiled cloth. "Got some old blades here. See if one of them feels right."

Morgin hesitated for a moment because he knew perfectly well what was coming, though his hesitation made Baldrak look at him oddly. He reached out and took one of the bundles at random, knew exactly what he'd find within it. He removed the oiled cloth and hefted the sword, his sword, his one sword, *the* sword, the blade that always found him. He held the steel up close to his face and whispered, "Old friend, old enemy, which are you?"

To Baldrak he said, "This one will do."

"Don't you want to try the other two before choosing that one?"

Morgin shook his head. "It wouldn't make any difference. And I didn't choose this blade, it chose me. How long have you had it?"

Baldrak frowned. "I don't know. It's just an old blade. We all have a few lying around. Might have had it for years. Couldn't really say. You know this blade?"

Morgin nodded, looking at the nicked and scratched steel. It hovered at the edge of his senses like an assassin waiting in the shadows. "Yes, we're old . . . acquaintances." He'd almost said something about knowing this blade for centuries, but Baldrak wouldn't understand.

"Well then," Baldrak said heartily, "let's work up a little sweat."

In pairs, the smiths had traced out sparring circles in the sand, and the ring of steel echoed throughout the camp. A small crowd of onlookers had gathered near the far edge to observe, and when they saw Baldrak and *the Elhiyne* tracing out a circle, a few called out cat-calls and derogatory comments about Morgin's heritage.

"We'll start easy," Baldrak said, "and warm up a little."

Baldrak and Morgin squared off and traded a few blows, nothing serious yet, more like two dancers at half speed. As Morgin's shoulders and arms loosened up, he and Baldrak, by unspoken mutual consent, picked up the pace a bit, though the sand made footwork difficult.

Baldrak disengaged and stepped back a pace. "Not used to the sand, eh?"

"No," Morgin said, "I'm not used to a lot of things."

They squared off again, and Baldrak flicked the tip of his blade toward Morgin's face, not a real strike but a test to gauge his reaction. Morgin merely sidestepped the half-hearted stroke and they squared off again, though again, by unspoken mutual consent, they both knew they'd get serious now.

Baldrak lunged with a cut to Morgin's face. Morgin parried it easily and they parted. Baldrak cut low, but somehow Morgin sensed it was merely a feint, that the real strike would be a chest high thrust. Knowing what to expect, he blocked the thrust easily and returned with a thrust of his own, stopping the tip of his blade a finger's width short of the man's chest.

They both froze for a moment, both quite surprised. Had they not been sparring, had this been a real fight to the death, Baldrak would have been a dead man with a sword thrust through his heart.

Someone shouted, "Stop playing with the fool Elhiyne, Baldrak. Show him what it means to be Benesh'ere."

Morgin, fearing Baldrak might react with hurt pride, lowered his sword and pleaded, "It was luck. Pure luck."

Baldrak shouted back at the heckler, "I promised him I'd be easy on him. And I'm a man of me word."

He looked at Morgin and spoke without animosity, "Let's try her again, man. And this time I'll come in a little faster, see how much you can take."

Baldrak cut and thrust at Morgin repeatedly, but as the pace of the fight increased, Morgin held back. He feared what the sword might do if he did go on the offensive. Would it take that as a signal to sate itself on the blood of the entire Benesh'ere tribe?

As Baldrak thrust at him, Morgin seemed to know what Baldrak's blade would do before it did it, and that gave him just the instant of foreknowledge he needed to deflect each strike. Baldrak picked up the pace, and Morgin stayed with him, even as the whiteface approached the legendary speed of a Benesh'ere swordsman. It was as if Morgin's magic had decided to return, but it didn't feel like magic, more like something unique to the sands, or the Benesh'ere, or the steel. But, even if his magic had decided to return, he didn't think he could control the blade if he went on the attack. So he stayed on the defensive, and he lost more matches than he won.

"Well done," Baldrak said as they returned to his tent, both dripping with sweat.

By the time they finished washing up in the lagoon, dusk was not far off; Yim had a fire going and a meal waiting for them. Morgin had learned she wore her debt collar because she'd been impudent to her mother and father regarding a young warrior she admired a little too brazenly, just as Tallik wore his for acting the bully. They both owed their parents a debt of honor.

Baldrak told Morgin to join them, and at that Yim gave Morgin a dubious look. The smiths all sat around an open fire in the midst of their tents, and Yim served them a meal of roasted goat, and some sort of cooked root vegetable. Yim gave Morgin his usual bowl of tasteless, boiled something-or-other, sometimes boiled wheat, today boiled oats.

One of the seven smiths, a fellow named Surnarra, called to Morgin across the fire. "You fought well, Elhiyne."

Baldrak added, "But always on the defense. Never went on the offense."

Morgin couldn't tell them why he'd held back, so he grinned at Baldrak and made a joke of it. "I didn't want to hurt you."

Baldrak frowned for a moment. Then Surnarra roared with laughter. "Got you there, he did, Baldrak."

Baldrak joined the other smiths in the laughter. "Still, you fought better than I'd expect of a plainface."

Morgin shrugged and said, "I've had a lot of practice recently."

     J. L. Doty

One of the other smiths asked, "You mean at Csairne Glen? We heard about that."

"No," Morgin said, and he described the almost daily gladiatorial contest he'd fought during his captivity in Durin.

"A Kull?" Surnarra asked. "One each day?"

Morgin said, "Not every day. Sometimes they skipped a few days if I had wounds that needed healing."

A strange silence settled over the smiths as the other smith asked, "And to the death, every time?"

Morgin just nodded.

Surnarra asked, "How many Kulls have you killed?"

Morgin thought about that carefully for a moment. "I'm not sure. I never kept count." He tried to recall all his many fights over the past few years. "The first two were in Elhiyne when the Tulalane and Valso held the castle through treachery. Then there were six or seven in the sanctum, and a couple more in the castle yard. Then on the Gods Road, maybe ten or twenty."

He recalled the day he'd broken up the ambush the Kulls had prepared for Tulellcoe and the small company of Elhiyne warriors. And there was the day he killed twelve twelves with the wall of water at Gilguard's Ford. But he didn't think these Benesh'ere would count that, because he'd done it with magic. "Maybe fifty, sixty, I don't know. I've never kept count."

Chagarin looked at him carefully and said, "You're not telling us something. I watched you consider it, and then decide not to say it."

Morgin grimaced. "There was one other time, but it was done with magic." Morgin described the wall of water he'd created with his magic, and how it had swept away twelve twelves. "But I didn't think you'd count that because of the magic."

For the longest moment the only sound that broke the silence was the crackling of the open fire. Then Baldrak reached out and calmly took Morgin's bowl of boiled oats. He handed it to Yim and said, "No man who's killed that many Kulls eats this kind of fare. Get this man some real food."

9

Without a True Name

THE BLADE HAUNTED Rhianne's dreams. It always haunted them. She awoke that morning exhausted, even though she'd slept through an entire night. She decided to remain in bed for a few moments with her eyes closed, and collect her thoughts.

She didn't understand the sword and its desires. It hungered for freedom, and it constantly pressed her to release it, but she couldn't allow it the independence it sought. Like a petulant child, it constantly hammered at her; tell an undisciplined child no, and it would wait only a few heartbeats to make the same request again: free me—free me—free me. Remaining vigilant through all hours of the day and night left her exhausted.

The sword demanded everything of her, as it had demanded everything of Morgin before his death. She despaired; she could not defeat the malevolence in the blade without Morgin. He was meant to defeat it, and she merely to assist him.

She recalled the moment when she'd entered the Hall of Wills after the sword had gone berserk, stepping through the vast doors into a room filled with a fog of stone dust. Morgin had knelt on the floor in the center of the room, both hands wrapped about the sword's hilt in a white-knuckled grip, the sword buried in the stone of the floor, his head bowed. Oddly, she now recalled that his head and shoulders had been covered in a fine sheen of that stone dust, something she hadn't noticed at the time.

And she recalled the glimpse she'd had of Morgin's power, compressed into a white-hot spark to contain the malevolence of the blade. She'd never had a chance to tell him he'd not lost his power, that it was instead consumed by the need to control the hatred within that talisman. She'd never told him, and he'd died thinking himself powerless.

There remained one thing she didn't understand: now that he was dead, what held the talisman's power at bay? Certainly, a piece of her was always devoted to that effort, but she alone could not contain such evil. And yet, with Morgin dead, the blade had not devastated the countryside. Perhaps Morgin had left his power behind somehow, left it in the blade as a counterbalance.

"Lady Mistress," Braunye said. "We have a busy day ahead of us."

Rhianne opened her eyes, lay for a moment and savored the quiet of early morning.

••••

Morgin and everyone in the camp bedded down right after dinner. They'd get a few hours' sleep, then rise in the early evening and head out onto the sands.

Shebasha visited him in his dreams regardless of when he slept. "When will you reveal yourself?" she asked him.

"What do I have to reveal? That I've been a fool; a fool about Rhianne, a fool about Olivia, a fool about Valso and everyone else?"

Shebasha lifted a hind paw and scratched her chin. "All you mortals are fools; it's just that some of you are more foolish than others. Give me your name, mortal. Give me your name and I'll give you a boon."

Morgin had nothing to lose, so he opened his mouth to say his name, but nothing happened. His tongue wouldn't move, his lips wouldn't move.

Shebasha smiled and licked at a paw. "You can't speak a false name in this dream, mortal."

Morgin understood now. Out of pure reflex he had tried to tell her his name was *Morgin*. But that was not a true name. The demon ElkenSkul had given him his true name, though now, after listening to

Toke, he doubted even that. As an experiment, he opened his mouth to speak the name *AethonLaw*, but again his tongue would not move, his lips would not move. He managed to utter only a crude grunt, and that confirmed his suspicion.

Shebasha laughed and stood. "The only place where you are truly a fool, mortal, is that you do not know your own name."

A very young Aethon appeared beside her. "Lord Mortal," he said, greeting Morgin. He glanced at Shebasha. "I told him to seek out The Unnamed King."

"Hm!" she said. "That would be wise."

Morgin's frustration grew with each word they spoke. "I would gladly seek him out, but I don't know how."

Shebasha looked at Aethon and said, "Sad, is it not?"

Aethon agreed, and then both of them turned their backs on him and walked away.

Morgin jumped to his feet and shouted after them. "Now wait, damn you. I'll go to the Unnamed King, but how do I find him? How do I find a myth, a legend that doesn't exist?"

He tried to follow them, but they ignored him and continued walking, and slowly they dissipated into the oncoming night. He stood there on the sands of his dreams pondering their words. To find the Unnamed King, where would he go? Certainly not in any of the clan territories, nor in Aud. Perhaps in Kathbeyanne, but that didn't feel right either. And then he suddenly realized what an idiot he'd been. The Unnamed King was also known as the King of Dreams; he would not find such a king on the planes of mortal men, nor on any of the twelve levels of existence. No, the King of Dreams would only be found in a dream. But how could he search in his dreams when he had no control over his dreams? He knew of no magic to give him that control, and it frustrated him that all he could do was stumble along hoping to somehow find the Unnamed King by pure luck.

He dreamt next of Aethon's tomb, looked upon the crypt and studied the tableau carefully as he remembered it: the skeleton king seated upon his throne, one skeletal arm resting casually on an armrest, the other on the hilt of the great sword. But as before there was some flaw in that picture, and it took him some time to realize exactly what. The first time he'd glimpsed the ancient crypt he'd been lying in the enchanted alcove in Castle Elhiyne, dying from a Kull crossbow bolt he'd taken in the chest. Then one wall of the alcove had shimmered and opened into the tomb. The skeleton king had been there on his throne with his magnificent sword, and all the arms and armor and trappings of a great king. And there'd been the body of a dead warrior lying on the floor of the tomb in front of the throne, a warrior dressed in simple garb and still clutching a plain and unadorned sword, very unlike the grand accouterments of a great king's tomb. And because Morgin had dropped his sword in the hall outside the alcove, the king had taken that dead warrior's sword and given it to him. But now, in his dreams, no warrior lay at the feet of the skeleton king, and the floor in front of the king's throne remained empty.

Baldrak shook Morgin out of his dream. "Come on, Elhiyne. We're going out onto the sands."

The entire camp had already shifted into frantic activity. In a very short time they broke down the tents and packed everything onto strange little pack animals akin to donkeys. The whitefaces called them chakarras. They were smaller than Benesh'ere warhorses, but like them they had large, broad hooves that didn't sink far into the sand. Packed up and ready to go, the entire camp moved out on the sands walking into the night.

••••

The Benesh'ere had about one thousand horses for mounted warriors, but only outriders and scouts who ventured out ahead of the main column rode. Most of the warriors walked with their mounts as part of a long, winding train of people and livestock. The moon hung in the sky at three-quarters, approaching full, and out on the yellow-white sand it lit up the night as if it were merely a shadow in the light of day.

Morgin trudged along with the smiths. Walking in the sand was difficult and exhausting, but they set a pace for the weakest of the Benesh'ere—old whitefaces and young children—so Morgin managed to keep up.

Chagarin joined him and walked beside him, some sort of bundle tucked under his left arm. "You'll develop the right muscles for the sand, soon enough. But until then you're going to be mighty sore, come morning."

Chagarin retrieved the bundle from under his arm, and by its shape Morgin knew it must be a sword wrapped in oiled cloth. Chagarin unwrapped the blade and held it out to Morgin. He took it, recognizing it immediately, and as they walked he threw a questioning look at Chagarin.

"Baldrak told me you know this blade."

Morgin shrugged. "Or one very much like it. But I left it back in Durin." And then he recalled that while he had left it in Durin, Rat had brought it to him that night out on the sands with Shebasha. "No," he said, "that's wrong. I forgot. I lost it out on the sands the night the sand cat attacked us." He wasn't about to try to explain how Rat had brought it to him in a dream. Let Chagarin think he'd carried it out onto the sands.

"That explains it," Chagarin said, nodding. "One of our outriders must have found it in the sand. They always turn derelict blades like that over to us smiths."

Chagarin held his hand out palm up. Morgin hesitated, wanted nothing more than to be done with the cursed blade, wanted to give it to Chagarin and never see it again. But he couldn't abdicate his responsibilities that way, for the burden of its power was his and his alone.

At his moment of hesitation, Chagarin's eyes narrowed. Morgin had no choice but to give up the blade at that moment, so he reversed it and handed it to the smith. But in his soul he made sure it knew that as long as it haunted the Mortal Plane, it would not be free of him.

Chagarin looked at it thoughtfully as they trudged through the sand. "Baldrak also told me you said this blade chose you, not you it."

Silence hung between them for a long moment, then Morgin said, "I was just speaking gibberish. I really don't know what I meant by that."

Chagarin continued to look at the blade. "It's unusual for a blade to make such a choice. But it's been known to happen."

He wrapped the blade again in the oiled cloth, all the while looking only at Morgin. "But I wonder how you knew it chose you. Most men are not close enough to the steel to sense such things."

With that, he turned and drifted off into the moon-lit night.

••••

At dawn the Benesh'ere stopped and set up their tents. They didn't circle together into one large defensive perimeter, but grouped into smaller encampments that stretched into the distance among the dunes. Several thousand whitefaces strung out in a long line over the distance of more than a league would take too long to reassemble each night.

The smiths didn't set up shop. Baldrak told Morgin the worst they might expect would be the occasional thrown shoe, or broken piece of tack, nothing that couldn't wait for them to get to the lake. They'd spend another night on the sands, and when they reached the Plains of Quam they'd shift back to sleeping at night and marching by day. Two days on the plains, then two days of travel through the forests just south of SavinCourt would bring them to their traditional camp on the east shore of the Lake of Sorrows.

Morgin could barely stand, and walked like an old man. Walking in the deep sand used his muscles differently than walking on hard ground. Baldrak laughed and said, "It's a shame you'll get your sand legs just as we're leaving the sands. When we return to Aelldie from the lake, we all suffer like that after a full season on hard ground."

With the reversal of their days the smiths had their hour of sword practice in the early morning, just after setting up their tents and before dinner. Morgin again participated, this time paired off with Surnarra, who had a distinctively different fighting style from that of Baldrak. Surnarra waded in with heavy blows, where Baldrak had been more surgical with his strikes.

Again, as their blades clashed, Morgin sensed where Surnarra's blade would strike an instant before it did so, and he fared rather well. It wasn't prescience; of that he was certain, for he'd been trained in sword magic, trained to use his power to strengthen his arm, but most importantly to speed up his reflexes and his perception of his opponent's moves. That quickness of perception often felt like prescience, but any experienced wizard knew the fallacy of that. Again, he lost more than he won, but the exercise renewed his hope that his magic had decided to return.

That night, as he trudged through the sand in the long column of the Benesh'ere, he sensed something arcane approaching. He turned about and saw Toke headed his way, with ElkenSkul hovering just over his shoulder. When Toke caught up with him he matched Morgin's pace, and merely walked beside him in silence.

Morgin didn't wait for Toke to spout his riddles. He simply asked, "What do the extra marks in my name mean?"

"Ah," Toke said, looking up at the moon above. "A good question, that."

Morgin looked at the faint shimmer hovering just over the old man's shoulder. "Surely, the *namegiver* knows the answer."

"No, young man, I wouldn't assume that."

"You can't mean the *namegiver* doesn't know the meaning of the symbols he scratches?"

Toke shrugged. "It is but a demon spirit, Elhiyne. I don't think it understands the concept of a name in the same way we do."

"Why is it also called *soul taker*? My grandmother called it *soul taker*."

"Now that, I do know. You see, without a name, do you truly have a soul?"

Morgin shook his head sadly. "Riddles! You and that damned sand cat give me nothing but riddles."

"Sand cat? Is it Shebasha you speak of?"

"She haunts my dreams just as you haunt my waking hours, and both of you haunt me with riddles."

Toke rubbed at the whiskers on his jaw. "Interesting! I'll have to ponder that."

Toke turned and walked away into the night.

10

The March

THE SHARPNESS OF the border between the sands of the Munjarro and the Plains of Quam surprised Morgin. In the space of only a few hundred paces they went from trudging through bottomless sand, to walking on a layer of sand only a hand's width deep, then to walking on the hard prairie dirt. And there they walked into a wall of mist, a light fog that clung to the ground and limited vision to a few hundred paces. Morgin remembered the plains well: a flat and barren land without shape or contour, broken only by clumps of sagebrush and brown grasses. The last time he'd visited the plains, he'd killed Salula.

Morgin noticed the difference in the temperature immediately. As the sun rose and climbed above the flat horizon, at this early hour the temperature would be rising quickly out on the sands. Here, it still held onto a hint of the spring night chill, which made the daylight hours bearable. The rising sun didn't burn off the mist, though he saw the clear, blue sky above so the layer of fog couldn't be too thick. To shift their sleeping schedule back to nights, they continued marching.

A difference arose in the Benesh'ere when they crossed that border between the oven of the sands and the horizonless prairie: a certain wariness descended upon them all, and everyone now carried arms. Out on the sands, a warrior might wander about the camp completely unarmed, or perhaps with no more than a utilitarian knife on his or her belt. Now, however, everyone—warrior, wife, debtor, old man, old woman, even small children—everyone carried a sword or a spear of some kind, many with a fabled Benesh'ere longbow and a quiver of arrows strapped to their back. And none wore the broad-brimmed straw hats beneath their hoods. Clearly, the whitefaces were preparing for some sort of battle or fight, and the straw hats would only hinder a fighter's ability to look quickly from side to side.

As they crossed onto the prairie, the leading edge of the column slowed slightly, bunching it up so they now walked about twelve abreast, whereas on the sand it had been no more than single or double file. Quite a few of the warriors with horses mounted up and rode out in squads of twelve, clearly outriders patrolling the column's flanks.

They stopped to set up camp around midday, and Morgin noticed another difference: the encampments were much larger. On the sands they'd clustered into small groups of one or two twelves, but the encampment he worked in now was more like one hundred twelves, with perimeter sentries posted.

The smiths followed their usual routine: hobble the horses, unload the pack animals, pitch the tents, stow their supplies, then time for an hour of sword practice and sparring. After that they cleaned up and ate a good meal. And to accommodate the change in their sleeping schedule, they'd wait until nightfall before bedding down.

"Elhiyne."

Morgin had been checking their water skins, making sure they were properly stowed and there were no leaks. He turned to find that Chagarin had approached him, silent as a hunting cat. They were all like that, the Benesh'ere; they moved with such stealth it seemed to be almost a magical talent.

Chagarin held out a sheathed sword and knife. Morgin accepted both, frowning. The sword he knew well, but the knife was new to him. He slid it from its sheath: it was a large, heavy blade, meant for fighting.

At Morgin's questioning look, Chagarin said, "From here on, you never go unarmed. And you don't leave the perimeter in a group with fewer than twelve blooded warriors. Once we step off the sands, we begin the March."

"The March?"

"Aye, the two-day March across the plains is Kull hunting season."

"You hunt Kulls?"

"They hunt us. We hunt them. From now on, be on the alert."

Morgin strapped on the sword and knife and went back to his chores. But he saw now that the whitefaces constantly scanned the perimeter of their camp, looking over their shoulders, jumping at the crack of a nearby twig, or the snort of a horse, or the bark of a dog.

Morgin was banking the cooking fires when Yim found him. "Lord Harriok wants to see you."

The Benesh'ere didn't use titles like *Lord*, but Yim was quite young and impressionable, and Harriok had made Morgin address him that way more as a jest, since Morgin was not Benesh'ere. "Let me finish this," Morgin said. "It'll just take a moment."

It took more than a moment, but Yim chattered on while Morgin worked, filling his ears with a stream of gossip about which young girl had her sights set on which young warrior. When he finished, Morgin stood, brushed ashes off his hands and said, "Lead on."

They crossed an open space to the next large group, which Morgin now understood was a well-structured defensive perimeter. Yim explained that Chagarin's instructions to not ". . . leave the perimeter in a group with fewer than twelve blooded warriors," didn't apply when crossing the short distance from perimeter to perimeter.

Morgin found Harriok sitting up in the shade of his tent, looking much better with color in his cheeks and a smile on his face. Branaugh sat beside him. Morgin greeted him by lowering his eyes. "Lord Harriok."

"Please, Elhiyne," Harriok pleaded, "don't call me that. That was just a joke."

"What should I call you?"

"Harriok. And I'll call you AethonLaw, not *the Elhiyne*."

"Actually, I'd prefer Morgin."

Throughout the exchange, while Harriok bantered happily, Branaugh sat stone-faced listening to the two of them. She seemed impatient, as if she had something on her mind and the banter irritated her no end for keeping her from getting to it.

Morgin asked them both, "What is it you're not saying?"

Harriok lowered his eyes while Branaugh continued to stare stonily. Harriok broke the silence. "I saved your life out on the sands and so you owed me a debt of honor. Then you saved mine, so the debt is repaid."

That seemed clear, but Morgin was just as clearly missing something. "So you'll remove the debt collar now?"

"I can't," Harriok said, his eyes still lowered. "My father will then be free to challenge you to mortal combat. And he'll kill you. I've stalled, made excuses, and we've been careful to tell them only that you gave me water, not that you carried me across the sands. But when we reach the Lake of Sorrows, I'm afraid I'll not be able to stall further."

The implications of that were rather clear. Morgin had a few more days to live, and then Jerst would kill him.

Branaugh still stared at him stonily, and he realized then that Harriok's confession was not the subject she waited so impatiently to discuss. She leaned forward and pleaded, "Did you kill the demon cat?"

Harriok winced at her outburst, looked at her and said, "Not that superstitious foolishness again."

"It's not foolishness," she said through gritted teeth, her eyes never leaving Morgin. "Well, did you?"

Morgin told her the truth. "I don't know."

"What do you mean by that? Either you killed her, or you didn't."

Morgin described the night Shebasha had attacked them, told them in detail what he remembered. "The last thing I recall was standing there with a sword, you unconscious, and waiting for her next attack. When she hit me I thrust out with the sword, but I have no idea if I struck true, and the next thing I recall was waking up in the heat of the day, no sign of the cat." He didn't want to discuss his dreams of Shebasha. He'd come to accept that his dreams and his reality were closely intertwined, but would these Benesh'ere accept that? If he claimed to have killed her based solely on a dream, would they think it an idle boast? He had come to like these two, and he didn't want them to think of him that way.

Branaugh shook her head, closed her eyes and let her chin drop. "That won't do."

Morgin asked, "What's the problem?"

Harriok sighed unhappily and spoke. "There is no question Shebasha struck me with the sixth claw, and left her venom in the wound. I should not be alive. My soul should be hers until she dies."

Branaugh opened her eyes and leaned forward, searching Morgin's face hungrily. "Yim says you were not touched by the sixth claw, that she marked you with the five but not the sixth. She also said you have an old scar about where the sixth would have been?"

Morgin nodded and said, "I'll have to trust Yim on that. I can't see them myself."

"May I look at it?"

Morgin nodded again.

Branaugh stood and walked around him as he opened his robe and exposed his left shoulder. She gently pulled the robe further down his back. "There is a scar here, next to the other five, and spaced about where the sixth would be. But they've all healed nicely."

She walked around Morgin and returned to her place beside Harriok. Morgin refastened his robe.

Branaugh looked at him intently as she asked, "Was that sixth scar an old one?"

Morgin owed them the truth. He shook his head resignedly, and Branaugh let out a faint whimper. "When I awoke that morning the sixth scar was swollen, and numb, and open. But it healed the first day, long before the others."

Branaugh buried her face in her hands and said, "That's just not possible. He can't have killed her. He's not Benesh'ere, and he hasn't completed the first four deeds."

At the mention of the deeds Morgin flinched, a reaction he couldn't have hidden, and Branaugh's eyes narrowed. "I know of the deeds," Morgin said. "Why do you speak of them?"

Harriok answered him. "Shebasha is thought to be the spirit of the sands, trapped within her own haunting. Killing her would free her of that. And there are many here who believe those old legends of the last SteelMaster returning to us. I do not."

Free the spirit of the sands!

"Is it possible?" Branaugh asked, almost pleading with him to deny it.

Morgin sighed and felt a great flood of weariness. "The Thane were giant, winged griffins, half eagle and half lion."

Harriok gasped, and Branaugh began to cry quietly.

Morgin continued. "They no longer exist. Aiergain of Aud is the hand of the thief."

With each revelation, Harriok's eyes widened further.

"The daughter of the wind was AnneRhianne, an ancient Benesh'ere princess who waited centuries for me to free her. WolfDane, the hell-hound king, is the Dane King. And now you tell me Shebasha was the spirit of the sands."

Harriok stood. "We have to tell them, tell everyone."

Branaugh stood beside him and pulled on his arm. "No. They'll never believe it. They'll think we're trying to save him from Jerst's blade. That'll only inflame them and they'll demand his death now."

"But—"

"No," she said. "Say nothing."

She looked at Morgin. "Can you prove any of this?"

"No, nothing."

She nodded. "Then we say nothing and you continue to wear the debt-ring. At least until we figure something else out."

••••

Morgin shot awake and sat up, his heart pounding, fear coursing through his soul. Still tangled in his blanket he pulled the heavy fighting knife. He'd slept out in the open under his blanket; he saw, by the faint bluish tint of the sky, that dawn was not far off. The thin mist still blanketed the prairie and Morgin could only see about fifty to a hundred paces into it. Some danger had awakened him, but what?

Nothing imminent, nothing nearby coming at him, so he tossed the blanket aside, stood and drew his sword. It came alive and tugged at his hand, though not forcefully. It pulled him toward the southern edge of the perimeter, so he walked that direction and that seemed to satisfy it. He approached one of the perimeter sentries, approached him well to one side. An armed man that chose to approach an armed whiteface in the misty-dark from behind, such a fool would probably not live long.

Morgin stopped at the perimeter half way between two sentries: one a swordsman, the other a pikeman. They were spaced so they could see each other easily in the mist. Morgin recognized the pikeman; he'd been one of the most abusive during his first days among the Benesh'ere, spitting on him and kicking him whenever the opportunity arose.

Both whitefaces looked his way and the swordsman said, "Elhiyne, you rise early, and carry both blades naked?"

Morgin glanced down momentarily, looked at the sword in his right hand, the knife in his left. "Yes," Morgin said, staring out into the early dawn of the prairie. "Something is wrong." The sword tugged at his hand, confirming that. "And I can only think of one thing that can be this wrong."

The swordsman on his left drew his blade. The pikeman on his right leveled his pike and dropped into a crouch. Then he whistled a single, sharp note, which Morgin heard repeated down the perimeter line and through the camp. Nothing happened for several heartbeats, then he heard a horse neigh, followed by the thunder of several horses charging across the hard prairie dirt, all hidden somewhere in the mist. And then a charging horse thundered out of the mist straight at him.

Morgin wrapped himself in a shadow, stepped to one side and ducked. The horse drove past him and a Kull saber sliced through the air where his neck would have been. Since the Kull's blade hadn't connected with a target the halfman knew he was there, and Morgin knew he'd not leave an enemy at his back. Morgin spun and charged after him, knowing what to expect. The camp erupted in chaos, shouts and cries and the ringing of blades clashing everywhere.

The Kull reined in his horse, pulled it to a stop and spun about. As Morgin crossed the distance between them in a sprint, he hoped all the halfman would see in the faint morning light was a dim shadow fluttering across the ground. The Kull hesitated, and that was the instant Morgin needed. He veered slightly to the right to avoid the horse's head, crossed the last few paces and leapt, drove the blade of the knife up under the Kull's chin as he hit him.

They both tumbled over the far side of the horse. Morgin hit hard, rolled, scrambled to his feet and turned to face the Kull. But the halfman struggled to rise with Morgin's knife buried in his throat. Morgin gripped his sword in both hands, swung it in a flat arc and half-severed the monster's neck.

A dozen paces outside the perimeter two mounted Kulls had a lone whiteface isolated. It was the fellow with the pike, whom Morgin had spoken to, and they were trying to herd him away from the camp alive, harrying him on both sides and driving him outward.

Morgin glanced at the Kull he'd just killed; no time to retrieve the knife. With the halfman's horse close at hand, he grabbed the saddle horn, got a boot in a stirrup and leapt into its saddle. He struggled for a moment to find the reins, then dug his heels into the horse's flanks and charged. Nothing fancy, he just charged into the midst of the two Kulls and the whiteface. With surprise on his side, he slashed out at one Kull, and felt his sword bite as his horse slammed heavily into the other Kull's mount.

Both riders and horses went down in a tangle of arms and legs, screaming horses and kicking hooves. A hoof grazed past Morgin's face, almost taking off his head. Still on the ground, he rolled over once to get out of the mess, tried to get to his hands and knees, but a Kull slammed into him, and they rolled together on the ground. The Kull came out on top straddling Morgin, raised a fighting knife over his head. Morgin's sword was too long for such infighting so he punched upward and hit the halfman in the nose with the sword's hilt. Then two hand-spans of steel blossomed from the Kull's chest.

The halfman froze; the knife held high, his eyes locked on the bloody steel protruding from his chest. A sword hissed and chopped through the wrist holding the knife high, removing the hand with the knife. The Kull lowered his arm, looked dumbly at the bloody stump of his wrist. Then his eyes crossed and he slid slowly forward off the steel protruding from his chest. He lay still on top of Morgin.

"Ahhh," Morgin shouted and pushed the dead Kull to one side. He sat up, the two whiteface sentries standing over him.

The swordsman said, "I think it's the Elhiyne. Sounds like him, at least."

The pikeman who had been so abusive looked at Morgin now, his eyes narrow and hard. "Does sound like him, but sure don't look like him."

Morgin didn't understand their banter for a moment, then he realized he was still wrapped in shadow, and with that, his heart leapt as he also realized his magic had returned. He quickly extinguished the shadows.

"Yup, it is the Elhiyne," the pikeman said, and Morgin braced himself for a kick, or some other abuse. But the pikeman merely looked at him for a long moment, his eyes still narrow and hard. Then he nodded, leaned forward and extended a hand to Morgin. "You fought well, Elhiyne."

Morgin took the hand cautiously, and as the pikeman lifted him to his feet the swordsman said, "Almost as good as a whiteface."

The Benesh'ere used the term *whiteface* casually among themselves, but an outsider would be wise to be very cautious doing so, for they might easily take the term as an insult. "Nah," the pikeman said. "He didn't fight that good."

11

Lost in the Mist

THE BENESH'ERE TOOK a couple hours to lick their wounds. As information passed up and down the column, Morgin learned that their perimeter had been the hardest hit.

"Them Kulls usually do it that way," the swordsman said as he checked a cut on Morgin's shoulder. "Throw a half-dozen feints with just a few halfmen testing several perimeters. That way Jerst don't know right away where to send help. He keeps a squad of six twelves of armed and mounted warriors in the middle of the column just for that."

The pikeman's name was Fantose, and the swordsman Delaga. The swordsman said, "This cut ain't too deep, but we'd better treat it so it don't fester." He reached into his pack and pulled out a small clay pot. He pulled the stopper on it, stuck his finger in it and retrieved a lump of brownish grease that smelled so bad it made Morgin's eyes water. When he rubbed it into the cut, Morgin's shoulder lit up with fire.

"Ow! That burns like netherhell."

Delaga grinned. "That means it's working."

Fantose approached them carrying some sort of dark, cloth bundle and leading one of the Kull horses. "You shouldn't let him put that crap on you."

Delaga turned on him. "But it works good."

"I know it works good," Fantose conceded as he tossed the cloth bundle to Morgin. "But he's going to smell like you now."

Morgin shook the bundle out to find that he held three Kull cloaks. "What are these for?" he asked. "I'm not going to wear them."

Fantose shook his head. "Of course you aren't. They're your kills, so your cloaks. We cut off the hood and keep it as a trophy."

Morgin had heard a little about that practice among the whitefaces. "But I didn't kill all three of them."

Fantose shrugged. "No, but you killed the first one, and if you hadn't taken his horse and plowed into the other two, they'd be stringing me guts up in a tree now. No, you get the kills."

The sound of a horse's hooves on the hard prairie dirt drew their attention. Blesset, riding one of the desert ponies at an easy trot, reined it in a few paces from Morgin. She held a naked sword in one hand, the reins in the other. Looking at the bundle Morgin held, she asked coldly, "What goes here?"

Fantose said, "They're his kills."

Delaga said, "They're his cloaks."

Jerst, his horse moving at an easy trot, brought his mount to a halt behind Blesset and sat astride it silently watching.

Blesset's face could have been cut from stone for all the expression it held. She reached out with her sword and rested the tip in the middle of the pile of cloaks in Morgin's arms. Then she pressed down with it, not a slash or a stab or any real kind of sword stroke. She merely pressed down, harder, and harder, and harder, until Morgin was forced to let the cloaks drop to the ground.

"He earned them cloaks," Fantose said.

She shook her head and smiled. "He earned nothing." She gently nudged her horse around, spurred it lightly and rode away into the mist.

Jerst merely sat astride his horse looking on. He looked down at the cloaks at Morgin's feet, his eyes hard and narrow, then into Morgin's face. Then he calmly reined his horse about, nudged its flanks with his heels and rode away.

••••

Casualties among the Benesh'ere had been light, so they were back on the March well before mid-morning. Fantose gave Morgin one of the Kull horses, with the explanation that, "You ride better'n me. Stay armed, stay close, walk 'er along the edge of the column and be ready to mount up in a wink."

Apparently, they gave Morgin credit for the light casualties; any advanced warning made an enormous difference. It gave everyone the instant needed to be awake, alert and armed before the Kulls hit.

"You smell 'em or something?" Delaga asked, marching beside Morgin.

Morgin, leading the Kull horse by its reins, shook his head. "No. I don't know what it is. I just woke up scared, and knew something was wrong."

Delaga thought that over for a moment. "Wish I could smell Kulls like you."

Fantose added, "We'd all have a better chance of smelling Kulls if we didn't have to smell you."

Morgin knew better than to argue the point.

Near mid-morning, they heard the clash of steel and cries of anger and pain somewhere down the column, all of it hidden by the thin mist. The March halted, and up and down the line warriors stepped a few paces out of the column and took up defensive positions. Morgin jumped into the saddle and drew his sword. He saw other riders nudge their horses to a position about twenty paces outside the line of warriors so he did the same. "Don't let them draw you out," Fantose shouted. "They want you to follow them. Then they'll surround you and take you alive. Then they get to have fun with you."

Morgin waited, trying to keep the tension out of his shoulders and sword arm. The mist had thinned further and he saw a little deeper into it. The plain appeared flat and featureless, when in fact it was fractured by gullies and washes. The Kulls used such features along with the mist to spring traps on the column. It was great sport for them, and they'd done it now for centuries.

When the excitement died Morgin saw the other Benesh'ere horsemen dismount and begin leading their horses again. He did likewise, and took up the March beside Fantose and Delaga.

One of Jerst's patrol twelves trotted past. They rode abreast, twelve warriors side-by-side, spaced about thirty to fifty paces apart. Any one man might be hidden within the mist, but he could see three or four of his comrades to either side. In that way they patrolled a swath several hundred paces wide on either side of the column.

Morgin asked Fantose and Delaga, "Why do you do this every year? Over and over. We're just targets out here."

Fantose considered that for a moment. "The March? We wait as long as we can. The mist thins a bit every day as we approach summer. Early spring it's so thick you can't see your hand in front of your face. We'd be dead meat fer them Kulls. So we wait until the heat of the sands is unbearable. We wait, and then we come in, hoping the mist ain't thicker than normal."

Morgin asked, "Is this normal?"

Delaga shrugged. "Pretty much average."

"Then why go back out? Why not just stay at the Lake of Sorrows."

Both of the whitefaces looked aghast, and both said at the same time, "It gets bloody cold."

Fantose shook with feigned shivering, and they both spoke what was apparently a common joke, "Wouldn't be able to get me manhood up when I needed it."

They considered that quite funny, laughed raucously and slapped each other on the back a few times. But when Delaga saw that Morgin was serious, he sobered quickly and said, "When you ask that question, that tells us you don't know the heart of the Benesh'ere."

••••

Cort and Tulellcoe followed what might have been Morgin's escape route. Like the farmers and their *thieves*, they discovered only small pieces of information here and there that could have been Morgin trying to escape going south. Then again, the obscure bits they uncovered might have nothing to do with Morgin at all. Someone stole an old mare at one farm, picked through a bin of cattle feed at another. It might have been Morgin, then again it might simply have been petty thieves.

Then, about four days south of Durin, while crossing an open field bordered by trees and hedgerows, Tulellcoe suddenly cried out. He reined his horse in sharply, dismounted and desperately tore open his tunic. He lifted the leather thong with the charms from around his neck and held it out at arm's length. On the end of it, tendrils of smoke drifted upward from the two charms they'd keyed to their memories of Morgin and Rhianne.

Cort dismounted and approached Tulellcoe. She leaned close to the charms and saw that they were burning their way through the leather thong. "Something happened here," she said. She looked about them and scanned the edges of the field. "Something happened in this field to both of them, something that generated very strong emotions. Can you tell more?"

Tulellcoe waited until the two charms had cooled enough to hold in the palm of his hand, then he cupped that for Rhianne in his left and that for Morgin in his right. He closed his eyes and stood that way for an interminable number of heartbeats. Then he opened his eyes, turned and began walking toward the edge of the field. Cort followed him, leading the two horses as he zigzagged back and forth, searching. Slowly he worked his way to the edge of the field and there stepped into a copse of trees. He walked about a hundred paces into the trees and stopped, looking about. He closed his eyes again and waited. Then he took a long, deep breath and let it out in a slow sigh. "Something happened to both of them, but not together. Something first to Morgin, and then to Rhianne, and the time between was not long, perhaps no more than a small portion of a day."

Cort asked, "You can tell no more than that?"

"No, nothing."

Tulellcoe replaced the thong around his neck. Then they mounted up and headed south. Two days later they came to the Ulbb, where they dismounted and stood on the north bank of the river looking out over the Munjarro.

Cort marveled at the oven of sand, yellowish dunes that extended to the horizon. Even here, on the edge of the waste, the heat rose off the sand in waves, making it an effort just to breathe. She watched blurry lines of heat play across the sand, and she wondered out loud, "You know, even in winter, out on the sands at midday the heat is oppressive."

Standing beside her, Tulellcoe said, "It cools at night, doesn't it?"

"In winter, yes. In winter it begins to cool even in late afternoon, and the night can carry a decided chill. But during the summer it's oppressive day and night."

Tulellcoe didn't respond to that. They were both thinking the same thing, and it had nothing to do with the heat of the sands. But it had to be him who voiced the thought.

"Nothing," he said. "Nothing now for two days' ride. No sign, no evidence, not even rumors. Nothing since that field where the charms reacted."

He stood statue-still staring out over the Munjarro for the longest time. Then he said, "They both died back there in that copse of trees, didn't they? The rumors were true."

••••

Morgin had come to realize that only his shadowmagic had returned, and it really didn't bother him all that much that the rest hadn't come back as well. He'd never been very good at most of it anyway, was plain terrible at complex spell-castings. But he had his shadows, and he could feel his power.

"Raw power," Olivia had chided him on more than one occasion. "That's all you have."

And it was then that AnnaRail would remind her, "Don't forget the shadowmagic, mother."

And Olivia would concede that point.

So shadowmagic must be intricate and refined, Morgin decided, like complex spell-castings—not crude and raw, like Morgin's simple, but rather intense, control of power. Power and shadows, with those two aspects he could do quite a lot.

Morgin pondered his shadowmagic throughout that day, as one skirmish after another erupted in the column, always hidden somewhere in the mist. Whenever they heard the noise of a Kull attack somewhere on the line, he jumped into the saddle, took his position, held his ground, and tried to keep himself alive. Though one time, sitting astride the Kull horse, staring out into the mist and waiting for a Kull to come charging out of it, he glanced over his shoulder at the Benesh'ere column, and knew he wanted to keep them alive as well, these strange whitefaced people he'd come to like.

Delaga and Fantose tried to teach him the sharp, whistled warnings they used. Morgin could whistle, but with nothing close to the volume the sentries needed. "Some can do it," Delaga said, "some can't. Just shout at me and Fantose and we'll do the whistling for you."

The two men kept up a constant banter about Delaga and his smell as they trudged along. Morgin enjoyed listening to them, and was chuckling at one of Fantose's remarks when the fear hit him.

He turned to the two whitefaces and shouted, "Shut up—Kulls—now—in force—here—us—"

He didn't wait to hear their response but leapt into the saddle. He drew his sword and slapped the horse's flank with the flat of the blade, took it out to the required twenty paces from the column. He heard the two whitefaces issuing those sharp, piercing whistles, heard them relayed through the column, but he was alone when the Kulls came out of the mist.

It was strange that his foreknowledge of a Kull attack allowed him to be out there a few heartbeats ahead of everyone else, strange that such a gift meant he now faced a full twelve of Kulls, faced them alone. He'd be a fool to just stand his ground and let them plow into him, so he wrapped a shadow about him and his horse, dug his heels into the horse's flanks and charged insanely at the twelve Kulls charging him.

He screamed as he charged, an angry cry of fear. An instant before he slammed into the lead Kull an arrow hissed past his ear. It came so close it actually cut his earlobe, and he wanted to shout back at the maniacs behind to hold their arrows, for he was out here, among the targets, an ally. And then the arrow punched into the right eye of the lead Kull. The halfman was dead an instant before Morgin and his horse slammed into them, and the Kull's raised saber was just one more obstacle he need not worry about.

They slammed together, a dead halfman and Morgin and their mounts. A good half-twelve of them went down in that instant, a repeat of the scene where Morgin had crashed into the two Kulls harrying Fantose. But this time the carnage was beyond imagining, a shrieking chaos of snapping limbs and twisted bodies.

Morgin tumbled into it, thinking that, like so many times before, now he would die. But he bounced once on the ground in a good shoulder roll, just as a massive horse tumbled over him, missing him by a hair's breadth. An arrow sliced under his left armpit, punching into the Kull in front of him. Another arrow sliced his right shoulder as it barely missed him and buried its barbed warhead into the breast of a Kull horse. Arrows right, left, up, down—one actually between his legs—slammed into every half-living thing near him.

The sword jerked and bucked in his hand, actually dragged him deeper into the fight. A mounted halfman loomed over him, and for just an instant Morgin saw his face clearly, split by a hateful grin as he thrust down at Morgin. But the sword deflected the thrust with ease and sliced out, killing both halfman and horse.

Another Kull thrust his saber at Morgin's head; he ducked and rolled to avoid it, came up next to a Kull mount without a rider. He climbed into the saddle, deflected a sword thrust aimed at his neck, couldn't find the horse's reins but dug his heels into its flanks anyway. And with its own will for survival it carried him out of the melee, carried him away from the fight, carried him into the mist.

He fumbled for the panicked animal's reins, got it under control and brought it to a stop. He turned about carefully; saw only mist in every direction, heard the fighting and screams of battle. But in the dim haze that surrounded him, the cries and clash of weapons seemed to come from every direction at once. The fight and the Benesh'ere column might be anywhere. Sitting there astride the Kull horse, breathing heavily and sucking air into his lungs in fitful gasps, he realized he was lost.

The fighting was within sight of the column, so it would be closer to his comrades than him. He pulled the horse about, tried to get some sense of direction from the sounds of the battle, then nudged the horse in the direction he thought might be right. His world narrowed to a mist-shrouded circle about a hundred paces wide, and he quickly realized he'd picked the wrong direction.

The column was heading west, and he'd been defending its north side, so if he headed south he should encounter some segment of the March. The sun was low on the horizon, dusk approaching quickly, so it was easy to pick that direction. But after some time he finally admitted he'd become hopelessly lost. And with the coming of night the mist thickened, so Morgin found a deep ravine, dismounted and led the horse down into it.

The Kull mount had been minimally provisioned. He had a blanket tied to the back of the saddle, a few bits of journeycake and jerky, but not much else. He ate what was there, tied the horse's reins about his wrist, wrapped the blanket around him, wrapped a shadow about him and the horse, and lay down in the ravine to pass the night.

12

A Feast for Flies

MORGIN SLEPT POORLY, was awake well before dawn and watched the mist thin as the sun rose. The strain of maintaining the shadows throughout the night took its toll, adding to his weariness.

He'd been close to the front of the column during the March, so he was probably ahead of them now. He turned west, let the horse walk to conserve its strength and figured he'd meet the whitefaces at the edge of the plains.

Sounds didn't carry far in the mist, and as he travelled he listened carefully for any noise that might signal danger, scanning constantly from right to left. He quickly discovered the ravines and gullies of the plain were often not visible until he was upon them, a trick of the mist. And while in the column they were never deep enough to require a detour, that was not the case now; the Benesh'ere probably followed a well-known path centuries old.

He came upon a deep ravine so suddenly he almost let his horse stumble into it. It spluttered angrily as he pulled on its reins, and the two mounted Kulls at the bottom of the ravine looked up at him. They were as surprised as he to find one another. They reacted quickly, drew their sabers and spurred their mounts, one slanting to the right and the other to the left, both charging up the slope hoping to trap him between them.

The ravine angled away from him to the left, so he yanked the horse's reins that way and dug his heels in. He wasn't too proud to run, drove the animal over level ground at the edge of the ravine. The Kull's animals wasted precious moments struggling in the loose gravel up the side of the ravine, and he got far enough away to hide in the mist. But staying with the gully gave the Kulls an easy trail to follow, so he turned the horse into the ravine and plunged down its side, then back up the other side. He rode away from the ravine at a random angle; when he didn't hear pursuit he slowed the horse's pace to a canter, rode that way for a few hundred paces, then slowed it to a trot, then finally a walk.

He'd been lucky.

The next time he encountered a Kull his luck didn't hold. He was at the bottom of a ravine crossing it, the Kull at the top about fifty paces down the ravine. Running wasn't an option as the Kull charged down toward him. He drew his sword, called upon his shadowmagic and charged at the Kull, met him just as he reached the flat bottom of the ravine. Just coming off the soft soil of the ravine's slopped edge, the Kull and his horse were a little off balance as Morgin hit them. He thrust and struck true, but the Kull cut his thigh in passing. Morgin glanced over his shoulder and saw the Kull fall from his saddle. He charged up the slope of the ravine and disappeared into the mist.

The day turned into a sequence of such encounters. And as it wore on, and he and the horse tired, he no longer had the option of running to avoid a fight. Luckily, only once more did he encounter more than one Kull at a time; his shadowmagic saved him more than his fighting skills. But with each encounter he paid a price of fatigue, for him and the horse; and a price of blood, as he slowly accumulated an abundance of cuts and minor wounds.

The mist thinned as he rode west, slowly crossing the width of the plains. When night descended he decided not to stop, reasoning that the Kulls would group and light campfires. He should see the glow from such fires in the mist long before encountering them. That worked rather well. Twice he spotted a cluster of campfires, and detoured around them carefully. In the wee hours of the morning, well before sunup, the horse could barely walk and he could barely stay in the saddle. So he sought out a deep ravine, dismounted and guided the horse into it, tied the reins to his wrist and wrapped the blanket around his shoulders. If he slept without the shadows he'd awake more rested, but then he might not wake at all if some Kulls found him asleep. He wrapped a shadow about him and the horse and sat down to rest.

••••

Something woke Morgin, some noise or sound. It was near dawn, the sky beginning to brighten, and the fear had come upon him, the fear that came with Kulls nearby. He still sat at the bottom of the ravine, the horse's reins tied to his wrist, his shadowmagic strong and active. He sat very still, careful not to move in the slightest, and he thanked the gods the horse was too exhausted to do more than stand silently beside him with its head hung low.

He heard a gruff voice say something, though the words were hushed and unintelligible. Another voice whispered a response. He was seated with his back to the edge of the ravine, so he turned his head very slowly to look both right and left: nothing. But to his right the ravine took a sharp turn.

He heard the hushed whispers again, so he stood, rising carefully and silently. He tied the horse's reins to some brush, lowered himself to his hands and knees and crawled slowly to the turn in the ravine. He checked his shadows, then peered carefully around the turn.

Like Morgin, two twelves of Kulls had tied their horse's reins to brush at the bottom of the ravine. Then they'd all climbed up the slope at the side of the ravine and were looking over its lip at something.

Morgin eased back away from the turn, climbed the slope and looked over its lip. In the predawn mist, about a hundred paces distant, he saw a line of shadowy figures he recognized immediately. It must be the sentry line for one of the Benesh'ere encampments. The Kulls were setting up a predawn attack.

Morgin crawled back to the bottom of the ravine, untied the horse's reins, then led it quietly away from the Kulls along the bottom of the ra-vine. He walked the animal about fifty paces and decided that was enough. He stopped, put a foot in the stirrup, reached up and gripped the saddle horn, and hesitated. When he climbed into the saddle the horse might splutter or make some noise, so he had to do this quickly for it to work.

In one motion he climbed into the saddle, got his right foot in a stirrup, drew his sword and dug his heels into the horse's flanks. It struggled to charge up the slope, exhaustion weighing heavily on the animal. He made the lip of the ravine, got the horse up onto the flat prairie and charged toward the whiteface encampment.

"Kulls," he screamed at the top of his lungs, "about to attack. Kulls—Kulls—Kulls!"

He was about fifty paces from the perimeter when a whisper of thought told him to duck to the left. He jerked that way as a Benesh'ere arrow with a steel-tipped warhead hissed past his right ear. Instinct flashed again and he twitched to the right as another steel-tipped arrow flew past. "It's me," he screamed, "the Elhiyne."

More arrows hissed past him, each missing him by only a finger's width, and then his focus locked on one particular arrow, targeted straight for the horse's chest. He didn't see it with his eyes, just knew that it was there, and he had an instant to realize that its steel warhead would pierce the horse's heart, and the horse would collapse beneath him. So as the arrow struck he jumped, the horse folded in on itself and he barely cleared its head; he hit the ground feet first going much too fast to stay on his feet. He tried to turn his landing into a roll, managed nothing better than a head-over-heels tumble that ended a few paces from the sentry line. He sat up just as a sentry lunged toward him with a spear, but the sentry hesitated, looked at him and said, "You're the Elhiyne."

Behind the sentry stood a dozen whitefaces carrying longbows. Morgin looked back toward the Kulls, saw a cluster of dead horses and halfmen, all badly feathered by arrows. His warning had given the whitefaces time to concentrate archers at this spot, and the battle had ended quickly.

He stood unsteadily and brushed dirt from his tunic. The sentry grounded the butt of his spear, leaned on it and said, "You sure got a crazy way of fighting Kulls. Ain't never seen anyone fight Kulls like that. You're kind of crazy, you know?" He considered that for a moment, half-grinned out one side of his mouth as if recalling some old memory. "Not the worst kind of crazy I've seen, but still crazy."

Morgin looked back at the dead Kulls and horses, and decided it was time to make a bow of his own. With Morddon's memories to guide him, he certainly knew how.

••••

As Olivia and BlakeDown argued in the middle of Castle Penda's great hall, Brandon found it hard to believe only a year had passed since the last meeting of the Lesser Council. So much had changed, and none for the better. Back then Elhiyne had been ascendant, and even some of BlakeDown's sycophants had begun looking to Elhiyne for leadership. With Morgin's almost single-handed defeat of the Decouix army, and his semi-mythical reputation as the ShadowLord-come-to-life, there was little BlakeDown could do to thwart Olivia's ambitions. Brandon would not have been surprised to hear her propose they crown Morgin—AethonLaw—king of the Lesser Clans. She might not have been able to push that through the Council, but still, it would have been a close call. Then that sword had changed everything.

Standing in the center of the hall Olivia spoke, using her public voice that carried to all. "With the four Lesser Clans united, we could field an army to challenge Decouix dominance. The White Clan was badly stung by their defeat at Csairne Glen."

BlakeDown countered, "We might have done that, a year ago, had not your grandson brought that talisman among us. Valso has had two years to rebuild, and I don't believe he is as weak as you claim."

Olivia gave BlakeDown a dismissive smile. "They lost six thousand men, and two years ago at Csairne—"

BlakeDown interrupted her. "At least, now that your outlaw grandson is dead, that blade seems to have quitted the Mortal Plane, and we can once again live without fear it will devastate the countryside."

Brandon shivered at the thought of Morgin and Rhianne dying in the jaws of the skree.

"Tis a cold and dreary place, isn't it."

Brandon turned to find that JohnEngine had quietly come up behind him. He said, "It's not the chill of Penda stone that makes me shiver. It's the chill in the hearts of the Council I fear most."

JohnEngine looked toward Olivia and BlakeDown, both of whom were red-faced with anger. "Aye. Even though Tosk and Inetka are leery of the growing rift between Olivia and BlakeDown, PaulStaff must support BlakeDown, and Wylow must support Olivia, and the Lesser Council is divided now more than ever."

They both turned their attention back to the two clan leaders.

Olivia sneered as she said, "You seem to fear your own shadow, Lord BlakeDown."

"And you, Lady Olivia, are foolishly fearless. That talisman was an embarrassment to all the Lesser Clans."

"You're embarrassed. My, my! The leader of Clan Penda is more concerned with how the Greater Clans perceive him, than with their constant threat of war. Perhaps you should go to Durin. Then you and Valso can pull out your manhoods and compare sizes."

Brandon saw Wylow and Eglahan approaching them through the crowd. Wylow was High Lord of Inetka, Eglahan, Marchlord of Yestmark, and both sworn to Elhiyne. Olivia held both in high regard, especially Eglahan, so they could be an important means of tempering her provocations.

"It's open insults now?" Eglahan asked.

Brandon said, "It digressed to that long ago. If Olivia were a man, by now she and BlakeDown would have probably tried to settle their differences with blades."

JohnEngine added, "They're just getting a bit more malicious."

"Look," Wylow said, nodding toward the center of the hall.

AnnaRail had stepped onto the main floor, awaiting acknowledgement before speaking. One of the counselors, obviously relieved to see someone step forward who might temper the situation, immediately said, "Lady AnnaRail, you may speak."

"Lords and ladies," she said. "We have much we disagree on, and yet we are united as the Lesser Council. There have been many proposals placed before the Council, and since it is just past midday, let us adjourn for lunch. We can satisfy our growling stomachs, and consider these issues for further discussion this afternoon."

Like almost everyone else, Brandon understood she was trying to diffuse the situation. A break for lunch would do that nicely.

One of the counselors said, "Excellent idea."

Another was about to agree, but Olivia shouted, "Wait. I have one more proposal we should consider over lunch." She paused for dramatic effect, and a knot formed in Brandon's stomach; he knew the calculating old woman too well. She continued. "We need unity. We have the unity of this Council, but we also need the unity of our armies. So I propose that we name, as Warmaster of the Lesser Council: Brandon et Elhiyne."

JohnEngine groaned; they all knew BlakeDown wanted that title for ErrinCastle.

No one responded, not a word, not an utterance. Then BlakeDown threw back his head and roared with laughter. "If you think Penda will play toady to some Elhiyne whelp, then you know nothing of the most powerful of the Lesser Clans."

They never did get to lunch that day.

••••

Morgin limped into the whiteface encampment followed by the sentry. The sentry said, "Heard you was lost in the mist. Figured you was dead by now."

Morgin hurt everywhere, but a dozen or more Kull saber cuts concerned him most. He rolled up his sleeve and showed the sentry a nasty cut on his forearm. "I've got about a dozen of these I need to treat before they fester."

The sentry looked at the cut and asked, "Kull saber?"

Morgin merely nodded.

"Come with me."

The sentry led him to a fire pit where a young girl knelt on her hands and knees, blowing on the embers still hot from the evening meal, trying to bring the fire back to life. The sentry told Morgin to sit down, and as he did so the girl's kindling caught, and a lick of flame crackled upward.

"Tamlea," the sentry said, addressing the girl. "The Elhiyne needs a healer. We'll take care of the fire while you find one."

She looked at Morgin curiously, then hopped to her feet and ran off among the tents.

Morgin sat there in silence watching the sentry build up the fire. Tamlea arrived with the healer, a middle-aged Benesh'ere woman with streaks of gray in her coal-black hair. The woman didn't introduce herself, just began cleaning his wounds silently, sewing some closed. Word spread quickly that *the Elhiyne* was still alive, and as she worked a small crowd gathered around them.

Morgin recognized one of the men: Jack the Lesser. They'd met shortly after he'd killed Salula. Jack stepped forward and said, "So, Elhiyne, we meet again."

"Aye," Morgin said.

Jack sat down opposite him. "Chagarin told me if you got back alive you can keep the sword, said something about it choosing you. Now why'd it do that, Elhiyne?"

Morgin shook his head tiredly. "That's just one of many questions no one seems to be able to answer."

"Well, you survived the last two nights. Sounds like you have a story to tell. Come, let's hear it."

Morgin told them about his two nights and a day lost in the mist. As he talked the sun rose above the horizon, and to his surprise, the mist dissipated completely, producing a bright clear day. The western horizon was no longer flat and unmarked, but now studded with trees blanketing low-lying rolling hills. Morgin had stumbled into the lead encampment of the March, and he estimated they were no more than an hour's march from the first trees.

Jack noticed him looking at the horizon and said, "Yes, the March is over. At least for this year."

Morgin finished the last details of his story. "So I ended up here by pure luck."

"But you kept your head," Jack said. "You stayed hidden and fought smart. And yes, you were lucky you didn't end up with your guts up in a tree."

Again, that curious phrase! "Fantose said something about *guts up in a tree*. What's that mean?"

Jack looked past Morgin to one of the whitefaces standing behind him and asked, "Mind lending the Elhiyne your horse? He knows how to ride."

Jack gathered up about a dozen warriors, all heavily armed, and Morgin rode with them at an easy trot toward the trees at the edge of the plain. As they approached the tree line they slowed, the whitefaces peering intently at the trees. Morgin tried to see whatever it was they were keen to spot, but not until they reined in at the edge of the tree line did he understand.

Four whitefaces had been tied upside-down high up on the trunks of four trees: two male warriors, one female warrior, and a small boy of no more than eight or nine years. They'd been tied upside down with their backs to the trees, each with his or her head about the height of a tall man off the ground, their feet tied above them. Then their abdominal wall had been slit with a saber, spilling their guts down over their chests, then over their faces, then onto the ground below. Flies swarmed about them in dense clouds. They all showed signs of mistreatment, but they'd clearly been alive when tied to the trees, clearly been alive when their abdomens had been slit and their guts spilled out, clearly been alive when they'd been turned into a feast for flies.

Without looking away from the corpses strapped to the trees, Jack said, "If we get separated from the March, lost in the mist, we try not to be taken alive. And you have to watch for a Kull that gets past the perimeter into the camp. They particularly like to take a child."

Looking at the four corpses tied to the trees, one of the whitefaces said casually, "Only four. A good year."

13

Ancient Lessons Remembered

NICKOLOT HAD LEARNED long ago that her small stature encouraged others to think of her as just a little girl, even though she was now a woman of marriageable age. If she wanted anyone to take her seriously about DaNoel, she would have to produce hard evidence. Otherwise, she'd be *just a little girl* having a spat with her brother. And too, she was not about to hurt AnnaRail—her own mother—by accusing her son of treason until she had fully convinced herself of his guilt.

She decided to start with the guard in the tower where they'd held the Decouix. She'd seen nothing truly incriminating the day Valso had escaped, just the guilt that flashed across DaNoel's face in the instant she'd surprised him crouching over the dead guard's body. And he'd been more concerned to point out that she had no proof, rather than denying any guilt, which bothered her no end.

After some careful inquiry, she learned that the guard's mother worked as an assistant cook in the castle. NickoLot found her in the kitchens during the brief period between lunch cleanup and dinner preparation.

"Yes, milady," she said in response to NickoLot's inquiry. "He was me son. A brawny good lad too."

"Do you still have any of his clothing?"

"Aye, milady. Me younger son wears it all the time."

NickoLot frowned. "Do you have anything of his that no one else has worn?"

The woman frowned. "Might be."

The women led her to a room she shared with two other assistant cooks, and three scullery maids. She opened a chest at the end of her bed, likely filled with all the belongings she had in the world. She dug through it, then pulled out a man's tunic. "I haven't altered this yet to fit the younger one, been saving it for when he grows into it."

NickoLot examined the tunic carefully, came up with a couple of reddish-blond, curly hairs. "What was your son's hair like?" she asked.

"Light red," the woman said. "And curly. Beautiful curls me boy had." She wiped another tear from her eye.

It took the rest of the afternoon to prepare the spell she had in mind; a charm to recall a person's memories for seven times seven heartbeats before the moment of death. It was a complex weaving, in which she had to tie power into the two hairs. To trigger the spell she borrowed a bit of spittle from the old woman, a blood relative, though she lied about the reason for wanting it.

She stopped just within the entrance to the tower where they'd imprisoned the Decouix. The room at the base of the stairs was little more than a small alcove, and she pictured again in her mind's eye the tableau of the guard lying on his back, his blood-soaked tunic, the blood pooling on the stone floor around him, DaNoel crouching over him. From the position of his feet, it was clear where he'd been standing. If DaNoel had murdered him—not if, when—his final memories would be haunting the stone there. Though, since time would slowly disperse them, she chided herself for having waited so long to do this.

She approached the spot cautiously, careful not to draw any power and contaminate the memories. She'd have only one chance, for once she triggered the spell, the memories would dissipate.

She stood where the guard must have stood, her back to the wall. Then she retrieved the charm, a small silver pentagram with the guard's hairs woven among the five points of the star. From her sleeve, she pulled the handkerchief into which she'd had the guard's mother spit; she could still feel the moisture in it. She closed her eyes, pressed the charm to her forehead and carefully rubbed the moist cloth across the pentagram.

The spell triggered nicely, and she felt some psychic remnant of the guard wash through her. She waited for his memories to fill her mind, and she waited, and waited. She counted fifty heartbeats, and only then realized there were no memories to be had. He must have been unconscious, or enspelled, long before he died.

••••

Rhianne and Braunye had just sat down to a meager dinner when a harsh knock on the door startled them both. "Mistress Syllith," a male voice shouted. "It's an emergency."

Rhianne stood, crossed the small hut, lifted the latch on the door and opened it. Outside stood the innkeeper, and behind him stood two men covered from head to toe in black soot. "There's been an accident at the mines," he said. "A land slide."

A problem with the mines was a problem for everyone. "How many injured?" she asked.

"We don't know yet. A dozen or more. Won't know until they dig them out." He hooked a thumb over his shoulder. "We have three at the inn right now. We're setting up lamps so you got light to work. They'll bring the rest down as they find them."

"Start boiling water," she said. "As much of it as you can. I'll need lots of boiling water. Braunye and I will gather our supplies and be there shortly."

"Right you are, mistress," Fat John said. He nodded toward the two men behind him. "These men will help you bring whatever you need."

She turned to Braunye. "Bring everything."

Rhianne and Braunye hurriedly gathered up all of their herbs and potions. They handed most of it to the two miners, but Rhianne had certain concoctions she'd augmented with powerful spell-castings. Those she carried herself.

The three injured miners had been laid out on the floor of the inn, two of them groaning and crying out in pain, one of them silent and still. Rhianne quickly determined that the silent one had already died, while another had a compound fracture of his lower right leg, and the third a crushed hand. Both men continuously groaned and cried out in pain.

Rhianne had never treated crush-wounds before; helped once, but never done it herself, wasn't sure if she could do this. But then Fat John took charge. "There's more'n one of us knows how to chop off a limb. We need you to keep them alive after." He glanced down at the two men and said, "That hand will have to come off, and that leg too."

Rhianne realized then that, in the past, with extremely serious wounds, their only recourse had been to simply amputate. But they didn't have power and magic to aid them. "No," she said angrily. "The hand, maybe. But the leg, definitely not."

Fat John frowned at her suspiciously, and considered her for a long moment. Then he shrugged and said, "You're the healer."

"Exactly," she said.

They set up one of the tables as a place for her to operate. She instructed Braunye and the innkeeper how to prep the wounds, then she and the innkeeper set the one man's broken leg, though he screamed with pain in the doing of it. She used one of her special potions to clean the wound so it wouldn't fester, then she went to work on the hand.

She'd barely gotten started when they brought more wounded in, and the night drifted slowly into a blurry haze of blood and broken bones and torn tissue. She did manage to save the one fellow's leg, but not the other's hand. In fact, she saved quite a few limbs during that night and the following morning, limbs that, without her, would have been lost to the bone saw.

About noon, exhausted and almost falling asleep standing up, she asked Braunye, "Who's next?"

"That's all, mistress," she said. "There ain't no more."

Rhianne staggered across the common room to a bench set in one wall, plopped down onto it and took stock of herself. Her simple homespun dress was a ruin of blood and bits of bone and flesh, her hair matted and sweat soaked. She'd come quite a distance from being a princess of Elhiyne.

Fat John handed her a clay cup of ale. She downed it hungrily, and asked him, "Why were they working at night, in the dark?"

"The whitefaces are coming," he said, as if that explained everything. And when he saw she didn't understand, he added, "We trade with them for their steel. One of them whiteface blades—a full sword—that'll fetch them a half ton of coke and two stone of smelted soft iron or pig iron."

Rhianne looked at the empty clay cup in her hand and realized her mistake in drinking it as the alcohol hit her and added to her weariness. "I'm going to rest for a moment," she said, and lay down on the bench, too weary to even bother cleaning up.

She must have fallen asleep, for a gruff voice awoke her. "This her?"

She opened her eyes. Fat John and a miner, covered from head to toe in black dust, stood over her. "Yah," Fat John said. "She's the one done it."

Done what? she wondered.

The miner nodded, turned and walked away without another word. She sat up and asked Fat John, "Who was that?"

He merely said, "Mine foreman," then he too turned and walked away.

Nothing more was said. She checked on the injured, applied more potions to prevent festering, staggered back to her hut and fell asleep.

The next morning she wandered down to the stream, lowered herself into the chill water still wearing the bloodied dress; both she and it did need cleaning. She wrung what water she could out of the dress, wore the damp thing as she walked back to her hut, but found a crowd of miners gathered there. As she approached, the crowd parted and she found herself facing the mine foreman. He looked at her disapprovingly, looked her up and down and said, "You need a new dress. We'll have to see to that too."

As he growled orders at his men, Braunye came out of the hut. "Mistress, come see." She grabbed Rhianne by the hand and tugged her into the hut. "Look," she said, pointing to a full coal bin. "They said we'll never have a cold night again. And look at this." She spun and opened their meager larder, and in it hung a full ham, and two wheels of cheese, and vegetables and flour, and dried beans. That night she and Braunye ate a wonderful dinner, the heartiest she'd had since coming to Norlakton.

The next morning one of the miners delivered three new dresses; one for Braunye, and two for Rhianne, homespun, but clean and fresh and new.

••••

Once in the forest the Benesh'ere relaxed a bit. Fantose told Morgin, "Bloody Kulls got rotten forest skills. Every now and then one or two try something, but most of them know not to, and them that don't, end up dead real quick."

Jack the Lesser asked Morgin, "Heard you handled yourself pretty good?"

"Right he did," Fantose said. "He can smell them Kulls like no one I ever seen. Warned us in advance several times—only a couple of heartbeats, but it made the difference. Killed his share of Kulls, he did."

Delaga added, "He took his share of hurt too."

Jack wrinkled his nose and sniffed at Morgin. "You didn't let Delaga put any of that stink grease on you, did you?"

Morgin grimaced. "Just at first. And it does work."

Delaga said, "See, I told you."

Jack shook his head. "I know it works, but it stinks enough to drive away nether demons."

Fantose added, "But it don't stink no worse than Delaga, so it don't make no difference for him."

Jack took notice of a large bundle Fantose had slung over his shoulder. "What you got there?"

"Hoods."

"Kull hoods?"

Fantose nodded. "Yup."

"You must have killed a lot of Kulls this year."

Fantose shook his head. "Nah, they ain't mine. They're the Elhiyne's."

"Then why you carrying them?"

Fantose looked at Jack carefully. "Jerst—well, Blesset actually—won't let him collect hoods."

Jack's eyes narrowed thoughtfully. "But he killed 'em, right?"

"Yah, he did."

"Looks like he killed quite a few."

"Yah, he did."

"And Blesset still won't let him have them?"

"No, she won't."

Jack went silent and mulled that over for a bit. Morgin noticed that several other warriors walking with them had gone silent as well, and seemed to be considering what they'd just heard. Morgin broke the uncomfortable silence by saying, "I shouldn't have insulted Jerst the way I did in your camp that night."

Jack considered that for a moment, then nodded and said, "No, you shouldn't have."

"I was wrong."

"Yes, you were."

"Any way I can make it up to Jerst and Blesset, get them to forgive me?"

All three of them considered that for a moment, then shook their heads in unison as Jack said, "Nah. Blesset is too cold-hard mad for any forgiveness."

"Then how do I get her to not kill me?"

Fantose said, "That's an easy one, man. She can't kill you 'cause Jerst is going to kill you first."

"Well then how do I get him to not kill me?"

Again, the three whitefaces considered his question as they traded glances among themselves. And again Jack answered, "Kill him first, in fair combat."

Morgin doubted there was any likelihood of that. "I doubt I can."

Jack threw a comradely arm about Morgin's shoulders and they began walking. "Yah, there ain't much chance of you winning any battle against him. And I was starting to like you, too. Shame, ain't it?"

They all agreed they were beginning to like Morgin, and it was a real shame Jerst would soon kill him. A real shame.

••••

Morgin moved silently through the forest, using Morddon's memories and reflexes to move with the stealth of a Benesh'ere. It was the first opportunity he'd had to try the ancient warrior's forest lore, and it amazed even him that he moved so silently. He had thought it would be difficult to translate those memories into this smaller, shorter body of his, this non-Benesh'ere body. But, to his surprise, like so many other of Morddon's ancient skills, it came naturally, almost instinctively.

He'd stepped away from the Benesh'ere column and into the forest to relieve himself, and once alone had instinctively shifted to the stealthy movements of a whiteface—when alone in the forest, silence meant survival. He hadn't even realized he was doing it until he'd traveled some distance from the main body of the Benesh'ere march. And he'd done it without shadows. It occurred to him then that his shadow magic and the Benesh'ere forest lore would be a powerful combination, and he wondered if the Benesh'ere didn't have a little magic of their own. Perhaps they weren't completely bereft of their magic, but retained something subtle that allowed them to move with such silence.

He found a good spot and relieved himself against a tree. But while doing so he heard a twig snap nearby and he froze. He dropped into a crouch, wrapped a shadow about him and danced among the shadows of the forest, moving about ten paces then freezing again. If some enemy had meant to sneak up on him, they wouldn't find him where they thought.

He heard another twig snap, saw a shadowy figure moving through the forest undergrowth. The figure approached the tree where Morgin had been only moments ago, and he recognized LillianToc, Jerst's youngest son.

LillianToc stood up straight and put his hands on his hips. "I thought he was here."

About five paces from LillianToc, Jack the Lesser stood up and said, "He was." Morgin hadn't seen or heard Jack approaching. "But he disappeared, and not even I could follow him."

He pointed a finger at LillianToc. "And you need to make less noise. He heard you."

Clearly, Jack was training the young boy in forest lore, so Morgin dropped his shadow magic, stood and walked toward them. "I did hear you."

LillianToc said, "Morgin, you move like a whiteface."

Jack frowned at that comment and said, "Yes, you do. Why is that? No plainface moves like a whiteface."

Morgin shrugged. "It was my shadow magic."

Jack shook his head. "No. You didn't use your shadows getting here, and I didn't hear you approach. No, you move through the forest like one of us."

At the unasked question that hung between them, Morgin said, "I learned it in a dream, long ago."

Jack shook his head. "That's not an answer I like."

"Nor I," Morgin said. "But it's the only answer I have."

••••

Chrisainne lay with her legs spread while BlakeDown lay on top of her and pumped in and out of her, grunting and sweating and abrading her cheek with his beard. She was careful to cry out with pretended pleasure, "Oh, my darling! Oh, my darling!"

He hesitated for a moment, looked in her eyes and grunted, "I'm not hurting you, am I?"

Damn! she thought. He'd stopped, which meant this might take longer, when all she wanted to do was get it over with. "Oh no, my darling. You're not hurting me, though your manhood is certainly of a size to do so. No, you give only the greatest of pleasure."

He didn't say anything, buried his face in her hair and resumed his pumping and grinding. He made love like a man pumping water from a well: push-pull-push-pull-push-pull. It was monotonous and without pleasure, like the man himself. She lay beneath him as he ground away at her, tried to pretend he was that young stable boy with the broad shoulders she so wanted to seduce. But with BlakeDown grunting in her ear, that fantasy brought her no pleasure.

Eventually BlakeDown's pumping grew almost frantic, until he growled with pleasure and climaxed. She cried out, timed her fake orgasm to match his peak of pleasure. Afterwards, he lay on top of her, his spent manhood slowly shrinking and sliding out of her. As always, he lay motionless for quite some time, and she prayed he didn't fall asleep on top of her.

Finally, he put his hands on the bed on either side of her chest and pushed upward. He paused and smiled at her, and she beamed back at him.

He said, "You enjoy that, don't you?"

She blushed, a trick she'd learned long ago as a young Vodah maiden. She could blush at any moment she chose, and used that ability to her advantage now. She looked aside, pretending embarrassment. "Women are not supposed to enjoy such carnal pleasures."

"But you're no ordinary woman," he said as he climbed off her and wiped his penis with her bed-sheet. As he put on his clothes he said, "I think I'll encourage your husband to spend more time at Castle Penda. And of course, you should accompany him."

She gave him a coy smile. "We would be honored to accept such an invitation."

While BlakeDown pulled on his clothes she threw on a robe, and once he was gone she retrieved that odd little coin from her purse. She'd been married off to a middling Penda lord, whose holding bordered on primitive, though it would have been worse without Valso's contribution to her dowry. Her husband knew full-well she'd seduced BlakeDown, was fully in favor of such a liaison if it advanced his standing in the Penda Clan, though she and he both pretended he didn't know. But Chrisainne's agenda did not include advancement in some backward Lesser Clan.

She sat down in a chair, then kissed the coin and closed her eyes to wait. That coin was a rather powerful spell-casting she could not have replicated.

Yes? Valso asked in her thoughts.

"The meeting of the Lesser Council will end tomorrow with little unity among the clans. And I think I can take some credit for that, Your Majesty. I've carefully fed BlakeDown's paranoia and his natural distrust of Olivia."

And after the Lesser Clans depart, will you be in a position to continue assisting me?

"BlakeDown wants my husband to bring me to Penda more frequently."

Good. But what about your husband? Might he be a problem?

"He's perfectly aware I'm spreading my legs for BlakeDown, and hopes it will improve his standing in the Lesser Clans. He's not able to look beyond such meager rewards."

Very good. I am pleased. Be assured that your rewards will not be meager.

14

Fire From the Blood of Our Kin

AT THE END of the second day marching through the forest the Benesh'ere arrived at their destination, a large rambling village sprawled along the eastern shore of the Lake of Sorrows, though the word *village* seemed rather inappropriate since it must house the entire tribe of more than seven thousand men, women and children. On the other hand, it had few permanent structures, though when Morgin saw the Benesh'ere pitching their tents, he realized it would not be in the heart of the Benesh'ere to live within wooden or stone walls.

He'd only seen the Lake of Sorrows once before, and then it had been by moonlight on a dark night, and he'd not grasped the size the body of water. Standing on the eastern shore, he could barely make out the far western shore, would have seen nothing had the day not remained clear and bright. He saw a rather large village—someone had mentioned it was named Norlakton—sprawled along the north shore a short distance away.

"Come with me, Elhiyne," Chagarin said. "We can use your strong back."

The Benesh'ere called the largest of the few permanent structures the Forge Hall, for it contained a dozen forges and was the smiths' hallowed domain. They put Morgin to work helping them unload their smithing equipment from the pack horses, though there wasn't enough left of the day to do more than pile the stuff against the back wall of the Forge Hall. Morgin and Baldrak then led the horses across the village and turned them over to Jack the Greater, who was busy overseeing a group of whitefaces repairing a large corral and stable.

Back at the Forge Hall they ate a quick dinner, then went to work cleaning four large anvils, each of which easily outweighed a grown man. In the Fall they'd packed them in grease before returning to the sands, and they worked late into the night scraping off the grease, wiping them down, then lifting and mounting each on a heavy oak stand next to the largest of the forges. At one point, sweating over one of the big anvils, Baldrak said, "You seem to know what you're doing around a forge, Elhiyne. Not like some novices I know. Where did you learn smithing?"

Morgin hadn't thought about it while he'd been busy bending his back to the labor of setting up the forges. He'd simply done the work that needed doing, had just known what needed doing without being told. He gave Baldrak the only answer he could, the same answer he'd given Jack the Lesser. "Long ago, in a dream."

Behind Baldrak, Chagarin frowned and looked thoughtful for a moment, then turned and went back to work.

The next morning at dawn Baldrak shook him awake. "Come on, Elhiyne. After all that work last night, I need to work the knots out of me muscles."

Baldrak led him to an open space behind the Forge Hall. They spent a few moments stretching and limbering up, then squared off, and as always, when sparring, they traded a few blows at half speed. But immediately Morgin noticed a fundamental difference. Each time his sword met Baldrak's, the ring of the steel had a harsh and uneven quality to it, a tone that irritated Morgin and grated on his nerves. It took more than a dozen blows for him to realize what he heard: the sound Morddon had identified as the ring of a flawed blade.

Morgin disengaged and back-stepped a few paces. "Do you hear it?" he asked.

"Hear what?" Baldrak demanded, catching his breath.

Morgin pointed at Baldrak's sword with the point of his own sword. "That blade, where did you get it?"

Baldrak frowned and said, "Just a spare blade lying about in the Forge Hall. And its weight and balance are right for me,"

"Have you used it before?"

Baldrak shrugged. "Maybe. Don't really recall. It's much like many common blades."

"But it's flawed." Morgin regretted the words as soon as he spoke them.

Baldrak's frown deepened. "And how would you know that?"

"I can hear it." Morgin extended his hand. "Here, let me see that blade."

Baldrak reversed the blade and extended the hilt. Morgin took the sword and held it up, looking at it closely. He saw nothing unusual or improper about it, but he couldn't deny what he'd heard. He tucked his own sword under one arm, lifted Baldrak's blade, and flicked the steel with a fingernail as he remembered Morddon doing so long ago. The blade gave out the faintest ring, a sound barely loud enough to hear, but buried deep in the sound Morgin heard the angry grate of the flaw. It resonated within his soul, and as he remembered Morddon doing, he took that sound into his heart and amplified it, let it grow until he identified the exact location of the flaw. But he didn't let the sound grow until the blade melted as Morddon had done. Once he knew the location of the flaw, he allowed the sound to die away, though a trace of it hung in the air about them both.

"There," he said, pointing to a spot about a third of the blade's length from the tip. "It's flawed there. It will eventually fail."

He looked to Baldrak for a reaction, but the smith merely looked at him oddly. Then the smith's eyes looked past him at something behind him, and Morgin turned to find Chagarin and the rest of the smiths gathered just outside the Forge Hall, all staring at him with that same odd look.

••••

As dusk approached on their first full day at the Lake of Sorrows, the entire tribe of Benesh'ere gathered at their equivalent of a town square. A massive pile of timbers and kindling had been erected in the middle of a large open area surrounded by tents, and Morgin stood with the smiths as twenty or more bodies were laid atop the timbers. Each Kull attack during the March had resulted in a death or two, and Morgin hadn't realized the Benesh'ere had carried their dead to the lake. The last to be placed atop the pile were the four who'd finished with their *guts up in a tree.*

Several warriors carrying torches touched fire to the kindling, and the tribe looked on silently as the flames climbed slowly up the timbers. Olivia would have made a grand speech, would have peppered the crowd with women paid to openly shed tears, and lackeys paid to cheer at just the right moments. But the whitefaces merely stood and looked on silently as the flames consumed their loved ones, and a column of gray smoke climbed toward the sky. Morgin surreptitiously glanced about, was careful not to be obvious, but found not a single tear shed by his newfound comrades. It was odd the way they all watched the flames with the same look upon their faces. They didn't look on with sorrow or fear or anger, and through most of the silent vigil Morgin was hard-pressed to identify what he saw in their faces.

The flames reached their zenith just about the time the sun disappeared behind the Worshipers, and still the Benesh'ere stood silently. Sometime later, full-darkness had settled upon them when the timbers collapsed upon themselves, reducing the pyre to a massive pile of glowing embers still too hot to approach any closer than about thirty paces. And only as the tribe dispersed did Morgin identify the look upon every face about him: determination.

As the other smiths turned and wandered back toward their tents, Chagarin didn't move, but stood silently, staring at the pile of embers, a pair of blacksmith's tongs gripped casually in his right hand and hanging limply at his side. Quite a number of the whitefaces didn't turn to leave, perhaps one in twelve, and, like Chagarin, each waited silently. Morgin decided to stay with Chagarin, though when he didn't move to go with the other smiths, the Master Smith glanced his way, looked at him for a long moment, then nodded silently, as if, by remaining, Morgin had done something significant, something appropriate.

As the embers cooled enough for them to approach the pyre without being driven back by blistering heat, Chagarin stepped forward and extended the tongs. He carefully selected a single ember about the size of

Morgin's fist and lifted it out of the pyre. He raised it up and examined it carefully, then said, "This will do."

He glanced Morgin's way, and at the questioning look on Morgin's face he said, "From this point on, all fires will be lit from this fire. The warmth we take on a cold night will be from fire from the blood of our kin. We'll cook our food with fire from the blood of our kin. And some day, though probably not in my lifetime, when the Seventh Wrong is righted, when we stand north of the Ulbb and are freed of the bonds that imprison us, on that day we will ride on Durin and exact revenge with blades forged in fire from the blood of our kin."

Chagarin turned, and holding the orange-red ember in the tongs, he marched toward the Forge Hall. That was apparently a signal for all of the other whitefaces who'd remained behind. Each stepped forward and thrust a wooden stave into the pile of embers, held it there long enough to ignite it, then turned and marched away, carrying a brand fired by fire from the blood of their kin.

Morgin followed Chagarin, watched him carefully light the forges from the ember he'd carried, watched the smiths and their wives light their cooking fires with embers from the forges. Because of the ceremony at the pyre they didn't sit down to dinner until quite late. The food didn't actually taste different just because it was cooked *with fire from the blood of our kin*, but the taste of it now carried meaning and purpose.

••••

"Let's get out of this castle, have a tankard of ale or two, and pinch the bottom of a barmaid or three."

At the sound of JohnEngine's voice, Brandon looked up from the papers on the table in front of him. His cousin stood just within the threshold of his room in Penda, and Brandon had trouble shifting mental gears. "Ale? Barmaid's bottoms?"

JohnEngine stepped further into the room. "Exactly. The atmosphere in this castle is stifling. It's a nice, warm night, and Wylow and one of his sons and one of the Pendas and I are going for a pint in that little inn in the village. Join us."

Brandon hesitated. "Are you sure that's wise? We're not terribly popular here right now."

"There won't be any trouble," JohnEngine said. "In any case, Perrinsall et Penda is coming with us. He's ErrinCastle's cousin, a decent fellow. He'll make sure we don't have any problems."

"You know," Brandon said, nodding. "I do need a break from this."

He stood, grabbed a cloak and said, "Lead on."

Wylow and SandoFall, Wylow's oldest son and Annaline's husband, and the Penda fellow waited for them at the main gate. After they introduced Perrinsall, they headed for the village, which lay just beyond the no-man's-land that surrounded the castle, a distance of about five hundred paces, well beyond the reach of the most powerful longbow.

The Happy Plowman was quite large and appeared to do a fair amount of business. The common room had a wood-plank floor, a bar along one side, a large hearth, a scattering of tables and chairs, with appetizing smells wafting from the kitchen. Quite a number of the tables were already occupied, but the five men had no trouble finding an empty one.

"How is Annaline?" JohnEngine asked SandoFall as they sat down.

SandoFall grinned happily. "Fourth child is due in about three moons. And she's not having any difficulties."

Wylow slapped his son on the back. "He's already got himself an heir and a spare, so the third and fourth must be for just plain fun, eh?"

A pretty barmaid approached them, they ordered the house ale and were served rather quickly. Perrinsall paid while JohnEngine filled five clay mugs from a large clay pitcher. They toasted Annaline and SandoFall, managed to forget the hostility and the schism in the Lesser Clans for a time. Perrinsall joined in, though he seemed a rather quiet fellow. Brandon, not one to frequent taverns, and not a big drinker, managed to enjoy himself—for a while.

SandoFall was relating the names he and Annaline were considering for the new child, when someone at a nearby table spoke the word *Elhiyne* in a noticeably harsh and angry tone. The room went silent, JohnEngine tensed and began to stand, but Brandon put a hand on his shoulder and forced him to remain seated. He said, "We don't need to finish the annual meeting of the Lesser Council with a tavern brawl."

Wylow nodded and said, "Listen to your cousin, John."

A couple of men at a nearby table stood, Penda armsmen, by the look of them. They staggered drunkenly across the common room to stand behind Wylow and SandoFall. Brandon watched Perrinsall nod to the innkeeper, saw the innkeeper nod back.

"Bloody Elhiynes," one of them said. "Think yer better'n us Pendas."

The innkeeper and a young man—probably his son—stepped into position behind the two drunks, both carrying heavy wooden cudgels about the length of a man's forearm. The innkeeper said, "Go back to your table and sit down. You'll not be starting trouble here."

One of the drunks turned on him. The fellow had trouble standing as he said, "But they're Elhiynes." He slurred his words badly.

The innkeeper was a large man, and he had the advantage of sobriety and the club. As the drunk staggered toward him, he buried the end of the club in the man's gut. The fellow grunted and let out a great whoosh of air, dropped to his knees and groaned. The innkeeper turned to his companion and snarled, "Get him back to his table."

As the two drunks staggered back to their table, one supporting the other, Perrinsall said, "I think we should leave."

The innkeeper agreed with him, "That's probably best."

The five of them tried to exit quietly, though they heard a few jeers from the table of drunken armsmen. They were only about twenty paces from the inn when the two drunks, with about a dozen comrades, spilled out into the street behind them. The five of them turned to face the armsmen, all instinctively not wanting danger at their backs. The armsmen carried swords, and not all of them were as drunk as the two who'd approached their table. Brandon noted that he and his companions merely carried utilitarian knives. They could defend themselves with power and magic, and probably come out of it reasonably unscathed. But it would be an ugly incident that would only widen the schism in the Lesser Clans.

Wylow said, "This ain't good."

The armsmen surrounded them quickly, though, as yet, no weapons had been drawn.

Perrinsall stepped forward and said to the armsmen, "You should think carefully before taking this any further."

Perrinsall was a rather minor Penda lord, so his warning didn't carry the weight it would have if it had come from someone like ErrinCastle. Brandon held his hands up, palms out, empty. "We apologize for disturbing your pleasure, and merely want to return to our beds."

One of the drunks staggered forward. "You can go to your beds, but only after we teach you a lesson or two."

They all stood there for a long, tense moment of silence, and Brandon knew that when the moment ended there would be violence. Then the night filled with the sound of hooves thundering on the road. The armsmen backed away momentarily as Brandon glanced over his shoulder.

ErrinCastle, leading a twelve of mounted Penda armsmen, charged down the road toward them. Brandon's first thought was that they'd stumbled into treachery, and would be murdered on the road. But ErrinCastle and his armsmen quickly surrounded them all and leveled their pikes at the drunken Penda armsmen.

ErrinCastle nudged his horse toward their leader, stopped the animal only inches from the fellow, who stood there swaying unsteadily. He leaned over the man and growled, "What in the netherhell do you think you're doing?"

The drunk lowered his eyes and said meekly, "Was just going to teach the Elhiynes some manners."

ErrinCastle lifted his boot out of a stirrup and kicked the man in the face. The drunk stumbled and fell to his knees as ErrinCastle said, "You idiot. These men are under Penda guestright."

He looked at the captain of his mounted armsmen. "Put all of these men in the dungeon for the night. Maybe they'll learn some manners."

The mounted armsmen hustled the drunken armsmen away. ErrinCastle remained and said, "Think I'll accompany you back to the castle." He nudged his horse toward the castle at a slow walk, and they walked beside him.

JohnEngine asked, "How did you know we were in trouble?"

Brandon answered him. "That's why he had Perrinsall accompany us."

"Why do you care?" JohnEngine asked ErrinCastle. "We're almost enemies at this point."

ErrinCastle stopped his horse and looked at JohnEngine pointedly. "This hostility between our clans; I agree with my father, about as much as you agree with your grandmother."

15

Debts Must be Paid

THE MORNING AFTER the pyre Baldrak awakened Morgin early. "We're going to see to the horses and chakarras," he said. "Should take most of the day."

They ate a breakfast of journeycake, jerky and hot tea, then crossed the camp to the corrals, Morgin hoping he'd get a chance to see Mortiss again. The smiths maintained a small forge near the corrals, along with tongs, nippers, files and the other tools of a farrier. Jack the Greater and his men had already cut a couple dozen animals from the herds—those that needed attention from the smiths—but they hadn't touched the smith's tools. To do so when not under direct supervision of one of the smiths would be a serious breach of propriety and custom. When Morgin and Baldrak began unpacking the tools and setting up the forge, Jack's men stopped working and stared at Morgin, and Jack raised a questioning eyebrow to Baldrak.

Baldrak paused and looked at them for a long moment. Then he said, "He's close to the steel, closer than most."

That seemed to ease their concern only a little. They returned to their work, but kept throwing surreptitious glances Morgin's way as he and Baldrak mounted the anvil.

When the forge was ready Baldrak walked back to the Forge Hall, then returned with a hot ember gripped in a pair of tongs. He lit the small forge and he and Morgin went to work on the animals.

At noon a couple of young girls showed up carrying baskets of food. Baldrak, Morgin and Jack and his men all broke from their work and sat down at various places around the forge and the corral. The girls served them steaming bowls of stew and Morgin ate in silence while he listened to the banter of Jack's men. They spoke of their work and their women and families, and Morgin realized these strange whitefaces shared the same joys and sorrows as any clansman or commoner or peasant. Then he recalled the March, with its few joys and many sorrows. It occurred to Morgin he might be the only outsider to have experienced the March, and seen the sad product of Kull brutality.

He wondered about Val, wasn't surprised he hadn't seen him. The *twoname*, like Morgin, was a prisoner, and probably closely watched, and Jerst had made it clear he didn't want the two of them interacting.

When he finished his meal he stood to stretch his legs. He walked over and leaned on the corral to look at the herds while Baldrak and Jack discussed horseflesh. The corral enclosed a rather large meadow in the foothills of the Worshipers. In the distance Morgin saw Mortiss, unmistakable because of her coal-black coat. She broke away from the other horses, trotted his way and stopped just within reach. Morgin reached over the corral and scratched her behind one ear.

"Look at that!" Jack said. He and his men and Baldrak had turned Morgin's way. "That demon of an animal lets him coddle her like a pet dog."

Mortiss snorted angrily, as if to say, *Don't compare me to some mutt.*

Morgin looked over his shoulder and said, "Be careful. She doesn't like being compared to dog flesh."

That brought a roar from Jack and his men, though Baldrak remained silent. Jack said, "So she understands what I say?"

"More than you know," Morgin said. He had a thought, and he said it before he really considered it. "Can I ride her?"

Jack gave him a sour look. "No you can't, because no one can ride her. She won't let anyone ride her. What makes you think you can?"

"I've ridden her before."

Jack shook his head. "Not possible. No one's ridden her."

One of Jack's men shouted, "Let him try, Jack." As he said it he nudged one of his fellows in the ribs, clearly expecting to have some entertainment at Morgin's expense.

"All right," Jack said. "If you want to try . . ." He glanced at his men and they shared a grin. ". . . but don't blame me when she dumps you on your ass with a broken leg."

Mortiss neighed and reared, affronted that these men thought she would allow a rider to be harmed. Morgin could almost hear her thinking: if she allowed a rider on her back, that rider would come to no harm. Of course, today she might choose not to allow Morgin on her back, and in that case Jack and his men would get their show.

Morgin asked, "Do you have a bridle and saddle I can use?"

That brought open laughter from Jack's men, who gathered around to watch what they clearly thought would be an entertaining spectacle. Jack just shook his head, ducked into the stable, returned with a saddle and bridle and handed them to Morgin. "She won't let you saddle her, but you can try."

Morgin had learned long ago that Mortiss allowed what Mortiss chose to allow, and today he'd learn quickly if she'd allow him to saddle and ride her. As Morgin approached her with the bridle, she turned her head and looked his way. Jack's men saw something in her look and roared with laughter.

Morgin cautiously slipped the bridle over her head, and she didn't react in the slightest. Jack's men responded with murmurs and whispers.

Morgin set the bit, then hoisted the saddle. The Benesh'ere preferred a light cavalry saddle, to which they might add saddlebags and other means of carrying weapons and supplies. But Morgin wasn't going anywhere soon.

Again, Mortiss turned her head and gave him an unfathomable look, and again Jack's men laughed. Morgin tensed as he threw the saddle over her back, but she didn't react and Jack's men responded with a wary silence.

Morgin quickly cinched the saddle in place, checked the tightness of the straps and asked Mortiss, "Are they comfortable? Are you ok?"

She turned and gave him that look again; she was clearly planning something.

No sense in delaying the inevitable, so he gripped the reins and the saddle horn, stuck his foot in the stirrup, and climbed quickly into the saddle. He sat there for a moment, waiting for her to surprise him in some way, but she just stood there complacently, while Jack's men's murmurs grew to exclamations of surprise and wonder. Mortiss spluttered, *They need to know who's in charge.*

Morgin had no spurs, so he lightly nudged her flanks with his heels, delicately pulled the reins to one side and she trotted out toward the center of the corral. As he'd long ago learned, Morgin didn't command Mortiss, he nudged with his heels, or tugged lightly with the reins, more suggestions what to do, never commands. She broke into a canter and he rode her in a wide circle, almost as if she had chosen to show him off, to show Jack's men a thing or two. Morgin was just beginning to feel a bit triumphant that he had successfully mounted the demon horse, that she hadn't chosen to humiliate him by throwing him on his ass. They were well out into the middle of the corral, a good hundred paces from the corral fence and moving at an easy canter back toward Jack and his men, and it was then, without warning, that she broke into a full gallop, charging directly at the high fence and the cluster of men. Morgin could do little more than hold on for the ride as she closed the distance between them quickly, the whitefaces all gaping with eyes wide and mouths open.

When she reached the edge of the corral she leapt, and Morgin found himself flying with her over their heads as they all dropped to the ground beneath him. She landed cleanly on the other side, and didn't slow down as she raced through the Benesh'ere camp, leaving a trail of amazed whitefaces behind them. She cleared the edge of the camp and broke out onto the open road, charged down it several hundred paces, and only then did she allow him to pull her to a stop. He reined her in, and turned her about to look back at the whiteface camp in the distance.

You're free now, she spluttered. *They cannot catch me unless I allow them to.*

Morgin looked down the road. There'd been no visible reaction yet from the Benesh'ere, no posse of angry whitefaces riding out to catch the Elhiyne. He could turn, ride on, and there was no doubt Mortiss was right. He could easily reach the Gods Road, and cross the Ulbb going north, or the Augis going south, and no whiteface could follow. And then he'd finally be free to throw off the debt collar, free to find the Unnamed King and his true name, though he still had no idea how he would do that. But he had obligations back in that camp, debts that must be paid, responsibilities that must be met before he might go on.

"No," he said, "I'm not free."

He turned her toward the Benesh'ere camp and nudged her forward.

She neighed, *You have grown, I see, and learned a thing or two.*

He rode back to the Benesh'ere camp at an easy trot. One of the sentries at the perimeter of the camp waved at him and called, "Eh, Elhiyne, you decided to return."

Morgin called back to him, "Of course," though there had been no *of course* about it. It had been a conscious decision, carefully thought out, though he couldn't be certain it had been the right decision.

A commotion in the middle of the camp drew his attention as he rode toward it. Blesset sat astride a mount, snapping orders at other riders to hurry, organizing a posse to come after him. The horses sensed her anger, making them skittish and difficult to control, difficult to mount. But as Mortiss trotted toward them casually, the frantic activity about Blesset slowly came to a stop as they all gaped at Morgin. Blesset, her back to Morgin, didn't notice him until he was almost upon her. As the silence among them grew and the frantic activity came to a standstill, she looked over her shoulder, saw Morgin, and that seemed to calm her. She grinned, not a nice grin.

She reined her horse about slowly until she could face him squarely. "For a bit there I thought you might deprive me of my justice. At least you have some honor, though it's not much, and quite hard to find."

••••

Valso sat upon his throne indifferently, his little demon flying snake on a perch on his left, while Carsaris, standing at his right hand, watched the Kull lieutenant march the length of the throne room, his heavy black cloak fluttering behind him, his helmet tucked under one arm. The half-man stopped the required twelve paces short of the throne's dais, dropped to one knee and bowed his head. Valso waved a hand in a bored gesture of acknowledgement. "You said you had important information for me."

The halfman grumbled, "Yes, Your Majesty."

"Then rise and speak."

The halfman stood, lifted his head, and seeing his face for the first time Carsaris realized he was seething with anger. Valso saw it too.

"Six twelves of us rode south for the spring sport, Your Majesty."

"Ah, yes!" Valso said. "I believe the whitefaces call it the March. Was the hunting good?"

The Kull shook his head. "No, Your Majesty. We lost more than forty, while we killed just over twenty of the whitefaces, and gutted only four."

"Why such poor results? Was it just a bad year?"

"No, Your Majesty. It was as if . . . the whitefaces . . . sometimes they seemed to know we were going to attack before we attacked; only a dozen heartbeats, but enough to give them a slight advantage, enough to save a life or two."

Valso leaned forward, his eyes narrowing, his interest obviously peaked. "That would seem to imply they had the advantage of some sort of magic. Some prescience, perhaps? But the Benesh'ere don't tolerate magic. Is it possible they've relented and hired some witch to aid them?"

The Kull shook his head again. "Perhaps, Your Majesty, but we don't think so. There was one among them whose fighting style we thought familiar. And he was shorter than any Benesh'ere I've ever seen, though a bit taller than average among normal men."

Valso considered the halfman's words carefully. "Perhaps a *twoname* traveling among them, a wizard who chose to aid them."

The halfman shrugged. "Again, Your Majesty, we think not."

"And why is that?"

"The one I speak of, he fought with more than a blade; he fought with shadows."

Valso remained seated, staring at the halfman, so still he appeared to not even breathe. Then he threw back his head and roared with laughter, startling the little snake. "I knew it. Yes, I knew it. That Elhiyne was never one to deprive me of good sport. We still have a merry chase ahead of us, and I'll have the pleasure of seeing him watch everything he values destroyed little by little. I was so disappointed that he might have died cleanly in the jaws of the skree."

The little snake took to the air and hovered overhead. "Ssshall I hunt him down and kill him, Your Majesssty?"

Valso shook his head. "No, Bayellgae. He's already tasted your venom, and I have other plans for him."

The halfman took a step forward, a breach of etiquette, but forgivable under the circumstances. "I can organize the guard, Your Majesty? Have them prepare to ride out after him?"

Valso stood, and began pacing back and forth on the dais. "No. No. Not yet. That will be a task for your leader."

"Our leader, Your Majesty?"

Valso stopped pacing and looked pointedly at the halfman. "Yes, lieutenant. You'll soon have your captain back."

Ever so slowly, the halfman's lips broadened into a grin that sent a chill up Carsaris's spine.

••••

Standing in the Penda courtyard by their mounts, JohnEngine met Brandon's eyes and they shared an uneasy look. The Council had ended badly, with Elhiyne and Penda almost declaring war over perceived slights and insults. At least, now that he knew where ErrinCastle's true feelings lay, he saw how the young Penda lord's actions were always aimed at calming the situation. JohnEngine did not question that, had it not been for the three of them working in unison, the Council could have ended in open war. They had even met once at the tavern in the village, met openly so no one could propagate rumors of a clandestine rendezvous. They'd all had to sup at the trough of paranoia far too much lately.

BlakeDown and Olivia emerged from the castle proper, followed by Wylow and PaulStaff, then ErrinCastle. BlakeDown escorted Olivia to her carriage, both of them beaming and smiling. One had to know them both quite well to see the animosity hidden beneath the pleasant demeanor.

ErrinCastle approached JohnEngine as a stable hand brought him a mount. "I'm riding with you," he said. "At least until you're clear of the crowds."

BlakeDown helped Olivia up into the carriage. They both paused and said some pretty words. Then BlakeDown turned to Brandon and said, "I bid you farewell." He turned without saying more and marched back into the castle.

ErrinCastle, Brandon, JohnEngine and the rest of the Elhiyne retinue mounted up. Brandon's horse neighed with nervousness, perhaps sensing the mood of its master. ErrinCastle and JohnEngine joined him at the head of the column, and they spurred their horses into an easy trot.

Brandon turned to ErrinCastle and asked, "It's so bad that you need to escort us?"

ErrinCastle grimaced. "I think it wise to be cautious. While I think there might be no difficulty without me, I know there will be none with me."

Crowds of Penda peasants and retainers lined the road out of the castle and through the village. They didn't cheer as they had upon the arrival of the Elhiyne contingent. They stood mute and silent, and JohnEngine felt their animosity radiating like the heat from a fiery red brand.

ErrinCastle rode with them for a league past the village and the crowds. There he reined in his mount and the column stopped. "I will continue to try to abate this schism that is growing like a cancer between our clans. You have my word on that. Do I have yours?"

JohnEngine nodded and said, "Aye. You have mine."

Brandon said, "And mine."

And there they parted.

Once alone, the two of them riding at the head of the Elhiyne column, Brandon spoke, his eyes still locked on the road ahead of them. "I fear we will fail."

16

To Find a Name

RHIANNE'S SENSE OF the blade had grown more acute in the past few days, and there was no doubt it had come physically closer to Norlakton. She couldn't point in a specific direction, for it felt as if the sword had taken up residence in her own soul, and waited there biding its time. And as to distance, she couldn't count off some specific length, couldn't say if it was closer than a hundred paces or farther than ten leagues. But for a certainty it had come closer, and that frightened her.

She'd gained some understanding of its vague and poorly defined desires. It wanted freedom; it wanted to be released, to be *free of the fires*—though she had no idea what that meant—and she could not allow that, would not allow that. At least its demands had recently tempered in some way, as if it had found some sort of peace or contentment; perhaps she had just grown stronger at resisting it, or simply ignoring it. With that slight lessening of its constant need, it required less of her power to resist it and she'd found herself a little more clear-headed each day. But then, any gain she'd made had been lost when it had come physically closer. She did not think it coincidental that its nearness coincided with the arrival of the Benesh'ere at the Lake of Sorrows.

With their arrival, Norlakton had transformed from a sleepy hamlet into a bustling hive of activity. The tall white-skinned Benesh'ere walked or rode about everywhere, wearing their dune-colored robes with the large hoods splayed out tent-like by the broad-brimmed straw hats they wore beneath them. They came to town and met with some of the miners, apparently trading for iron and coke; she'd never heard of coke, learned it was some derivative of coal, much like charcoal came from wood. Interestingly enough, she learned they also traded for bow staves.

"They're quite picky about their staves," the innkeeper told her. "Got to be cut from just the right part of the yew, and then dried for at least two years. Got to be cut the right way, and dried the right way, and the gods help anyone fool enough to try to shape it. Them whitefaces just want a simple stave, and they'll shape it themselves. But they make a longbow can shoot an arrow near three hundred paces."

Rhianne worked through the afternoon preparing her herbs and potions, the blade hovering ever at the edge of her consciousness, an invasion of her soul she knew not how to banish. It occurred to her she should not banish it, that maybe it needed someone to control it, though the gods forbid it should be her. But with Morgin dead—

At the thought of Morgin, an unbidden tear touched her eye.

"Is something amiss, mistress?" Braunye asked.

"No," she lied, wiping away the tear with her sleeve. But then she realized she owed Braunye a small bit of the truth. "There was someone . . . once . . . but he's dead, and it still hurts when I think of him."

Braunye tried to comfort her, and she thought perhaps it had been a mistake to tell her even that much.

That afternoon Fat John sent one of his sons to summon her to the inn. They'd brought one of the miners down from the mines with a crushed finger, and for something serious like that they always brought them to the inn. She had far more room to work there if she needed her full surgical skills. With so much experience, she was becoming quite adept at surgical procedures, though that day she failed to save the finger. But while working on the poor fellow, three Benesh'ere entered the inn's common room, paused and looked briefly at her, their faces hidden by the shadows of their hoods. Then they conversed quietly at some length with the innkeeper. She finished sewing up the stub of the man's finger just as the Benesh'ere departed.

As she packed up her small surgical kit, Fat John hovered over her protectively. And then he said, "You know, now them whitefaces are here, we'll have them witches from Inetka and Elhiyne snooping around. They'll probably want to talk to you."

A knot formed in the pit of her stomach, and she must have blanched, for the innkeeper asked. "Why does that frighten you?"

She lied. "Those women are truly powerful, and a common hedge witch like me is wise to avoid their notice."

She'd become quite adept at lying, though the look on Fat John's face made her wonder if she had so easily fooled him.

••••

The smiths had given Morgin his own tent, one of the small desert tents only large enough to accommodate about two people. It seemed to be a symbolic gesture on their part, some sort of recognition that he belonged among the men who worked steel, though he knew better than to believe it meant they considered him one of them. He would always be the outsider here, and not just because of the color of his skin.

A whiteface's tent was his abode, whether it be a large pavilion-like affair like those of the tribe's leaders, or just a few strips of canvas sewn together to make a small lean-to. It was a sanctum into which no one ventured without specific permission. Beyond providing a place in which to sleep out of the weather—the Forge Hall was much too hot for a good night's sleep—the tent was also a place in which he could store his meager possessions: a blanket, a spare change of clothing, one of those woven straw hats, a water skin, a small pack with a few strips of cratl jerky, a knife and some other trail implements, and the blade that haunted his soul during every waking and sleeping moment.

The smiths had pitched Morgin's tent among their own, though his was by far the smallest, which was appropriate for a single man living alone. At that thought, a string in his heart twanged painfully, and he tried not to think of Rhianne dying in the jaws of the skree. One more debt for which, someday, he would extract payment from Valso.

After a day assisting the smiths at the forges, a clear, cool evening had settled over the whiteface camp. Morgin ate dinner with the smiths and their families, a communal affair in which all shared happily. Then he and the men sat about a fire and he listened to their banter while they shared a crock of weak ale.

Morgin retired to his tent and arranged his few possessions carefully, and then rearranged them. He had so little he could have just tossed them in one corner of his tent. But he felt at ease in the small tent in a way he didn't feel among the whitefaces. Perhaps he now thought of the tent as a home, his home. While arranging and rearranging his possessions, his mind had really been focused on his future. He needed to mend the rift with Blesset. Interestingly enough, Jerst seemed less blood-thirsty than his daughter, and Morgin wondered if the father might be more amenable to reconciliation than the daughter.

"Elhiyne."

Morgin recognized Toke's voice, and he'd left the tent flap pulled back so when he turned he saw the whiteface standing in the light of the half-moon. The demon ElkenSkul hovered beside him.

As Morgin crawled out of his tent, the whiteface sat down on the ground, so Morgin sat down facing him.

Toke said, "You've come a long way, plainface. A tent of your own, and all."

Morgin shrugged. "I guess the smiths find some value in my help."

Toke turned to the demon and said, "He's modest. Is his modesty real, or feigned?"

Toke cocked an ear, as if listening to a response from the demon. Then he threw back his head and laughed. "Yes, yes. We're all fools that way. And you and I, friend, perhaps more than most."

To Morgin, Toke said, "The demon thinks your modesty is real. It says you don't yet know your true nature, that you're foolish that way."

Morgin thought that, for once, Toke wasn't mocking him. "And I don't know my true name either, do I?"

Toke frowned and gave Morgin a dubious look. "And why would you say that? You were properly named by the demon, weren't you?"

"Was I properly named?" Morgin asked. "Or was my grandmother mislead? I know my name is not AethonLaw, because I cannot claim it in a dream, nor in the demon's presence. And *Morgin* is merely a moni-ker, a label by which I can be called. No, I saw the demon's deceit. I saw the extra marks it placed in the sand the instant after my grand-mother looked away. I saw her obliterate the symbol before she noticed those extra marks. But I saw them; me, only me. Only I knew those extra marks existed, and now the demon has shown them to you. Why? Why you?"

Toke flashed his teeth in a broad grin. "I am merely a messenger, Elhiyne. You need to find your true name, for you can't defeat your enemy without it. And if you do not defeat your enemy, the exile of the Benesh'ere will be as nothing compared to the slavery of the entire Mortal Plane."

Morgin leaned forward and snarled, "Then stop playing games. Stop taunting me with riddles and tell me my damn name."

The grin disappeared and Toke's face softened with sympathy. And too, Morgin thought he saw pity. "I don't know your name. Like you, I only know what it is not."

Toke stood; Morgin remained seated and the old man looked down on him. "I wish I could help you, but I can't. The only one who might help you is the Unnamed King, though he's just a myth, so you're rather stuck there, aren't you?"

"But I may have an inkling of how to find him. I think I can only find him in a dream."

Toke turned and strode off, asking the demon, "You think he's right?"

Toke listened to the demon's response, but when he again spoke, he was too far away for Morgin to make out the words, though the conversation between the whiteface and demon continued rather animatedly.

••••

Morgin slept poorly that night, drifting in and out of a light slumber, never truly finding any sort of deep sleep, though he did dream of Aethon's tomb, and again the simple warrior no longer lay at the skeleton king's feet. Toke's words haunted him, and when he awoke well before dawn, he knew he would not again find sleep, so he arose, dressed, wandered down to the lake and washed up. Then he returned and sat down in front of his tent and pondered Toke's words, and he pondered his name.

Toke didn't know his true name, and apparently neither did ElkenSkul, not in the sense that the demon could interpret the symbol and voice his name. Morgin had to find his true name to defeat his enemy, but who was his enemy? Certainly, Valso, but Valso alone couldn't enslave all of the entire Mortal Plane, though as King of the Greater Clans his rule did feel a bit like slavery, but that was clearly not the kind of slavery Toke had meant. Morgin's thoughts returned to that vast chasm of unnatural power he'd sensed in Valso, and how, in Durin, after he'd witnessed the Dark God's power at Csairne Glen through Morddon's eyes, Valso's power now had the same taste as that ancient power. Was the source of that power his enemy? If so, he would need an enormously powerful weapon to defeat it. Perhaps his cursed blade was meant to defeat that power. Perhaps he was meant to unleash it, remove all restraint from it, but how could he focus its hatred and bloodlust on Valso and the source of his power. It had proven time and again uncontrollable; unleashed, it wanted blood, any blood, the blood of the innocent as well as that of the truly evil. No, his cursed sword was not the answer.

Perhaps, the AethonSword. He recalled the skeleton king sitting on his throne in the crypt, his bony arm resting casually on the hilt of that great sword. He himself, as Morddon, had put the lifeless body of Aethon on that throne, had arranged him carefully to match the image of Morgin's dreams. But Morddon—or was it Morgin—knew without doubt the great jeweled sword was not the blade to defeat the Dark God, that it had to be one of the blades Morgin had forged during the centuries he'd spent at the forges in netherhell.

There! Without truly thinking about it he'd subconsciously thought of himself as the forger of those blades, not Morddon. But how could he have spent centuries forging those blades when he'd yet lived only a little more than twenty-four years. Were the gods so casual with time that they had created such a dichotomy? Or was it all just one big hallucination he'd imagined in a dream?

Morgin, through Morddon, had given Aethon one of the two swords he'd forged in the hell of his dreams, hoping it might defeat the Dark God. But with his last dying breath Aethon had told Morgin—Morddon—that the sword he'd forged, the sword he'd given Aethon, had meant nothing to the ruler of netherhell, and the Dark God had destroyed it.

Morgin looked at the sword he now possessed. Was this the one remaining sword he'd forged so long ago; and was it meant to defeat the monster that now haunted Valso's soul? But still, perhaps it was not the sword alone that must defeat the Dark God. Perhaps such a weapon must be wielded by the proper hand.

Morgin lifted his hands and stared at them. False dawn had lightened the sky, and he could count the many scars on his hands. Was he meant to wield that sword? Was that what his name meant, that perhaps the sword's power could not be properly unleashed unless he did the unleashing. Should Morgin, as Morddon, have wielded the great sword all those many centuries ago?

••••

I have a task for you.

This time DaNoel managed to neither grimace nor flinch at Valso's intrusion into his mind. *I am with Olivia. I cannot speak now.*

Very well. But when you are free, just think of me and I will know.

"DaNoel," Olivia snapped. "Pay attention."

"Yes, grandmother."

DaNoel decided he hated the old woman too, hated her almost as much as he hated the whoreson. But at the thought of Morgin his guts twisted. What if he was still alive? What if Valso's hints that Morgin may have survived were not merely an attempt to make him ill-at-ease? What if he somehow came back and exposed DaNoel's treachery. NickoLot had her suspicions, but no proof. Did Morgin have proof? Because if he did, and he came back, Olivia would do more than simply exile DaNoel. The humiliation would be intolerable. But, if Morgin yet lived, he would still be a hunted man, and if DaNoel cooperated with Valso, he would only be doing so to help capture and execute such a wanted outlaw. Now that would not be treachery.

DaNoel watched Brandon attempting to placate the old woman. Olivia didn't want outright war with Penda any more than Brandon, but her ambition had sparked a fire in her soul, and her mutual animosity with BlakeDown had blinded her to her own provocations. DaNoel had to give Brandon credit, for he had managed to blunt some of the sharp edges of her acrimony.

These meetings of the clan leadership bored DaNoel. He had nothing to contribute, didn't really care what was decided. So he listened, but didn't listen, nodded at the right moments, frowned at others, and when it ended, he chatted politely with his kin as they left Olivia's audience chamber.

He returned hurriedly to his room, a simple bachelor's bedchamber where he slept, or to which he occasionally brought some barmaid. He'd fended off AnnaRail's attempts to find him a bride, but perhaps he should not resist her efforts. As a married man, and a direct member of the ruling clan, he and his wife would be given a small suite of rooms, though he bitterly realized they'd be nothing compared to what they'd given Warmaster Whoreson.

Alone in his room, he allowed thoughts of Valso to enter his mind. He pictured the face of the Decouix king, and heard his voice.

I take it you are now free to talk?

Yes.

Good. I have a simple task for you. Brandon and ErrinCastle have been secretly conspiring, and JohnEngine has been aiding them. They're seeing to it the patrols on the border between Penda and Elhiyne are commanded by their hand-picked lieutenants.

DaNoel saw some advantage to be gained from this information. Brandon had managed to ingratiate himself to the old woman, and everyone now thought of his cousin as a possible future leader of Elhiyne. It rankled that no one looked at him that way. *I'll tell Olivia, expose Brandon's treachery.*

And when she asks how you know this, how will you prevent her from learning of your treachery?

Valso was right. He couldn't simply expose Brandon without exposing himself.

I have a better idea, Valso said. *Be sympathetic to Brandon and JohnEngine's concerns. Express concern and worry at the rift between the two clans. Speak quietly but directly of placating the two leaders. Tell them what they want to hear, so they'll include you in their counsel, and you could gain considerable standing as a man who helped prevent a disastrous war.*

DaNoel considered Valso's idea carefully. Not only would that be more effective than trying to expose them, but it would finally bring Da-Noel into the inner counsel of the clan's future leadership. *Yes,* he said, *an excellent idea.*

You see, DaNoel, subtlety can be a very powerful tool.

17

The Freedom to Die

"FELINA WANTS TO learn to swim too."

Morgin looked up from sharpening the knife for the old cook Satcha and turned around. LillianToc stood facing him; a young girl about his age hid shyly behind him and peeked out past his shoulder. Morgin had been teaching LillianToc to swim, and he'd progressed to the point where he could keep his head above water with a decent dogpaddle.

"Who's Felina?" Morgin asked.

"I am," the girl whispered, looking at Morgin with wide, almond shaped eyes. He'd seen her about the camp a few times, thought she might be the daughter of one of the smiths, though the smiths' children were raised in a communal way by all their wives, so he didn't yet know which. She would be a real beauty when she grew up.

"Whose daughter are you?"

Blushing, she said, "Baldrak's."

"And you want to learn to swim like LillianToc?"

She grew bold and stepped out from behind the young boy. "Yes. Will you teach me?"

Morgin nodded. "Ok. When?"

"Now."

"Yes," LillianToc said. "Let's do it now."

Morgin glanced toward Satcha. The old woman smiled and nodded her permission.

Morgin pointed to the lakeshore. "All right, down to the lake with you."

LillianToc and Felina danced down to the lake stripping off their clothes. Morgin was only slowly adjusting to the casual attitude the Benesh'ere displayed regarding nudity. He stripped down, but didn't throw his breeches off until the last moment before he dove into the lake. He surfaced about twenty paces from the shore, treading water. LillianToc and Felina stood in the shallows watching him.

"See what I mean," LillianToc said. "It's like he's standing on the bottom, but there is no bottom."

Felina took to swimming like a fish, and by mid-morning could dogpaddle alongside LillianToc. The two of them made for a noisy swimming lesson.

"Elhiyne," Baldrak called from the shore. "Chagarin wants to see you in his workshop."

Morgin hollered back, "Tell him I'll be right there."

LillianToc and Felina protested mightily that the lesson shouldn't end yet. Morgin told them he had no choice, for one did not ignore the Master Smith's summons. He toweled off, returned to his tent and changed into a fresh Benesh'ere robe, then marched across the camp to the Forge Hall. But when he entered Chagarin's workshop, a separate room at the back of the Forge Hall, he knew immediately this would not be a simple discussion with the Master Smith. Chagarin sat at a workbench, but standing to one side were Harriok and Branaugh. Harriok looked healthy and hale, with no sign of the illness that had come from the venom of the sixth claw. He stood and clasped Morgin's hand with a hearty shake.

"You are well," Morgin said. "I'm glad."

Branaugh said, "He still has some weight to gain before I'll let him do anything strenuous."

Harriok grinned at Morgin and said, "Remember, my friend, if you ever take a wife, you also take a new lord and master."

If he ever took a wife, Morgin suspected something showed on his face since both Harriok and Branaugh sobered.

"Elhiyne," Chagarin said. "Come here. I want you to look at something."

Morgin walked over and stood beside Chagarin at his workbench. On it lay something long and thin wrapped in an oiled cloth, two short to be a sword, too long to be a knife. Next to that lay three cold puddles of dull metal, each about the size of a man's hand with fingers spread. They appeared to have been poured without any specific shape in mind, and allowed to cool as-is, but Morgin recognized them as the steel bloom from a smelter. Chagarin picked up one and handed it to him. "What do you think of this?" Clearly, it was meant to be some sort of test.

Morgin looked at the metal closely, almost sensed a terrible imbalance within it, knew immediately with his ancient memories what it meant. He said, "This was fired or smelted with stink coal, coal contaminated with the yellow earth. It'll be hard to forge, nearly impossible to quench properly, and then it'll be brittle and likely shatter easily at the first impact."

Chagarin nodded without saying anything, took that piece from him and handed him another.

Morgin didn't need to look at it. "Pig iron," he said. "Very brittle, but not a bad start for steel. Needs to be treated properly in a forge, possibly combined with softer iron."

Chagarin exchanged that piece for the third. The instant it touched Morgin's hand he knew the metal. "Mild steel," he said. "It'll hold an edge, but not the best. Again, treat it properly in a forge, and a good blade can be had. Harden it up a bit and it could serve as the backbone for a blade. Maybe wrap the pig iron around it to hold an edge. Though, I'd still adjust the hardness of both a bit before doing so. It would make for a better blade."

Chagarin took the third piece back and said, "Right, right, and right. Three out of three."

Branaugh said, "You knew, without performing any tests. Master Chagarin spent half the morning testing those pieces before he knew what you knew by merely touching the steel."

Morgin looked at Harriok and Branaugh and said, "You told him, didn't you?"

They ignored his accusation as Chagarin reached for the oiled cloth and unwrapped its contents: a sword broken into two pieces about a third of the blade's length from its tip. Morgin immediately recognized the blade.

"You said this was flawed," Chagarin said. "You knew that from nothing more than the sound of its ring. I tested it as well, and you were right; it broke at the flaw."

Morgin locked eyes with the smith and refused to acknowledge any of this.

Chagarin nodded toward Branaugh and Harriok and said, "These two tell me you killed the demon cat. And they told me what you told them about the first four deeds."

Morgin didn't answer him and he continued. "Both you and he were touched by the sixth claw. You were completely unaffected and he eventually survived."

Morgin closed his eyes and said nothing. He felt Harriok put a hand on his shoulder in a light, easy grip. He just rested it there, not attempting to hinder Morgin, more a gesture of friendship. "Be at ease, friend."

Morgin opened his eyes and looked into his friend's face, and he saw sorrow there. He was not surprised when Harriok pulled a small knife from his belt, and raised it to Morgin's throat. He said, "I'm sorry, my friend. I cannot postpone this any longer."

He cut the debt collar, slicing cleanly through it and lifting it off Morgin's neck. He said, "I think it would be best if you waited in front of your tent."

Morgin turned and walked from Chagarin's workshop, walked through the Forge Hall and out into the light of day. He hesitated for a moment; felt that the lack of the debt collar must shine like a beacon slicing through a dark night. Then he calmly walked through the Benesh'ere camp, walked proudly to his tent, sat down in front of it, his legs crossed in front of him. And he waited.

He didn't have long to wait. In the distance, he saw a commotion build in the center of the camp. Then he saw a crowd of white faces walking his way, with Blesset in the lead. She, like the rest of them, carried her longbow in her left hand, strung and ready for war. In her right hand, she carried a single arrow with a steel-tipped warhead. She stopped just a little more than one pace from Morgin, a look of triumph lighting her face with joy. She said not a word, but calmly and carefully nocked the arrow, lifted the bow, drawing the string back as she did so. She aimed the arrow directly at Morgin's heart and held it there for several heartbeats. Then without warning she lowered her aim and released the bowstring. It twanged loudly in the silence that surrounded them and the arrow struck the ground not a finger's width from Morgin's boot, buried half its length in the dirt. Blesset had exercised the traditional form of challenge for mortal combat. She smiled and stepped aside.

The warrior immediately behind her stepped up, nocked an arrow and shot it into the earth just behind Blesset's arrow, then he stepped aside. The man behind him stepped up and shot his arrow into the earth immediately behind that. And one-by-one the warriors that followed Blesset each took their turn, shooting an arrow into the earth until a small forest of shafts carpeted the ground in front of Morgin's tent.

When they'd finished, the small crowd of them parted, and Jerst and Jack the Lesser walked down the path created through their midst, both carrying a longbow and a single arrow. Jerst stopped in front of Morgin and looked at Jack questioningly. Jack shook his head and said, "No, my honor is satisfied without killing him." Jack looked carefully at the forest of arrows. "And I find it interesting only about a hundred of us still feel that way."

Jerst looked pained, as if he'd been betrayed by a good friend, and Morgin realized it was quite possible the warmaster didn't want to do this. But then he nocked his arrow, raised his bow and shot it into the earth just in front of Blesset's. The warmaster had taken precedence in this challenge.

He looked into Morgin's eyes and said, "Tomorrow." Then he turned and walked away.

••••

The smiths' wives cooked a feast for dinner, goat prepared in a spicy marinade, then roasted on steel skewers over glowing coals. There were also vegetables and tubers Morgin hadn't tasted before, some wrapped in leaves and placed at the edge of the coals, others also roasted on skewers.

It was all quite delicious, though it had the air of a condemned man's last meal.

Afterward, Jack the Lesser, Fantose and Delaga joined them, and the smiths broke out a keg of strong ale. They all sat around a large fire, drinking mugs of ale and trading stories about Morgin's fighting prowess, and counting up the number of Kulls he'd killed. There was no talk of any possibility that he might defeat Jerst, for no one cared to discuss the impossible. No, this little gathering was a wake to grieve over Morgin's impending death. "It's a shame," Jack kept repeating. "A cryin' shame."

Morgin held back on the ale, only sipped a little, just enough to get a bit light-headed, not enough to get truly drunk. He didn't want to die with a hangover. Baldrak and another smith drank enough that their speech slurred noticeably, and Delaga out did them all, ended up staggering about and barely able to stand. Jack and Fantose helped him stay on his feet as the gloomy festivities ended and they returned to their tents.

Chagarin, oddly enough, sat quietly throughout the evening, frequently looking at Morgin with an odd sideways glance. As Morgin turned and headed for his tent, the Master Smith joined him and walked silently beside him. They had to navigate around the forest of arrows buried in the ground to reach his tent, and there, Chagarin turned to face him. He said, "Don't kill Jerst tomorrow. He deserves better."

He said nothing more, but turned and walked away into the night.

••••

Morgin actually slept quite well that night. He did think on Chagarin's words for a short time, but sleep quickly found him, and he slept deep and long, with only normal, ordinary dreams to remember in the morning.

He awoke just after dawn feeling quite refreshed. He dressed, washed up and ate a light breakfast, just a couple of bites. The entire Benesh'ere camp had arisen early like Morgin and he saw many whitefaces moving among the tents. Everyone's movements appeared slow and tentative, and an odd, oppressive silence muffled all sound, even the clanking of pots and pans.

Morgin sat down in front of his tent to sharpen and oil his sword, and await whatever would come. He didn't have to wait long before Baldrak approached him and sat down facing him. "We smiths have to remain neutral in this, but that doesn't mean I can't tell you what to expect."

Morgin wanted to ease the obvious discomfort he saw in Baldrak's eyes. "I thank you for that. And I thank you and the other smiths for the friendship you've shown me."

Morgin's words appeared to increase the smith's discomfort rather than ease it. "You're allowed only a sword; no knives or other weapons beyond your fists and knees and elbows and teeth. When I stand and walk away, you should walk to the center of camp. There you'll find a large circle fifty paces wide and marked by small stones. Wait outside the circle until Jerst joins you. Outside the circle, neither of you can draw a weapon against the other. Jerst will approach you directly and issue formal challenge. After that, the two of you will part and walk to opposite sides of the circle. Wait until Jerst steps into the circle, then you do likewise. Once inside the circle, it is you and your sword against Jerst and his, and you cannot again leave the circle until one of you is dead. If either of you attempts to do so, you'll be shot by a dozen archers stationed outside the circle. And if anyone enters the circle to aid either of you, they'll be shot by the same archers."

Morgin said, "A well-defined formula."

Baldrak considered his words for a moment, then said, "A formula we have lived by for centuries." With that, he stood and walked toward the Forge Hall.

Morgin had dressed carefully that morning with an eye toward the coming contest: loose breeches, his boots and his knee-length Benesh'ere tunic. He stood, stripped off the tunic, stripped to the waist and belted on his sword. Then he walked slowly and calmly to the center of the camp, accompanied only by an oppressive circle of silence. No one greeted him and he greeted no one. The circle of stones had been laid out just as Baldrak had described, so he stopped one pace outside it and waited, and he felt no need to fidget nervously or look about, but stood there staring at the other end of the circle. And he waited.

Slowly a crowd gathered around the circle, though they maintained a distance of about ten paces from the stones. They spoke among themselves and chatted amiably, though that oppressive silence muffled their words. The sun rose farther into the sky as the crowd built, and Morgin realized every whiteface in the tribe had come to see his execution. He looked for Val, but saw nothing of the *twoname*, hoped the whitefaces hadn't chosen to execute him outright.

He stood in the midst of seven thousand men, women and children, and while they were not loud, as a crowd they emitted a low background of voices and quiet murmurs. But then, in a single heartbeat, that murmur disappeared and an utter and complete silence descended upon them all. He heard gravel crunching beneath a pair of boots behind him, too close to be just another onlooker, and without turning, he said, "Warmaster Jerst."

Jerst stepped up beside him. At the far side of the circle the crowd parted. Two warriors carried Angerah's throne through the opening created, and placed it at the front of the crowd outside the circle. Angerah followed, the crutch under one arm, the walking stick held in the other, Merella beside him. He sat down on the small throne, looked across the circle at Morgin and Jerst, and nodded.

Neither Morgin nor Jerst looked at the other; standing side-by-side they both faced the center of the circle, and Jerst said amiably, "Elhiyne, I hope you slept well last night."

They sounded like two merchants casually greeting one another on the street. Morgin said, "Quite well."

Jerst's voice was oddly bereft of anger as he said, "I challenge you, to the death."

Morgin needed to right the wrong between them, even if doing so was no more than a meaningless gesture. "And I accept. But before we start this, I owe you an apology. The words I spoke more than two years ago were wrong and uncalled-for."

"Thank you," Jerst said. "I accept your apology . . . but I still must kill you."

"If you can."

For the first time Jerst looked at Morgin, so Morgin turned and looked at him. They stood that way for a long moment, then by some sort of mutual consent they both turned away from one another, and walked to opposite sides of the circle.

Morgin stopped as he'd been instructed, turned and faced the center of the circle, standing just outside the perimeter of stones. Jerst, already standing on the other side of the circle, drew his sword and handed the sheath to a whiteface standing beside him. Morgin unbuckled his sword belt, drew the blade from the sheath, and laid the sheath and belt on the ground beside him.

Jerst stared across the circle at Morgin and nodded almost imperceptibly. It was a question, and in return Morgin answered with one, single nod of his head. Jerst stepped into the circle, so Morgin did likewise. They stood there fifty paces apart, and the crowd about them uttered not a sound. And then, again, as if by some mutual understanding, as if they could communicate on some level beyond that of sight and sound, they both simultaneously charged.

18

SteelMaster

NORLAKTON SEEMED RATHER subdued this morning. With the arrival of the Benesh'ere several days ago, the dirt street running through the middle of town had seen a steady stream of activity. From the earliest hours of the morning, and even well into the evening, any number of whitefaces could be seen about the town, or, if the whitefaces themselves were not visible, their presence was marked by their desert ponies tied up here and there. But this morning, none were visible, not a single one.

Out of curiosity Rhianne wandered down to the inn, stepped through the crude, wooden door and into the dirt-floored common room. Fat John stood behind the bar, wiping a tin mug with a bar rag. She asked him, "Do you know why the Benesh'ere have suddenly disappeared?"

He shrugged and said, "There's something up with them whitefaces. My guess is they're settling a dispute between a couple of their warriors. Can get pretty bloodthirsty. Best to stay clear of their camp until it's over."

Rhianne opened her mouth to ask for further details, but in the distance an odd sort of rumbling, thunder interrupted her. The sound continued without letup, though the walls of the inn muffled it considerably.

The innkeeper nodded, put his rag down and stepped around the end of the bar. Rhianne followed him out into the street, and there, even though distance still muffled the sound, there was no mistaking the roar of several thousand voices raised in a vast and deafening shout.

She wondered if she should go there, took a step toward the stables, but Fat John grabbed her arm. "You stay away from them whitefaces, mistress, today, and for several days after. When they start killing like this, it ain't healthy for us plainfaces to be near them."

Rhianne was torn, and yet she knew nothing of these strange desert people; it would be foolish to act on such an impulse. She had no good reason for going to the Benesh'ere camp, so she nodded, resolved to take Fat John's advice.

Most of Norlakton had stepped into the open air to listen just like Rhianne and the innkeeper. "Yup," Fat John said, "someone's gonna die today. It's bad for business when them whitefaces get to killing each other."

••••

Morgin and Jerst met in the center of the circle charging at full speed. Jerst's blade swung toward his knees, but Morgin sensed from the steel that it was a feint, that the blade would swing upward at the last instant and go for his throat, so as it began to rise he dropped and rolled beneath it. He came up behind Jerst, and as the warmaster spun to face him Morgin swung his blade in a flat arc. Jerst deflected the blow clumsily and they separated, the roar of the whitefaces' shouts and screams a deafening backdrop to the ring of steel.

He and Jerst faced each other, both in a crouch, breathing heavily, circling warily. It happened again, that odd sensation that he knew what Jerst's steel would do before it did it, as if the steel itself were alive and talking to him. Jerst came in with a two-handed overhead strike. Morgin deflected it to one side, spun and elbowed Jerst in the ribs, twisted out of reach and turned to face him again. Again, crouched at the ready they circled warily. So far Morgin had gotten the best of Jerst, probably because the warmaster had started out overconfident. Morgin saw in his eyes that would not happen again.

Don't kill Jerst tomorrow, Chagarin had said, and for the first time Morgin thought that, with the steel aiding him, he just might win. But he couldn't win, not by killing Jerst. He owed Chagarin that.

Morgin lunged with a two-handed strike, slicing in at an angle. Again, Morgin knew what Jerst's steel was about to do, so he was ready for the warmaster's parry. The blades struck and rang loudly, but Morgin slid his cross-guard down the length of Jerst's blade, forced it high and stepped beneath it, only to meet Jerst's fist as it slammed into his temple. He hit the ground hard and rolled dizzily away as the tip of Jerst's blade bit into the earth next to his head. Then he staggered to his feet and back-stepped away from the warmaster, blood dripping down his cheek from a gash Jerst's fist had opened there.

The Benesh'ere tribe went insane.

Morgin continued to back step and circle, Jerst stepping forward and circling with him. The warmaster didn't fight with anger or rage, but with cold determination masked by a hint of sadness, as if carrying out an unpleasant task that must be done.

Jerst stepped in and swung. Morgin met his blade squarely, and responded with a strike of his own. They traded four blows that way then separated, again circling warily.

Morgin felt his muscles tiring, slowing, his lungs demanding more air. But the warmaster had slowed also, gulping in air with each breath. The roar from the tribe had grown so deafening, Morgin could no longer hear Jerst's struggling breaths, could almost not hear his own.

Morgin attacked, feinting with a low slice that he turned into a lunging jab. Jerst skipped out of the way on his tiptoes, but Morgin felt his blade bite into the man's side, a glancing cut that wouldn't kill him, but might slow him. But the warmaster was better than that; he spun away from Morgin's blade, and with Morgin overextended he chopped toward Morgin's neck. Morgin deflected the strike with a clumsy, glancing parry, Jerst's blade slicing across his upper arm. They both danced away from each other, Morgin thankful the cut had not been on his sword arm. But it would limit his effectiveness in a two handed stroke, though with Jerst clutching at his side they were even on that score.

Again and again they engaged, Morgin's uncanny awareness of Jerst's steel keeping him alive, but Chagarin's demand he not kill Jerst preventing him from taking advantage of the strange sentience of the steel. Each time they met, each time they engaged, they both moved slower and slower. And heartbeat by heartbeat, as the sun climbed toward noon, the cries of the whiteface onlookers grew muted and restrained.

Morgin could barely lift his blade, could barely stagger into the next engagement, then stagger away from it. He had a dozen minor wounds on his arms and legs, and the effort to swing his blade frequently threw blood in Jerst's face. Once, it even gave him some advantage as the warmaster was momentarily blinded by a few drops of Morgin's blood. But Morgin's footwork had turned clumsy, oafish and heavy, and he missed the opportunity to take advantage of it. Though Jerst fared no better, and each time they engaged Morgin suspected they both looked like two inexperienced novices clumsily slapping their blades at each other.

They separated, staggered away from one another, the sun now well past its zenith. They'd fought through the morning and into the afternoon, and Morgin realized Jerst bled from as many wounds as he. They'd knocked each other to the ground several times, and rolled about chest to chest a couple of times. The warmaster's face and arms were covered with sweat and blood and dirt, and when Morgin looked at his own arms he realized he was in no better shape.

They both stood there for a long moment about ten paces apart, swaying unsteadily from side-to-side, too weary to lift their swords, the tips resting in the dirt in front of them. "I won't kill you," Morgin said.

Jerst lifted his arm and used his sleeve to wipe blood encrusted dirt from his eyes. "Won't . . . or can't?"

Morgin shrugged. "A bit . . . of both."

"Why?" Jerst asked, clearly perplexed.

Morgin sensed the weariness in Jerst's steel, sensed the weariness in his own steel. An eerie pall hung over the tribe as they looked on in mute silence, no longer cheering, no longer shouting for blood. "The steel doesn't want me to. And your steel won't let you kill me."

Jerst nodded as if he understood. "But we've fought this way for centuries. We can't leave the circle of stones until one of us is dead."

At that moment Morgin understood more than fatigue held Jerst back. It was not just the exhaustion of his body and his steel, but the weariness of his heart. He wanted Morgin's death no more than Morgin wanted his, so Morgin said, "Perhaps it's time to change."

Jerst shook his head. "I don't know how," he said, then staggered forward, raising his blade in a clumsy, overcommitted strike. Morgin had had enough, and to the warmaster's steel he said, "No."

Jerst staggered, struggled to hold his blade up, trembling with bunched muscles as if its weight had grown unbearable. Slowly, the weight of the blade grew, forcing him to lower it to the ground; fighting against it Jerst stumbled over his own feet, and fell to the dirt in front of Morgin. On his hands and knees, Jerst looked up, and instinctively Morgin raised his sword for a death stroke.

Don't kill Jerst tomorrow, Chagarin had said.

Morgin hesitated, and in that instant Jerst saw his opportunity, he rolled forward and threw his weight against Morgin's ankles. Morgin went down on top of Jerst, and in a tangle of arms and legs they rolled over several times. Jerst came out on top, reared up and slammed a fist into Morgin's eye. The world spun, and before Morgin could act, Jerst had regained his feet and stood over him with his sword raised. But just as Morgin was about to command the steel again, the warmaster hesitated, a frown of indecision on his face.

The moment drew out, the crowd deathly still, and then a single male voice crowed with laughter. Toke stood on the edge of the circle next to Angerah, laughing hysterically, tears streaming down his cheeks, the demon *namegiver* hovering at his shoulder. Jerst lowered his blade and looked about uncertainly, frowning, glancing from right to left as if Toke and ElkenSkul were hidden in one of Morgin's shadows.

"Have you . . . found your . . . name yet?" Toke shouted, having trouble spitting the words out in the midst of his own laughter. "Or do you . . . still claim . . . a false name?"

Toke's riddles only served to inflame Morgin's anger. Ignoring Jerst, he lurched to his feet, crossed the short distance between them staggering like a drunk. He stopped at the edge of the circle only a handsbreadth from Toke, and shouted in his face, "Enough!" He leaned forward, careful not to cross the line of stones that marked the limit of the circle, and in Toke's eyes he saw only laughter and derision. "Why do you torment me with your riddles, old man?"

Toke's laughter died, and in the stillness that ensued Morgin noticed several whitefaces glancing back and forth between him and Toke, as if they couldn't believe their eyes. While Angerah and Merella both smiled and nodded knowingly, as if privy to some dark secret. "You see all . . ." Toke said, ". . . and yet you see nothing."

Morgin heard Jerst's footsteps behind him, so he spun to face the warmaster. But Jerst paused just outside the reach of his blade. He lifted his sword and looked at it for a moment, then tossed it to the ground. He walked up to the edge of the circle and, like the other whitefaces, his gaze shifted back and forth between Morgin and Toke. Then his eyes settled on Morgin and he asked, "You see Toke?"

Morgin shouted, "Of course I see him." He pointed at the old man. "He's standing right there. I see him as easily as you."

Jerst shook his head, a look of wonder and awe on his face. "But I don't see him. No one has ever seen him . . . not until you. He is invisible to us all, was born that way, and has lived his life that way."

Harriok stepped out of the crowd, reached out like a blind man searching with his hands in a dark room. One hand touched Toke's shoulder, the other his cheek, and Harriok said, "He is here." He looked at Morgin. "It was said that you would see all, and yet see nothing."

A single voice cried out, "Nooooo!"

Blesset, on the far side of the circle, ran around it staying just outside the perimeter of stones. She stopped at the closest point to them, leaned forward and said, "No. It's time to kill him. So let's be done with it"

Jerst shook his head and said, "No, it is time for us to change."

"Kill him," Blesset demanded. "Kill him, damn you. Where is your honor?"

Jerst looked at her carefully as if seeing something other than his daughter. "I don't know where my honor lies, but it's certainly not here with his death."

Blesset staggered backward as if slapped; her eyes narrowed into hard, angry slits, staring at Jerst as if accusing him of betraying her. She turned her head slowly, looking for someone to support her, someone to agree that Jerst should execute Morgin. And in response the entire tribe seemed to sigh and lean back, as if distancing themselves from her. She saw it and her eyes hardened even further. Then she reached for the sword at her side and spoke in a cold, hard whisper, "Well if you'll not do it then I will."

In a single motion she drew the blade, stepped into the circle of stones and raised her sword. Shebasha materialized in front of her, sprang into the air and hit her in the chest. Blesset and the demon sand-cat tumbled in a sprawl of arms and legs and paws. Then both jumped to their feet, facing each other, and Shebasha let out a scream that resonated in Morgin's soul.

Harriok shouted, "Blesset, he killed the demon cat. Don't you understand? He killed it and that is why I live. And before that he righted the first four wrongs."

Shebasha licked one paw and calmly said to Blesset, "We have invaded the circle, for which the penalty is death. But I am already dead, so that leaves only you."

Morgin had forgotten about the archers, but the steel warheads on their arrows warned him, dozens of them knowing they were now destined to pierce Blesset's heart. Standing only two paces from Morgin, she looked down at her feet, and only then realized what she'd done.

As the archer's raised their bows Morgin heard the whisper of the steel, telling him that this must not end in mortal bloodshed, and only he could save Blesset. And now, as if the steel controlled him, he screamed, "No," and lunged for her. He heard the twang of a dozen bowstrings as he stepped in and wrapped his arms around her, closed his eyes and waited to feel the steel pierce his own heart. And he waited. And nothing happened.

He opened his eyes, looked into Blesset's face. Her eyes were focused over his shoulder, awe and wonder on her face. Still holding her, he turned his head slowly and found a dozen arrows hovering in the air only a hand's breadth from the two of them, steel warheads aimed at their hearts.

Morgin said to the steel, "Please, no."

The warheads glowed a little, a faint orange shimmer that grew slowly to a bright, cherry red. The wooden arrow shafts emitted trails of smoke, then flared into white-hot flame, and moments later ash and molten steel dropped to the ground.

Blesset tore herself out of Morgin's arms. She stepped away from him and pleaded, "It can't be. It's not possible. He's a plainface. How can he free us of our debt to the Shahotma?" Tears streamed down her cheeks. "How can a plainface free us of our sin of betrayal?"

Morgin shook his head. "You have no debt to the Shahotma. History has it wrong. It was not the Benesh'ere who betrayed him. It was an archangel, and the Benesh'ere were the last to remain loyal to the Shahotma. Even unto the end."

She whispered, "No. Impossible. How can you know this?"

Morgin looked slowly from Blesset to Jerst, and then to Harriok and Chagarin standing just outside the circle. "Because I was there. Because Aethon died in my arms, and I laid him to rest in Attunhigh."

Chagarin nodded, as if Morgin had just answered a question he'd long wondered at.

Angerah called out to Chagarin, "Help me, old friend."

Chagarin crossed the distance between them, and helped the old man stand. Then, with Angerah leaning on him heavily, they stepped across the line of rocks and into the circle. Angerah said, "I do believe you bring great change upon us." Then carefully, with Chagarin helping him, he dropped to one knee in front of Morgin, bowed his head and said, "SteelMaster, command me."

19

The Obsidian Blade

JOHNENGINE WONDERED IF the small stream had a name. Perhaps the local peasantry called it by some term or designation other than "the stream." It certainly wasn't big enough to be called a river, but its small size masked it true importance. It was one of the many features that defined the traditional border between Elhiyne and Penda lands.

JohnEngine and Brandon had decided all border patrols should be headed by someone they could trust to keep a clear and calm head. They only had a few lieutenants who fit that requirement, so that meant JohnEngine must share their duties and spend a lot more time in the saddle these days. He and Brandon had been relieved to learn DaNoel shared their disdain for Olivia and BlakeDown's provocations. It gave them one more soul they might trust to share these duties. And Brandon had a new wife to worry about, a rather pretty blond. JohnEngine hoped that when it came his turn, Olivia and AnnaRail would find him someone as attractive.

"Lord JohnEngine," one of the scouts said, standing up in his stirrups and pointing across the stream.

JohnEngine didn't need to stand up in his stirrups. Across the stream and several hundred paces distant, a cloud of dust rose from a Penda border patrol riding their way. They rode at an easy canter, not at a full gallop or charge, so their approach did not alarm JohnEngine. He and his men had been riding about a hundred paces from the stream and parallel to it, so they halted, and he had them wait there. The Pendas likewise stopped about a hundred paces from the stream, and with no apparent hostility in the air, JohnEngine said, "Wait here." Then he nudged his horse forward. The Penda lieutenant did the same.

As they approached JohnEngine was pleased to see that he was dealing with Perrinsall. They both stopped a few paces from the stream and on opposite sides, an old formula that worked to keep the borders safe, and peaceful. JohnEngine said, "Good day to you, Lord Perrinsall."

The Penda nodded and said, "And good day to you, Lord JohnEngine."

ErrinCastle had been good to his word, had made sure a calm head was in charge of the Penda patrol.

They compared notes on border activity, confirmed that neither clan had experienced any real cross-border banditry. Perrinsall was hunting one highwayman who'd proven to be a nuisance to a few of the local merchants, but the fellow hadn't attempted to perpetrate his crimes on the lands of one clan, then escape across the border onto those of another. If he had, JohnEngine would work closely with Perrinsall to ferret the fellow out, and see him hung from a gibbet.

JohnEngine finished by saying, "Perhaps some time you'll allow me to buy you a pint."

Perrinsall said, "Gladly. I look forward to it."

They parted and returned to their men.

••••

Carsaris walked carefully down the corridor, his every sense focused on the Kull captain behind him. He heard the creak of the halfman's leather armor, the thump of his boots on the stone floor, the occasional clink of a piece of metal harness, but nothing more. The halfman moved with an eerie silence that sent a shiver up Carsaris's spine. No man felt at ease with Salula at his back, and Carsaris had now worked closely with the captain long enough to know the halfman cultivated such fear, actually enjoyed it.

When the two Kulls standing guard at the entrance to Valso's apartments saw them approaching they perked up. And when they realized

Salula accompanied Carsaris, one of them actually smiled, a strange sort of sharp grin, with no joy or happiness in it, merely hunger and anticipation. Carsaris always found it unnerving to see a Kull smile, and he hoped never to see it again.

Carsaris was expected, so they opened one of the double doors without preamble. He paused, stepped aside, and with a wave of his hand indicated Salula should precede him, saying, "After you, Captain."

Doing so was merely an excuse to no longer have Salula at his back, but the Kull captain recognized it for what it was, and he smiled knowingly. And where the common Kull soldier's smile had truly seemed evil incarnate, Salula's grin hinted at depravity far beyond anything imaginable.

"No, Lord Carsaris," Salula said, his voice a low growl with none of the light and pleasant tones that had once come from the swordsman France's throat. "After you."

Carsaris capitulated and stepped through the door. He heard Salula fall into step behind him, knew he heard Salula only because the halfman wanted him to.

Valso awaited them in a comfortable sitting room, seated casually on a chair and dining on his morning repast, with the little demon snake curled about a nearby perch and preening itself like a cat. Carsaris approached him, bowed deeply and stepped aside. Salula stepped up to Valso, dropped to one knee and lowered his head. "My king."

Valso carefully finished chewing on something, then delicately dabbed at his lips with a linen napkin. He turned his head slowly and looked at the kneeling halfman for a long moment, then he looked up and met Carsaris's eyes. "Is he ready?"

"Almost, Your Majesty."

Valso's eyes narrowed angrily, the snake hissed and a lump formed in the pit of Carsaris's stomach. "Outwardly the swordsman is fully subdued, but apparently there is yet some inward turmoil. I think Captain Salula might explain better than I."

Both the head of the snake and that of Valso turned slowly to look upon the Kull, and they stared at him for several heartbeats, their stillness eerie in its similarity. Valso finally said, "Rise, Captain."

Salula rose and stood silently looking upon the king. Impatiently, Valso said, "Speak."

The rumble of Salula's voice sounded like rolling thunder in the distance. "This France fellow is stronger than any of us would have thought, and inwardly, like a poorly trained dog, he still pulls at his leash, which could prove to be a lethal distraction at an inopportune moment. But such incidents grow less frequent with each day, and like any dog, he will be properly trained."

Valso demanded, "How long?"

"Not long, Your Majesty. A few more days, four or five at the most. After that, nothing will remain of him but a memory."

Valso stood and tossed his napkin onto the table. "I had hoped for sooner, but . . . that will have to do."

He walked slowly around Salula, examining him from every angle, then stopped in front of him, facing him. He looked into the halfman's eyes, and Carsaris saw none of the unease a normal man would feel looking into such a face. Then he looked down at Salula's leather armor and said, "This will not do."

He turned back to the dining table, retrieved a sharp knife, turned back to the halfman, reached out and took hold of a steel buckle. He sliced through the leather holding the buckle, had to saw at it a bit to make it come loose, then tossed the buckle onto the table next to his meal. "No steel," he said. "None whatsoever. Not on you, on your leathers, on your horse, on its harness, in your packs. We'll have wooden harness fashioned for you where it will do, soft iron where it will not. Absolutely no steel whatsoever."

Salula's head nodded, an almost imperceptible tilt of his chin. "As you wish, Your Majesty. But what of my knife and sword? Soft iron will not hold an edge."

Valso grinned, and it reminded Carsaris of the halfman's grin. "I've thought of everything, my good captain. Unbuckle your sword."

While Salula did so, Valso turned and walked across the room to a large chest against one wall. He opened the chest and retrieved a long, thin bundle wrapped in an oiled cloth, then returned and placed the cloth on the table. He unwrapped the bundle to reveal a sheathed sword and sheathed knife. He lifted the sword carefully, almost reverently, and turned toward the halfman. By that time Salula had unbuckled his sword belt, and held his own sheathed blade in his left hand. Valso extended the hilt of the sheathed sword he held toward the halfman and said, "Draw the blade."

Salula reached out cautiously and gripped the extended hilt, and as he pulled on it a black, obsidian blade slid from the sheath, wicked, serrated edges glinting unnaturally in the room's dim light. "Glass?" Salula asked. "It'll shatter at first contact with steel."

Salula still held his own steel blade by the sheath in his left hand. Valso, as fast as the little snake on the perch behind him, reached out and pulled Salula's steel blade from its sheath. He held it up, looked at it carefully, then walked to the center of the room, which Carsaris noticed was oddly bereft of any furniture. Valso had planned this.

He stopped, turned toward Salula, swung the blade a few times through the air, then said, "I need a little sword practice, Captain. Will you oblige me?"

Wary and ill-at-ease, Salula walked to the center of the room and stopped, facing Valso. He hesitated, looked at the king uncertainly, then carefully swung the obsidian blade in an overhead strike. Valso parried the strike easily with the steel blade; the steel on obsidian rang in a higher pitch than steel on steel, and like steel on flint it released a shower of bright sparks.

Salula raised the obsidian blade and looked at it dumbly. It remained whole and undamaged.

"It's magicked," Valso said. "With the aid of my master, I've spent a good part of winter and most of spring preparing that blade and its companion with the most powerful spells I could fashion."

Salula's teeth flashed in an evil grin, and he struck out with the obsidian blade more confidently, one, two, three strikes. And as Valso met each one, a cascade of sparks brightened the dim light of the room. Salula stopped, looked again at the blade, and laughed, an ungodly roar that struck fear in Carsaris's heart.

Valso tossed Salula the steel sword and he caught it easily in his left hand. Then Valso strode across the room and sat down at the table. "As

I said, absolutely no steel." Valso lifted the sheathed knife off the table and held it out to Salula. "Here is its companion."

Salula crossed the room and took the knife, pulled the obsidian blade part way out of the sheath, looked at it carefully and smiled. Then he shoved it back into the sheath with a snap.

He looked at Valso and asked, "I assume you have a reason for this."

Valso smiled. "The Elhiyne still lives, the one that dances in shadows, the one that killed you the first time. And he now has unusual powers over steel."

Salula dropped to one knee again. "I thank you my king for the boon of devouring his soul. This time I will not fail."

"Yes, kill the Elhiyne," Valso said. "But he's living among the Benesh'ere, and not even you can fight seven thousand of those maniacs, so you'll probably have to bide your time, watch and wait. You won't be able to get to him until he leaves them, which he will eventually do. Perhaps you could spend the time making sure his wife is dead as well. It makes me uneasy that I do not have positive confirmation of her death. So sniff about as you travel, see if you can find any hint of her. She hasn't surfaced at any of the Lesser Clan strongholds, but that doesn't necessarily mean she's dead. She could be in hiding, so if you do find her, kill her as well."

Salula's voice grumbled like thunder in the distance. "I have a thought, Your Majesty. A bit of knowledge gleaned from the swordsman's soul. This France knew the two of them well, and they were connected in some way. When the Elhiyne leaves the Benesh'ere, I might have trouble tracking him. But if I found her, might there be a way to use her to do so?"

Valso threw back his head and laughed. "Wonderful, my dear captain! I so missed having you around."

Valso stood and paced back and forth in front of the kneeling Kull. "She stayed here only recently, and when she left I had her rooms carefully swept. We have strands of hair, a few clippings from her finger nails. And I have everything of the Elhiyne, his blood, his feces, name it and I have it. Yes, I can craft a powerful spell, one to control her, and one to take advantage of that connection you say is there."

Valso stopped pacing and turned to face Salula. "Yes, if she still lives find her and kill them both. But there is something far more important than their deaths. There were once three swords, one a magnificent, jeweled work of art, the other two plain and unadorned. Like the jeweled sword, one of the plain blades was flawless. But the other plain blade contained a minute and undetectable flaw. My master faced the flawed blade and destroyed it centuries ago. The Elhiyne possesses the other, and I want you to bring it to me, for it is a blade of limitless power."

Salula asked, "But the great, jeweled sword, isn't that the Aethon-Sword? Isn't that the talisman?"

Valso shook his head. "Do not be fooled by the beauty of the jeweled blade; it is without power. The real blade of power, the AethonSword, is the remaining simple blade. My master cannot manifest on the Mortal Plane while we do not control that blade, for it is the only thing that can defeat him here. Bring me that blade. Yes, kill the Elhiyne. And if his wife still lives, after using her against him, kill her too. But bring me that blade."

Valso turned back to his meal, a clear sign of dismissal.

Salula grinned, and as he spoke Carsaris shivered. "With pleasure, Your Majesty."

••••

BlakeDown grunted like a pig and jerked spasmodically as he spilled his seed in Chrisainne's mouth, grasping the back of her head and jamming his manhood into her throat so hard she almost gagged. He lay on his back in his bed, and when he relaxed and finally let go of her head, she rolled off him and pretended to be tangled in the sheets for a moment as she quietly spit his foul slime into a fold in the bed-linens. She rose up on her knees, and when he opened his eyes, she pretended to swallow.

He smiled and said, "You are a little minx."

She smiled back at him. "I take pleasure from your pleasure, my lord."

He grasped her by the shoulders and pulled her down on top of him, and she snuggled her cheek against his beard, pretending the coarse hairs didn't irritate her delicate skin.

Her husband had contrived an excuse to be away from Penda *on busi-ness.* The two of them never openly acknowledged the fact, but they both knew his real purpose was to get out of the way so she might spend more time with BlakeDown. *More time beneath BlakeDown,* she thought, *while he grunts and sweats on top of me.*

BlakeDown dozed for a time, and she lay there patiently while he snored and breathed heavily. She thought of the young stable boy with the broad shoulders. It had been easy to seduce the young fellow, and she longed to feel again the straw beneath her back as he lay on top of her, making sweet love to her. With his experience limited to climbing on top of peasant girls, he knew nothing of pleasuring a woman, and had turned out to be a most eager and apt pupil. The stable master had learned of their liaison, which might have been a problem, but she pleasured the stable master as well, so he dare not be indiscreet. BlakeDown would execute them both.

"This Vodah," BlakeDown grunted, surprising her. She'd not realized he'd awakened. "This kinsman of yours that arrived two days ago."

Chrisainne lifted herself off the man, threw a leg over him and strad-dled him. She wanted him to see her breasts clearly, and she was careful to straddle his limp manhood, both distractions she knew how to use well. She said, "A distant kinsman, my lord."

"And what does this distant kinsman want?"

She felt his manhood coming to life, knew there was no need to en-courage him in his distraction. "To meet with you, my lord. Beyond that, I know nothing."

"But you know of the man."

A messenger from King Valso, he was here to propose a face-to-face meeting between the two clan leaders. She would be foolish to display too much knowledge of such matters. Valso wanted her to ensure that the messenger got a private audience with BlakeDown. Beyond that, it was up to the messenger to make the meeting happen. She said, "I be-lieve he has the king's favor, and is a trusted confidant."

"He has the king's ear?"

"I know little of these matters, my lord." She turned on her blush. "I am merely a woman, after all. But I do recall my father speaking of him, said he spent quite a bit of time in the king's presence."

BlakeDown considered that carefully, nodded and said, "Then I'll have him summoned before me."

Valso wanted it to be a *private* meeting. "Would that be wise, my lord? A public summons."

BlakeDown's eyes narrowed in thought for several heartbeats. "You're a smart, little one. Yes, a public meeting between The Penda and a messenger of The Decouix, word of that would spread quickly. We'll make it a private meeting, just this messenger and me. And you'll arrange it."

"Yes, my lord."

His manhood had grown fully erect. He lifted her hips and shoved it into her, jammed it into her painfully. Oh well, she'd try to pretend he was the stable boy.

20

The Schemes of the Witch

AFTER THE BATTLE in the circle with Jerst, Morgin staggered down to the lake and washed off the sweat and blood and dirt, stripped down completely and washed his clothing as well. Truly exhausted, he staggered back to his tent, lay down on his blanket and slept for a couple of hours.

He awoke to the smells of fire roasted meat, found Yim and Branaugh waiting outside his tent in the fading light of dusk with a hearty meal and bandages for his wounds. Yim fed him while Branaugh salved the cuts and slashes on his arms and legs; he winced and grunted as she stitched up a particularly nasty one in his side. But both young women remained completely silent, Yim without her usual girlish chatter, and Branaugh without her usual probing and challenging questions. They kept their heads bowed, wouldn't meet his eyes, refused to respond to his comments, and answered a direct question with little more than a grunt. So he ate mostly in silence, trying to think through his new situation, occasionally thinking out loud and talking to himself. When he finished the meal and Branaugh finished her ministrations, she and Yim scurried away almost fearfully. He went back to his blanket.

He awoke well after sunrise and crawled out of his tent. Carefully placed just outside the tent flap he found a bow stave wrapped in oiled cloth. Since joining the whitefaces he'd felt naked without a good Benesh'ere longbow at hand, really a remnant of Morddon's memories more than his own. And he vaguely remembered mumbling during the meal the previous evening that he'd have to get a good bow stave and make one. Branaugh must have paid more attention to the off-hand comment than he had.

He examined the stave carefully. It was the highest quality of yew, fine-grained, and properly dried. He'd heard that the townsfolk of Norlakton cut such staves to Benesh'ere specifications, then dried them carefully and traded with the whitefaces for good steel. He ate a light breakfast of jerky and journeycake and water, then sat down in front of his tent to work on the bow.

Making a bow took great care and careful concentration. He began shaping it with his knife, cautiously removing only a tiny sliver with each stroke. Any mistake that removed too much wood would render the stave useless, or result in a bow of inferior quality. So he always removed less than he thought necessary and cautiously edged his way slowly toward the finished product. He'd long ago learned to be patient with such work. Centuries of making such bows had taught him patience. Centuries of—

That thought wasn't his, so he cut it off abruptly and shouted, "No."

Every whiteface within earshot paused and looked his way. Yim, waiting patiently nearby, jumped to her feet, crossed the distance between them at a running shuffle, stopped in front of him, bowed and said breathlessly, "Does the SteelMaster wish for something?"

He almost snarled sarcastically, *No, the SteelMaster does not wish for something.* But he shouldn't take his frustration out on the poor girl, so he merely said, "Yes. I want you to call me Morgin, and please stop referring to me in the third person like I'm not here." It had come out more harshly than he'd intended.

She blushed and lowered her eyes. "Master Chagarin might think that a sign of disrespect. He might not like—"

"Tell Master Chagarin I ordered you to. The SteelMaster ordered you to call him Morgin. And tell all the other girls they're to do the same. Tell everyone they're to do the same." Again, his frustration had made it come out harsh.

She bowed. "Yes, SteelMaster—uh, Morgin." She scurried away fearfully

Oddly enough, while the camp had come fully awake, no whiteface came near him. There were more than seven thousand of them going about their daily business, and yet they gave him and his tent a very wide berth. Near midmorning Yim and Branaugh approached him, stopped a few paces away and bowed their heads. Branaugh said, "If the SteelMaster will permit, we'll—"

Morgin interrupted her. "Did Yim tell you what I said, that I wish to be simply called Morgin?"

Yim blurted out, "I did tell them, but they don't believe me."

"Believe her," Morgin said to Branaugh, and he thought he caught a hint of a smile on her lips. But it disappeared quickly.

"Very well," she said. "If Morgin will permit—"

"And please stop addressing me in the third person."

"Very well . . . Morgin. We've come to pack up your belongings."

"Why?"

"We have a tent more appropriate to your station."

"But I like this tent just fine."

"But it's not—"

"No," Morgin snapped.

She described his new tent, a pavilion even grander than that she and Harriok shared. He liked his little tent, and a streak of frustrated stubbornness crawled up from his gut, so he shook his head and said, "I'm not moving. I'm staying right here."

Branaugh turned to Yim, though when she spoke to the young girl her words were clearly meant for Morgin. "Did I not tell you all he would be stubborn about this?"

Morgin spent the morning sitting in front of his tent, working on the bow, and slowly, little by little, the whitefaces stopped taking a wide detour around him. It started with one of the young girls rushing past him on some errand. She stopped abruptly, looked at him fearfully, realizing she'd unintentionally breached whatever sacred space they'd all decided to adopt about the SteelMaster. Morgin laughed, shook his head and said, "I won't bite."

She giggled and hurried on.

By noon the movement of whitefaces around his tent was that of a normal, large Benesh'ere camp, though he did notice the Benesh'ere women now gave him odd looks in passing, the same coy looks barmaids used when they wanted to make a little coin on their backs. A young girl passing by gave him that look now, then turned and walked away, a little extra sway to her hips. He watched her recede into the middle of the camp, couldn't help but find her attractive.

"She's a looker, ain't she?"

Morgin turned his head and looked up to find Delaga, Fantose, Baldrak and Jack the Lesser standing over him. They'd approached from behind his tent and he hadn't seen them coming. Fantose nudged Delaga in the ribs and said, "She's wondering what kind of steel the SteelMaster has between his legs."

Delaga answered him with, "Blasted SteelMaster! Every woman in camp's wondering the same thing."

Baldrak shook his head sadly and sat down as Fantose said, "Me own wife's wondering at it." Fantose plopped down beside Baldrak and continued. "Sad day when a man can't count on his wife pleasuring him because she's all atwitter about some SteelMaster."

For the first time since the fight with Jerst Morgin relaxed. "You're not going to treat me like some god?" he asked.

Baldrak considered that for a moment. "We never had a SteelMaster before. We don't know how to treat you."

"Well, how about like you always did?"

Fantose's eyes narrowed in careful thought. "So I should come over and spit on you and kick you a few times like I did when you first come to us?"

They all got a good laugh out of that. When the laughter died, Jack asked, "What will you do now?"

Morgin didn't understand. "What do you mean by that?"

"You're now free to do as you wish," Jack said. "To go where you will. No one will hinder a SteelMaster."

Morgin considered that and shook his head. "I'm a wanted man in the clans, with a price on my head. Any clansman can kill me without penalty."

Jack's eyes narrowed and he said, "Oh, I wouldn't be too certain of that."

Whether that was a statement of confidence in his ability to defend himself—after all, he had defended himself against the warmaster—or an implicit declaration that the whitefaces would seek retribution if someone killed a SteelMaster, Morgin could not be sure. Morgin said, "In any case, I'd prefer it not be known outside the tribe that a plainface is among you, and especially that a SteelMaster is among you."

All four of them nodded thoughtfully at that, and Jack said, "We'll spread the word. But what do we do about the *twoname*?"

Val! Morgin had completely forgotten about him. "What does he know?"

"Nothing," Jack said. "We've kept him in a tent under guard."

Morgin considered that carefully. Deep inside he knew he could not spend the rest of his days with these whitefaces, these friends of his, though they probably hadn't yet realized that. "He's a friend," Morgin said. "Tell him Jerst killed me in the circle of stones. Keep him under guard in a tent as far away from the Forge Hall as possible. Then, when we go back out onto the sands in the fall, let him go."

Delaga said, "Plainfaces come among us quite regularly, so we need to make sure you always look like one of us. Yer taller than most plainfaces, tall enough to pass for a short whiteface."

Fantose added, "Just keep yer hood up, don't let no one see yer face."

Baldrak chimed in, "And wear gloves or gauntlets. Don't let them see yer hands."

Fantose leaned toward him conspiratorially. "And you know, you might do me a favor. Pleasure me wife, but do a really bad job of it."

Delaga thought that was the funniest thing, but Jack asked again, "So what will you do?"

Morgin looked pointedly at Baldrak. "I think I'd like to work with some smiths on some steel, see what I can really do." He looked at the bow stave in his hands. "But first I think I'll finish this bow."

Fantose eyed the stave and gave him a sour look.

"What's bothering you?" Morgin asked.

Fantose grumbled, "Waste of a good stave."

Jack put a fatherly hand on Morgin's shoulder and said, "He means that while you may be a SteelMaster, when it comes to making a bow, and using a bow . . ."

Delaga finished for him. "You ain't no whiteface."

"So only a whiteface can make and shoot a bow."

Jack shrugged uncomfortably. "It takes a lot of knowledge to make a proper longbow. And a lot of strength to pull one. Don't be disappointed."

"I'm strong enough," Morgin said. "And I'm going to make the bow of a proper size for me, not a whiteface. And I've made bows before. I have the knowledge."

Fantose's eyes narrowed. "When did you learn to make a proper whiteface longbow?"

Morgin almost answered, but held his tongue as he realized it was an answer from a dream. But in that moment he realized that hiding from his dreams had never served him well, so maybe it was time to embrace them, especially if he was going to use them to find the Unnamed King. He said, "I learned about twelve centuries ago, before the Great Clan Wars."

The four whitefaces went silent as they pondered that, uneasy looks on their faces.

Morgin continued. "In any case, I'm tired of goat." He held up the stave. "I'm going to finish this bow, then do a little hunting. Anyone care to join me?"

••••

Tulellcoe's horse crested a small rise southwest of Lake Savin. Built centuries ago on the peak of a distant hill, Castle SavinCourt commanded the countryside. Even larger than Elhiyne, its parapets, ramparts and bulwarks lent it a decidedly formidable air.

Tulellcoe and Cort let their horses walk at a leisurely pace. They followed a road little more than a cart path, deep ruts forcing them to keep to the edge of the road where they found much better footing.

"What do you think?" he asked Cort, gauging the distance to SavinCourt. "Mid-afternoon?"

She stood up in her stirrups and arched her back, stretching the kinks of a long ride out of her muscles. "Yes, mid-afternoon, or even earlier."

At noon they were close enough that they decided to continue on without stopping for lunch. They found the gates of the castle open, a continuous stream of carts, people on foot and mounted riders coming and going. The sergeant at the gate recognized Cort. "Why, it's the Balenda!" He bowed his head. "Lady Cortien, are you expected?"

"No," she said. "We were just riding by, and are a bit tired of trail rations."

The sergeant eyed Tulellcoe, obviously not recognizing him, so Cort said, "This is Tulellcoe et Elhiyne. Lord Eglahan knows him well."

The sergeant's back stiffened, and he bowed from the waist. "Lord Tulellcoe. I'll send a runner to let Lord Eglahan know you're here. Do you need a guide?"

Cort answered him. "No, I know the way well."

SavinCourt occupied the better part of the hill, with the inner keep at its crest, and while much of it sprawled outside the outer bulwarks, the interior contained what amounted to a small city. This wasn't the first time Tulellcoe had come to SavinCourt, but without Cort's greater knowledge of the place, he might have had to search a bit to find the inner keep.

Eglahan awaited them there. "Tulellcoe, Cort," he said as he descended the steps from the main entrance. "What brings you to SavinCourt?"

Tulellcoe said, "Just passing through, and we're hoping you can provide us with a soft bed and a decent meal."

"Of course," Eglahan said. "Have you eaten anything today?"

"Just some jerky and journeycake this morning."

Eglahan ordered up a hearty lunch from the kitchen and they talked while they ate. Tulellcoe asked Eglahan, "We've been away from Elhiyne for more than a year, but I've been hearing rumors of disunity in the Lesser Clans."

Eglahan's eyes narrowed warily. "There is some disagreement, perhaps a bit more than usual."

He had clearly chosen his words carefully, spoken as one diplomat to another. Tulellcoe speared a piece of cheese with a knife, and said, "Come now. Speak freely. We've known each other far too long for you to fear I'll be carrying tales to Olivia."

Eglahan rubbed the top of his bald skull. "There is a fearful schism growing between Penda and Elhiyne, and both Olivia and BlakeDown seem bent on provoking one another."

Cort asked, "How so?"

Eglahan hesitated and glanced at Tulellcoe, clearly reluctant to say the wrong thing in the presence of a member of the ruling family of Elhiyne. He spoke carefully. "At the meeting of the Lesser Council Olivia proposed Brandon as warmaster of all the Lesser Tribes."

Tulellcoe couldn't believe what he'd heard. Cort groaned and said, "That is poking the beehive with a stick."

But something didn't add up, so Tulellcoe said, "But that is such a blatant provocation, and my aunt is not that blind."

Cort raised a questioning eyebrow, so Tulellcoe added, "Yes, she's a scheming old woman who'll use any of us to gain even the slightest advantage, but she's neither foolish nor stupid, especially not when it comes to BlakeDown. She's always known exactly what levers to push with him."

Eglahan rubbed his beard and his eyes narrowed in thought. "You do have a point there. But she is provoking him. There is no doubt of that. So the question is: why? What does she hope to accomplish?"

21

A Journey Remembered

AT THE KNOCK on the door of her hut, Rhianne looked up from the herbs she was preparing. She stood, crossed the small room and opened the door. Fat John stood there, his hand raised, ready to knock again. "Ah, Mistress Syllith, good day to you. Lady Jinella wants to see you."

Rhianne asked, "The Elhiyne witch?" She tried to hide the fear in her voice, but failed.

The innkeeper simply said, "Aye, but you've nothing to fear from her."

Rhianne shook her head. "For simple people such as you and me, gaining the attention of a noblewoman is never wise."

"True. But you can't avoid it, mistress."

Rhianne had acquired a shawl, simple homespun, but still a nice touch that added a hint of formality to her attire. She put it on now, closed the door to her hut and walked beside Fat John down the dirt, main street of Norlakton.

Rhianne knew of Jinella, was thankful she'd never met her face-to-face. A Tosk of high rank but middling power, Olivia had spoken of her as a possible bride for one of her grandsons. If she was now *esk et* Elhiyne, then she had likely married either JohnEngine or Brandon.

As they walked down the street, Fat John said, "She's taken up residence at a table in the common room. Sittin' there like a queen on her throne, she is. Ruinin' me business, she is. Be glad when she goes."

As they approached the inn Rhianne looked carefully at her hands. The illusion she had spent so much time crafting gave them the appearance of middle age, with the creases and lines and calluses of a woman just a step or two above the status of a peasant. The spell would do the same for her face.

When she stepped into the common room, Jinella's power hovered at the edge of her senses, like a cat waiting patiently for movement in the brush where a mouse might hide. Rhianne almost reacted instinctively, almost fortified the spell, but the spell's subtlety might be broken by such an overt act, so she willed herself to calmness and didn't touch her power.

Rhianne hadn't been in the presence of another witch since she'd left Durin, and she sensed now that she could command far more power than this Jinella. That surprised her; she herself had been a witch of middling power, but she realized now that she had grown, that her power had blossomed and matured far beyond the simple spells she'd learned as a young girl. That reminded her of the blade, and she wondered if resisting its pull had strengthened her power, just as a blacksmith's muscles grew and thickened with use.

"Come, child," Jinella said.

Rhianne hesitated, surprised at the audacity of a woman who would call another woman, apparently twice her age, *child*.

Jinella misinterpreted her hesitation as fear. "Don't be afraid. I won't bite. Come and sit with me." With a wave of her hand she indicated a stool at her table.

Rhianne kept her eyes downcast as she shuffled across the floor, imitating the fear-filled walk she'd seen Braunye adopt so many times. She stopped at the table.

"Sit down," Jinella said impatiently. "Don't be so fearful."

Rhianne sat down on the stool and kept her eyes downcast, though out of curiosity she looked up for just an instant. Jinella was quite beautiful, blond hair, shining blue eyes, and she actually had a pleasant smile hidden beneath the arrogance. Rhianne remembered looking beautiful herself, what seemed ages ago. But now, even without the illusion that added decades to her age, she had none of the trappings of a young noblewoman, and a piece of her longed to return to that life, to be young and beautiful again.

Jinella said, "I'm here to understand your capabilities. We take our responsibility as rulers of these people quite seriously, and would be most displeased were we to find a charlatan preying upon them."

"Charlatan, Your Ladyship?" Rhianne asked, knowing her best defense would be to pretend to a very limited education. "I don't know what that word means."

"A faker," Jinella said. "An imposter with no real power who mixes false potions and takes advantage of these people."

Rhianne didn't answer, though her confidence grew as she realized she could easily fool this witch with her far greater command of power, and with the spells she had so carefully crafted. Jinella, like any witch, could sense the magnitude of another witch's power. But Rhianne had learned to mask her power, had learned to cast a veil that hid her own capabilities from other witches, and allowed them to glimpse only the tiniest hint of her abilities. In Mistress Syllith, Jinella would find a low-level hedge witch of rather limited strength, but not a charlatan.

Jinella quizzed her for a good portion of the afternoon, asked her to demonstrate her *most powerful* spells. Rhianne pulled out a few spells young witches were taught in their first lessons, and pretended to struggle mightily to summon even that limited ability. Jinella sent her back to her hut to bring samples of the herbs and potions she'd prepared. She didn't bring anything strong or powerful, nothing she might use on a truly bad injury. Jinella examined them carefully and seemed satisfied. Yes, she would leave under the impression Norlakton had a middle-aged witch with only a very limited command of true power, and that would suite Rhianne well. No one would learn Rhianne esk et Elhiyne still lived. No one, especially not that old witch Olivia.

"Well, Mistress Syllith," Jinella concluded. "You'll be a good thing for this village. A good sized village like this needs a healer, and should you need help, don't hesitate to call on those of us more capable." And with that, she dismissed Rhianne.

She walked back to her hut, careful to keep her eyes downcast, the meek and mild commoner. And not until she stepped through the door and closed it behind her did she relax. She sat down at the small table that served as a place to dine, and as a work place for preparing her herbs and potions, and there, once again alone, she breathed a sigh of relief.

But wait! Where had Braunye gotten to?

"I sent her on a meaningless errand."

Rhianne gasped and jumped up from her chair; only then did she see the shadowy presence in the corner of the room. She sensed the vast power it commanded, though she understood she sensed it only because the witch before her wanted her to.

"She thinks it was you who sent her on the errand, so when she returns, don't confuse the poor girl by denying it . . . Mistress Syllith. But shouldn't I call you Rhianne?"

Rhianne gasped again, and the shadowy presence floated toward her. "You have grown in power since we last stood face-to-face, grown considerably."

The shadowy presence snapped her fingers; the veil of illusion hiding her features vanished, and before her stood a tiny woman dressed in black from head to foot, a veil of thin material now hiding her features. She lifted the veil and said, "And don't worry. I won't give you away to grandmother."

Rhianne blinked her eyes, and had to look twice to realize NickoLot stood before her. "Nicki," she said, and rushed forward to wrap her arms around the tiny woman. And then it hit her: Nicki, AnnaRail, Roland and JohnEngine, people she loved.

"Oh Nicki," she cried, tears streaming down her cheeks. "I miss you so much."

"Then why don't you come back?"

Rhianne released her and shook her head. "I can't. I can no longer tolerate that old woman's meddling."

"But AnnaRail and Roland and JohnEngine all miss you; they mourn you."

"Give me time," Rhianne pleaded. She stepped away from NickoLot, threw out her arms and said, "Look at me."

NickoLot raised a sardonic eyebrow. "You look like a common laborer."

"No!" Rhianne said, spinning about once to take in the entirety of her small domain. "Not that. Oh, yes, I'd love to wear beautiful dresses and look pretty again. But I'm doing something good for these people, doing it without the aid of the clan—doing it in spite of the clan."

NickoLot hesitated, and looked skeptically about the small hut.

Rhianne continued. "When I'm ready I'll get a message to you somehow, and you can tell them I'm still alive. But right now, Olivia would just find some way to use me. And I can't let that happen anymore. I need to be my own woman. So please, keep my secret for now."

"But what of Morgin? Why don't you go find him wherever he's gotten to?"

"Oh, Nicki, you know he's dead."

"I don't believe it," NickoLot said with absolute finality.

Rhianne hugged her again. "I'm certain I would sense his soul in some way if he were still alive. But there's nothing; all I sense is that cursed sword. You have to accept reality."

"You sense the sword? Where is it?"

"I don't know. I can't sense direction or distance. I'm not even sure if it remains on the Mortal Plane. But how did you find me?"

"I'm here with Jinella. Mother thought it would be good for me to get away from grandmother for a while, and I must admit, she was right. But you've spent quite a bit of time at the inn, haven't you? And you've practiced some magic there, right?"

"Ah," Rhianne said. "I see. You recognized the residual scent of my magic."

Nicki smiled, the first time she'd shown any happy emotion that day. "Yes, so I went sniffing about. And since Jinella has never met you, she didn't. She's Brandon's new wife, you know, and I rather like her; she's quite a pleasant person."

Nicki helped her dry her tears and they spent a brief time together. Nicki promised she'd keep her secret. But after she left, all Rhianne could think about was the strangeness in her eyes, old eyes for such a young girl, very old eyes.

••••

Morgin moved carefully through the undergrowth of the forest, strung bow in hand, an arrow nocked, ready to pull the bow string back and release it. He moved with Morddon's Benesh'ere stealth and reflexes. Deer droppings not two paces in front of him told him he was close to his prey, a large buck he'd spotted from a nearby hill. He'd circled to approach the animal from downwind. Like Morgin, Harriok and Jack the Lesser were tired of goat, and they'd decided venison steaks would make for a nice change. With summer approaching, the deer and elk had sought higher pastures to graze on spring's bounty, so the three of them had ridden south of the lake, and then quite a ways up the side of Attunhigh.

About two hundred paces distant a raspberry bush shaking violently caught his attention, and he glimpsed the buck's rack visible above it. He looked to the left where Jack stood crouched on another game trail. He raised a hand, caught Jack's eye, pointed two fingers forward to let Jack know he'd spotted the buck. Jack nodded, so Morgin slowly turned his head to the right. There, Harriok nodded to indicate he too had seen Morgin's signal.

The three of them moved forward one careful step at a time. Even Jack had finally admitted Morgin moved with the stealth of a whiteface, and that appeared to be proof enough that Morgin had told the truth when he'd spoken of living through the Great Clan Wars in the soul of a Benesh'ere warrior.

Morgin was about a hundred paces from the buck when it wandered out from behind the raspberry bush, nibbling on ripe berries. He had a good line of sight to the buck, so he rose from his crouch with exaggerated care. Since he had been the first to spot the buck, the first shot was his, so Harriok and Jack remained in a crouch.

With the same, slow wary motions, Morgin drew back the bow string and raised the bow. He sighted down the length of the arrow, sighted on a spot just behind the buck's shoulder. His arrow would pierce its heart, giving it a quick, clean end. But something in the far distance caught his eye, and he hesitated. It hadn't been a movement, or a flash of light, but something that had triggered a memory deep in his subconscious.

He lowered the bow and took in the sight of two spires of rock, two sharp peaks side-by-side in the far distance. He'd seen them before in a distant memory, though he couldn't recall when. And too, he had never been this high up the side of Attunhigh before, at least not in this life.

That was the key that brought his memories back. He had seen those peaks through Morddon's eyes, seen them as he'd ridden down the mountain after laying Aethon to rest in his crypt. And the memory was not a recollection stolen from the Benesh'ere whose soul he'd haunted. No, this was a memory of Morgin's, his and his alone, a memory acquired by looking through the ancient warrior's eyes.

An arrow hissed through the air and thumped into the buck's side. It jumped, trumpeted a painful cry, staggered and fell to its side. Harriok cried out, "Good shot, Jack," and the two of them ran forward to make sure the buck was finished.

Morgin remained still, transfixed by the two spires in the distance. If he moved south a few leagues, the two peaks might appear separated exactly as they had appeared twelve centuries ago. Morddon had ridden down from Aethon's interment in sadness, while Morgin had concentrated on memorizing every feature of the land, every peak, every spire, though he'd memorized only features of rock and granite that would not—had not changed in all that time. A league or two south of the Lake of Sorrows, he guessed, and then higher up the side of Attunhigh, and he'd be standing on the trail Morddon had followed down from the mountain that sad day. With a dozen other such reference points rolling around inside his head, Morgin realized he might, after all this time, be able to backtrack up that trail and find that crypt.

••••

As they rounded a sharp bend in the trail, BlakeDown reined in his horse. Tharsk stood above them, a cold, black monolith carved from the solid granite of the mountain face. He always marveled at the fortress that commanded Methula.

The trail too had been chipped out of the solid stone of the mountain. Travelers tended to hug the uphill side away from the precipitous edge, and centuries of traffic—the constant wear of boots and hooves and cartwheels—had worn the rock there into a smooth and almost glassy surface, while the edge nearest the drop remained rough and une-ven. The trail skirted the base of the fortress wall for a good distance, then entered the black shadow at the mouth of a tunnel, part of the fortress itself. Any traveler wishing to cross the Worshipers through the Pass at Methula must either pass into that tunnel, or climb the sheer rock of the fortress wall above it, and those in the fortress would have an easy time dislodging such a fool.

It had taken quite a bit of effort to arrange this meeting. The Vodah messenger had ridden back and forth between Durin and Penda several times, all in secret, carrying messages sealed by powerful magics.

Valso frequently went unseen by any but his closest advisors for days at a time. So it had been easy for the King of the Greater Clans to sneak away, to arrange a few ruses to leave the impression he remained closeted in the palace in Durin, while in fact he had ridden to Tharsk. But BlakeDown had ruled Penda for more than thirty years in a very public fashion, so doing something like that would have been impossible for him. Instead, he'd arranged a hunting trip to Methula.

He and PaulStaff had an agreement that he could hunt the bighorn sheep near Tharsk, and PaulStaff could hunt the wild boar that roamed the forests on the river Ella. Of course, they each required the other to give notice well in advance of such an encroachment on their lands, and to keep their numbers small enough that there would be no question of an armed incursion. In any case, PaulStaff was a boot-licker, and wouldn't dare deny him. But such a hunting trip got him relatively high into the pass at Methula, within an easy ride of Tharsk.

He'd selected the members of his hunting party from those he knew to be loyal and discreet, and they'd set up a base camp a few hours' ride from Tharsk. But hunting the big sheep couldn't be done in large groups, so each morning he selected three of his liege men to accompany him, then set out for a day of hunting. They'd actually hunted the sheep for two days now, and bagged one kill. But on this, the third day, BlakeDown had selected three companions whom he could trust implic-itly, and they rode directly to Tharsk. They could spend a good three hours at the fortress, and still return before dark with tales of an unsuc-cessful day of hunting.

BlakeDown looked up to the battlements at the top of the fortress wall. He saw a few dim shadows standing there, so he called out, using the false name they'd agreed upon. "I am a simple hunter named Doagla. I and my friends seek shelter for a few hours."

A voice from above said politely, "You may enter the tunnel."

A portcullis just within the shadows of the tunnel rose with a clanking rattle of chains dragging across stone. Behind it another portcullis rose slowly, and behind that another, and another, and another. When the way was clear, BlakeDown spurred his horse forward and his companions followed. Behind them the portcullises descended with the same noisy scrape of steel chains on stone, and BlakeDown realized they were at the Decouix's mercy. Perhaps he'd just have them murdered. They wouldn't be the first men to disappear in the vastness of Methula.

The tunnel followed the curve of the mountain, and at its center they found a massive stone portal slowly opening with the grind of old hinges echoing in the close air. The portal let them into a circular courtyard open to the sky, surrounded on all sides by high walls cut from the same black rock as the tunnel, with another portcullis on the opposite side of the courtyard. Valso awaited him there, standing confidently and smiling. "Lord BlakeDown. Thank you for coming. It is a pleasure to see you again after so long."

"The pleasure is mine, Your Majesty," BlakeDown said, lying as easily as Valso.

He dismounted, and he and Valso shook hands, though BlakeDown did not bend the knee, for Valso was not his king. Valso showed no displeasure at the omission.

He led BlakeDown into the fortress proper to a small, comfortable room with a large hearth containing a blazing fire. Even with summer approaching, the mountain air held a decided chill. The room also contained a table onto which a hearty meal of meat, cheese, bread and ale had been placed, though the table contained only two chairs.

Valso smiled charmingly and said, "My men will entertain your men while you and I share this repast."

"Excellent," BlakeDown said, sitting down at the table, not waiting for Valso.

Valso's men ushered BlakeDown's companions out of the room and closed the heavy plank door. Valso threw the latch on the door, then returned to the table and sat down opposite BlakeDown.

They ate, and spoke of hunting, and the bighorn sheep, and other subjects about which neither of them really cared. A goodly amount of time passed before Valso casually said, "I've heard the annual meeting of the Lesser Council didn't go so well."

BlakeDown grunted angrily and wiped grease from his chin with his sleeve. "That old witch Olivia, she's a thorn in all our sides."

"Aye," Valso said, "We do have that in common."

"Isn't that about all we have in common?"

Valso considered that for a moment, then delicately wiped his chin with a linen napkin and stood. He turned his back on BlakeDown, walked to the hearth and held out his hands, warming them. "Perhaps we have more in common than you think."

"Like what?"

Valso turned to face him. "I would think you'd like to see that thorn removed as much as I do."

BlakeDown prompted him, "And?"

Valso grinned. "And we'd both benefit from a more stable and less disruptive rule in the Lesser Clans. I would greatly like to see an ally on the throne of the Lesser Clans."

BlakeDown's heart raced as he said, "The Lesser Clans have no throne."

Valso shrugged. "That can easily be changed. The Lesser Clans can have a throne and a king. But it would have to be the right king."

"You would support the right king?"

Valso smiled and nodded. "As long as that king swore fealty to me, yes I would. But that king must also help rid me of that thorn we spoke of."

BlakeDown changed the subject and they talked of other things for a time, more matters about which neither of them really cared. When the time came to leave, they both stood and clasped hands.

"You have given me much to think on," BlakeDown said. "We should communicate further on these matters." And then, for the first time in centuries, a leader of one of the Lesser Clans bent the knee and kissed the hand of the King of the Greater Clans.

22

Striking the Steel

CHAGARIN HAD CALLED Morgin to the Forge Hall where all the smiths had gathered, and as he walked into the room, the smiths all stepped back and waited expectantly. They'd laid an array of swords on one of the workbenches, naked blades, unsheathed and shining in the glow from the forges. The smiths looked at Morgin, then the blades on the workbench, then back at Morgin again, and he realized they wanted him to do whatever it was a SteelMaster did.

Morgin said to Chagarin, "I don't know what it means to be a Steel-Master."

The shoulders of all the smiths slumped with disappointment. Morgin knew he should at least try, so he walked up to the workbench and picked up the nearest sword. It had a good heft and a fine balance, so he held it upright and tapped his fingernail against the blade. The tone it emitted was pure and sweet, and a single note resonated in his soul clean and crisp.

He laid that blade down and picked up the next. He pinged it with his fingernail, and it too rang clear and pure. He took up that sound with his soul, fed it power and life, and it spoke to him of many battles and the chaos of war. He let the note die as he turned to the smiths. "This blade has taken many lives."

The smiths nodded in unison.

He tested each blade that way, and each blade spoke to him, some with the voice of a kind woman, others with the command of a warmaster on the battlefield. One blade, though, rang with a harsh and guttural tone. He crossed the room and handed that blade to Chagarin with the words, "This blade is flawed."

Chagarin accepted the blade and nodded.

Baldrak said, "Try commanding the steel as you did in the circle."

Morgin turned and looked back at the workbench covered with blades. It was about five paces distant, so he concentrated on the first blade he'd touched there. He held out his open hand and said, "Come."

The blade trembled, visible only as a faint shimmer in the reflected glow of the forges, as if it wanted to obey him, but found it difficult. The blade next to it trembled also, so Morgin concentrated on the one blade to the exclusion of the others. Off to one side he heard the creak of wood straining under pressure, but he ignored that and focused his will on the blade. Several of the blades on the bench near it trembled, so he redoubled his effort to focus only on the one.

The smiths stood silently watching him, almost as if they feared any sound they might make would dampen the SteelMaster's power. And in that silence the room was actually alive with sounds: the crackle of the fires in the forges, wood creaking and straining as if under enormous pressure. The smiths were all focused on Morgin, mute and silently watching him, not working at any of the heavy wooden benches, so no wood should be straining so. The silence ended with the sound of wood tearing and splintering somewhere behind him.

"Morgin, duck."

At Baldrak's shout Morgin let his knees buckle, dropping to the floor and spinning to see what had happened. A massive anvil, splinters of wood still clinging to it, almost took off his head as it sailed past him and thudded into the hard dirt floor. The sword on which he'd focused his concentration shot toward him, the other swords on the bench following it, all tumbling end-over-end. Morgin hugged the dirt floor and willed the steel to stillness as one blade—he no longer knew which—stuck its point in the ground near his hand. The other swords clattered on top of him in a heap, a hammer thumped into his ribs, and other smithing tools slammed into the pile of swords and tools atop him.

It ended abruptly, and into the silence that ensued Chagarin whispered, "Is anyone hurt."

"Not me," one of the smiths said.

"Nor I," said another

As each of the smiths chimed in, Morgin took stock of himself; bruises definitely, but no serious wounds. "I'm ok too," he said, trying to rise, tools and swords clattering off him as he did so.

Baldrak lent him a hand, helped him get to his feet, looked at him closely for a moment and said, "Bloody SteelMaster. Could of got us all killed." Then he burst into laughter.

The other smiths joined him, and Morgin did too, his stomach almost cramping he laughed so hard. One of the smiths slapped him on the back and said, "Next time you try that, make sure I ain't in the room."

That brought on even more laughter.

••••

Morgin swung the heavy sledge high over his head and brought it down onto the block of cherry red steel. Welded to the block was a thick rod of steel a bit longer than a man's arm, glowing red hot where it met the block, but cool and dark at the other end where Chagarin gripped it. By tradition, when striking a sword, the master smith stood on the north side of the largest anvil in the Forge Hall. Morgin, one of three strikers, stood on the west side, while the other two completed the remaining points of the compass.

When Morgin's sledge struck the hot metal it produced a muted clang; steel heated to the point of softness did not ring as clearly as cold metal. The striker next to him brought his sledge down, followed by the third striker. The three of them created a three-beat tempo, with a slight pause before Morgin again raised his sledge to repeat it. During one such pause, as Morgin swung his sledge high over his head, Chagarin rotated the block onto its side.

Clang clang clang . . . clang clang clang . . . clang clang clang.

It was mindless work, and Morgin relished it for that. He swung the sledge time and time again, his mind drifting through a hundred different thoughts. At moments like this, he sometimes mourned Rhianne, and vowed revenge on Valso for her murder. But that pain was too raw to dwell on, so he thought on that glimpse he'd had of the two spires, and his long-ago memory of them. Buried within him he had a collage of such memories, but he could retrieve only the memory of the two spires. He certainly retained other reference points that might help him find Aethon's tomb; he'd already ventured out twice on his own in attempts to find them, and twice now he'd failed. Only the two spires stood out as distinct and well defined. The rest swirled about in his thoughts, confusingly tangled into an ever-changing pattern of mixed memories. Perhaps each memory would coalesce properly only when he actually looked upon the feature he'd memorized so long ago.

Clang clang clang . . . clang clang clang . . . clang clang clang.

Chagarin turned the block on its side several times, and it lengthened a tiny bit each time a sledge slammed into it. But it was not yet time to strike it toward its final shape as a blade, and the cherry red glow had dimmed. When it was next Morgin's turn to swing his sledge he held back and said, "The color's not right. And it's time for a fold."

Chagarin nodded, lifted the block on the end of the bar and shoved it into the forge. As they waited for the color of the steel to return to bright, cheery red, Morgin put down his sledge and lifted a heavy steel wedge mounted on the end of a long iron handle. Chagarin removed the block from the forge, placed it on the anvil again, and Morgin placed the point of the heavy wedge on top of it in the middle of the block. The other two strikers hammered down on the top of the wedge several times, slowly forcing the wedge through the block of metal. When they'd almost, but not quite, separated the block into two pieces, Chagarin and Morgin used tongs to fold the block back on itself. Chagarin returned the folded block to the forge and looked at Morgin questioningly. "I can still hear a faint echo of a flaw in the block," Morgin said. "Two or three more folds should eliminate it completely."

Morgin's sense of the steel had grown considerably in recent days, and it had turned into an ability to know exactly when to move on to the next step in the process. The smiths had wanted him to forego the heavy labor of a striker, but with his ancient memories hammering at his thoughts, he wanted to again experience every facet of making a blade.

No one smith made an entire blade. Each man had his own specialty, be it striking the steel, shaping, quenching, finishing the blade, or finishing the hilt. One man might, on his own, make a pot for the cooking fires, or a small knife, but not a blade. A blade required a team effort overseen by Chagarin, and now Morgin with him.

Clang clang clang . . . clang clang clang . . . clang clang clang.

They returned to the rhythm of striking the steel.

••••

Five straight days of striking steel, folding, striking, folding, striking—they'd worked into the night on this fifth day, folding and striking until the last block whispered to Morgin that it was ready. Then he and the smiths all took a dip in the lake to wash off the grime and sweat. He washed his clothes, put on his breeches and carried the rest slung over his shoulder, and in the cool night air his hair had almost dried completely by the time he returned to his tent utterly exhausted. But where his tent had stood he now found a giant pavilion, with Harriok waiting for him at the entrance.

"Where's my tent?" Morgin demanded.

Harriok glanced over his shoulder and looked at the pavilion. "This is your tent."

"Just had to have it your way, eh?"

Harriok winced at Morgin's words. "It's not having it my way that matters. You are the first SteelMaster to come among us in centuries. You freed the spirit of the sands, and righted the first four wrongs before that."

He looked at the pavilion again, then turned back to Morgin and swept his arms out to indicate the entire camp. "You are our future, the end of our exile. You've already given us new heart by telling us it was not we who betrayed the Shahotma, that we stood by him unto the end. Every whiteface walks with their chin held a little higher now. No longer must we bear the burden that history falsely laid upon us. So can you blame us if we try to give you every comfort we can—if we revere you just a little?"

Morgin opened his mouth to protest, but Harriok held up a hand to stop him. "Don't worry. My father and I have spread the word, made everyone aware that we'll only make you uncomfortable if we go too far.

We also pointed out that if we make too much of it, the clans will learn you are with us, and they'll come after you. So it's in every whiteface's best interest to pretend a SteelMaster has not come among us."

Harriok looked back at the pavilion again. "It is a bit much, but please honor us by accepting it."

Harriok didn't wait for an answer, but turned and walked calmly away. For the first time Morgin realized how much he meant to them, realized he let them down by not accepting the honor of their gifts, though he resolved he would only let it go so far.

He ducked under the tent flap and into the pavilion. A small lamp dimly lit the interior, and he saw that a thin curtain divided the tent into two rooms. He unbuckled his sword belt, was about to lay the sheathed blade to one side when he heard another blade slide from its sheath. He reached for the hilt of his sword, but someone behind him laid cold steel on his shoulder; the tip of a sword hovered near his throat just within view. "Don't," Blesset said.

She caressed his cheek with the steel and it glinted in the dim light only a finger's breadth from his eyes. Then the sword's tip rose from his shoulder, and it disappeared as he heard the hiss of a blade slashing through the air. He flinched, waiting for her to attempt to kill him, not wanting to call on the steel unless he had to. When nothing happened after several heartbeats, he turned about slowly, his sheathed sword in his left hand. She stood facing him, holding her blade lowered to her side, and because the lamp behind her made her a black silhouette, he could see nothing of her features.

"SteelMaster," she whispered. "Bah!"

He said, "I don't want to be a SteelMaster—*the* SteelMaster. But the gods haven't given me any choice in the matter."

"You would have me believe they haven't given *us* any choice in the matter. What if I choose to kill you where you stand right this moment? That would be a choice."

"No," Morgin said, "you couldn't. I wouldn't allow your steel to do so."

He tensed, ready to command the steel if she decided to exercise her choice, but she just stood there staring at him, her sword held loosely by her side.

Knowing in his heart she needed to know the truth, he said, "Let me tell you a story." She didn't respond, so he told her of the first five deeds. He told her his story in its entirety, told her of SheelThane, Aiergain, AnneRhianne, WolfDane and Shebasha. He told her of Morddon, Aethon, Gilguard, Metadan and Ellowyn. He told it all.

"So you see," he finished. "I'm not some hero who has quested to right the seven wrongs. I'm just trying to stay alive, and somehow I stumble into each deed. I'm just a fool, that way."

Again, she said nothing, stood there regarding him. But after the longest moment, she turned, and carrying her naked blade at her side, she walked out of the tent. As she'd turned, he'd caught a glimpse of something glistening on her cheek, and he thought it might have been a tear.

23

The Curse of the Benesh'ere

JOKATH HELD OUT his tankard to the bartender. "I'll have another."

Wiping a clay mug with a bar-towel, the bartender shook his head and said, "Not until you clear your tab. No more credit for you."

A tall man leaned on the bar next to Jokath. "How much is his tab?" he asked. "Maybe I'll cover it."

As the bartender said, "Two silvers," Jokath looked at the man carefully. Tall and gangly, blond hair just short of shoulder length, long, blond mustache, its ends waxed and curled.

"Now why would you do that?" Jokath asked.

The blond stranger turned slowly to face him. Jokath looked into his eyes, but something there sent a shiver up his spine, so he looked away. *Inhuman*, Jokath thought, *and dangerous*. He wondered if he should walk away from this, but he could not resist the idea of a little profit.

The stranger spoke in a growl, his voice like the rumble of distant thunder. "I heard you say you've just come up from the south. I'm traveling south for the first time, and I'd like to know what I'll find down there."

Jokath smiled, but knew better than to look again into the stranger's eyes. It wouldn't hurt to give the fellow a little information, especially if he was buying. "I make the trip regularly, and I know the way well. It's part of my business." Jokath didn't add that his business was thievery. He hadn't crossed the line into outright robbery, for the clans tended to hunt highwaymen down and hang them. But small groups were easy prey if they didn't know enough to post a proper guard.

The stranger paid his back debt, ordered two fresh tankards of ale, handed one to Jokath and said, "Let's take a table where we can speak in private."

Jokath spoke at length of every minute detail concerning the Gods Road going south. He knew it well, for he'd haunted it for years, and carefully gave out more facts than were really necessary, stretching the conversation out as much as possible. The longer he spoke, the more tankards the stranger would have to buy to wet his parched tongue.

The stranger didn't drink much, was still nursing his first tankard when Jokath finished his fifth. The stranger had sat quietly listening to his every word, sat there with a strange stillness that seemed almost in-human. There it was again, that word *inhuman*. But Jokath had just men-tioned something that broke the stranger's stillness—though he was now quite drunk and couldn't remember what. The stranger leaned forward, his eyes narrowing, and his voice again reminded Jokath of distant thun-der. "You say Norlakton has a healer now?"

"Yes, yes," Jokath said, his words slurring badly. "Snotty bitch, she is. Turned me down when I offered her good coin for a roll in the hay. Used her cursed magic on me, threatened to turn me into a toad."

"How old is she?"

"Middle aged. Thought she was younger the first time I seen her, but it was dark. Seen her since, and it would have been a waste of good coin."

"How long has she been there?"

"Since early spring."

The stranger smiled, not a pleasant smile, more a nasty grin of antici-pation. He stood. "Come. You look a little wobbly. I'll help you to your room."

Jokath had trouble focusing on the stranger. "Don't have no room. Don't have the coin."

"Well you've earned a room," the stranger said. "But it'll have to be at the inn where I'm staying. This one's too expensive. And we can have a last tankard there before calling it a night."

Jokath stood, had to lean on the table to keep from falling down. "Well I thank you much, kind sir."

The stranger helped Jokath out of the inn and into the street. They turned left and walked with Jokath leaning heavily on the man. Then Jokath remembered that there were no other inns in town. "Wait," he said, halting near the open mouth of a dark alley. "There ain't no other inns here."

"I know," the stranger said, pulling him into the alley.

Jokath saw the moon glint off a blade, then a horrible, intense pain washed through his chest as the knife pierced his heart. His knees gave out and he collapsed to the ground. The stranger leaned over him and wiped the blade on his tunic. Then the stranger turned and left him lying in the mud. And the last thought that crossed his mind before he died was that the stranger's knife had been made of obsidian, and it radiated darkness in a way no simple blade of glass should.

••••

Morgin and Harriok followed the trail of blood through the forest undergrowth northeast of the Lake of Sorrows, tracking on foot, their horses following behind them. It had been pure coincidence that a pheasant had spooked and taken to the air just as Harriok had released his arrow. The pheasant had in turn spooked Harriok's target, a young buck, and it had bolted just an instant before the arrow struck. The arrow pierced the thigh of its left hindquarter, an injury that would eventually kill the animal, but not disable it enough to prevent it from leading them on a leagues-long chase. No hunter left a wounded animal to die slowly. They would track it, find it, dispatch it, and make good use of the meat it provided.

Morgin suspected that if it had been an arrow from his bow it would not have missed. Not that he was better with a bow than Harriok. He was as good, or better, than most clansmen, but any Benesh'ere displayed much more skill with bow and arrow than him. No, something in the steel made his arrows strike true in an uncanny way. He'd begun to suspect the steel warhead on an arrow understood his desire, and somehow found the target regardless of any mischance or ill luck. He kept such thoughts to himself.

They broke out of the undergrowth and onto the Gods Road just south of Gilguard's Ford. Morgin heard the rest of their hunting party not far behind them. He looked up the road and caught a fleeting glimpse of the buck staggering into some undergrowth just north of the Ulbb. "There it is," he shouted, pointing. He climbed into Mortiss's saddle and spurred her forward at an easy gallop.

When he hit the ankle-deep water of the wide ford, Mortiss's hooves sent water spraying ahead of her, splashes of it glinting in the bright summer sun. Once across the ford he reined her in at the edge of the road near the brush where he'd seen the struggling buck. He dismounted and didn't need to tell Mortiss to wait there.

He carried his strung bow in case he might need to down the buck from a distance. But he found the animal just off the road, lying on its side, spent and no longer able to run. He felt a pang of sorrow and pity for it as he thrust his sword into its heart.

He stepped out of the brush. The hunting party had gathered in the road just south of the ford: Jack the Lesser, Jack the Greater, Harriok, and Jerst. He waved an arm and shouted, "Come and help me. This buck's too big for me to handle on my own."

After he'd said it, only then did he recall that his Benesh'ere friends, in their exile, could not cross the ford and stand north of the Ulbb, and he felt shame that he had so callously taunted them, even if not intentionally. In his forgetfulness, he had reminded them of the greatest of all torments for a whiteface. They sat astride their horses waiting for him silently.

He wiped his sword on some leaves and sheathed it. The buck was not the largest he'd downed, so he thought if he gutted it first, he might just be able to lift it onto Mortiss's saddle on his own. He threw a rope over a convenient branch, tied one end about the buck's neck, but could only hoist it just off the ground. He gutted it quickly, and with its weight reduced he managed to hoist it high enough to drape it across Mortiss rump. He stood panting by Mortiss's side for several heartbeats after doing so. He'd damaged the hide and some of the meat in the process, but there'd been no avoiding that. He'd come back for the guts later, since every part of a kill had some use.

He cinched the buck in place with a few short lengths of rope, then walking ahead of Mortiss he led her down to the ford. They crossed it quietly, and when they reached the rest of the hunting party no words were spoken. In silence Jack the Lesser and Jerst lifted the carcass off Mortiss's back and began butchering it. They'd break it up into pieces to distribute among the five of them, making it easier to carry it back to camp.

"Why not," Jack the Greater said loudly, standing with his back to them at the edge of the ford looking north. "Why can't we cross the Ulbb? It's just legend. Has anyone ever challenged it?"

Jack the Lesser, Jerst and Harriok straightened from dismembering the carcass. "Don't," Jack the Lesser said.

Harriok added, "You know it's been tried. And you know what happens."

"That's legend too," Jack the Greater shouted angrily, and he took one step into the ford. "Just tales told around the fire after dinner." He took another step forward, the water of the ford rushing around his ankles. "It hasn't been tried in my time, or my father's time, or my father's father's."

He took another step, then another, then he marched like a soldier going to battle, his footsteps spraying water in front of him much like Mortiss's hooves had. He stopped just short of the center of the ford and turned back to face them. "See," he shouted. "Just tales, stories, legends with no truth to them. Since we never go north of the Ulbb, how do we know we can't?"

He spun and marched further into the ford, and as he crossed its center he started laughing, loud maniacal cries that echoed through the forest. "Just stories," he screamed as he marched toward the north shore. "Tales to fool stupid and foolish whitefaces."

Nothing hindered him or slowed him, and he did not falter as he crossed the entire width of the ford, his cries and shouts growing more unintelligible with each step. "A joke made by kings to fool us all. Skeleton kings and great, giant wolves and enormous half-birds, and dog warriors."

Morgin recognized his references to the distant past, even if the rest of the hunting party did not.

Jack reached the far shore, stepped onto it, put both feet on dry land and stood there with his back to them at the very edge of freedom. Then he turned about, and they all gasped at the sight of his face. Trails of blood streamed down his cheeks from his eyes. More blood streamed down his neck from his ears, and blood flowed freely out his nose and mouth. When he spoke he spit gobbets of thick brown blood, a color that told them the blood had already begun to clot. "You seeeeeee!" he cried, looking up to the heavens, his arms outstretched. "I can stand north of the Ulbb."

He stood there silently for several heartbeats, his arms outstretched, his face turned up toward the heavens as if praying to the gods, then he toppled forward like a tree felled with an ax. He hit the water face down with a mighty splash; his body bobbed in the shallow water for a moment, and then the current took him. The body floated in the shallows of the ford, drifting slowly downriver, the water around it turning red. Then it drifted out of sight around a bend in the river.

With tears in his eyes, Jack the Lesser said, "I guess now I'm Jack the Only."

He turned to Morgin. "Will you try to retrieve the body? If it washes up on the north side, none of us can do so."

Morgin simply said, "Sure. I'll bring it back to the camp."

He climbed into the saddle and let Mortiss pick her own way east. Just past the ford the Ulbb narrowed into a raging torrent, then further still it opened up again, and flowed calmly northeast. Just a few leagues down from the ford he found Jack's body washed up on the south shore. Oddly enough, he had only a little difficulty lifting Jack onto Mortiss's back, for all that remained of the towering whiteface was a bloodless husk.

He tied Jack across Mortiss's back, then led her on foot up to the top of a low-lying hill to survey his surroundings. He'd never traveled through this part of the forest and didn't want to get lost. But as he stood there he recalled that Morddon knew this country well. And Morddon remembered the Ulbb flowing south of the hill on which he stood, not north of it as it did now. And he could even make out the ancient riverbed where it had once flowed, dry now, and overgrown with brush.

Curious, he followed the crest of the hill west, the dry ancient riverbed on his left, the flowing Ulbb on his right. As the crest of the hill led downward, the two riverbeds converged about a league east of the ford. There, a massive tumble of stone and earth had spilled into the old riverbed, an ancient cataclysm that had diverted the flow of the Ulbb. The stones were rounded and smoothed by time, telling him the massive slide had occurred centuries ago. And yet, above the tumble of rocks stood a tall cliff of raw basalt, and he thought that if the gods ever wanted to have another cataclysm, they could divert the Ulbb back to its original course.

He shrugged the thought away and began the long walk back to the Benesh'ere camp with his sad burden.

••••

Rhianne had intended to be back in her hut well before dark, but a sky filled with gray, dreary clouds and constant drizzle had brought dusk early to the town of Norlakton, catching her off guard. As she guided the horse into the town at a slow walk, Braunye walking beside her, she glimpsed a dark shadow at the edge of her vision, and it startled her. She looked toward it, but saw nothing there.

"Is something amiss, mistress?" Braunye asked.

"No," she said, chiding herself for being so skittish. "Just jumping at shadows that aren't there."

"Ye done a lot of that lately."

Yes, she had done a lot of that lately. It had started three days ago with a sense of foreboding, as if something malevolent stalked her from the shadows. Since then she'd had that feeling of a watcher hovering nearby, and had been startled several times by a dark shape moving in the periphery of her vision. She trusted her witch's intuition, had even attempted a seeking in the hope she could uncover any danger that might be haunting Norlakton, but she'd turned up nothing.

　　　　　　　　J. L. Doty

She left her horse with the stableman at the inn, then she and Braunye walked back to her hut to prepare dinner. *I'm just jumping at shadows,* she thought. *Just shadows.*

She'd spent the day up at the miners' camp, treating quite a number of them for a nasty cold making the rounds from miner to miner, and child to child. She couldn't cure a cold, not without resorting to some powerful healing spells, but she did relieve some of their symptoms, for which the miners and their wives were quite grateful.

The blade pulled at her constantly now, unrelenting in its demands. It hated *the fires*, feared them in fact, seeking always to be free of them, and for some reason it seemed to think she held the key to its freedom. And she'd come to understand it didn't want freedom merely so it could devastate and destroy. It wanted its freedom so it could escape from the fires. In some way they tormented it. But what fires? The fires of a hearth, of a cook's oven, of a campfire, of a smith's forge—

She almost vomited at the rush of hatred that washed through her soul. That must be it. In her entire life she'd seen a smith's shop only once or twice, and then only in passing, had had no interest and hadn't paid any attention at the time. She knew of that kind of fire only as an academic concept, though with the way Benesh'ere blades and steel had recently come to mean so much to Norlakton's economy, the smith's craft was in the forefront of everyone's thoughts.

This time she steeled herself, prepared for the blade's reaction as she again thought of the fires of a smith's forge—

Again, hatred washed through her soul, so intense she cringed under the onslaught. And she resolved to not again think such thoughts. But she'd learned something, though she still could not be certain what.

24

The Blade is Near

SOMETHING ABOUT THE town of Norlakton drew the attention of the steel, and Morgin felt compelled to go there. But he didn't act on that until Harriok and Jack the Lesser came to the Forge Hall to pick up a few steel arrowheads.

"We're going to the plainface town," Harriok said.

Jack added, "Need the arrowheads to trade for some nice things for our ladies."

Morgin stood up from his workbench and said, "I'll go with you."

All activity in the Forge Hall ceased as Chagarin said, "No."

Harriok and Jack said, "No," as well, and so did the smiths.

"It's too dangerous for you to walk among plainfaces," Chagarin said.

The steel agreed with him about the danger, but Morgin still knew he must find out why the town drew its attention. He said plainly, "I'm going."

They had quite a loud discussion about that, but Morgin refused to relent. So a short time later he found himself standing outside the Forge Hall in the bright morning sunlight as Chagarin, the smiths, Harriok and Jack the Lesser looked him over carefully. He'd donned a hooded Benesh'ere tunic, with a straw hat turning the hood into a tent-like affair that hid his face in deep shadow. And he'd augmented it with a bit of shadowmagic just to be sure. A pair of riding gloves hid the skin of his hands.

Harriok said, "He looks Benesh'ere."

Jack added, "A short Benesh'ere. But I guess he does."

Chagarin said, "Keep your face and hands hidden. And we can't call you by your real name, so what should it be?"

"Call me Morddon," he said.

They all agreed that Morgin had chosen a good Benesh'ere name. The smiths also agreed that they and their sons should all accompany him as bodyguards, but Morgin pointed out that a large, heavily armed troupe of whitefaces riding into town would draw more attention than just the three of them. They compromised; Chagarin and Baldrak would go as well.

As they rode into town Morgin noticed that the plainfaces eyed them curiously, and he realized that if he were in their shoes, curiosity would compel him to do the same.

"Let's start at the inn," Harriok said. "The innkeeper's ale is not bad. And he keeps a small stock of trade goods on hand. And on a nice day like this he'll have tables outside. It'll be nice to sit in the sun instead of that sweaty common room of his."

They stopped in front of the inn, Morgin swung his leg over Mortiss's rump and stepped down onto the dirt of Norlakton's main street—its only street, actually. His comrades dismounted nearby and they tied their horses to metal rings hammered into the side of the inn. They took one of the outside tables and the innkeeper introduced himself as Fat John. The innkeeper fit his name.

Harriok and Jack dropped their hoods, while Morgin, Baldrak and Chagarin kept theirs up. Five tankards of ale and a lunch of bread and cheese cost them only four steel arrowheads. Until that moment, Morgin had not truly understood the value of Benesh'ere steel.

The innkeeper brought out his trade goods, and while Harriok and Jack haggled with him, Morgin leaned back and let the lunch and ale settle in his stomach.

He was simply staring down the street, not really paying attention to anything in particular, when he saw her. From a distance he couldn't make out her face, but she walked like Rhianne, moved like her in every way, and in that moment his heart climbed up into his throat. But as she came closer and he saw her features more clearly, while there certainly was a resemblance, it was slight at best. Up close there were so many differences between this woman and Rhianne; she carried far too many years in her face, her nose and chin were square and rough like those of a laborer, and her eyes were a dull brown.

As she approached she slowed and hesitated, looked at Morgin and his whiteface comrades fearfully. Harriok and Jack had warned Morgin that many of the plainfaces reacted that way; the stature of the Benesh'ere apparently intimidated them quite a bit. Then Fat John approached her and greeted her warmly as Mistress Syllith. He escorted her past their table and into the inn.

"Bit old for my taste," Jack said.

Harriok added, "Take a couple decades off her and I'll bet she was a pretty one once." To Morgin he said, "You like them older, huh?"

For just an instant, he had hoped they had gotten it wrong. He'd had a moment to believe Rhianne still lived, but then reality had intruded painfully. "No," he said. "She just reminded me of someone I once loved. But she's dead now."

Harriok frowned. "Sounds like you still love her."

••••

"What can I do for you, Mistress Syllith?"

Rhianne had to shake herself to focus on Fat John's question. As she'd stepped from her hut to walk to the inn, the sword's influence had suddenly begun to grow rapidly, and it now pulled at her painfully. Ever since the Benesh'ere had arrived at the lake, it had hammered at her with such force there was no question it was now near. She had concluded that one of the Benesh'ere had found it, and brought it here to their camp near Norlakton. But this! She'd only felt it this strongly once before: when kneeling in front of Morgin in the Hall of Wills after the blade had gone berserk, and it muddled her thinking now.

"Are you ill?"

Focus, she told herself. "No, just a little addled. I've never been so close to the Benesh'ere before."

"They're fearsome, ain't they?"

"Yes, they are." She had to think for a moment to recall why she'd come. "I need a new mortar and pestle. Mine is broken."

"Well, you come to the right place."

Fat John happily gave her a new mortar and pestle, as long as she agreed to spend at least two afternoons every twelve-day ministering to her patients from his common room, though he also agreed to feed her and Braunye dinner afterwards. She could probably have struck a better bargain, but it took so much energy to remain focused, her heart wasn't in it. She bundled up the mortar and pestle in a cloth sack she'd brought, then stepped out of the inn onto the street. She hesitated on the inn's threshold, trying to catch her breath and steady her nerves.

She took a tentative step forward, unsure if she could walk without falling, and wanting to avoid such embarrassment. She took another step, then another, and began the short walk to the other end of town and her small hut. The intensity of the blade increased for a few steps, but as she passed the table occupied by the five strange Benesh'ere, it started to wane. It had done the same when she'd approached the inn earlier, but she'd been too addled to notice it.

She gasped, stopped and turned toward them; two had removed their hoods and hats, but the faces of three remained deeply hidden in shadow. She had to ask, had to know if they'd come across a dangerous talisman. But as she opened her mouth to speak, the two with their hoods thrown back stood and stepped between her and the other three, towering over her menacingly. She'd never been this close to a whiteface, never truly understood how enormously tall they stood.

"Did you want something?" the older one said warily, and his tone made it clear they only wanted to hear one answer.

She stepped back fearfully and gave them what they wanted. She shook her head, then turned, lowered her eyes and walked hurriedly down the street toward her hut. She'd been a fool to try to approach such barbarians that way.

••••

Carsaris watched the Kull lieutenant—Qartan was his name—march across the floor, drop to one knee in front of Valso and bow his head. Behind Valso the little flying snake lay coiled about its perch.

"Rise, rise," Valso said impatiently, waving a hand to emphasize the point.

Qartan's leathers creaked as he slowly rose to his full height. He faced the king impassively, his left hand resting casually on the hilt of the sword strapped to his waist, the look on his face not even remotely human.

Valso said, "I've brought Salula back."

At that, Qartan's lips spread slowly into a broad grin. "I had heard rumors. I look forward to seeing him again. He is a leader I can respect, a strong leader, as are you, my king."

Valso said, "I think you respect his ruthlessness."

"Aye, my king, as I respect yours."

"But you'll have to be patient," Valso said. "It will be some time before you work directly with him again. I've sent him on a special undertaking, something of great importance to me. And you can help, my dear Lieutenant."

Qartan nodded and lowered his eyes. "Whatever you require, Your Majesty."

"Salula will need a diversion, something spectacular to focus the entire Benesh'ere camp away from Norlakton. And I have devised the perfect distraction. And you, Lieutenant, are the perfect man—halfman, I should say—to carry it out. I think it will also be the kind of thing you Kulls enjoy doing."

The halfman bowed his head slightly and said, "I enjoy serving you, my king."

Valso smiled. "No doubt, that is because of the nature of the tasks I assign you."

"There is that, my king."

Valso turned and paced back and forth as he spoke. "Take however many men you need. I'll leave you to be the judge of that. Travel incognito. Wear common livery, and let no one see that you are Kullish. Travel only in small groups and take enough supplies so you need not stop in any town or village for more. Do bring your Kull cloaks, but keep them hidden in your saddlebags until after you've acted. Then wear them openly, for they are your signature livery. We wouldn't want some common thug to take credit for the deed I wish you to perform." Valso stopped pacing and faced the Kull. "Do you understand?"

"I do, Your Majesty. And this diversion you have devised?"

Valso's smile broadened. "That will be the fun part, at least for you halfmen, a vicious little display of your depravity. But with the diversion, you must also deliver a message to the Elhiyne."

••••

The kitchen maid hurried up the hallway in Penda, carrying a tray of food for BlakeDown. When the lord of Penda reviewed his accounts he usually took lunch in his study, and Chrisainne had learned it could be a good opportunity to catch him alone. She intercepted the kitchen maid just outside his study, held out her hands and nodded toward the tray of food. "I'll take that into Lord BlakeDown."

The maid curtsied and said, "Yes, milady," and handed the tray to Chrisainne. "Will that be all, milady?"

"Yes, thank you."

As the maid turned she had a little trouble suppressing a knowing smile, but she managed to keep it to no more than a slight upturn at the corners of her mouth. The servants, like all servants everywhere, knew everything that went on inside the walls of this castle. And had the girl been indiscreet enough to let the slight smile turn into an actual smirk, Chrisainne would have reported her to BlakeDown. She'd be quietly disciplined, and possibly dismissed.

Holding the tray in one hand, Chrisainne knocked politely on the door to BlakeDown's study. "Enter," he said, though the heavy planks of the door muffled the sound.

She pulled the latch and eased the door open. BlakeDown sat behind a large desk covered in parchments and ledgers, and without looking up he waved a hand casually and said, "Put it to one side. I'll get to it in a bit."

Good, she thought. *He is alone.* He sometimes called in one of his stewards to clarify some point or other in the accounts, but not today. Chrisainne crossed the room and put the tray down on the small table he'd indicated. Then she turned around and approached BlakeDown from the side. She curtsied and leaned forward, holding her face up toward BlakeDown. The gown she wore hugged her waist tightly and exposed plenty of cleavage. She summoned the most sensual tone she could manage and said, "Will that be all, my lord?"

BlakeDown started, looked up from his accounts and down at her. She didn't miss the fact that his eyes lingered on her breasts for several heartbeats. He smiled, and she saw the lust in his eyes as he reached out to her.

She stood quickly and skipped out of his reach, saying, "Oh my lord, I am but a lowly serving maid. What is your intention?"

He laughed as she stepped around the desk, putting it between them. "I'm suddenly very hungry for lunch," he said. "But the lunch I hunger for is standing before me."

She must be careful. Once he started pounding his manhood in and out of her, she had little control over him. And while his lovemaking was crude and artless—the man himself even cruder and more artless—at least he was gentleman enough to acquiesce to her timing and not force himself upon her prematurely, though she'd never pushed that to its limits. It occurred to her now that his acquiescence was probably more self-serving than any gentlemanliness. She'd subtly taught him that if he allowed her to tease him a bit, to build his desire to an intense demand, he would find far greater pleasure in the act itself. But Valso had a very specific task for her, and she had to accomplish that before she allowed BlakeDown to descend into his mindless rutting.

"Eat your lunch, my lord. You must keep up your strength." She let a little glint appear in her eyes. "There'll be time for dessert afterwards."

He laughed again, and turned to the tray she'd placed on the small table. He lifted a goblet and gulped some wine, tore off a hunk of bread and chewed at it. While he did so she crossed the room, stood behind him and massaged the muscles of his neck.

"You're tense, my lord," she said, carefully easing toward the subject Valso wanted her to broach. She dare not bring it up directly, for that would seem too inquisitive, too probing. "Is it that old witch Olivia? She seems to be a thorn in your side."

"Thorn," he growled angrily. "More like a sword, or a spear." He turned and faced her, chewing on a hunk of cheese that soured his breath. "She turned the meeting of the Lesser Council into a circus with her proposals."

She turned away from him and crossed the room to an open window that looked out on the inner bailey below. "We've all heard rumors, my lord. But the subtle ins and outs of such politics are beyond me."

She heard his footsteps as he approached behind her. "Well don't worry your pretty little head about it."

"I don't worry, my lord, not with you in command of the situation. And you have your son at your side. He seems such a smart, intelligent, young man."

"Yes, ErrinCastle, the only good thing that cow of a wife ever gave me. He's organized the border patrols nicely."

There, he'd brought up the subject of the border patrols, not her. "Border patrols, my lord? I thought the borders were stable and secure."

"They were. But I worry those Elhiynes might try something, though I draw comfort from ErrinCastle. He's chosen a select group of lieutenants to assist him, just the right men."

She turned to face him, let him have a good look at her cleavage. "Oh really, my lord. Who might that be?"

She saw his lust growing. He rattled off three names, and as he did so she frowned, which peaked his curiosity. "What is it?" he asked. "I saw it in your eyes: a bit of doubt."

"Oh it's nothing, my lord. You know I know nothing of these matters."

"No. What is it? I value your opinion."

She hesitated and blushed a bit. "Well, I don't know the others well. But young Lord Perrinsall, he seems . . . Oh, I shouldn't say."

"No. Speak your mind. I demand it."

"Well then . . . Perrinsall seems a rather . . . indecisive young man. I wonder how he will fare when faced with those arrogant Elhiynes."

BlakeDown's eyes narrowed in thought. "You know, I think you might be right. He might let those Elhiynes walk all over him. I'll have to personally review ErrinCastle's choices."

"Oh, pay no attention to me, my lord."

He smiled and looked at her cleavage, so she lifted an eyebrow and said, "Perhaps it's time for dessert."

That was all the permission he needed. He lifted her skirt and petticoats, fumbled at his breeches for a moment, pressed her against the wall and thrust his manhood into her. She cried out, pretending to be in the throes of passion as he pounded in and out of her. At least with her petticoats raised up between his face and hers, she didn't have to smell his sour breath.

Valso would be quite pleased. She'd sown exactly the doubt needed. And the next time she screwed BlakeDown she'd help him think of the right men for those border patrols, men Valso could count on to do exactly the wrong thing.

25

A Deadly Diversion

MORGIN ALLOWED MORTISS to pick her own way up the steep trail, and when they reached the crest of the hill, he reined her in. He sat in the saddle and slowly scanned the panorama around him, the steep and jagged mountain directly in front of him, the foothills of Attunhigh behind him. Ahead and to his left the two spires now appeared exactly as they had long ago, which told him Mortiss now stood somewhere close to the route Morddon had followed after leaving Aethon's tomb.

The spires had haunted him since he'd first seen them. His glimpse of them back then had been from a far different angle, and every time he thought of them he felt compelled to find the proper viewpoint, to prove to himself he could stand on the ancient route Morddon had followed. He'd hunted back and forth carefully all day to get the angle right, frequently striking out through the forest where no game trail led. Thankfully, the forest undergrowth grew thin and sparse this high in the foothills below the great mountain.

Six times now he'd ridden Mortiss out to find that back trail, and six times he'd failed after spending an entire day seeking back and forth. Each time he'd returned to the camp he'd felt even more compelled to find it.

The sun was dropping toward the horizon, and he knew he had just enough time to get back to the camp for a late dinner. He turned Mortiss about, ready to admit his sixth defeat, but a little to the right, almost directly ahead, an outcropping of rock drew his attention. He nudged

Mortiss forward, had her follow the crest of the hill where no undergrowth impeded travel. As she moved at an easy walk, the shape of the outcropping changed subtly as the angle from which he viewed it changed. But not until he'd traveled about half a league did he recognize it, and then it came to him in a flood of memory. Its shape reminded him of the head of one of the great winged griffins, another feature he'd memorized so long ago, and now he knew for a certainty he'd found Morddon's back trail. And with that realization he understood his mistake. He'd been searching for the features from below, always looking upward. But centuries ago, as Morddon had ridden down from Attunhigh, he'd memorized many of the features from above, looking downward.

"So what will I do now?" he asked Mortiss.

She spluttered, *If you don't know, then I can't tell you.*

In any case, the thought of backtracking Morddon's trail was, at least on this day, a moot point. It would take days to carefully search out each memory, to find each feature he'd memorized so long ago, and then move on, searching for the next. He'd left the Benesh'ere camp with sufficient provisions for only a few days of travel, and he had a few blades to finish. He and the smiths had reached the final quenching stages on several, and he must be there for that. No matter how much that tomb compelled him to find it, the unfinished blades demanded even more that he complete their forging and give them life. No, he'd have to plan this more carefully, come prepared next time for a longer trek.

He'd used up most of the day with his hunting and searching, but a direct route back to the Benesh'ere camp should see him there shortly after dusk. It occurred to him that any indecision about whether or not he would return and find the ancient crypt had now vanished; or perhaps someone else had made the decision for him long, long ago.

●●●●

Morgin and Chagarin watched Baldrak carefully chip the dried clay off the blade, while the other smiths had paused at their forges and anvils to look their way. The final quenching had gone well and the blade appeared to be in good shape. They must still mount the cross-guard, wrap the tang, sharpen, polish and buff the blade, but if testing proved the quench had truly gone well, the hard part was done.

"Daddy, can I go to the plainface town with LillianToc?"

At the sound of the girlish voice they all looked up from their concentration on the blade. Felina stood just inside the door to the Forge Hall, LillianToc hovering behind her.

"Go ahead," Baldrak said. "But you have to help your mother with dinner, so be back early."

Felina turned and skipped out the door, shouting, "Father says I can go."

Morgin and the two smiths returned their attention to the blade. Baldrak picked up a pumice stone and carefully scraped the last vestiges of clay from its surface, exposing the slight gradations of color due to the many layers formed during the striking of the steel. He stroked the edge a few times with the stone and said, "The edge is good. Very hard. It'll be some work sharpening this blade."

He handed the blade to Morgin, who accepted it in both hands. The steel in the blade whispered an incoherent cacophony of voices at him. Morgin turned, marched across the Forge Hall, and with all the smiths following close on his heels, stepped through the door into the bright sunlight. The eyes of every whiteface in the vicinity turned his way and all activity ceased, for they all knew a blade would be born today, though the question still remained if it would be born healthy, or stillborn.

In the sunlight Morgin examined the blade, and slowly the cacophony of voices calmed, though still they could not speak as one. He gripped the tang with his right hand, then lifted the blade and held it high, let the stark light of the midday sun glint off its surface. He raised his left hand and flicked his middle finger at it, tapping it with his fingernail, producing a very faint and dull ping. But the sound reverberated in his soul and he embraced it, took it into his heart and amplified it, and the dull ping grew into a sharp, clear, loud tone. He amplified it further, noticed in the corner of his eye that many of the whitefaces had covered their ears with their hands, painful grimaces on their faces. One-by-one he spoke with each voice, like a choirmaster tutoring the individual members of his choir. Deep within his heart he sang the note this blade must sing, and nudged each voice toward that single, pure tone.

He wondered about this strange choir of voices. If he couldn't get them to harmonize properly, was it a flaw in the SteelMaster, or merely a flaw in the blade? Two days ago they'd finished a blade, and Morgin had taken it out for *testing*. The smiths and all the whitefaces thought he merely tested each blade as it had been made, but he had learned through trial and error that all blades were incomplete after the final quenching, and in them he always found this untrained choir of untrained voices that needed a master to guide them. Two days ago that blade had failed, and he'd finished holding melted pieces of flawed steel. The entire camp had mourned his failure that day.

One-by-one he encouraged the voices like a parent teaching a child, as AnnaRail had taught him, demanding, but never appearing to demand, finding the strength of each voice and helping them to understand themselves. He must be a bit irrational since, once introduced to a sword, he quickly came to think of each voice as almost human, but then most people had always considered him a bit odd. Or perhaps he was just a SteelMaster, and most people didn't—would never—understand a SteelMaster.

One-by-one the voices came in line with the tone they must sing. It reached a grand crescendo, and then he allowed the tone to die away, let it drift on a netherwind. And as the last faint remnant of the blade's note echoed through his soul it whispered to him in a single, clean voice.

No one could teach him what it meant to be a SteelMaster. He'd contributed bits and pieces of forgotten lore to each step in the process of making a truly superior blade, the forging, striking, shaping and quenching, and the smiths had greatly valued such bits of information. But that had all been no more than pieces of forgotten knowledge within the craft. Whereas quelling the cacophony of voices in the freshly quenched steel, appeasing their fear and disunity, that he had discovered purely by accident. That, only a SteelMaster could do. And once treated with the magic of the steel, such a blade struck true even in the hand of a less experienced swordsman, for it struck with a single voice.

He let his eyes wander the length of the blade one last time, listened to the single, clear voice within it. Then he turned to face the smiths and repeated its words, "And so must a blade be born."

The smiths cheered, and the whitefaces around them all joined in.

••••

JohnEngine reined his horse in one hundred paces from the ancient rock wall that demarked the Penda-Elhiyne border. At one time the wall had probably been cleanly crafted of carefully placed stones about waist high, with straight, almost vertical sides, and a crown of finished, flat slabs. But weather and time had turned it into a line of tumbled stones, a good source of materials scavenged by local peasants in need of building supplies.

Following the normal formula, the Penda patrol had halted a hundred paces on the other side of the line of tumbled stones. The Penda leader nudged his horse forward into an easy walk, and JohnEngine did the same. From a distance of about forty paces he saw the man's face clearly and did not recognize him, though that did not raise any alarms.

They both halted a few paces short of the stones. The Penda nodded his head, the formal equivalent of a bow when in the saddle. "Lord JohnEngine," he said. "It is an honor to finally meet you."

JohnEngine nodded his head. "You have the advantage of me."

The man spoke clearly and proudly. "I am Lewendis et Penda, third son of Cyril who is second cousin to Lord BlakeDown."

Lewendis, not a name on ErrinCastle's list of those they could count on to keep a calm head; a distant relative of BlakeDown, so probably from the north bordering on Tosk lands.

"Lord Lewendis, it is a pleasure to meet you."

"You are kind, Lord JohnEngine." Lewendis seemed wary; not ill-at-ease or intimidated, but distrustful, and his tone carried a note of cynicism.

JohnEngine said, "I wonder that we have not met before."

Lewendis's upper lip curled up slightly, an involuntary sign of distaste, as if he took some insult from JohnEngine's words. "I've just been assigned to the Penda border by Lord BlakeDown himself. I consider it a true honor to guard our borders against incursion . . . by anyone."

That was an odd way to put it, almost as if he felt the need to specifically fear Elhiyne incursion, not just the usual stray cow or bandit problems. JohnEngine asked, "Assigned by BlakeDown himself? Not ErrinCastle?"

Lewendis gave him a smug grin. "Exactly, Lord JohnEngine. Lord BlakeDown is taking a more personal interest in our border with Elhiyne. He's quite pleased with ErrinCastle's oversight, but felt his greater experience in these delicate matters warranted his particular attention. I assume Lady Olivia has done the same, since she has one of her grandsons riding border patrols."

JohnEngine avoided the obvious probe. "We all pay particular attention to our borders. If we don't, then something as simple as a stray cow or itinerant bandit might cause a misunderstanding."

Lewendis's lips narrowed into a hard, straight line. "And what do you mean by that?" he demanded. "Do you accuse us of sending bandits across the border to rob your people?"

"Of course not," JohnEngine said, angered by Lewendis's prickly nature. "Petty thieves and bandits are always a problem, whether they're yours or ours. And we've always worked together to eradicate them."

That appeared to appease Lewendis a bit. JohnEngine steered the conversation to the usual cross-border comparison of local problems, and slowly Lewendis calmed. But when they parted JohnEngine left with a most uneasy feeling.

••••

The door to Rhianne's hut burst open without warning. She started and dropped the potato she'd been peeling, while Braunye jumped to her feet fearfully. One of Fat John's sons stood in the doorway, breathing heavily, fear plain on his face. "Mistress Syllith," he panted. "There's been a fight. You must come right away."

"What kind of injuries?" she demanded.

He shook his head. "I don't know. Knives and cuts and blood, and stuff like that."

She had a little kit prepared for such emergencies and stowed in a small canvas duffle. She snatched it up and said, "Come, Braunye." To the boy she said, "Lead the way."

Once out in the street she saw the crowd gathered near the smith's shop and didn't need the boy's guidance. But as she approached a wall of tall backs she had to shout, "Make way. I'm a healer." And even then it took the smith elbowing several of them aside, shouting, "Make way for Mistress Syllith."

One of the whiteface warriors lay on the ground at the entrance to the smith's shop, clutching his side and gulping shallow breaths, blood coursing between his fingers. Seated on the ground next to him, a young, whiteface boy held a knife clutched in his right hand, blood oozing from a wound on his thigh. The boy had gone into shock, trembling badly, his eyes staring into a far distance.

Rhianne knelt down next to the boy and said, "It's all right now." She gently took the knife out of his hand. There was blood on the blade.

As she used the knife to cut away the legging of his breeches, the wounded warrior hissed through clenched teeth, "Someone send word to the camp."

Fat John stepped out of the crowd. "Already done. Sent one of my boys for that when I sent the other for the mistress."

The warrior reached out and put a hand on Rhianne's arm. "Yer a witch, ain't you?"

She paused and looked at him. "Yes."

He shook his head. "We don't abide magic."

"I'm a witch and a healer," she said. "So I won't use magic, but I'll use my healing skills."

He let go of her arm. "Good enough."

The cut on the boy's leg was shallow, probably a slice from a knife or sword, and while it bled a great deal it wasn't pulsing. She gripped Braunye's wrists, put her hands on the boy's wound and said, "Put pressure on it like I taught you. I need to check the man's wound."

The warrior had a nasty puncture wound just beneath his ribs on his left side, probably a thrust from a sword. If the blade had entered the man's side at an angle shallow enough, there'd be no damage to vital organs. If he didn't bleed internally, she could treat it with herbs to prevent festering and he had a good chance of living. But if the blade had gone straight in, he'd have a gut wound, and even with magic to aid her, it would likely fester and he still might not live.

She looked up at Fat John, was about to tell him they needed to get the man off the street so she could work on him, but the rumble of a large number of horses riding hard drowned out any sound she might make. She heard neighing and spluttering and men dismounting nearby. The crowd around them parted and several whiteface warriors towered over her with drawn swords. The man who appeared to be their leader dropped to one knee beside the wounded man and asked, "What happened?"

Rhianne said, "He can't talk now. He's hurt."

The man on one knee ignored her. The wounded warrior ignored her as well, and grimacing with pain he said, "Kulls . . . About six of them . . . Weren't dressed like Kulls . . . didn't look like Kulls. And didn't seem to be together until they all turned on us and attacked. LillianToc hurt one—" He cried out and shook with pain. "I hurt a couple more . . . but there were too many . . . and they took Felina. Headed east, I think. Took her alive."

Fat John interposed. "They did go east. I seen 'em. And they wore Kull cloaks when they rode out of town."

The wounded man gripped the leader's arm desperately. "You got to get her back, Jerst. Got to get her back."

The leader turned to Rhianne. "We'll take him and the boy from here. But we thank you for your aid."

Though she argued, the whitefaces gave Rhianne no choice in the matter. They summarily, though gently, ushered her to the other side of the street. Their leader issued orders for certain whitefaces to remain behind, then he and his men rode out hard and fast. Rhianne told Braunye to return to their hut, while she refused to leave until certain the wounded man and boy were properly taken care of. She stayed until a group of their women arrived on horseback. She watched them bandage the man and boy's wounds, and had to admit they knew what they were doing. But she stubbornly waited until they'd brought two litters, and carried the man and boy away to their camp. And for the first time in more than a moon, not a single Benesh'ere could be seen on Norlakton's only street.

26

The Steel's Revenge

MORGIN AND THE smiths were preparing to quench another blade when they heard voices throughout the camp raised in a general uproar. They stumbled out of the Forge Hall into the late afternoon sun, and got a confusing story of Kulls attacking somewhere. With each heartbeat they learned more: the attack had been in the town, on whitefaces, and they'd taken Felina alive and ridden east.

They buckled on swords, grabbed their bows and quivers then sprinted to the corral. Saddling their horses seemed to take an eternity, but each knew that doing a sloppy job of it now would just leave him on his butt in the road, probably with a broken bone or two. As they climbed into the saddle, Baldrak shouted at Morgin, "They're headed for the Gods Road. They'll try to make for Gilguard's Ford."

Morgin spurred Mortiss hard, knew she could easily outpace the Benesh'ere mounts, could outdistance them and out endure them. Even he would normally consider such a tactic foolhardy, but if he could catch the Kulls before they reached the ford, use his shadowmagic to protect him and Mortiss, perhaps use it to spirit away Felina if they stopped to rest their mounts, or use it to harass and slow them if they didn't, there might be a chance. So he gave Mortiss her head and let her ride like the netherwind.

He'd long known she had few of the limitations of a normal horse, guessed she'd been born of some netherlife, and she confirmed that now as she pulled him into a state slightly removed from simple mortality.

Thank you, old friend, he thought, knowing she could cover leagues at a pace beyond that of any mortal horse. He didn't know if she sensed his desire, or if she just knew what was needed, but tendrils of the nether-world brushed through his soul as she raced down the road, and he prayed she would find some way to cross the distance before the halfmen reached the ford.

When she reached the Gods Road, he reined her in for a moment and looked back down the smaller road to Norlakton. Far back he saw the leading elements of his Benesh'ere brethren charge into view. He turned Mortiss north and spurred her on, and she screamed a hellish cry, an oath that she would not fail him.

About a league up the Gods Road Morgin and Mortiss rounded a curve in the road and he saw two Kulls a hundred paces distant, seated atop their horses, swords drawn and waiting for him. The Kull leader had left a few halfmen behind to slow him, and when they saw him they spurred their horses into a charge. He and Mortiss bore down on them, the distance closing between him and the two Kulls. The two halfmen rode their horses on either edge of the road, intending to force Mortiss to ride between them. But at the last instant Mortiss swerved; she didn't charge off the road as Morgin thought she might, but instead swerved right into the path of the Kull horse on the right.

The impact produced a monstrous crash that threw Morgin into the air. He kept his balance, hit the ground feet first, turned it into a tuck-and-roll, which, after one roll, turned into a tumbling sprawl. He jumped to his feet, amazed he was still alive, amazed he didn't have any broken bones. The Kull horse and rider they'd rammed lay sprawled in the road, unmoving. Mortiss, her eyes glowing pits of red fire, faced the other Kull horse and rider, reared once and crushed the horse's skull. The horse went down; she reared again and crushed the Kull's chest.

When she turned to Morgin and trotted up to him he wasn't sure if the glow in her eyes stemmed from the fires of netherhell, or the flow of godmagic, and he didn't care. He climbed into the saddle, spurred her on, and again she rode like the netherwind.

Twice more he met Kulls waiting in the road for him, and twice more Mortiss dispatched them rather handily. A league after the third such encounter the rear of the main Kull column came into view far in the distance, riding hard up the road. From the terrain about them Morgin knew they were nearing the ford, and he spurred Mortiss harder, racing to intercept the Kulls before they reached the ford. But when he saw water fountaining up in giant splashes from the pounding hooves of the Kull horses, he knew then that he'd lost the race. His heart dropped, and he sat up in the saddle, relaxed the reins and Mortiss slowed from a charge to a gallop, then a canter, then a trot, then she slowed to a walk that brought them up to the bank of the ford. He got there just in time to see the Kulls spurring their horses up onto the north bank of the Ulbb.

The Kull lieutenant had a small bundle strapped across his saddle, and he reined his horse around to look back at Morgin. He threw his head back and laughed, braying a loud caw of triumph that echoed off the nearby hills. "ShadowLord," he shouted. "Oh mighty Elhiyne."

The bundle across his saddle remained deathly still, and as he untied the straps that held it there, Morgin's whiteface friends caught up with him, riding horses that staggered with exhaustion. Morgin looked into their faces, and again he saw no sorrow at the knowledge of what had just transpired, saw only that grim resolution he'd seen at the funeral pyre after the March.

"ShadowLord," the Kull lieutenant called.

He finished untying the bundle, then raised tiny Felina up, holding her under her arms, raising her high above his head. Her head lolled to one side, lifeless, and like Jack the Greater, blood flowed freely from her eyes and ears and nose and mouth. "ShadowLord," the Kull shouted, "look at your triumph."

Morgin leaned forward in the saddle, and with rage coursing through his soul he was about to spur Mortiss forward and be damned with the consequences, but beside him Jerst held out an arm, blocking him. "No. You'll just waste your own life."

Morgin couldn't stop tears from streaming down his face, and on a sudden impulse slid out of the saddle and dropped to the ground beside Mortiss. He grabbed his bow, had it strung in an instant and reached for an arrow, but Jack the Lesser put a hand on his shoulder. "It's too far. They know the range of our bows, and they're standing just beyond it."

"ShadowLord," the Kull cawed, still holding Felina's corpse high for them all to see. "My king has a message for you. If you live among the whitefaces, they will pay your rent in lives." He shook Felina's lifeless body. "And this is the first of many payments. If you live among peasants, they will pay your rent in lives. Wherever you live, someone will pay your rent in lives."

Morgin shut his eyes and tried to tune out the braying sound of the Kull's boast. Valso would never allow him peace. With everyone thinking him dead, he'd thought he might find harmony in anonymity among the Benesh'ere. Somehow, Valso had known.

The voices in the steel around him, the voices in the swords and arrowheads did bring him a kind of peace. As he soothed them, as he taught each piece of steel to speak with a single voice, it brought him some peace in return. He listened to them now, hoping to find a greater peace, but instead he found the same determination he saw on the faces of the Benesh'ere. And too, he found a confidence the whitefaces did not have, a belief that no exile could limit the steel. He still held his bow with one arrow nocked, and he focused on that one, single warhead, and when he heard its message he raised the bow, drew back the string, and released the arrow into the air. Only then did he open his eyes.

He'd shot the arrow so quickly he'd startled his Benesh'ere friends. Jack the Lesser looked at him and shook his head. "A waste of a good arrow," he said.

Morgin smiled and simply said, "I asked the steel to help."

Jack and several of them heard him, and their eyes widened as they turned to look hopefully at the arrow arcing high over the ford. The Kull lieutenant saw the arrow also, and crowed with increased laughter. The arrow reached the zenith of its arc, then started its slow descent downward. But even long before it reached the ground, all there saw that it would fall thirty or forty paces short, and the anticipation on the faces of the Benesh'ere died. But just as it reached the same height as the Kull seated atop his mount, it turned unnaturally, and streaked a flat, level trajectory above the ground. The Kull lieutenant, still crowing with laughter, still holding Felina high, looked down just as it punched into his eye and out the back of his head.

Morgin pulled another arrow from his quiver, nocked it, raised his bow, pulled and released. In rapid succession he nocked, pulled and released five more arrows, each time picking out a specific Kull and asking the steel warhead in the arrow to strike true. As the six arrows arced out over the ford, no one but Morgin yet realized the Kull lieutenant was a dead man. Not until he wavered in the saddle, dropped poor Felina's lifeless body to the ground, then tumbled to the ground himself, not until that moment did any of them realize the steel had obeyed the SteelMaster. There came a moment of utter stillness, surprise and silence from them all, then the six arrows punched into the eyes of six more Kulls.

The remaining Kulls panicked, tried to rein their horses about, but they were too tightly packed to do so quickly. Morgin started releasing arrows, one after the other, asking the steel warhead in each to give him the boon of a Kull death. He drew and shot until no arrows remained in his quiver, looked dumbly at his empty hand for a moment after he'd reached for an arrow that wasn't there. At that moment Jerst placed an arrow in his hand.

He continued to loose arrows until the last Kull disappeared around a bend in the road on the other side of the ford, though he noticed, interestingly enough, that the arrows didn't hesitate to follow the Kulls around the bend. Of the three twelves the Kull lieutenant had brought with him, six halfmen lay dead back on the road where Mortiss had killed them, and another twenty lay dead on the opposite shore of the ford.

Dusk had settled over the land as Morgin unstrung his bow, wrapped it in its oil-cloth case, and then tied it to his saddle. He looked at Baldrak and said, "I'll go fetch Felina's body. We won't leave her for the crows."

He took Mortiss's reins and walked her across the ford, feeling no need for any great hurry, and wanting to delay the moment when he must look upon the young girl's body. Mortiss picked her way between the bodies of the Kulls he'd killed, and among them lay Felina where she'd been dropped. She lay sprawled with her limbs at an odd angle, her body desiccated and shriveled much as Jack the Greater's had been.

Morgin bent over her and straightened her arms and legs carefully. He glanced about for something in which to wrap her, but he'd saddled Mortiss hastily, hadn't bothered with saddlebags or a blanket. And the only alternative was one of the cloaks of the dead Kulls strewn about the riverbank. He would not bring Felina home wrapped in a Kull cloak, so he stood and pulled off his sand-colored, Benesh'ere robe. Knee length, it would provide a good burial shroud for the child.

He wrapped her in it carefully, then lifted her into his arms. He didn't want to strap her across his saddle like a sack of potatoes, so he held her in his arms as he walked back across the ford, Mortiss following behind him. His Benesh'ere friends parted quietly as he walked through them to find Baldrak. He handed the girl to her father and said nothing.

••••

As the Benesh'ere carried away the wounded warrior and boy, Rhianne turned toward her hut and began walking. Dusk had already arrived, and night would soon be upon them. At least the nights had grown warmer, and didn't require as many blankets or as much coal for their small hearth.

As she approached their hut she noticed that no light leaked past the shutters of their small window. Braunye should be preparing dinner, and she wouldn't do that in the dark. Perhaps she'd gone out on some errand.

Rhianne pulled the rope latch on the door and opened it. The only light in the room came from the dim glow of their small hearth, and it provided no more than a faint reddish illumination. But the dying light of dusk that splashed through the door showed her that Braunye had fallen asleep in one of their two rickety chairs, her back to the door, her arms on the table, her head resting on her arms. She hadn't bothered to light a lamp, probably because it had still been daylight when she'd fallen asleep. The poor girl had been badly traumatized by such a violent assault on the man and boy, and must have been exhausted by the experience. Rhianne herself stifled a yawn, for the afternoon's events had stressed them all.

When she stepped into the hut the smell hit her: the stench of blood and feces and urine. She gasped, left the door open so she had some light by which to see, rushed across the room and gripped Braunye by the shoulders. She shook her. "Braunye, what's wrong?"

The girl remained totally unresponsive, so Rhianne pulled, needed most of her strength and grunted with the effort to raise the girl's shoulders. When she succeeded, Braunye's face peeled away from her arms with a sticky, sucking sound. She pulled the girl's shoulders upright, though her head remained tilted downward.

"Braunye, girl, what's happened?"

She pressed the palm of her hand to the girl's forehead and raised her head. But when she got it upright, the girl's head fell back to an angle beyond anything humanly possible, almost tumbling from her shoulders. Her hair stuck to the side of her face, glued there by blood, and her open eyes stared blankly at nothing. Someone had cut the girl's throat so viciously and deeply that only her spine connected her head to her shoulders.

The door slammed and a deep, grumbling voice growled, "She ain't going to wake up,"

Before Rhianne could react, an arm wrapped around her throat with crushing force. She struggled, kicked and spit, tried to scream, but the vice-like clamp on her throat only tightened. Then a hand slapped something against her forehead and she felt a strange magic wash through her, though in some way it felt oddly familiar.

"Stand," her captor said, "make not a sound, and do not move."

The arm about her throat slackened, allowing her to breathe again, but though she wanted to, she could not cry out. He released her completely, and her first thought was to run, or cry out or scream, but her muscles refused to move or respond in any way. He'd left her standing in the middle of the floor, the door to her hut on her right just barely visible in the corner of her eye. She caught a fleeting glimpse of a shadowy figure as it approached the door, but try as she might she could not turn her head to look his way.

She heard him pull the latch, heard the door creak open, though only a crack. She saw enough to know he peered out into the night, checking the street carefully. Then he said, "Good," and threw the door wide.

He gripped her by the collar of her dress and said, "Come with me."

Her legs obeyed without any conscious volition on her part, but she didn't move fast enough for him and he dragged her stumbling out into the street, then around to the back of her hut. There, he marched her into the forest and led her along a small game trail. She stumbled and landed painfully on her hands and knees, her dress tangled in the undergrowth.

"Blast you, woman. Stay on your feet."

He picked her up by her collar again, choking her. She coughed and struggled to breathe as he dragged her further into the forest. She stumbled again, and again fell to her hands and knees in the brush.

"By the name of the Dark God himself," he snarled. He gripped her around the waist, lifted her as if she weighed nothing and tossed her over his shoulder. She tried to struggle, but he snarled, "Lay still and be quiet," and her muscles went limp.

He carried her to two mounted horses tied to a tree deep in the forest, then hoisted her into the saddle of one. He tied her hands to the saddle horn, then mounted the other horse. And holding the reins of her horse in one hand, he nudged his gently forward, leading her deeper into the forest.

Consciousness seemed a distant thing as she remembered the feeling of this magic. Valso had done something similar to her when she'd tried to kill him with a poisoned needle in Castle Elhiyne. As awareness and sanity eluded her grasp, she remembered this magic well, for it tasted of Valso's corruption.

27

Spinning, Spinning, Spinning

THE BENESH'ERE BUILT a small pyre for Felina. Morgin, and the smiths, and the members of her family, and those close to her, each contributed a piece of wood to the pyre until it stood about waist high. Baldrak laid her wrapped corpse gently upon it, then turned and strode to the Forge Hall. He returned, carrying a hot coal from one of the forges in a pair of metal tongs. He placed the coal on a small pile of kindling at the base of the pyre, then knelt down and blew on it until flames licked upward.

He stood beside Morgin as they watched the pyre burn, watched it consume the wilted husk of her body in fire from the blood of our kin. Morgin couldn't suppress the tears that streamed down his cheeks. But the whitefaces stood stoically, and looked upon the fire without sorrow or tears, just that determination he'd seen before.

When the pyre had burned down and nothing but ash remained of Felina, Baldrak used the same tongs to retrieve a hot coal from the embers, then turned and carried it to the Forge Hall. Other whitefaces followed his example, retrieving burning embers in various ways, some carrying them on a bed of leaves in the palms of their hands, some with tongs like Baldrak's. Morgin understood then that the whitefaces were adding them to their cook fires and forge fires so that Felina's fire would burn with the fire from the blood of their kin.

The Benesh'ere retreated to their cooking fires while Morgin stood alone and watched the pyre cool and slowly dwindle to ash. He could not put the Kull's message—Valso's message—out of his mind, that wherever he went someone would pay the rent of his freedom with the lives of the innocent. He could not escape the fact that Felina had died a most horrible death because he lived among her people. He struggled to think of a way he might continue to do so without paying that horrible price. But no matter how vigilant the Benesh'ere might be, Valso's Kulls would always find a way to make someone pay.

"Come, Elhiyne," Baldrak said. In the dark, and with his concentration wholly focused on the ash of the pyre, Morgin hadn't noticed him approach. "Come and eat something."

Morgin couldn't look away from the remains of the pyre. Baldrak cleared his throat and said, "If you are like me, or my wife, or any number of us, you're trying to find many ways to blame yourself for this. But this is the life of the Benesh'ere, the heart of the Benesh'ere . . . the heart of the sands."

Morgin got a little drunk that night, knowing he'd have trouble finding sleep and hoping the alcohol might help. But when he climbed into his blanket he lay there awake and relived time-and-again the events of the afternoon. If he could discover in those events a way he might have prevented it, then perhaps he might stay with his Benesh'ere friends. But as he struggled with that thought, he realized it didn't matter. Aethon's tomb called to him. Something remained unfinished there, and he knew now that he must answer that call.

Once he made that decision sleep came easily, and he dreamt of the blade and its hungry, demanding power. When he thought of killing Valso, the blade hungered to help him do so. And when he thought of more pleasant things the blade still hungered, but without a specific target for Morgin's anger, it merely hungered to take life, any life, friend or foe.

He dreamt of Felina laughing and skipping out the door of the Forge Hall to go to the plainface town. At that moment, he could not have believed that such a day would end in such tragedy.

He dreamt too of Aethon's tomb and it pulled at him. He knew now that his destiny demanded he backtrack up Morddon's trail and find the ancient crypt. "I'm waiting for you," the skeleton king told him in his dream. "One last time you must come to me."

"But why?" he asked in the dream. "Why now?"

The skeleton king turned the black pits of his eyes on Morgin and said, "Because the time is now right for the forging."

Morgin awoke tangled in his blanket, groggy, his stomach twisted in knots. He'd turned and struggled so much in his sleep he had trouble extracting his feet from the snarled mess. But after a few moments of effort he pulled free, stood and walked down to the lake. He splashed water on his face, hoping the chill would clear the fuzzy thoughts clouding his mind, but Felina and the sword and the crypt refused to give him peace.

When he stepped into the Forge Hall, Chagarin took one look at him and said, "You look like netherhell."

"Didn't sleep well."

"No," Chagarin said. "None of us did."

"I'm leaving," Morgin said.

Chagarin nodded. "I know."

••••

Rhianne awoke, her head resting on the ground, the embers of a small campfire still smoldering. As the sun rose in the east it cast long shadows across the ground on which she lay. She recalled a collection of fragmented memories, her captor telling her what to do, her body obeying him under the control of a powerful compulsion spell. She struggled to remember that he'd dragged her out of her hut, lifted her into the saddle of a horse and tied her hands to the saddle horn. Then he'd mounted another horse, and they'd ridden for quite some time through the dense forest.

South, she thought. *We rode south—or was it east?*

The spell muddled her thoughts, made it impossible to think of anything more complex than simple bodily commands: raise her hand, lower her eyes, walk, stop, sit. Her forehead felt odd, so she reached up and found some sort of medallion attached there. She tried to peel it off, but it defied her efforts and remained attached to the middle of her brow.

"Sit up," a gruff voice said, the same voice that had assaulted her in her hut.

She didn't recall going through the motions, but she now found herself sitting on the ground, her legs crossed, facing the smoldering fire. A piece of wood landed in the embers of the fire, sending sparks flying, then another, and another. A man in simple livery stepped into view, bent down with his back to her and began blowing on the wood. It took three or four huffs of breath for the wood to catch, then it crackled and flames fluttered upward.

The man straightened, stood tall and blocked the rising sun for a moment, then stepped around the fire and sat down facing her. Recognizing the sparkling blue eyes, the long blond hair and heavy blond mustache waxed at the tips, she gasped and said, "France?"

The man grinned, the kind of unpleasant grin she'd never seen on the swordsman's face. "Well now, pretty one," he said, this man who was France, and yet not France. "I wear him well, do I not?"

He said it as if discussing wearing a suit of clothing. When she looked more closely, she saw that the sparkle in the swordsman's eyes had been extinguished. His eyes remained blue, but flat and unflattering. She'd seen such eyes before, the night Valso had given her to his Kulls. "You're a halfman."

"Aye, but not just any halfman."

She shook her head frantically, trying to keep one coherent thought connected to the next. She snarled, "France would never have consented, and it takes the consent of the man to make a halfman."

He nodded, agreeing with her. "And yet, there is one exception."

She had heard of an exception, hadn't paid attention at the time, never thought she'd need to know such details. The man's consent was not required for the most powerful of the demons that made a halfman. She gasped, and couldn't stop herself from hissing, "Salula!"

His grin broadened. "Not only pretty, but smart. And that's a good thing."

Instinctively, almost as a reflex, she called forth her power and reached for it. But it burned her, seared a hole into her soul and the contents of her stomach spewed forth, splattering bile down the front of her simple homespun dress. She choked and coughed as her stomach heaved, though nothing remained to disgorge. She lay on the ground, panting as the spasms slowly diminished.

"Not so smart after all," Salula said. "But still, a lesson well learned."

He stood abruptly and barked, "Stand."

Again, her body obeyed with no conscious thought on her part, and she stood up immediately. He stepped around the fire toward her, and she started to step back away from him but he snarled, "Stay."

Like a dog ordered to heel by its master, she froze in place. He stopped less than a pace away, leaned forward and sniffed at her neck. "I'll not forget your scent, pretty one."

He leaned back, gripped her by both shoulders with his hands and said, "Now close your eyes." Again, she could not have disobeyed. Then he gripped her shoulders and spun her, spun her about her own axis, spun her like a top. She twirled, could not stop herself from doing so, felt the spell washing through her, and she became acutely aware of the blade. It seemed to be spinning about her, circling her rapidly, but she knew the blade remained stationary while she spun, conscious of its direction, most conscious of it each time she spun to face it, and then spun on. Her spinning slowed, then finally stopped altogether with her facing the direction from which she sensed the power of the blade, for this spell had not allowed her to face any other direction.

"Good," Salula said. "Due north. He hasn't begun to move yet. But he will."

••••

JohnEngine waited in silence while Brandon read the parchment carefully. When he finished he put it down on the table in front of him, then tiredly ran his fingers through his hair. "ErrinCastle writes that BlakeDown has repeatedly overridden his choices for border patrol lieutenants."

JohnEngine crossed the room, reached down and picked up the parchment, scanned it as he asked, "And this Lewendis?"

Brandon turned away from the table between them, crossed the room to a small table against one wall and filled a goblet from a pitcher of wine. JohnEngine's cousin usually drank only in moderation, had never really joined in when the rest of them went whoring and drinking, but now he gulped at the wine hungrily.

He turned and faced JohnEngine. "ErrinCastle writes that Lewendis is a hothead, just as you surmised. They've kept him on a short leash on the Tosk border for years for exactly that reason. With Tosk sworn to Penda he could do no harm there. BlakeDown's intervention worries ErrinCastle; it's as if someone is counseling BlakeDown to assign command of the patrols to the worst possible leaders. It makes me wonder if someone truly desires war between Penda and Elhiyne."

JohnEngine joined his cousin at the small table and filled a goblet for himself, saying, "The Decouix wouldn't mind seeing us ripping each other's throats out."

"Agreed," Brandon said angrily. "But Valso has very little influence in Penda. And I can't believe BlakeDown would be stupid enough to let the Decouix drive a wedge between us."

Brandon frowned and asked, "Who've we got on the border now?"

"DaNoel," JohnEngine said.

"Good," Brandon said. "He'll keep a calm head."

JohnEngine dearly hoped Brandon was right about that.

••••

Morgin gathered up his few belongings while the smiths' wives packed his saddlebags with twelve days of compact trail rations. As he saddled Mortiss and packed up his gear, a continuous stream of whitefaces came to see him: Jerst, Harriok and Branaugh, LillianToc, Jack the Lesser, Baldrak, Delaga and Fantose. They all tried to talk him out of leaving, but he'd made up his mind somewhere in that dream, and his dreams rarely left any room for argument.

Angerah and Merella came to him last, but did not try to dissuade him from leaving. They said their farewells, and Merella finished by saying, "We know you must leave."

Angerah said, "And we know you must return."

Morgin said a quiet farewell to Chagarin and Baldrak, then rode out of the Benesh'ere camp.

••••

Rhianne spun like a top, spinning, spinning, spinning, conscious of the blade and its malevolent power, conscious only of the blade and its direction. When Salula spun her like this her will evaporated completely. Each morning she awoke, and each morning she resolved not to aid him, and each morning he spun her. He spun her at dawn, midday and dusk, and each time he spun her she betrayed the man who now carried that blade.

The spinning slowed and she tried to come to a stop facing away from the blade, facing any direction but the blade. But the spell overpowered any choice or desire on her part, and she came to a stop facing it squarely. She could not have done otherwise.

"Ahhh!" Salula growled happily. "This morning, due north. And now, northwest. Maybe he's on the move. We'll have to wait until dusk to be certain."

Rhianne sat down by their campfire and sobbed openly, shedding tears of frustration and anger. Salula interpreted them as the tears of a frightened young woman. She chose not to correct him on that matter, for if that tiny bit of misdirection gave her some advantage at some point, she would be a fool to give that up now.

Salula sat down opposite her. "He's moving slow and careful, so we'll take our time and be sure."

She asked, "How did you know something in me could be used to find that blade?"

Ignoring her question, Salula grinned and laughed, but said nothing.

She now knew to a certainty they were camped due south of the Benesh'ere camp. They hadn't moved since he'd brought her here with her hands tied to the horse's saddle horn. He fed her, not well, but well enough. He kept the fire low, clearly not wanting to draw attention with a trail of smoke during the day, or brightly glowing embers at night. But he did burn a fire and kept it just high enough to give her the warmth she needed so she didn't take a chill and fall ill. No, he had to take care of her so she might betray whoever now carried that blade. But how did he know she could sense the blade so?

France, and Salula, both and yet neither. She wondered if anything remained of the swordsman, or if his soul had been completely destroyed by the demon Salula. He caught her staring at him, turned the swordsman's blue eyes upon her, and she shivered at the emptiness of his gaze. Nothing human remained in that look, but perhaps something human remained in the soul. She looked away, and he laughed, his voice sounding like rock grating on stone.

The last meal she'd eaten in Norlakton had dried on the front of her dress, and at most she'd been able to peel away desiccated bits and pieces of it. But there still remained the stain of the bile and other fluids from her stomach. There must be a stream or brook nearby, for several times the halfman had ordered her to, "Stay. Don't move and don't make a sound." And she'd remained frozen like a statue while he'd left the camp briefly and returned with water.

"I need to bathe," she said. Slowly, those blue eyes turned her way and stared right through her. "I'm filthy."

He considered her for a moment, then stood and said, "Follow me, pretty one, but say nothing louder than a whisper."

She obeyed, for she had no choice. He led her about fifty paces from their camp to a small stream, stopped there, pointed at it and said, "Go ahead. Bathe."

The water in the stream flowed barely ankle deep, so she couldn't immerse herself completely. "Do you have soap?" she whispered.

He laughed at that. "What do you think, pretty one?"

She stepped around him and stopped at the edge of the stream, and waited for him to walk away, or at least turn his back, but he stood unmoving, staring at her in that eerie silence of his.

She asked, "Can't you at least turn your back so I have some privacy?"

"You didn't need much privacy that night you pleasured my men in Castle Elhiyne."

That angered her. "And you know that was not by my choice."

"Aye, they did tell me you were a lifeless doll. A pretty doll, but still lifeless. Still, if you want to bathe, then you'll bathe with me watching you, or you'll not bathe at all."

She had intended to clean the dress anyway, but she was not about to voluntarily disrobe in front of this monster, so she laid down in the stream and let the cold water wash over her. She turned over to completely soak the dress down, then stood and ran her hands over her body inside her dress in an attempt to clean herself. Then she wrung as much water out of the dress as she could.

He led her back to the camp and she sat down on a log near the fire. Thankfully, the fire was warm and the dress reasonably dry by dusk. And of course, since dusk had arrived, he spun her again.

"West-northwest," he said. "He is on the move. We'll get up early and follow."

28

Attunhigh

MORGIN RODE STRAIGHT to the place on Morddon's back trail where time had weathered the outcropping of rock. He sat in Mortiss's saddle and looked at it carefully, knew quite well it took a real flight of imagination to see the head of a great, winged griffin in the jagged angles of a piece of granite. But that mattered not, for he'd memorized that feature all those centuries ago, and even if it didn't look exactly like the head of a griffin, it was the feature he remembered. He could begin his search knowing he'd at least started on Morddon's back trail.

It took most of the morning to get to that starting point, and then he spent the afternoon coursing back and forth, always trying to move higher up the side of the mountain in a zigzag pattern, turning frequently to look back down the trail. The other features he'd memorized so long ago weren't stored in a nice, ordered list in his memory. He never knew what feature he would find next, couldn't even name the features he sought. He hadn't known he needed to find an outcropping of rock that looked like the head of a griffin until he happened to look upon it and recognize it. Only then had he remembered it.

At the end of that first day, he'd travelled only a short distance up the mountain, and had yet to spot another feature he recognized. He stopped searching well before dusk, found a good sheltered spot for a campfire, strung his bow, left Mortiss to graze and went out to find something for dinner. He shot a medium sized rabbit, gutted it and skinned it. He built up a small fire, roasted it and ate well. He was happy to find he'd have a little left over for breakfast.

••••

"My hands hurt," Rhianne pleaded as her horse quick-stepped up a small embankment. The knots in the rope binding her hands to the saddle horn seemed to tighten whenever her horse jostled her a bit. "The knots are too tight. Please."

In front of her, Salula reined his horse to a stop, and hers stopped obediently. Salula turned about in the saddle and stared at her without moving for several heartbeats. Then he pulled on the reins of her horse, making it step forward until it stood beside his. He looked down at her hands. Coated with grime and dirt, her fingertips had turned a bluish-white, with no color beneath the nails.

Saying nothing, he reached over and carefully untied the rope. With her hands free she lifted them and opened and closed her fingers, trying to restore the circulation, though when it did return it came in painful spikes and searing flashes. He gave her a few precious moments, then said, "Always keep one hand on the saddle horn."

Her left hand shot down of its own accord and gripped the horn. Thankfully, he hadn't ordered her to grip it tightly, for she guessed doing so continuously would become as painful as the rope had been.

"Even if you fall from the horse, you'll keep one hand on the horn."

He nudged his horse's flanks with his spurs, it walked forward, and when the slack in her horse's reins tightened, it followed. She closed her eyes and tried to nap in the saddle, as she'd heard experienced soldiers could do. But the blade hammered at her senses and refused to allow her a moment's respite. It must be close, though she couldn't sense distance, only direction, and even that was little more than a vague sensation, nothing as accurate as when he spun her and Valso's spell took hold.

At noon, he reined his horse to a stop, dismounted and tied its reins to a bush. Then he said, "You can let go of the horn and dismount."

The way he'd phrased it released her from the compulsion of holding onto the saddle horn, and allowed her to dismount, but did not compel her to do so. From such little clues she was slowly gleaning the limits of the compulsion spell. She dismounted quickly so he'd have no inkling of his mistake.

She touched the medallion that had somehow adhered to the center of her forehead, and wished for a mirror of some kind. She felt the outlines of some sort of rune there, and she dearly wanted to try to understand its nature. *Patience*, she thought. *Patience is needed here.*

When he said, "Come here," she crossed the few paces separating them. She wanted to resist, but knew it was fruitless, knew to bide her time and learn more of the limits of the spell.

He gripped her by the shoulders and spun her, and as Valso's spell engulfed her she lost all sense of time and place. Spinning, spinning, spinning, for her there existed only the blade and its malevolent power, a beacon that called to her, though she knew if ever she truly answered its summons, it would be her undoing.

The spinning had stopped some time ago, though she hadn't realized it and had just stood there, her eyes closed, overwhelmed by the siren call of such power. She struggled, and with an effort of will opened her eyes. Salula sat on a nearby rock, staring at her with those pale blue eyes.

"Due north again," he said, standing. He turned and faced north, stepped to the edge of their small camp and stopped near a small pile of kindling he'd gathered. "He's zigzagging, searching for something."

Salula had clearly expected to corner his prey much sooner than this. And had the fellow traveled in a reasonably straight line, or followed some well-defined path, they probably would have. But by now, both she and the halfman knew that if they followed the direction provided, if they travelled due north as indicated, by dusk they'd find he was east or west of them, some direction that would force them to turn once again from a simple, straight line.

"Blast and damnation!" the halfman snarled. He kicked the pile of kindling, scattering it about their camp. Then he turned to Rhianne and said, "We'll wait a bit before going on, see if he changes direction again. So sit down."

The compulsion dropped Rhianne to the ground where she plopped awkwardly onto her butt. She said, "Might I at least sit in a more comfortable place?"

Salula considered that for a moment, then nodded toward a nearby boulder and said, "You can sit there."

That had released her from the compulsion to sit in place, but the way he'd phrased it had not induced her to go sit on that rock. Still, she picked herself up quickly and did so anyway. Let him think his words had bound her to the compulsion of sitting on the rock, while she remained free to do otherwise.

She had no illusions that she'd find an opportunity to take advantage of it, not this time, not here and not now. But there would come a time, perhaps at a critical moment when his life hung in the balance. Yes, there would come a moment, a single instant in time, and then she would act.

••••

DaNoel waited with his men the prescribed one hundred paces from the Penda-Elhiyne border, in this case a dry-wash that cut deeply through arid fields at the western end of the boundary. The Penda patrol had stopped at the prescribed distance on the other side, and when the Penda lieutenant nudged his horse forward, DaNoel turned to his sergeant and said, "You know what to do."

The sergeant, an old veteran of many campaigns, nodded and said in a surly tone, "Yes, my lord." He didn't approve of DaNoel's tactics, but DaNoel cared nothing for the man's opinion, and had made it quite clear he was not to express it. His only concern should be to obey DaNoel's orders.

DaNoel spurred his horse forward into a walk and crossed the distance to the dry-wash slowly, watching the Penda lieutenant closely for any sign of treachery. He didn't recognize the man, and thankfully the fellow wasn't foolish enough to try anything. They each stopped a few paces short of the dry-wash, and DaNoel called out, "I am DaNoel et Elhiyne. And you?"

The fellow frowned, his eyes narrowed and he said, "Lord DaNoel, I am Lewendis et Penda, third son of Cyril who is second cousin to Lord BlakeDown."

A distant relative of BlakeDown, so distant he was barely one step removed from a commoner. DaNoel didn't need to recite his pedigree, and he'd be damned if he'd honor Lewendis with the title *Lord*. "Lewendis," he said. "I haven't heard that name before."

Lewendis almost flinched, and his lips hardened into a straight, angry line. "Until recently I've spent most of my time protecting Penda's northern border."

"Protecting!" DaNoel said, laughing. "I should hardly think Penda needs protection from those Tosk toadies of BlakeDown's."

Lewendis's spine stiffened. "The Tosks are a valued ally."

The right moment had come, so DaNoel reached up, lifted his hat and wiped his brow with the sleeve of his forearm, giving the signal he'd told his sergeant to watch for. He didn't need to look over his shoulder to see the sergeant deploying the archers: the look on Lewendis's face told him all he needed to know. And behind Lewendis, the Pendas were hastily trying to set up some sort of response.

Lewendis demanded, "What treachery is this?"

With a dozen archers deployed, DaNoel now had the upper hand. It pleased him to see this Penda humbled so. "No treachery, Penda. Merely cautious insurance. You Pendas are known for speaking with a slippery tongue."

"Will you kill me now?" Lewendis demanded. "Murder me right here?"

"Of course not."

"Then I'm free to leave?"

"Of course."

"And receive an arrow in the back."

DaNoel shook his head. "No, that would be a Penda type of treachery. You're free to go, and do so alive. And you have five heartbeats before I give the signal for my archers to loose their arrows."

Lewendis's eyes widened, he wheeled his horse about and spurred it hard, wisely reining it left and right in a zigzag pattern. DaNoel gave him the five heartbeats, then raised his hat and waved it. Laughing at the fool Penda, he looked up and saw twelve arrows arcing overhead. He watched them reach their zenith, then descend among the Penda patrol. None of them struck home, but the Pendas retreated in a chaotic rout.

It was time those arrogant Pendas learned a lesson. DaNoel laughed again, laughed all the way back to his men.

••••

One by one Morgin had found five memorized points of reference, though he'd had to course far and wide to do so. He'd lost an entire day before realizing that one of the points, an unusual rock pillar, no longer existed. It had long ago tumbled into a pile of large boulders. But as he and Mortiss climbed higher up the side of Attunhigh his options grew fewer, which proved to be to his advantage. Standing on the crest of a ridge with a precipitous drop to either side, he had no choice but to follow the ridge, which led him nicely to the next point of reference; fewer choices, less coursing about, faster progress.

That morning he crossed above what would be the snow-line in winter, though now all that remained were a few patches of white clinging to the shadowed side of a gulley, or to the bottom of a ravine. Tall pines dotted the hillsides, with almost no undergrowth to impede him, and Morddon's back trail no longer seemed a fragmented sequence of memories, so he now moved with much greater confidence.

••••

"He's definitely searching for something, pretty one," Salula said as they set up camp for the night.

This high up the nights took on a decided chill, so Rhianne huddled in her blanket, snuggled close to the small fire and tried to ignore the halfman's manic ramblings.

"And I wonder what. What is he trying to find? What is so important to him? He already has the sword. So what else matters that much?"

She had learned that the spell did not compel her to answer his questions, unless he first ordered her specifically to do so.

"My curiosity is up. So I think I'll let him find what he seeks first . . . then kill him."

Rhianne could only pity the poor fellow, whoever he might be.

••••

Tulellcoe and Cort dismounted in the inner bailey of Elhiyne. Avis rushed breathlessly down the steps of the main entrance accompanied by a young squire. "Lord Tulellcoe," the old man said, breathing heavily. "Forgive me. We didn't know you were coming. Nothing is prepared."

Tulellcoe put a hand on his shoulder. "Calm down, man. I know I've arrived unannounced, so I don't expect anything to be ready. Are my old rooms still available?"

"Aye, my lord. The Lady Olivia would not allow them to be assigned to anyone else, though they're a bit musty. We should air them out and change the linens. I'll have someone on that right away." He looked at Cort. "And I'll arrange a room for the Balenda."

"There's no need," Tulellcoe said as the squire took the reins of the two horses. "She'll be staying with me."

The young squire glanced sidelong at Cort, but the old man showed not the slightest reaction to such a revelation. Cort, being Cort, neither blushed nor lowered her eyes, but smiled at the young squire. He blushed and lowered his eyes.

Tulellcoe glanced at the sky, gauging the time of day by the height of the sun: a little before midday. "Please see the Balenda to my rooms, and arrange a bit to eat. I assume my aunt is in her private chambers."

"Yes, my lord."

Tulellcoe left Cort in Avis's care and headed for Olivia's private audience chamber.

"Nephew," she greeted him, seated among cushions on a comfortable couch. "Welcome back. What has it been, more than a year?"

Today she wore a dark, reddish robe, almost a deep brown the color of dried blood. And her black hair contained more streaks of gray than he remembered.

"A bit more," he said.

She patted a spot beside her. "Come. Sit beside me."

Anyone fool enough to take that invitation and sit beside her would find himself intimidated by the nearness of her power, a tiny bit of which she always allowed to leak into the room for just that purpose. He crossed the small room, leaned down and gave her a chaste kiss on the cheek. "I'll stand," he said, placing his hands in the small of his back and stretching. "Been in the saddle for days, and I need to walk the kinks out."

"As you will," she said, a knowing smile on her face. They both knew he was wise to her tactics. She asked, "What have you been up to this past year, besides bedding the Balenda?"

News of that sort traveled fast in the castle; she had quite a number of informants tasked with reporting even the most trivial details to her, probably even had someone in SavinCourt that reported to her some time ago. But he was up to the game, so he said, "Mostly just bedding the Balenda."

She threw her head back and laughed, then said, "Come now, you must have something to tell me."

He gave her a brief and highly edited summary of his travels with Morgin, and his drifting about with Cort after they'd been separated. He finished, saying, "He's dead now, and you seem to care little about that."

She shrugged, poured herself a small goblet of water. "He became more a liability than an asset, and I have other things to worry about."

"Like the border situation with Penda?"

"Ah, you've heard rumors."

He crossed the room to a window overlooking the inner bailey, stared down at the courtyard below. "More than rumors, I've heard a few unsettling details."

"Like my nomination of Brandon as warmaster of all the Lesser Clans?"

"Aye, and it sounds like you knew exactly how volatile that would make the situation."

She took a delicate sip of water and said, "Someone has to keep BlakeDown in his place."

"But why provoke him so? I know you're not the foolish, old woman some believe."

"Well I thank you for recognizing that, even if others don't."

They sparred back and forth like that for quite some time. Unlike other members of the family, such evasive tactics did not frustrate him.

He'd grown up dealing with her like this, knew she enjoyed the competitive interplay of their words, and if one were careful, and willing to put in the time, she did yield up bits and pieces of information. But one had to take the time to put those bits and pieces together carefully. Tulellcoe would later recall every word, and meticulously replay them in an effort to do so.

She dismissed him with some excuse about needing to speak with one of her stewards. But when he opened the door to her chamber to leave, NickoLot stood in the hallway, and she stepped hurriedly in his way to block his path, a tiny thing dressed in black as if in mourning. "Uncle," she said, and the strength of her voice surprised him.

Standing in the doorway still holding it open, he greeted her, "Nicki!"

She looked him up and down carefully, the kind of look Olivia might use to intimidate, but on Nicki's face it was really just a cold, piercing appraisal. "Rhianne isn't dead," she said. "I know it. And neither is Morgin. He can't be."

"Oh really!" Olivia said, sarcasm punctuating every word. "With all your powers, child, where is your proof that they live?"

NickoLot opened her mouth to say something, but hesitated fearfully.

"Exactly," Olivia said. "I tire of this little fantasy you're perpetrating. Leave us, and take your childish games elsewhere."

NickoLot lowered her eyes, turned and walked away in silence.

Tulellcoe frowned and looked at Olivia. The old woman said, "She refuses to accept reality. It's not healthy."

He stepped into the hallway and closed the door quietly, his thoughts roiling in turmoil.

••••

Morgin now recognized the trail clearly as Mortiss carefully picked her way up a twisting track of steep switchbacks. They'd climbed above the tree line that morning, and at this altitude the vegetation was limited to lichen and mosses. Trees and scrub no longer masked the trail with their ever changing growth and regrowth, and near mid-morning he'd passed the last of his memorized features.

Mortiss gave a last burst of effort and climbed up onto a flat shelf of rock, a wide expanse where long ago Ellowyn and the other legion commanders had awaited Morddon in a solemn, silent throng. With them had waited the royalty of the House of the Thane and what remained of the Benesh'ere command. Morgin nudged Mortiss forward slowly to the center of the shelf and dismounted.

The black slash of the crypt's entrance remained as he remembered it, filled with rocks and small boulders piled there by the angels, and obscured by the shadows Morgin had cast. He marveled that after all these centuries his shadowmagic still remained strong and undiminished.

He let Mortiss wander off to graze; perhaps she would find some of the lichen to her liking. He laid his sword to one side, leaned it carefully against a boulder well out of the way, then set to work removing the stones from the cave's entrance.

••••

Salula stopped at the bottom of a steep rise, up which the trail led in a series of sharp switchbacks. He climbed out of the saddle and tied his horse's reins to a scraggly bush that had managed to send out a few dried and withered shoots among the rocks. With the command in place to keep one hand on the saddle horn, Rhianne was forced to remain mounted. Salula finished with his horse and approached her, stopped beside her horse and said, "You may take your hands off the saddle horn and dismount."

Not a compelling command, but she obeyed nevertheless.

Using a piece of rope he tied one end around her left wrist, leaving a tether about the length of a man's arm. He leaned toward her, lowered his voice and whispered in her ear. "I'm leaving your hands free so you can climb. You will follow me. You will say nothing. You will make no noise and utter no sound. You will move only as far as required by my pull on this tether. If I release it, you'll stay in place."

Salula drew his sword, and she saw it for the first time, a black shadow of obsidian gloom. She sensed the magic in the blade, some sort of spell-crafting she did not understand.

They started up the switchbacks on foot, Salula leading, she following at the end of her tether. It was an arduous climb in muddy skirts that kept twisting about her ankles, made even harder since she could make no sound, could not utter a grunt or a moan on a particularly difficult stretch of trail. She marveled that Salula moved with absolutely no sound, climbing up the switchbacks in a silence truly unnatural and inhuman.

As they neared the crest of the trail she heard someone above them occasionally grunting with effort. She heard the dull clap of stone against stone. From below it appeared the trail opened out onto some sort of shelf in the side of the mountain.

Salula hesitated about the height of a man from the top of the trail, turned back to her and whispered in her ear, "You can wait here." He didn't realize it, but with that non-compulsive statement, he'd broken all of the compulsions he'd laid upon her.

He left her there and climbed slowly, silently to the top of the trail, paused there and peered over its lip. Then he moved forward with that deadly silence only a Kull could affect, and when he stepped onto the shelf above, he disappeared from sight.

Rhianne scrambled upward, trying to do so silently, knowing she could not abandon the poor fellow who now possessed that blade. She managed not to stumble or fall, like some witless maiden, reached the top of the trail and looked over the lip of the shelf. Salula stood no more than an arm's length from her, crouched, creeping forward silently. At the far end of the shelf a man stooped over a heavy stone, his back to Salula, grunting as he tried to lift the block of granite.

Off to one side she spotted the sword, and that was the oddest thing, for this close her sense of direction to the blade and its power had grown quite acute; and that sense pointed not at the steel sword lying to one side, but at the man grunting with effort to lift the stone.

The man finally lifted the stone with a great effort, and staggering under its weight, he backed out of a strange crease in the rock. He dropped the stone onto a pile to one side of the shadowy crease, then glanced their way, and at the sight of his face, she froze in disbelief.

Looking at Salula, Morgin's eyes gladdened with joy as he straightened. He said, "France! My old friend, I thought you dead and gone."

Morgin opened his arms and walked toward Salula to embrace him. Rhianne climbed desperately up onto the shelf. Her ankles tangled in her muddy skirt as she stumbled toward Salula screaming, "Nooooo! It's Salula."

Morgin froze with his eyes wide just as she hit Salula from behind, wrapping her arms around his waist. She let her knees buckle and tried to pull him down or hinder him with her weight, but he snarled, "Let me go," and her arms opened as the compulsion overcame her. He swung his fist around behind him, and slammed the hilt of his sword into the side of her head.

29

The Crypt of the Sunset King

MORGIN STAGGERED TO a stop when Rhianne scrambled onto the shelf of rock and screamed, "Nooooo! It's Salula."

Rhianne! His Rhianne! Alive! Not dead! Filthy and bedraggled, her hair clumped and matted with dirt, wearing a common, homespun dress of course fabric caked with mud. His Rhianne! But as she charged France, her words hit him.

Salula! No, it couldn't be. Salula was dead. But then as Rhianne wrapped her arms around France, his friend growled, "Let me go," and his words came out in Salula's voice, the harsh rumbling tones of the halfman Morgin would never forget.

Salula batted Rhianne in the side of the head, and she crumbled to the ground like a rag doll. Then Salula turned to face Morgin, and he realized that nothing of his old friend the swordsman remained in that face.

"Well, Elhiyne," Salula growled. "Or should I call you ShadowLord? We meet again."

A hundred thoughts raced through Morgin's mind. The entrance to the crypt was now almost clear. If he could rescue Rhianne, who lay unconscious on the ground behind Salula, he could climb over the last few rocks in the slash, and gain access to the crypt. But what then?

He glanced toward his sword, sheathed and leaning against a large boulder far to one side. It would be a race between him and the halfman, but Salula had a sword in his hand, and he completed Morgin's thought for him. "No, Elhiyne. I'll cut you down before you get there. Then I'll kill the pretty one behind me, and take that blade to my king."

He slashed the obsidian blade through the air between them, threw back his head and laughed, an evil caw that sent waves of fear coursing through Morgin's soul.

He had one chance, and he remembered that Benesh'ere lore told him he must not command the steel, *for the steel always commands*. So he held out his hand toward the blade, palm open, and he said, "Please, come to me."

As Salula stepped in and thrust with the obsidian blade, Morgin's sword teetered toward him, slid out of its sheath and shot across the space between them, the hilt smacking into the palm of his hand. He turned the blade's momentum into a slashing parry, and a blinding cascade of sparks erupted where steel met glass. Salula staggered backward, so Morgin lunged, but the halfman parried, and again the two blades showered them with sparks as they met. They disengaged, separated and stood facing one another in a crouch.

Salula showed Morgin the grin he hated. "I like the sport you give me, Elhiyne."

He charged in with a high two-handed, overhead strike. Morgin met it squarely with his sword, a cascade of sparks lighting up the rock around them. Slash, parry, strike, the two of them traded blows, dancing back and forth on the shelf of rock. Salula drove Morgin back toward the entrance of the crypt with a series of heavy blows, but Morgin glimpsed a momentary opening, deflected the halfman's sword, couldn't bring his blade to bear so he hit him in the side of the head with its hilt.

Salula staggered and stumbled back several steps. He straightened, still showing Morgin that grin. "Good sport, indeed."

The halfman spoke those words with the same cocky confidence he'd always shown. But Salula had neither the finesse nor speed of the swordsman, and Morgin had grown since they'd last met, in physical size, maturity, and understanding of his powers. The halfman could no longer count on his advantages of strength, brutality and ruthlessness to win this match. When Morgin met Salula's eyes, he saw that the halfman also understood these things.

Salula smiled, danced backward a few steps, stepped over Rhianne's unconscious form, looked down at her and raised his sword high. Morgin screamed and charged as the halfman brought his blade down, clumsily deflected it so it bit into the earth near her head, then slammed into the halfman.

The two of them tumbled to the granite of the shelf, and something bit sharply into Morgin's side as Salula's head slammed into the rock. They came to a stop with Morgin on top of the semiconscious halfman, but a sharp lance of pain in his chest prevented him from taking advantage of it. He rolled off Salula, felt blood coursing from a wound in his chest just under his right arm.

Salula groaned as Morgin staggered to his feet still holding onto his sword, and he saw that the halfman held a blooded, obsidian dagger in his off hand. He tried to raise his sword to strike at the halfman, but a lance of pain slashed through him and he could barely maintain his hold on his sword, let alone strike the halfman down with it. The ground teetered beneath him, he staggered backward into the shadows hiding the entrance to the crypt, stumbled over one of the rocks he hadn't yet removed and fell deeper into his shadowmagic. He barely managed to climb to his feet as waves of dizziness sent him staggering about in the shadows he'd created centuries ago.

••••

Morgin staggered into the skeleton king's crypt, struggling to hold onto consciousness, clutching at the stone wall of the tunnel entrance to stay on his feet. Blood pulsed from the wound in his side, and had already soaked his tunic and breeches all the way to his boots. He had no idea how long it would take Salula to find his way through the shadowmagic obscuring the entrance to the crypt. It would slow the halfman, but not for long, so Morgin probably had only a few heartbeats before Salula found him.

He tried to turn back because his Rhianne was out there, but the ground tilted crazily beneath his feet and he dropped to his knees, then fell forward onto his hands. He tried crawling, no real destination in mind, driven by a stubborn refusal to simply give up and let the halfman have his way. He ended up lying on his chest, the sword still gripped in his right hand, dragging himself through the dust that centuries had deposited on the floor.

The skeleton king still sat upon his throne as Morgin remembered him, unchanged from the first time he'd seen him in this crypt, when he lay dying in the enchanted alcove in Castle Elhiyne. And then later—or was it earlier, centuries earlier—he and Morddon had carefully positioned him in his crypt, using Morgin's memories to properly lay the king to rest. In life Aethon had been a majestic king, filled with vigor and vitality, while in death he was no more than a skeleton of bones and tufts of hair, seated upon his throne, one skeletal arm resting casually on an armrest, the other on the hilt of the great sword.

Aethon's hand seemed oddly indistinct, as if the bleached white bones of his fingers were changing, fleshing out. Morgin's eyes moved to the crowned skull, a grinning white mask of death framing eye sockets of black shadow. The skeleton moved; its head turned; the eyeless pits looked upon Morgin, then looked past him.

Morgin turned his head and looked back, following the skeleton king's gaze. The wall of the crypt now opened into the enchanted alcove in Elhiyne, and there he saw his own past as he lay there dying from a Kull crossbow bolt through the chest. When Valso and the Tulalane had occupied Castle Elhiyne, he'd tried to sneak in with the help of his shadows, but Valso had discovered him and the Kulls had given chase. He'd stumbled into two halfmen in an empty corridor, one had put a crossbow bolt through his chest, and he'd crawled into the alcove to die. Back then he'd thought the connection between the alcove and the skeleton king's crypt was merely a figment of a dream. But now he understood that the gods twisted time and reality to suit their purposes. The skeleton king would heal that Morgin from the past, and he and Nicki would kill the Tulalane in the sanctum, Olivia would accuse him of cowardice, and he'd ride against Illalla's army, ride to meet MorginDeath at Csairne Glen. And now, more than two years later, he found himself dying again in Aethon's crypt, looking back upon his own death in the past.

With his last bit of strength, he turned his head and looked once again upon the skeleton king. Aethon's flesh continued to form; the face filled out: a young face he and Morddon remembered well, strong, handsome. The eyes were no longer pits of shadow but pools of sorrow and mercy, and Aethon was once again a king of life and health, seated upon his throne dressed in a suit of golden mail and glimmering silk and rich leather. The tapestries on the walls shone with the brilliance of their colors again, and the assorted trappings of arms and armor were clean and bright once more.

Something turned over in Morgin's chest. He coughed up a mouthful of blood, saw himself as if from a great distance lying helpless on the floor of Aethon's crypt. He had many regrets: that he wouldn't be there to save Rhianne from Salula, that he couldn't save his friend France from Salula. But most of all he regretted that he wouldn't be there to see that untamed lock of hair once more escape the tangle of tresses atop Rhianne's head. With his last breath, he regretted that most.

••••

Aethon watched in sadness as his friend, Lord Mortal, died once more, still clutching his simple and unadorned sword. He could never think of him as Morgin, for that was not a real name. Hopefully, someday in the future or the past, the poor fellow would find his true name.

Aethon waited, and in a few heartbeats, Lord Mortal's corpse decayed into ruin. Aethon looked across the crypt to the enchanted alcove where the fatally wounded Lord Mortal of two years ago had stumbled in to die the first time. Just a moment ago for the older Lord Mortal at his feet, two years ago for the younger Lord Mortal in the enchanted alcove; all the same in this place where the gods had brought the past and present together.

He stood, and slowly crossed the floor of the crypt, entered the enchanted alcove in which the younger Lord Mortal had died. He knelt beside him and mourned him briefly, then he placed a hand gently on the mortal wound in his chest, a wound from which the pulse of life had ceased. With both hands he lifted the younger Lord Mortal's lifeless form, holding him tightly against his own breast. Looking old and sad, he closed his eyes and bowed his head, whispering softly, "Forgive me, mortal, for what I must do."

After a time, he laid the younger Lord Mortal gently on the dust-covered floor of the enchanted alcove. The wound in the young man's chest had disappeared, though dried blood still caked his tunic. He turned back to his throne, noticed that the older Lord Mortal lying on the floor of the crypt was now no more than a skeleton dressed in rags, the bones of his hand still clutching the plain and unadorned sword. As he walked past him, he had a thought and looked back to the younger Lord Mortal lying in the alcove with no sword or weapon. The younger Lord Mortal would need a sword, while the older one was done with that blade. So he bent down carefully over the older Lord Mortal and removed the simple, unadorned sword from his skeletal grasp, then returned to where the younger Lord Mortal lay in the alcove. He stooped down, placed the sword's hilt in the young man's hand and curled his fingers about it. "You will need this, Lord Mortal," he said. "May it stand you in good stead."

He stood straight again and returned to his throne. He sat down, resting one arm casually on an armrest and the other on the hilt of the great jeweled sword. Then slowly, inevitably, the decay returned. The tapestries lost their brilliance and the weaponry lost its shine, the enchanted alcove was no longer visible through one wall of the crypt, and the king, powerful and majestic in life, was once more a skeleton of brittle bone and rotted flesh.

••••

A harsh grunt broke the silence of the crypt, and Salula staggered into the tomb. "Where are you?" he growled, blood dripping down his face from a cut where he'd smashed his head on the rock of the shelf. "You can't hide from me, fool mortal, and after I have your life, I'll have that blade that my master fears."

He looked at the skeleton on the throne, and at the one on the floor, then his head jerked from side-to-side as he searched angrily. "There's no place to hide in here," he shouted. He strode across the crypt to a shield leaning against one wall, kicked it aside and looked behind it. "Nothing," he screamed.

He ripped a moth-eaten tapestry off the wall. The centuries had not served it well and it shredded in his hands, so he tossed it aside. He looked toward the heavens and screamed, "Where is that blade?"

He flew into a maniacal rage, kicking arms and armor aside, breaking anything that got in his way, careful to look closely at each sword he found and declare it, "Not the one." He kicked shields and spears and other weaponry aside, cared nothing for the wealth of jewels that encrusted them. "Pretty weapons," he growled. "Useless junk in a real fight."

In desperation he kicked the skeleton king's bones apart, stomped them into the dust, overturned the throne to look beneath it, then hacked at it with the obsidian blade, cleaving it in two. He ignored the skeleton of the ancient warrior on the floor, for he saw it possessed no sword, nor any means of hiding one. He turned to the broken and shattered throne, screamed curses and hatred at the bones scattered about it.

He finally stopped in the middle of the crypt, breathing heavily, the air thick with dust. He'd destroyed everything but the jeweled sword, and that he merely spat upon and said, "Another pretty, useless thing."

He turned his head slowly and looked one last time about the crypt. There were no recesses in the walls, nothing, no place to hide a blade, and no place to hide the body of a badly wounded Elhiyne. He looked toward the entrance and the shadowmagic that obscured everything there. "You and your blasted shadows. Used them to elude me, did you? I stumbled right past you while you hid in those shadows, didn't I? Well I'll find you and that blade. No matter where you go I'll find you."

He stormed out of the crypt, back into the shadows at the entrance, and left behind only silence, and a floor strewn with the scattered bones of the skeleton king.

••••

Rhianne rolled over, managed to get to her hands and knees, but could make it no further as dizziness made the ground shift and sway beneath her. She must get up, must help Morgin. She had almost summoned the resolve to get at least one foot on the ground beneath her when Salula's gauntleted fist crashed into her cheek.

She tumbled painfully on the rock of the shelf, tried to roll away from him, but his boot slammed into her ribs and she almost lost consciousness. Then he picked her up, grabbed her by the shoulders and spun her. She spun once, but not even the spell could support her and she tumbled to the ground in a heap. A moment later she wished she had lost consciousness as he picked her up by the front of her dress and held her face tight up against his, so close she could look nowhere else but into those horrible eyes. "We're going to find that husband of yours. And when we do, you're both going to watch each other die, and it will not be a quick death. That I promise you, pretty one. That I promise you."

He threw her over his shoulder, and somewhere between the rock shelf and the horses she lost consciousness.

••••

The crypt embraced the silence of the dead for a time, and then the bones of the skeleton king shimmered and glowed with an ancient light. The shattered throne came together, its bits and pieces reassembling as if it had never been damaged. The tapestries reformed as well, though they remained moth-eaten and old. The armor and arms returned to their ancient resting places. Then the bones of the skeleton king slid across the floor, and one by one reformed in the shape they'd held for centuries. And once again the skeleton king sat upon his throne, one arm resting casually on an armrest, the other on the hilt of the great sword.

Once again his flesh reformed, the face filled out, the eyes were no longer pits of shadow but pools of sorrow and mercy, and the king was once again a king of life and health, seated upon his throne dressed in a suit of golden mail and glimmering silk and rich leather. The tapestries on the walls shone with the brilliance of their colors again, and the assorted trappings of arms and armor were clean and bright once more.

He stood, this young and vibrant king, and crossed the room to the body of Lord Mortal lying in the middle of the crypt. The poor fellow's body had fleshed out and was no longer a shriveled skeleton. The king stood over him and looked at him carefully, and he said, "Thrice, we have come to this, Lord Mortal. Thrice now, I must torment you with life. I know you understand not the reason for such blooding, but without it we are all doomed to a future of slavery and degradation."

He knelt, rested a hand on the wound in the warrior's side. With each healing Lord Mortal grew more reluctant to return, and too, this third time crossed a certain threshold, a boundary beyond which control of this mortal would quickly diminish.

Lord Mortal gasped, coughed out a glob of clotted blood and sucked a breath of air into his lungs. But he quickly quieted and remained unconscious, breathing raggedly and unevenly.

The young king stood, looked down upon his handiwork and asked, "Did you ever find your true name, Lord Mortal?"

He considered the poor fellow at his feet. "No, I suppose you didn't. But you must, you know, for without it you will suffer a fate far worse than all of us."

He sighed, turned about and returned to his throne, sat down upon it and looked at the unconscious Lord Mortal who lay sucking in ragged breaths of air. The young king nodded, as if acknowledging a painful and difficult task finally completed. He spoke, his voice a faint whisper, "And so must a blade be born."

He rested one arm casually on an armrest and the other on the hilt of the great sword. Then slowly, inevitably, the decay returned. The tapestries lost their brilliance and the weaponry lost its shine. The king, powerful and majestic in life, was once more a skeleton of brittle bone and rotted flesh.

••••

And so ends *The Heart of the Sands*, the third book of *The Gods Within*, in which Morgin has learned the heart of the Benesh'ere and tasted the magic of steel. In the fourth and final book, Morgin must save Rhianne and France if he is to save himself.

Some Notes About Steel

THE AUTHOR SPENT a considerable amount of time researching old and new methods of making steel, though he does not purport in any way to be an expert. And if he has made any mistakes, he would appreciate hearing about them.

Pure iron is a fairly soft metal, and as Salula pointed out, will not hold an edge well. Add carbon to it, and it gets harder—it becomes steel; the more carbon added, the harder it gets, and the better the edge it will hold. But if too much carbon is added, while the steel will hold a good edge, it becomes brittle, and a long, thin blade like a sword could easily break, or shatter on impact. So a swordsmith must draw a careful balance between enough carbon to provide a hard edge, but not so much that the blade shatters during a fight.

An alternative approach is to make the backbone of a blade using steel with less carbon that is more flexible, then wrap a layer of high-carbon steel around it that will hold a good edge. In this way, the sword-smith can make a blade with an extremely hard edge, but flexible enough to maintain its integrity on impact. Morgin alludes to this technique when Chagarin tests his knowledge of steel.

High-carbon and lower-carbon steel are often combined by the folding process that Morgin and Chagarin used. The process of striking hot steel and folding it forge-welds alternating layers of the two types of steel. The alternating layers provide a balance of hardness and workability. Folding evens out the carbon content and removes impurities, which can produce localized flaws in the strength of the blade. If the smith starts out with five layers of alternating types of steel, then folds it sixteen times, the blade has 5 x 2^{16}, or 327,680 layers.

Sulfur in very controlled, small amounts can make steel easier to machine, but too much will make it extremely brittle. Hence, Morgin's comment that one of the steel blooms had been ". . . fired or smelted with stink coal, coal contaminated with the yellow earth."

Chromium is added to make stainless steel, steel that is resistant to oxidation. The iron in simple carbon steel can oxidize when exposed to oxygen and water vapor, producing hydrated iron oxide: rust. Rust is active and accelerates corrosion by forming thick layers of iron oxide which then flake away. The addition of chromium impurities (as much as 11%) allows the steel to produce a chromium oxide layer on the surface that is passive. Due to the similar size of the steel and oxide ions they bond very strongly, producing a microscopically thin protective layer of chromium oxide that doesn't progress. *Stainless* steel is not truly stainless; it can be discolored in many ways. But the thin chromium oxide layer isolates the iron in the steel from oxygen and water vapor, preventing the active formation of rust.

Iron ore is a mixture of rocks and minerals that contain high concentrations of about five different types of iron oxides. Smelting is the process of extracting the iron from those oxides and removing other contaminants in the ore. It uses heat and a chemical reducing agent (usually some source of carbon) to drive off undesired elements as gasses or slag, yielding raw iron or steel. Coke, and in times past charcoal, is most often used as the reducing agent. Coke, derived from coal, and charcoal, derived from wood, are produced by burning off all volatile elements, leaving behind relatively pure carbon. If simple coal or wood is used to smelt or forge steel, the presence of the volatile elements can contaminate the iron, producing an inferior grade of steel.

An experienced smith can control the contaminants in the steel by controlling the contaminants in his flame. Residual oxygen in the flame can combine with carbon in the steel to reduce the carbon content, driving it off in the form of carbon dioxide. But residual oxygen can also combine with the iron in the steel to produce iron oxide, which can result in seriously inferior steel. Conversely, residual carbon in the flame, with no residual oxygen present, can increase the carbon content of steel. Hence, Morgin's comments about adjusting the hardness of the pig iron and mild steel when Chagarin tested his knowledge.

Only a knowledgeable and experienced smith can successfully make use of these techniques.

Dramatis Personae
The Heart of the Sands

Clan/Tribe	Color	Ward	Leader
Decouix	White	Tertius	Valso
Rastanna	Gray	Undecimus	Valso
Vodah	Blue	Duodecimus	Valso
Elhiyne	Red	Octavus	Olivia
Inetka	Yellow	Nonus	Wylow
Penda	Green	Quartus	BlakeDown
Tosk	Violet	Primus	PaulStaff
Benesh'ere	**Black**	**Septimus**	**Angerah**

The Greater Clans

- Decouix (dominant among the Greater Clans)
- Rastanna
- Vodah

The Lesser Clans

- Elhiyne (dominant among the Lesser Clans)
- Inetka (sworn to Elhiyne)
- Penda
- Tosk (sworn to Penda)

Clanless

- The Benesh'ere, the exiled tribe

Personae Decouix

- Illalla—King of the Greater Clans and head of all three (deceased)
- Merriketh Alaella—wife to Illalla and mother of his children
- Valso—only living son of Illalla and Merriketh, and heir to the throne of the Greater Clans
- Haleen—only living daughter of Illalla and Merriketh, called *The Mad Whore* by some
- Andra—minor Decouix nobleman
- Thandin—an emissary to Elhiyne
- Degla—minor Decouix nobleman
- GeorgeAll—minor Decouix nobleman
- Carsaris—an advisor to Valso and one of his most powerful sorcerors

Personae Rastanna

- Oubba—Commander of Tharsk, the fortress at Methula
- Carri—Oubba's wife
- Tarkiss—Oubba's son
- Andrew—an old country nobleman
- Stetha—Andrew's son

Personae Vodah

- Xenya—a young noblewoman with a rebelious attitude regarding Valso
- Alta—Xenya's brother

Personae Kullish

- Salula—Captain and commander of all Kulls
- Verk—a Kull captain, subordinate to Salula
- Mook—a simple Kullish guardsman
- Brakke—Kull officer in command of the Kullish forces at Tharsk

- Salya—a Kull lieutenant in Durin
- Qartan—the Kull lieutenant that kidnaps Felina

Personae Elhiyne

- Olivia—Head of Clan Elhiyne
- Bertak—Olivia's father (deceased)
- Hillell—Olivia's mother (deceased)
- Karlane—Olivia's husband (deceased)
- Malka—Olivia's oldest son and heir to the leadership of Elhiyne (deceased)
- Marjinell—Malka's wife
- MichaelOff—oldest son of Malka and Marjinell (deceased)
- Brandon—youngest son of Malka and Marjinell
- Jinella—born Tosk, now Brandon's wife
- Roland—Olivia's youngest son
- AnnaRail—Roland's wife
- DaNoel—1st child of Roland and AnnaRail
- Annaline—2nd child of Roland and AnnaRail
- JohnEngine—3rd child of Roland and AnnaRail
- NickoLot—4th child of Roland and AnnaRail
- Morgin—adopted child of Roland and AnnaRail
- Rhianne—the 4th of Edtoall and Matill's four daughters, and now Morgin's wife
- Hellis—Olivia's younger sister, took her own life in suicide (deceased)
- Tulellcoe—Hellis' only son, conceived by Illalla in an act of rape
- Vergis Caladan—an alias used by Tulellcoe
- Alcoa—Marchlord of the western reaches that border on Penda
- Eglahan—Marchlord of Yestmark, sworn to Elhiyne
- Packwill—a scout, sworn to Eglahan of Yestmark
- Annen—bastard son of Eglahan
- Abileen—a sergeant of men
- Dannasul—a childhood friend of Morgin and JohnEngine
- Durado—an old man who maintains the waystation at Kallun's Gorge

- Samull—Durado's son
- Gorguh—Elhiyne stable master
- Erlin—Elhiyne stable boy
- Valken Surriot—a *twoname* who fought with Eglahan at the battle of Yestmark
- Seurrak Aldwith—an alias used by the Surriot
- Cortien Balenda—a *twoname* who fought with Eglahan at the battle of Yestmark
- Thenda Sa—an alias used by the Balenda
- Hwatok Tulalane—a *twoname* advisor to Olivia (deceased)
- France—a common swordsman
- Rindal—an alias frequently used by France

Personae Aud

- Aiergain—Queen of the free port city, aka the Queen of Thieves
- Pandorin—a lieutenant in Aiergain's guard
- Sacress—Aiergain's physician
- Terrikle—a manservant provided to Morgin

Personae Penda

- BlakeDown—Head of Clan Penda
- Doagla—an alias used by BlakeDown when he meets Valso at Tharsk
- ErrinCastle—Blakedown's oldest son and heir to the leadership of Penda
- Anja—a very young girl of minor status
- Tarare—a nobleman known to be a mouthpiece for BlakeDown
- Chrisainne—born Vodah, married minor Penda lord, seduces BlakeDown for Valso
- Perrinsall—ErrinCastle's cousin, and trusted to keep a calm head
- Lewendis—distant relative of BlakeDown's and a bit of a hot-head

Personae Inetka

- Wylow—Head of Clan Inetka

- Carmet—Wylow's wife
- SandoFall—Wylow's oldest son and heir to the leadership of Inetka
- Edtoall—a minor Inetka lord and father of Rhianne
- Matill—Edtoall's wife and mother of Rhianne

Personae Tosk

- PaulStaff—Head of Clan Tosk

Personae Benesh'ere

- Angerah—ruler of the Black Council
- Merella—Angerah's wife
- Jerst—WarMaster of the Benesh'ere tribe
- Blesset—Jerst's daughter
- Jack the Lesser—a bowman and scout
- Harriok—Jerst's oldest son
- Branaugh—Harriok's wife
- LillianToc—Jerst's youngest son
- Jack the Greater—Jack the Lesser's twin brother
- Delaga—a common swordsman
- Fantose—a common pikeman
- Chagarin—the Master Smith
- Baldrak—a smith
- Felina—Baldrak's daughter
- Surnarra—a smith
- Yim—an impressionable young girl
- Tamlea—a young girl
- Tallik—a young bully
- Satcha—the cook for Jerst's extended household

Personae Celestial

- Attun—a mythical god
- Unnamed King—knows all names but his own
- Erithnae—god-queen and consort to the Unnamed King
- Aethon—the last Shahotma King

Personae Angelicus

- Metadan—an archangel
- Ellowyn—an archangel
- Laelith—a faerie
- Cynaban—Metadan's senior lieutenant

Personae Common

- Raffin—a merchant, also known as Fatpurse
- Mathal—a fruit vendor
- Ott—a peasant
- Gulk—Ott's wife
- Ikth—Ott and Gulk's son
- Darma—captain of the *Far Wind*
- Bakart—first mate of the *Far Wind*
- Braunye—a peasant girl sold to Rhianne in exchange for healing her father's cow
- Chiren Tesha—guardmaster of a merchant caravan out of Anistigh
- Katha—leader of the scouts reporting to Chiren Tesha
- Jokath—a common thief that preys on travellers on the Gods Road
- Mistress Syllith—Rhianne's alias in Norlakton

Personae Nether

- Beayaegoath—the Dark God and ruler of the ninth hell of the netherworld
- Bayellgae—the venomousss demon flying sssnake
- ElkenSkul—the demon *namegiver*
- Mortiss—Morgin's unusual horse, also known as the DeathWalker
- Soann'Daeth'Daeye—a shadowwraith that Morddon meets outside Kathbeyanne
- Shebasha—a great sand cat whose soul is haunted by a demon

Personae Ancient

- Morddon—a bitter and angry Benesh'ere warrior, and Morgin's alter ego
- AnneRhianne—a Benesh'ere princess and Rhianne's alter ego
- WindHollow—a young Benesh'ere boy and AnneRhianne's nephew
- Gilguard—warmaster of the Benesh'ere
- Sarker—a Benesh'ere scout
- Takit—a Benesh'ere scout
- Bendaw—a Benesh'ere scout
- Binth—the pipist, Morddon's father
- Eisla—the SteelMistress, last of the SteelMasters, and Morddon's mother
- Jander—a Benesh'ere warrior, one of Gilguard's senior lieutenants
- Magwa—the jackal queen
- TarnThane—the griffin lord
- SheelThane—the griffin queen
- AuelThane—a griffin warrior
- TearThane—a griffin warrior
- WolfDane—the hellhound king
- Perrik—a nobleman with a flawed blade

Acknowledgements

I'D LIKE TO thank Durelle Kurlinski for fixing all my dotted t's and crossed i's, Karen for both supporting my dream and being my most valuable critic, Kelley Eskridge for helping me turn an ok manuscript into something I can be really proud of, and Steve Himes, and the whole team at Telemachus, for getting a quality product out the door.

Books by J. L. Doty

Series: The Dreadmark Covenants
Dread Child (available 3/1/2024)
Dread Spirit (6/1/2024)
Dread Soul (9/1/2024)
Dread Lord (12/1/2024)
Series: The Treasons Cycle
Of Treasons Born
A Choice of Treasons
Stand Alone Novel
The Thirteenth Man
Series: The Gods Within
Child of the Sword
The SteelMaster of Indwallin
The Heart of the Sands
The Name of the Sword
Series: The Dead Among Us
When Dead Ain't Dead Enough
Still Not Dead Enough
Never Dead Enough
Series: The Blacksword Regiment
A Hymn for the Dying
A Dirge for the Damned
A Prayer for the Fallen
A Requiem for the Forsaken
Series: Commonwealth Re-contact Novellas
Tranquility Lost

About the Author

JIM IS A full-time SF&F writer, scientist and laser geek (Ph.D. Electrical Engineering, specialty laser physics), and former running-dog-lackey for the bourgeois capitalist establishment. He's been writing for over 30 years, with 19 published books. His first success came through self-publishing when his books went word-of-mouth viral, and sold enough that he was able to quit his day-job, start working for himself and write full time—his new boss is a real jerk. That led to contracts with traditional publishers like Open Road Media and Harper Collins, and his books are now a mix of traditional and self-published.

The four novels in his new coming-of-age epic fantasy series, *The Dreadmark Covenants*, are scheduled for release beginning in early 2024.

Jim was born in Seattle, but he's lived most of his life in California, though he did live on the east coast and in Europe for a while. He now resides in Arizona with his wife Karen and Julia, a little being who claims to be a cat. But Jim is certain she's really an extra-terrestrial alien in disguise.

Visit the author's website at https://www.jldoty.com/
Contact the author at jld@jldoty.com